In the moonlight, I could see the sign of the crescent moon on the upper swell of her breast.

The mark of QualiKa! The rumors are true. The QualiKa are active again. Cautiously, I rose to my feet. My hands were shaking, and I took a deep, calming breath. "I wouldn't think the QualiKa would like human music any more than I do," I said loudly.

The QualiKa spun around with a clatter of stones, daggered claws sliding from wide pads of her fingertips and the great ripping claws on her feet rising. I didn't move, I didn't react, though I trembled inside.

The QualiKa's stance relaxed slightly as she saw me, though the claws remained out and threatening. She moved smoothly to block the entrance to the path down the steep hill, cutting off any chance I had to retreat. She had strange, pale eyes that were piercing and deep, and her face was extraordinary.

"I'm alone and no threat to you," I told her. "Or have the QualiKa lost their respect for Sa, also?"

Other Avon Eos Books by
Stephen Leigh

DARK WATER'S EMBRACE

SPEAKING
STONES

STEPHEN LEIGH

AVON • EOS

AVON BOOKS, INC.
1350 Avenue of the Americas
New York, New York 10019

Copyright © 1999 by Stephen Leigh
Inside cover author photo by Denise Parsley Leigh
Library of Congress Catalog Card Number: 98-93285
ISBN: 0-380-79914-6
www.avonbooks.com/eos

First Avon Eos Printing: March 1999

AVON EOS TRADEMARK REG. U.S. PAT. OFF. AND IN OTHER COUNTRIES, MARCA REGISTRADA, HECHO EN U.S.A.

Printed in the U.S.A.

WCD   10   9   8   7   6   5   4   3   2

To Susan
For the smiles

And, as ever, to Denise

ACKNOWLEDGMENTS

The Miccail "Lullaby to a Sa Child" is based on a Zuni lullaby quoted in *Daughters of the Earth: The Lives and Legends of American Indian Women* by Carolyn Niethammer (Collier Books, Macmillan Publishing Company, 1977). I highly recommend Ms. Niethammer's book to anyone interested in Native American culture as seen from the female viewpoint (a difficult perspective to find among historical books on the subject of Native Americans), and I have "borrowed" a few customs quoted there for the Miccail society.

From *The Book of the Hopi* by Frank Waters, I borrowed aspects of the Miccail mythology and language, as well as some details grafted onto the QualiKa sect.

I also read *The Dull Knifes of Pine Ridge* by Joe Sarita (Putnam, 1995), which gave me insight into generational cultural conflicts. The Valentine T. McGillicuddy quote which starts the "Circumstances" section is from this book.

In researching the subject of prejudice on the internet, I came across the Anti-Defamation League website, from which I look the Farrakhan, Netanyahu, and Arafat quotations.

Yet another book important to the development of this novel is *Rebels: The Irish Rising of 1916* by Peter de Rosa (Ballantine Books, 1990), a fascinating study of the beginnings of the end of seven centuries of British rule of Ireland, and a cultural conflict with which my own ancestors were intimately familiar.

The Patrick Pearse and Sean Heuston quotes are from this source.

I'd like to thank Dr. Rebecca Levin for her input into the biology of the Miccail and the Sa. Any errors of extrapolation and science are mine, not hers.

And a great "huzzah!" to Jennifer Brehl, my editor at Eos. Your enthusiasm, energy, and support have been a constant blessing. Jen, I hope you know how much you're appreciated!

If you're connected to the internet, please check out my web page at www.sff.net/people/sleigh/— you're always welcome to browse through!

A MICTLANIAN GLOSSARY

THE LANGUAGES OF MICTLAN, HUMAN, AND MICCAIL:

The crew of the *Ibn Battuta*, drawn as they were from a multinational crew, adopted English as their *lingua franca*. However, most of the crew were at least bilingual, if not relatively fluent in three or four languages. Inevitably, words and phrases from other languages crept into their everyday speech. Well before the *Ibn Battuta* was launched, during the period when it was being constructed in orbit and the crew members were learning their roles, a subtle *patois* of many languages had come into common use among the crew and support personnel. The emerging language was almost a Creole, though the largest portion of the vocabulary derived from American English. By the time of their arrival at Mictlan, despite the ship-decades of LongSleep, this convention was firmly in place. New terms and descriptions might as easily be drawn from Cantonese, Japanese, Russian, Spanish, or Kiswahili as English, or even (as was the case with the world-name itself) an ancient Native American language such as Nahuatl. For the most part, we have stayed with English for the sake of readability. However, where it seemed appropriate, the terms used by the colonists have been appropriated here.

The sections from the viewpoint of the Miccail themselves contain words drawn from their own language, again where it seemed appropriate. As in Japanese (for instance), the Miccail created conglomerate words composed of smaller, monosyllabic nouns. Thus, "nasituda," the word for the carved stelae which were the first, most visible signs of the Miccail presence is Stone ("na") Carved ("si") Past ("tu") Speak ("da"): literally, the Carved Stone that Speaks of History, or as we have (more romantically, perhaps, and certainly more freely) translated it here, Telling or Speaking Stone.

The list of human and Miccail words below is by no means exhaustive, and is provided only to give some insight into derivations and meanings.

aabi	Miccail. Literally, "Ears hearing." An acknowledgment that you've heard and understood what was said to you.
AnglSaiye	Miccail. The island, sacred home of the Sa
brais	Miccail. Literally, "Sun's Eye"; the pupilless third eye set high on the forehead of the Miccail. The brais cannot focus and the Miccail do not properly "see" with it. Instead, it serves as a "skylight" and warns them of sudden shifts in light which might signal the approach of a predator.
Cha'akMongTi	Miccail: The "crier with a god's voice" or GodMouth. A prophet, one who speaks with divinely inspired words.
Chali	Miccail. The larger of Mictlan's two moons, dubbed Longago by the human colonists.
Che'Veyo	Miccail: Spirit Warrior.
CieTiLa	Miccail. Literally, "Those Touched By The Gods." More simply, it means "The People," referring to the Miccail as a whole.
culear	Human. From Spanish: literally, one who has sexual intercourse with the rear. A gay male.

da
: Human. Etymology uncertain. The closest meaning is perhaps "Uncle." Da refers to any male of a person's Family who is of a generation or more older.

danjite ikenai
: Human, from Japanese: "Absolutely not"

dottó
: Human, from Italian: a contraction of "dottore," or doctor. The English equivalent might be the colloquial "Doc."

Geeda
: Human. Etymology uncertain. The eldest male of a Family

Geema
: Human. Etymology uncertain. The eldest female of a Family

hai
: Human, from Japanese: "Yes."

hakuchi
: Human, from Japanese: "Idiot."

hand
: Miccail counting: a "hand" equals four.

Ja
: Miccail. A suffix indicating a female in servitude

Je
: Miccail. A suffix indicating a male in servitude

jitu
: Miccail. A narcotic drink used in Sa rituals.

kahina
: Miccail: the spirits or minor deities who control the earth, the wind, and the waters. These spirits are responsible for rain, for storms, for floods, for earthquakes. The earth kahina dwell in rocks and trees and sometimes take on animal aspects as well; the water kahina live at the bottom of lakes and underneath the sea, and sometimes manifest themselves in fish; the air kahina live in the clouds, and may sometimes speak to the Miccail through the birds.

kami   Human, from Japanese: a local spirit or
                minor deity, often inhabiting particular
                trees or stones. Kami are usually con-
                fined to a specific location, and could be
                helpful or not, depending on whim.
                Sometimes the souls of particularly
                strong dead people could become kami,
                inhabiting a place or an object special to
                them.

kasadi   Miccail. Ducklike amphibians who con-
                gregate on shorelines during their brief
                spring mating season.

kav   Miccail. An herbal tea

khudda   Human, from Syrian (vulgar): used as a
                profanity: human excrement

Kiria   Human, from Latin: Priest or Priestess.
                Probably derived from Kyrie.

komban wa   Human, from Japanese: "Good eve-
                ning."

KoPavi   Miccail: literally, "Open Door," or the
                religious rits and etiquettes of the Miccail
                which opened their souls to the Shad-
                owWorld where the gods lived. The
                QualiKa believed that strict adherence to
                KoPavi was necessary to sustain the Mic-
                cail's well-being as a people.

lansa   Miccail: spear.

lavativo   Human, from Italian: "Lazybones"

mali cvijet   Human, from Serbo-Croatian: "Little
                Flower"—a term of endearment.

mam   Human. Etymology uncertain. "Mother."
                Since it was entirely unlikely that anyone
                could be certain of the father, there is no
                analogue word for the male parent on
                Mictlan.

marset   Miccail. A small mammalian animal hunted for both its food and fur.

mi   Human. Etymology uncertain. The closest meaning is perhaps "Aunt." It refers to any female of a person's Family who is older than you, and of whom you're not a direct descendant (i.e., not your mother, grandmother, etc.)

Miccail   Human, from Nahuatl: "The Dead." On Mictlan, the extinct race of sentient beings who perished a millennium before the arrival of the *Ibn Battuta*.

Mictlan   Human, from Nahuatl: "The Land of the Dead." In Aztec/Mayan creation myths, this is the Land of the Dead, from where the god Quetzalcoatl brought the bones of man. This was used as the world-name after the bones of a sentient race were found here.

mojo ljubav   Human, from Serbo-Croatian: "My love"

nasituda   Miccail. The Speaking Stone of the Miccail, the carved stelae of crystal which are the most prominent remnants of that extinct race.

nei   Human. Etymology uncertain: "Absolutely not!"

Njia   Human, from Kiswahili: "The Way." This is the principal religious/philosophical belief system among the humans on Mictlan.

Quali   Miccail. The smaller of Mictlan's two moons, dubbed Faraway by the human colonists.

rezu   Human, from Japanese via Europe: a lesbian.

Sa   Miccail. A suffix indicating a Miccail
                     midmale. Nearly all the rare midmales
                     belonged to the Sa sect, a religious col-
                     ony based on an island.

shangaa   Miccail. The long, caftanlike robe that
                     was the main item of clothing worn by
                     the Miccail. Shangaa, woven from the
                     pulp of a native plant, were dyed many
                     bright colors, and varied from plain, util-
                     itarian robes to fine ceremonial costumes.

sib   Human, from English: "sibling." On
                     Mictlan, a sib is anyone of your Family
                     of the same generation, regardless of who
                     the mother was.

Ta   Miccail. A suffix for the dominant female
                     in a Miccail tribe, also known as the
                     OldMother.

Te   Miccail. a suffix indicating that the per-
                     son is the OldFather of a Miccail tribe,
                     the dominant male.

terduva   Miccail. A segment of time equal to 512
                     (or $8 \times 8 \times 8$) years. The Miccail, with
                     hands consisting of three fingers and a
                     thumb, counted in base eight.

Ti   Miccail. The suffix used for a deity.

Tlilipan   Human, from Nahuatl: "place of black
                     water." Name given to a peat-stained
                     lake near the colony site.

Tu   Miccail. The suffix used to designate the
                     head of the Community of Sa.

una tortillera   Human, from Spanish: in extremely vul-
                     gar usage, a lesbian.

VeiSaTi   Miccail. One of the gods of the Miccail,
                     the one most sacred to the sect of the Sa.

verrechat	Human, from French: "glass cat." A small, catlike marsupial with transparent or lightly tinted skin and muscles. Sometimes domesticated.
wizards	Human. A contraction of "winged lizards"—a type of flying reptile found near the human settlement.
Xa	Miccail. A suffix indicating a female of the free caste
Xe	Miccail. A suffix indicating a male of the free caste
xeshai	Miccail. Literally, "Second Fight"—a ritualbound two person combat that was the usual method for solving severe disagreements between Miccail tribes. Each Te or Ta would choose a champion from among the Xe or Xa to represent them. In rare cases, *xeshai* might be group combat, but even then there were specific rules limiting how the conflict would be handled.

And I say to my people's masters:
    Beware.
Beware of the thing that is coming,
    Beware of the risen people.

—PATRICK PEARSE
First President of
the Irish Republic

PRELUDE:
CosTa

CosTa's belly ached, her stomach muscles drawn taut from lack of food over the last three days. The sips of water she allowed herself did nothing to stop the constant burning in her gut. The vision still refused to come to her. Colors pulsed behind her eyes and hidden shapes drifted mockingly just at the edge of her sight, but there was no clear image, nothing she could claim as the sign she must have. Every year, since the first time her moon-driven bleeding had begun, she had undertaken this dreamquest, and every year had held disappointment.

She knew she was to be called, yet her god, GhazTi, would not answer.

CosTa fell to her knees under the stars and the razored crescent of the moon Quali, the cold salt wind whipping her as she wavered at the edge of the precipice overlooking the bay and the distant island. She prayed again to GhazTi, begging for a sign that the time was now, that CosTa should at last take up the unfinished task of her grandfather NagTe and defend their land from the humans' plundering. The moon was falling to the west behind the island—once it had vanished beyond the sea, this year's dreamquest would end. Though CosTa could fill her stomach once again, her deeper hunger would still go unfed for another turn of the seasons.

Sudden brilliance fell across her *brais*, the third, light-sensitive eye on her forehead, and CosTa looked up. Between the horns of the moon, a new star had appeared, flaring brighter than anything except the moon. As CosTa watched, the star tracked across the sky, streaking higher

1

until, overhead, it exploded in a fireball and vanished.

The track of its passage was a spear of red in CosTa's vision, the dying fireball its fiery head.

CosTa cried aloud and fell prostrate on the ground, the nagging emptiness of her body forgotten. Unbidden tears tracked down her cheeks. She stayed huddled on the cold stones, giving thanks to GhazTi until Quali had left the sky behind the island, as the shapes and visions which until now had remained hidden filled her mind with the path of her destiny. Then, the memory of GhazTi's spear-star still burning in her eyes, CosTa left the cliff and slipped into the forest.

She would go to her people and she would tell them what GhazTi had spoken.

At last, she would take her grandfather's legacy and fulfill the long dream.

The QualiKa, those dedicated to defending the birthrights of the CieTiLa, the people, could now return, and CosTa would be their Cha'akMongTi.

CIRCUMSTANCES

"It is a mere waste of time to attempt to teach
the average adult Indian the ways of the white
man. He can be tamed, and that is about all."

—VALENTINE T. McGILLICUDDY,
First Agent assigned to the Oglala Sioux,
report to Washington, 1879

JOURNAL ENTRY:
Anaïs Koda-Levin, O'Sa

I WAS THE FIRST. I WAS CERTAIN THAT BEING "THE First" meant that it was up to me to create the rules for everyone who came afterward.

And to show how ignorant I can be (and, probably, just how ill suited I was for the task), for a long, long time, I thought that this was something good. I wanted to thank all the *kami* for choosing me to be the one.

Now, looking back with the wisdom of hindsight (and a little less ego), I realize that it's a hell of a lot more fun to be a critic than a creator.

I do wonder whether I made a mistake in grafting together a skein of ancient and alien Miccail rites and mores, weaving them with our human viewpoint. I was convinced that it was necessary back then: after all, the Miccail had dealt successfully with the complications of a 'midmale' sex for millennia, and this was new for us. Why *not* borrow from their experience and their culture? Why not take the best of both of our cultures? Why not re-create the religion that the Miccail had nearly forgotten and shape it in an image that would help us?

The Miccail had fallen so far from the height of their civilization that their remaining leaders seemed grateful for our help in restoring AnglSaiye and reconstructing the Community of Sa. I truly believed that, given a few decades, we would learn how to coexist, and we would help each other move forward in cooperation. My new religion, my *KoPavi,* would help us get to that idyllic place.

Which maybe *would* have happened, except that the Miccail idea of "progress" and ours didn't particularly match. I should have known . . .

5

CONTEXT:
Matsunanga Allen-Shimmura
of the Rock

"DAMN!"

Matsu poked his whitewood staff at the feathered mass that had just nipped his calf. The goathen chick hissed at him, snapped once again, then ran off to join the rest of the flock, flapping its vestigial wings angrily. Matsu rubbed at his shin and then rolled up the pant leg to examine the bite, knowing he'd have a nasty welt by evening. "God*damn*, that hurt . . ."

Matsu's *da* Isaac claimed that as recently as a century ago, goathens didn't even have teeth. Matsu wasn't certain whether that was true or not, though Mictlan's wildlife certainly had a history of rapid mutation. However, he knew goathens had teeth *now*, well, toothlets, anyway: Matsu could see the imprint of stubby beak ridges in his inflamed skin. At least it was only the younglings that tended to bite—the adults were less aggressive.

It was Matsu's week to tend the goathen flock. In addition, his *mi* Fra had given him Fianya to watch, which was another royal pain in the ass. Fianya was just a little over two years old, a few months past the age when all Sa—the midmales—were supposed to be sent to the island of AnglSaiye to be educated by the Community of Sa. Matsu wished Geema Euzhan had sent ker away. He didn't understand why Geema had refused, but he knew that most of the adults in the Rock *and* on the island were upset about it, one way or the other.

Fianya had been trouble since birth. Matsu still remembered the night Komoko gave birth to Fianya, and the uproar Geema Euzhan had caused when she realized that the baby was a Sa, a midmale. "Now you see what can happen when you've been with one of *them* . . ." Matsu had heard Geema Euzhan shout before his *mi* and *da* had hustled him away from the vicinity of the birthing room.

Geema Euzhan had been furious and unapproachable for weeks afterward, and all the Family children avoided her. Not long after, Komoko had tried to leave the Rock with Fianya, and *da* Gerald had caught her on the highroad to AnglSaiye and brought her back. Since then, Kokomo usually stayed inside the compound, and Geema seemed to have finally calmed down. She even seemed to *like* Fianya. She must, or why would she have refused to send Fianya to the Sa?

Fianya was an unruly and defiant child—because ke was a Sa, Matsu believed. Matsu knew that the midmales from the other Families were handled like they were cut glass and might shatter if handled too roughly, so no wonder they grew up thinking they were special. Matsu had never seen Geema Euzhan correct the child, nor did the rest of the Family. Just last week, Fianya had tugged on the tablecloth before dinner, breaking a glass and two plates, and *mi* Vivian, who'd been right there, hadn't even scolded ker, only made ker help clean up the mess.

If Matsu had done the same thing, he'd have been mucking out the middens the next day. Geema Euzhan *should* have sent Fianya to AnglSaiye and the Sa and gotten rid of ker while she had the chance. It's what Matsu would have done.

"Fianya! Where the heck are you?" he called.

"I'm over here, *da* Matsu!" Peering into the sun, Matsu could make out Fianya, waving ker little arms from atop a stack of cut-peat blocks about a hundred meters away.

"Climb down from there and get back over this way," Matsu called to ker. He rubbed at the goathen bite again and let his pant leg back down. "I can use some help with these damn animals."

Matsu had taken the goathens out into the fields around Tlilipan, a small pond of dark, peat-stained water a half-kilometer or so from the foot of the massive stone called the Rock, the original home of all the Families. He was beginning to regret his choice. The fields were muddy from the late snow yesterday, and the wind was coming in from the north, obliterating any warmth the sun might have lent. From off near the river, there came a sudden low, mournful hooting, and Matsu felt icy fingers run his spine. His head came up, his eyes narrowed, and he checked to see if his rifle was still propped against the knob of blueferns to his right. Even the goathens seemed to have heard the grumbler—they were all standing quiet, each of their ugly, feathered heads turned toward the river's tree line.

Matsu didn't like grumblers, and he wasn't much impressed by the fact that they had turned out to be the fallen, mutated remnants of the people the original human colonists had named the Miccail—"the Dead": an extinct civilization who had left ruins all over the area. The AnglSaiye Families might live with grumblers peacefully (for the most part, anyway), and the Sa midmales even seemed to genuinely enjoy the creatures' company, but there was no way to tell the smart ones from the stupid ones except that the smart grumblers usually wore clothing, and the stupid ones were just animals, who might attack without warning. Grumblers were ugly, with their leathery, snouted faces, tympanic ears, and a third, sightless eye set in their foreheads. Their four-fingered, clawed hands were nasty weapons, and the great ripping claw on each of their feet was supposed to be worse. Matsu remembered Cita Allen-Shimmura after he'd been laid open by a wild grumbler. Matsu hadn't been supposed to see, but he'd pushed his way between the adults when they brought Cita back to the Rock, and Matsu still could recall the image of blood-drenched clothing, and the rictus of pain on old Cita's face.

Cita had died, two days later.

The grumbler howled again, and another one answered from just upriver. Matsu wished he knew some of the grumbler language—maybe he'd be able to tell if these two were talking or whether they were just wild ones making noise. "Fianya!" he called loudly. He thought he saw movement out of the corner of his eye, just at the edge of Tlilipan,

but when he turned to look, nothing was there. A shiver
went through him at that—he'd heard tales of *kami* inhabiting the marsh. The ghost of the ancient Miccail that old
Anaïs, the O'Sa, had found in the peat bog was supposed
to live out here. Matsu rubbed at his eyes, and multicolored
sparks exploded silently in front of him.

Fianya didn't answer Matsu's shout, though another
grumbler howled, this one behind Matsu, somewhere out
in the swamp around Tlilipan. "*Khudda!*" Matsu swore,
and snatched up the rifle. He made sure a cartridge was in
the chamber. "Fianya! Damn it, get over here!" The goathens had huddled together in instinctive protection, the
larger males facing outward. They hissed and muttered,
their long necks swaying nervously.

"Fianya!" Matsu spun around slowly, scanning for the
child, blinking into the sunlight. Ke simply wasn't there—
not by the peat pile, not along the hummocked shore of
Tlilipan, not on the marshy ground between here and the
river. "Come on, Fi! Answer me!" Ke could be hiding—
behind the peat, between the hummocks of long grass, behind one of the boulders, but that was unlike her. Matsu's
fingers tightened around the stock of his rifle, clenching and
unclenching nervously. He didn't hear the grumblers anymore, and the goathens were tentatively spreading out and
starting to feed again.

"Fi!"

He heard only his own voice, accompanied by the
faintest echo from the Rock. Strangely, it was irritation that
filled him, not fear. Fianya was hiding, and when Matsu
found ker . . . The words were already filling him, angry
and edged. He stalked over to the peat, turned with a huff
of fury to look behind, ready to pluck ker up and scold ker.

But there was no one hiding there. Matsu felt the flutter
of cold down his spine once more. "Fianya!" he called
again, and this time there was a tremor in his voice.
"Fianya!"

Ke didn't answer. The goathens glanced curiously at
Matsu and returned to their grazing. Matsu stood, turning
slowly, his breath making a cloud around him.

Somehow, he knew that Fianya was gone. Somehow, he
knew that no matter where he looked, he wouldn't find ker.

He wondered how he was going to tell Geema Euzhan,
Komoko, and the rest of his Family.

SONG:
"Lullaby for a Sa Child"
(traditional Miccail chant)

Nu tasa, ojal tasai
Egdi senludi nu
Yalota heote saam
Nu tasa
Kalasi nu tasa!

TRANSLATION:
Little Sa child, little sweet one
Though this baby playing
Will soon be traveling on
Little Sa child
Little Sa so delightful!

CONTEXT:
Taira and Terri Koda-Schmidt
of the Sa

ALL TAIRA NEEDED TO DO WAS GLANCE AT TERRI—
that was sufficient. As with many identical
twins, a psychic shorthand generally operated between the
two of them. At least, it always had in the past.

Taira was no longer quite so sure. Not anymore.

"*Hai*, I'm *entirely* serious," Terri said in response to the question contained in Taira's uplifted eyebrow. "Caitlyn Koda-Schmidt has the qualities we need for this. I've *seen* it, Taira."

Word of Fianya's disappearance had come to the island of AnglSaiye and the twin heads of the Community of Sa via a runner dispatched from the Family Koda-Schmidt. Taira still found it difficult to believe. In a few days, they would need to react officially. As yet, they'd not even discussed the situation with YeiSa, the FirstHand of the Miccail portion of the Community, even though the runner had told them that "grumblers" had been heard in the vicinity just before Fianya had vanished, and half the Rock suspected the newly reborn QualiKa to be responsible for the incident.

Taira had the feeling that this was going to be political dynamite, and ke had no intention of having it blow up in their faces.

Euzhan Allen-Shimmura's refusal, two months ago, to send Fianya on to AnglSaiye to be raised in the Community had already precipitated a minor crisis—both between AnglSaiye and the Rock, and among the various branches of the five Families. What Fianya's sudden disappearance might mean none of them could guess.

All of which was enough of a headache for Taira. And now ker twin Terri was claiming divine inspiration on the choice of whom to send to investigate the matter.

"I agree that Caitlyn is empathetic and understanding," Taira said to ker twin. Ke poured steaming *kav* from the pot over the fire into the two raku cups on their shared desk, handing one to Terri. They blew steam away from the fragrant liquid and sipped as one. "But I think that you've been indulging in too much *jitu* if you truly believe that ke's ready for this kind of responsibility."

Taira expected Terri to shrug then. It was what ke would have done. But Terri was wrapped in that serious, strange melancholy that afflicted ker more and more often lately.

"It's just the Work . . ." That's how ke'd respond if I asked, with the capitalization prominent in ker voice. *"It's just the Work . . ."* The corners of Terri's mouth drooped like branches under snow as ke frowned. "Don't mock me, Taira," Terri thundered. "The Sa have always taken *jitu* to better hear VeiSaTi's words, and I'm only following the *KoPavi* as we all should. I heard this clearly, Taira. The vision was crystalline. Perfect. Caitlyn must go, because ker presence is essential."

"Terri . . ." Taira nearly sighed and gave up before ke even started, knowing that this was the argument they'd been having for the last year or more. *An old, trodden road, with the rhetorical ruts worn so deep we can barely see over the top of them . . .* "As SaTu, we've both read O'Sa Anaïs's journals. We both know that ke didn't believe in the *KoPavi*. Read the last entry the O'Sa wrote . . ."

"I have. Many times. And what did ke say, at the very end? 'I'm afraid.' The O'Sa was afraid—because ke realized that all the time, the *KoPavi* was there, that it was true."

Taira was already shaking ker head, abandoning that path. "All right. I'm not going to start that argument again. Let's talk about Caitlyn. Caitlyn has performed in a mediocre fashion in all the programs in which ke's been involved. " Taira automatically took the devil's advocate position. It was the way the two of them had always made their decisions over the decades, casting objections at each other until the solution became obvious. Taira hurled doubts back at ker dour twin. "Ker teachers all say ke's a lackluster student. I'll admit that most people seem to *like* ker, but that doesn't mean that anyone will *follow* ker, or that ke'll exercise the careful good judgment that would be necessary with this."

"Caitlyn *must* go. It is VeiSaTi's wish. There's no argument past that."

Taira frowned and put ker cup down on the desk with a growl of annoyance. Ke rose from ker chair and walked slowly to the window, uncomfortable with ker twin's insistence. Invoking god was totally unfair, in Taira's mind.

This wasn't like Terri—no, any more it was *too* much like ker. The connection between them had frayed over these last several months. Sometimes, Taira wasn't sure that ke knew Terri at all now. Ke was fast becoming an ascetic, living only for the rites and ceremonies ke performed as SaTu. Devout, and utterly dedicated to the religion the O'Sa had founded. And far, far too interested in the Work.

The Work. Two years ago, crews shoring up the foundations of the ancient Sa temple had broken through a stone wall and discovered a passage. There, reclining on slabs of polished marble dusted with thousands of years of darkness and isolation, were half a hundred *nasituda*, the carved stelae on which the Miccail had written their histories, their stories, their legends. Translation was slow because not even the current Miccail could read all the symbols of their long-dead ancestors, but it was clear that these *nasituda*, these Speaking Stones, contained the ancient *KoPavi* of the Sa, the rituals and codes on which the Sa community of the Miccail had been based, millennia ago.

A century ago, O'Sa Anaïs had taken the nearly lost oral tradition which was all that had remained of the *KoPavi*, and created it anew. Now the ancient original, believed to be entirely lost, had been found. This was fascinating material, Taira agreed. Historically important. And, *hai*, religiously important as well. But for Terri, it was an obsession.

From the window, Taira could see the temple grounds and the orange-robed Sa, both human and Miccail, walking in the gardens or hurrying to appointments or classes. Beyond the walls, the green, tall plateau of the island rose; in the mists beyond were the blue-tinged hills that enclosed Crookjaw Bay. "Terri, you'd be throwing Caitlyn at that buzz-saw anachronism Euzhan. Talk about a trial by fire."

"Fire hardens and tempers steel," Terri answered firmly.

"Or it destroys," Taira responded. Ke was still staring out at the landscape; ke didn't need to turn to sense the rigidity in Terri's body language. "We should send Rashi. Ke's your choice to succeed us as SaTu, after all."

"*Nei!* Absolutely not! We can't!" The vehemence of

Terri's reply brought Taira's attention back to the room again, puzzlement crossing ker lined face. Terri must have sensed ker twin's consternation, for ke waved a hand to ker. "Not Rashi," ke said, less angrily. As ke continued to speak, ker voice become almost soothing, gentle. "Rashi's already left AnglSaiye, and will be in Warm Water in a few days. It would take a week to get word to ker."

Still studying ker twin's face, Taira carefully shrugged. Rashi wasn't *ker* favorite—ke thought Rashi a sycophant, too obviously fawning over Terri, but Terri seemed impressed by ker abilities. "All right. Perhaps Linden, then."

Terri was already shaking ker head. "It must be *Caitlyn*," ke said again firmly. "Taira, if nothing else, we need to discover whether or not Caitlyn has the skills we both suspect ke has. This gives us the chance to find out."

"I'd rather ke failed on something trivial. We'd already told Euzhan that she only had another month to send Fianya here or we would go to the Elder Council. This could be a nasty situation. For all we know, Euzhan's snatched the child and hidden ker away because of that."

"I know this is a serious matter, Taira, but I also know what VeiSaTi has told me. We can't ignore Ker, can we?"

I'm not even sure I believe Ke exists, Taira wanted to say, but that would just be the old argument again. "So we must send Caitlyn because of a *jitu* vision."

"We must send Caitlyn because it's what our god wants."

Taira knew there was no winning this battle, and ke was suddenly too tired to continue fighting. "I won't send ker alone."

Terri almost—almost—smiled. "Linden can go with ker, then."

"And YeiSa will want to send a Miccail Sa along as well."

"But Caitlyn will lead the group. We must make that clear. They will both follow Caitlyn's orders."

"I would still rather send Rashi."

Terri's face clouded again, a flush crawling up ker neck

like the mark of hands. "Rashi has other work to do, Taira. Important work."

Taira sighed. "All right. We'll send Caitlyn, if that's the only way we can reach agreement. I just hope we can find Fianya alive . . ."

Terri's eyes widened at that. "Of course," ke said, ker voice carefully flat. "Of course that's our hope. Whatever VeiSaTi wills . . ."

VOICE:
Caitlyn Koda-Schmidt of the Sa

WITH A SHOUT, I CURLED MY HAND INTO A FIST and punched at FerSa's face, but the Miccail wasn't there when the strike arrived, having stepped aside. I felt more than saw ker alongside me, and before I could turn, ke had grabbed my by the collar of my *shangaa*, ker claws snagging the cloth, and ker other hand coming swiftly up toward my head. FerSa's bony hips were under mine, and as ke turned and stepped, I went flying. Reflex sent me into a high fall, slapping the mat hard as I landed. As usual, it was a spectacularly lousy fall. I landed mostly on my back.

I lay there for several seconds making sure I could breathe.

YeiSa's clap came as FerSa leaned over me with a quizzical look on ker long, snouted Miccail face. Ker nostrils flared as ke helped me up, and I limped over to line up for the end of class. We bowed out, and YeiSa, our sensei and FirstHand of the Miccail Sa, came over to me as we started to sweep the woven straw mat. Ker seeing eyes squinted toward me, and ker *brais*, the third eye higher on ker forehead, was clouded with concern. Ke rubbed a hand along ker graying spinal mane. "You are hurt?" ke asked in the growling Miccail language.

"I'll live. But I'll bruise nicely, though."

"You know I admire your determination, Caitlyn."

"But not my skill."

YeiSa answered my smile with own of ker own. "You have the rest of your life to master this. Be patient. You have many bruises still to come."

Normally, I would have smiled politely and nodded, accepting YeiSa's platitudes. Maybe it was because I really *was* hurting, but I found myself speaking my frustration to YeiSa, something I'd never done with ker before. "YeiSa, I don't think it's going to matter how many bruises I get. I'm never going to get this art, not really. It's just another in a long list of things I'm not very good at."

Ke didn't reply at first. I heard ker take a long, deep breath, hold it for several seconds, then let it out again with the husk of a sigh. "What would have happened if FerSa had thrown you that way on your first day of practice with me?"

"It would have been my last day of practice, at least until all the broken bones had healed."

I saw YeiSa's lips twitch as if ke wanted to smile. "Sometimes when you always look ahead, you only see how far you have to go. Occasionally, you need to look behind to see how far you've come."

More platitudes. I could have continued the discussion, could have told ker "*hai*, but I look at everyone else who started when I did, and I'm the only one who still funbles through even the basic moves. I'm the only one who still hasn't learned to easily roll and fall." I could have said that, but I didn't. I figured YeiSa would have a bromide for that as well.

YeiSa, not accepting my silence, waved ker hand at the mat and the practice hall. "All you'll ever see here is a reflection of what you bring to the mat, CaitlynSa. Nothing more. Like anything else, it works best when you bring with you a passion."

I started to answer, but I saw Linden at the same time,

coming toward us from the east entrance to the training room. "YeiSa," ke called. "Have you managed to teach Caitlyn here anything yet?"

"I've taught ker how little ke knows," the Miccail answered. "That's the most important lesson I have."

"I'm fairly sure I have a grasp on that one," I told ker, and looked at Linden. Ke was grinning at me. "What's up?" I asked.

"Come on," ke told me. "My *da* Ely's about to try flying again. It should be great fun, if he doesn't kill himself."

"The last time he tried, nothing happened at all," I reminded Linden

"He's been fiddling with the engine. Evidently it starts every time now."

I glanced back at YeiSa, who nodded to me. I grabbed my clothes from the dressing room and, toweling off my hair and face, followed Linden out of the training hall and into the chilly afternoon breeze, fragrant with brine. A knot of humans and Miccail were gathered near the cliff edge closest to VeiSaTi's temple, and we hurried over toward them. This was one of the things I loved about the island: here was the one place on Mictlan where both human and Miccail lived together in relative peace. Most of the Families had relatives living here—it was not only the Sa who made the island their home.

One of our SaTu (Taira, I knew, since ker gray hair was shorter than ker twin's) was standing at the edge of the crowd, and Ghost was with ker. I went toward them while Linden plowed into the crowd, greeting friends and family.

"Caitlyn," Taira said as I approached. "Good to see you. Did the FirstHand give you a workout?"

"Ke damn near killed me, SaTu," I answered, addressing ker by ker title as head of the Community of Sa. A faint smile touched the corners of the old Sa's mouth. "Hey, Ghost," I said. "You look . . . ummm . . . different."

A computer projection, an artificial intelligence, and the last remnant of the crippled starship *Ibn Battuta* still in orbit

around Mictlan, Ghost changed appearance at will. Gabriela
Rusack, one of the original nine colonists, had been the
head programmer for the *Ibn Battuta*, and Ghost was the
primary personality she had created for the ship/personnel
interface. Her programming had been as quirky as her own
personality, and as brilliant. Gabriela would have been
pleasantly surprised with Ghost—he had learned, he had
grown, he had evolved within the limitations of the crippled
and ancient computer network in which he resided. Our
continued contact with Ghost has been crucial to us over
two centuries. There were still two working holographic
projectors, one here on AnglSaiye and the other back on
the Rock; when the *Ibn Battuta's* erratic path takes it directly over us, Ghost can activate the remaining network,
consult with the Elders, and do the necessary system main-
tenance.

Today, Ghost was a man, dressed in clothing that looked
to be from old Earth. I didn't recognize the face.

"Orville Wright," Ghost informed me. "Kitty Hawk.
Earth Date 1903." I shrugged, and Ghost shook his head.
"No one studies their history anymore," he muttered. "I
know *you* didn't. I saw all your schoolmasters' reports."

"We have you to remind us about it," I told him. "In-
cessantly."

"You won't have me forever." Ghost glowered melo-
dramatically, and I laughed. "Go ahead, make fun of your
poor AI," he said into my amusement. "Just because I'm
a construct doesn't mean I don't have feelings."

I glanced at Taira, who usually seemed to enjoy banter-
ing with Ghost, but Taira wasn't listening to us. Ke was
staring at the crowd around Ely's machine, but ke didn't
seem to be seeing it, and the frown on ker face was in
contrast to the gaiety everyone else was exhibiting. Mito
Allen-Levin had set up his bulky still camera on its tripod
and was recording the moment.

"SaTu, you're looking troubled."

Taira gave me a quick smile and a half shrug. "Ghost
has brought us news from the Rock," Taira said. "Actu-

ally, I'm glad you came over, Caitlyn. I need to talk with you about it.''

"Me?" I said, puzzled by that. While Taira was pleasant enough to me—as ke was with all the Sa—I was also not one of ker favorites, the ones ke chose to confide in or entrust with the community's responsibilities. "Is it something to do with my Family, SaTu?''

"No," Taira began, but any elaboration ke might have made was interrupted by a sudden roar and cough from Ely's machine. A cloud of smoke erupted from the nose of the thing, and the crowd moved back quickly, the Miccail barking in consternation. I could see the airplane now, twin wood and canvas wings, a boxy body and exhaust pipes belching a bluish fog. The plane was set at the top of a long, inclined ramp that ended at the cliff's edge, with a sheer drop to the gray sea below. The engine was spectacularly noisy and dirty. I coughed as the wind blew fumes toward us.

"She's mostly a WWI biplane," Ghost was shouting over the erratic, mad drone of the plane. Ely was climbing into the open cockpit, waving at the gathering. "Ely asked me to provide the design, and that seemed best. The Sopwith Camels were relatively simple and reliable machines. Even if the engine quits, Ely should be able to glide in safely.''

"And precisely why do we need this?" Taira shouted back.

"It's progress," Ghost answered.

"That's exactly what I was afraid you'd say.''

Ely waggled the flaps and revved the engine; it backfired with a visible gout of flame from the exhaust, sending the crowd scrambling back even further before the engine caught again and the propeller became a blur. The engine settled into a steadier whine. Ely waved—Linden and one of ker sibs yanked the blocks from the front of the wheels, and the plane rumbled down the ramp, picking up speed. The end of the ramp curved back upward, and the plane lifted gracefully as it left the ramp . . .

. . . then dropped like a stone past the cliff's edge.

We all surged forward, and Linden shouted, pointing out and down. "There he is! He's flying!" I could see the biplane, a hundred feet below and out above the bay's choppy waves, and climbing again. As I watched, Ely turned the plane into a long, slow banking turn as the crowd—the humans, at least—gave a ragged cheer. The Miccail mostly just watched, the expressions on their snouted faces impossible to decipher, their dark and wide eyes following Ely's flight. He was nearly level with the cliff's edge and still rising, beginning to circle the island as a blue-white cloud streamed behind.

The droning engine coughed again. Sputtered. Died. The exhaust trail cut off, and the biplane made a sharp turn back toward us. "*Khudda!*" Linden cursed, and waved at the crowd. "Move back! Hurry! Give him some room!" Ely had the nose turned back to us now, the plane moving in eerie silence, the wings dipping first left, then right. The propeller rotated slowly in the wind, useless. I could see Ely's goggled face, peering over the windshield, his hair ruffling wildly. I could see that he was aiming for the level clearing next to the launching ramp, but he was already low and losing altitude rapidly as he approached the island. "Ghost?"

"He'll make it," Ghost answered. "I think."

The wings dipped again as Ely came over AnglSaiye's cliffwall, and his left wheel hit the stones. The wheel and support went pinwheeling away, pieces of whitewood spraying toward us as everyone ducked. The plane hit the ground hard, running for a few meters on one wheel before dropping with a ripping crash onto its bottom left wingtip and spinning wildly. Pieces of the wings broke away, while the fuselage came to rest a few feet from the rear of the temple's stone facade. After long seconds of stunned silence, Ely emerged, slowly limping, from the dust and wreckage as his Family rushed toward him.

"Amazing! Wonderful!" Ghost shouted. Taira lifted an eyebrow toward the hologram. "This is a historic moment: Mictlan's first successful powered flight."

"You have a strange definition of 'successful,' " Taira told Ghost.

" 'Any landing you can walk away from is a good landing.' That's an old test pilot adage. After all, this is the first step back toward the stars. People will talk about this for centuries." Ghost looked at me. "*If* they remember their history," he added.

"I think I'll remember it," I told him. "I really do." A small fire had started near the engine; Ely and Linden started shouting, organizing a bucket brigade to throw water on what was left of the craft. Since most of the populace of AnglSaiye, human and Miccail, seemed to be milling around, it didn't look like one more person's help was going to make any difference. "SaTu, you mentioned needing to speak to me?"

The reminder erased Taira's amused smile. Ke seemed to draw in; age lines creased deeper in ker face. Ke put ker hand on my shoulder, and I felt ker fingers press tightly against me.

"Not here," ke said. "Bring the projector so we still have Ghost, and we'll go to my chambers to discuss it." Taira was staring somewhere beyond the wrecked airplane. "We're sending you to the Rock, Caitlyn," ke said softly. "It seems someone there doesn't like the Sa."

"To the Rock?" I asked. I'd been there once. I'd hated it. It was everything AnglSaiye was not. "SaTu?"

But ke didn't answer. Ke started walking toward the temple entrance. I picked up the projector and followed.

When we entered Taira's rooms within the temple complex, I set the device down again. Ghost, who had "walked" with us, shimmered and dropped the image he'd been holding, becoming a dark-haired female in the dress uniform of the *Ibn Battuta*. From old pictures (despite my admitted lack of attention in history class) I knew the face: Captain Roberts, the *Battuta*'s commander, killed in the shuttle explosion that nearly destroyed the starship.

"Actually," Ghost said to Taira as ke shut the door, "I have another bit of bad news. The trouble with Fianya's bad enough—though you could have at least pretended it was the first time you'd heard it, Taira. Now I can tell you the other.'' She paused, her lips pressing together grimly, and she seemed to stiffen. "I'm dying,'' she said.

"*What!?*" Taira and I both shouted the word at the same time.

She held up her hand. "It happened over a month ago,'' she said. "I was just out of range of the projectors, or I'd have actually been talking to you when it happened. I haven't mentioned it before because I wanted to work out all the scenarios. I suppose this was inevitable, but . . .'' A shrug, a toss of her long hair. She seemed incredibly nonchalant for someone discussing her coming death. "The ship was hit by a meteorite. The impact tore off one of the fuel tanks—in fact, if someone was watching the sky that night a few hours later, they'd have seen the tank hit the atmosphere. It was quite spectacular for a few minutes as it burned up. A huge, brilliant red shooting star . . .''

"This happened more than a month ago?" Taira said. "Why haven't you told anyone before? I must have spoken to you twice since then.''

"Could you do anything about it, Taira? Could you help me? Are you going to fly up here in Ely's plane?''

To that, there was no answer either one of us could make.

"But you're intact?" Taira asked Ghost. "The computer system wasn't damaged?''

"I'm intact,'' Ghost agreed. "But the impact also increased the ship's tumbling. Just keeping the antennae focused on the projectors is taking several of my processing cycles at the moment. As you know, since the original shuttle accident, I've been using the remaining attitude jets to keep the ship's orbit from decaying totally. I always knew I would die—simple orbital decay would have claimed me in time. But I'd calculated that with judicious use of the fuel and a little luck, I could keep the *Ibn Battuta* from becoming another shooting star for a few centuries more. Not now. The luck part didn't pan out. The tank that was destroyed held the majority of the remaining fuel. What little I have left . . .'' Another shrug.

"How long, Ghost?" Taira asked. Ker words sounded heavy and slow.

"The calculations took time, and I kept hoping I'd overlooked something. But . . ." She looked from Taira to me, and back.

"Another three months," she said. "Not much more."

I was shocked.

But what SaTu Taira said then shocked me more.

JOURNAL ENTRY:
Anaïs Koda-Levin, O'Sa

I SPOKE WITH GHOST LAST NIGHT, SINCE THE FAMilies finally consented to give one of the Rock's projectors to those of us who have moved to AnglSaiye. It was so wonderful to hear from her once more—"her," since as usual with me, she'd taken on Gabriela's aspect. I didn't realize until I was away from the Rock how much we needed Ghost, how much we depend on the knowledge in the ship's databank. I realized again that though Ghost might only be an artificial intelligence, a construct of light particles and not flesh, she's still as real to me as the rest. I would mourn her death the way I mourned when Geema Anaïs, my namesake, died last year.

In many ways, Ghost is as crucial to our existence here as anyone. I don't think anyone could deny that fact. Certainly without Ghost's input, my ancestors would never have survived in the beginning. We depended on the knowledge in the broken starship's databanks, and Ghost was the conduit through which that information flowed. We needed an unbiased opinion to guide us, and often enough, that was also Ghost. Without Ghost, we humans would never have survived the first years on Mictlan, and if we hadn't clung to existence, the Miccail might never have arisen from their own long slumber. There would have been two dead races buried on Mictlan, and we would never have come to know each other.

When I raise my eyes to the sky for guidance, it's Ghost I'm looking for.

VOICE:
Ishiko Allen-Shimmura of the Rock

"ISHIKO!"
        Sometimes when I hear Geema Euzhan screeching like that, as if I had nothing better in the world to do than to immediately drop whatever I was doing and run to answer her summons, I just continue working and pretend I don't hear her. Childish?—absolutely, but it does drive Euzhan crazy, and—childishly—I still get a twinge of pleasure from that.

I kicked the wheel to spin the embryonic pot a little faster, dipping a hand—my left, the stiff and unmoving flesh-lump—into water and then easing the clay upward to shape the bowl. Porfiera, my apprentice, was watching me without saying anything. I glanced at her; she looked back at me with her strangely mismatched eyes (one large and ice-blue, the other small and as richly dark as stained wood), then shrugged and went back to painting the greenware with the underglaze I'd prepared.

I hunched over the wheel again.

"Ishiko! Damn it, girl, where are you?" Geema's querulous voice was nearer now, echoing in the stairway that led down to my studio. I could hear her cane tapping at the stones, then mam Dana's voice: "Now, Geema, you shouldn't be going down these stairs. Please, I'll find Ishiko and send her to you; she's probably in the middle of something. Matsu, please escort your Geema back to her rooms, would you? Thank you.''

"All right," I heard Euzhan say. "But make damn sure the girl gets up here quickly. I'm not going to wait for her all day. And someone tell Gerald I'm going to my rooms now. I expect him there in one minute. One minute, do you hear?''

Porfiera glanced at me sidewise as Euzhan's voice faded and we heard Dana come down the stairs. I didn't turn around, but I felt her staring at me from the doorway. I spun the bowl, pulling more clay from the bottom.

"Geema Euzhan was calling you," mam Dana said finally. Since I couldn't ignore her any longer, I turned on my stool to look at her. She has extraordinarily long fingers; they crawled like scurrying spindle-legs across her arms as she stood, arms crossed. I've always admired those fingers. I used to pray to the *kami* of the Rock that they'd come one night to fix my left hand and make it like mam's. "Why didn't you answer her? Did you know she was ready to come down the stairs looking for you? She could have fallen.''

"Geema is harder than the stones. She'd have bounced and cracked the steps." I regretted the words as soon as I'd said them, but mam's frown made me lift my chin defiantly, pretending that I didn't care that I'd been cruel.

Fingers like dark twigs bunched the cloth of her sweater. "Would you go see her, please?''

I displayed my clay-draped right hand (the left half-hidden behind the bowl) and gestured at the spattered wheel with its fledgling piece. "Mam, I promised Theodora a set of bowls before the next Gather and I lost all that time looking for Fianya—which gives me exactly five more days to finish, decorate, and fire them.''

"Ish . . ." Mam sighed. "Is a few minutes too much to ask?''

I shook my head, biting at my lip and looking away from her. "Fine," I said at last, curtly. "A few minutes.''

As Dana turned and left, I kicked the wheel again—too fast. The bowl's fragile walls wobbled outward; when I tried to save the piece, I pressed too hard with my left hand. The sides curled in and collapsed. "Damn! Oh, *damn!*" I stared at the ruined piece twirling off center in the middle of the wheel, then pounded the clay back down, taking what little satisfaction I could in squeezing the rebellious clay back into a wet ball again. I got up from my seat and draped a damp cloth over the clay, then went over to the sink to wash. Porfiera watched as I took off my apron and started rinsing the clay slip from the fingers of my right hand and the fleshy spatula that was my left.

"I'll finish these up and start the kiln going," she said. "By the time you're back, we can start them firing."

I nodded, shook my hands to dry them, then wiped them on my hopelessly smeared pants. "You're Geema's favorite," Porfiera said. "That's why she's always asking for you."

"I'm Geema's disappointment," I answered. "That's why she won't leave me alone." A strand of hair had escaped from my scarf; I blew it away from my eyes and tried to smile at Porfiera. "Thanks, Por," I told her. "I'll be back as soon as I can, and we'll start firing what we have."

When I arrived at Geema's rooms, my *da* Gerald was just leaving. His face was grim, as if he and Geema had just had a nasty argument, his splotchy, discolored skin reddened with anger. "I take it she's in a good mood," I said.

Gerald grunted. "She'll probably let you keep your ass, since she's already chewed mine off," he said. "Go on in. She's waiting for you."

"Any luck out there?" I asked.

Gerald grimaced and shook his head.

We both sighed.

Geema Euzhan was standing at the window overlooking the center courtyard of the Rock. Seeing her outlined against the sun reminded me again how doll-like she appeared: like a sculpted version of the person she must once have been. At 106, she is far and away the oldest human on Mictlan—in fact, Aleksandr Allen-Levin, our current historian, says that Euzhan may be the oldest human *ever*, since 106 on Mictlan translates to about 143 solar years. Euzhan is sixth generation in a world where the seventh is already dead and most of the eighth are already gone; she'd known and talked with people who were only old tales to us: Anaïs the O'Sa; Elio the Betrayer; the Kiria Tozo, who is now considered almost a saint . . .

The vagaries of mutation, which had touched all of us so much, especially within our Family, had gifted Euzhan with long life. At first glance, from a distance, you might think she was no more than twenty, with a young woman's figure and a fall of magnificent dark hair. The cane she used seemed to be an anachronism in her hands, an affectation. In twilight, she could still appear to be stunningly beautiful. But when you see her up close you notice the fine network of wrinkles that cover her skin, or realize that the firm, young body is *too* firm, that all her joints move stiffly. Touching her hand is like stroking the raku glaze on a pot. Euzhan is an ancient shell of youth, and one day might shatter and dissolve into brittle dust.

"Geema, you wanted me?"

She turned like a statue on a turntable, her head held stiffly. Her skin was glossy, as if stretched too tightly over the frame of her face, but she was still pretty.

I worry sometimes that Euzhan's gift has been passed on to me. Everyone says I still look the same as I did when I was fifteen, and certainly my sibs Edznài and Nobe, who were born only a few years before me, are looking their age now. I'm not certain I want that—to be trapped in eternal youth like a honeydipper preserved in an amberdrop's sap. I don't want to be Geema Ishiko, the Ancient Curiosity.

"You didn't answer me," Geema said. Her voice was that of a young woman as well, but if you listened carefully, you could hear the tremor of age in it, hidden deep under the surface.

"I'm sorry, Geema. I was working. I'd blocked out the rest of the world, I'm afraid."

She sniffed, and her fine nostrils flared. "And Porfiera didn't hear me either, I take it."

"Even if she did, I'm afraid that Por is someone else I sometimes tune out."

"Hmm." Her scowl drew taut lines from her mouth to her cheekbones as she decided how much satisfaction she could wring from continuing to complain about my lack of attention. Evidently not much, since she finally sighed. "Well, I wanted to talk to you. Sit." With her cane, she pointed to a leather chair next to her desk. I saw the ornate head of the cane through her fingers, the oaken wood from old Earth itself and carved by the patriarch Shigetomo. There was also the black, jagged line of an old repair halfway down the shaft—the Betrayer had once broken the cane in half, back when it had belonged to Geeda Dominic, a century ago.

I brushed at the gray mess on my pants, which only raised a small cloud of clay dust, then sat—whoever in the Family had the job of cleaning Geema's office today was going to hate me. Geema Euzhan moved behind the desk, grimacing as she bent slowly at the waist. Her doll's face smoothed as she moved papers aside and placed her hands on the polished wood. "I've just finished talking with Gerald."

"They haven't found Fianya." I felt the same apprehension choking my throat that I'd felt when little Euzhan, my own dear Euz, whom I'd named after Geema, had started coughing up blood that winter night. Tears stung my eyes, unbidden, at the memory. I could see her face, and poor Timon's, too, and my three babies who had never made their Naming Day, and the dozen or so miscarriages in between. . . . I shoved them all back into that safe box in my head, where their voices, calling for their mam in pain and fright, couldn't be heard.

I took a breath. *A lot of mothers have lost their children here. You're not unique in that . . .*

Three days ago, almost everyone on the Rock had been looking for Fianya after Matsu had come back bawling about grumblers and a *kami* and other strange sights. There were rumors about a revival of the QualiKa—the violent sect of Miccail who, over half a century ago, had killed O'Sa Anaïs and several other humans in the Hannibal Massacre. Even though the QualiKa had all but disappeared since then, some were saying that the sect had never been entirely disbanded. At least half of my Family were still out searching, even though it had been frigidly cold last night—too cold for a near-infant to be outside and survive. By this time, nearly everyone believed Fianya to be dead. I believed it myself.

I wondered how Geema felt about that.

Euzhan frowned, the way she always did when a Sa was mentioned. "No, they still haven't found her," she answered. Euzhan never used the Sa pronouns "ker" or "ke." Never. Fianya had always been "she." "Gerald has most of them out combing the woods downriver from the Rock. We've sent word to AnglSaiye via Ghost, since it can't be avoided, though I'm sure they heard of this long before now. That means that the damn twins will be even more upset than they were already." Her fingertip traced the wood's grain; we both watched the slow, deliberate movement. "It also means that we'll end up with the Sa here, looking into things that aren't their business . . ." Her voice trailed off, then she looked up at me again. "They're going to suspect us," she said.

I looked at her doll's face, and the faint, faint lines around the eyes and the way she pinched her mouth together. I remembered Geema's reaction after Matsu had come back saying that Fianya was gone—there had been no guilt there. The anger and concern had been genuine, I was certain. "No, Geema."

"*Hai*," she answered. "They will, and you know half the Families wonder the same. I want you to help with this," she said. "We need one of our people involved when the Sa start looking for answers."

I could feel puzzlement twist my face. "Geema, we're innocent in this. I've heard that the new QualiKa . . ."

Geema sniffed derisively. "You think the Sa will believe that grumblers are to blame, when they're so thick with the animals? Or will they instead start looking at a Family whose genes remained pure of the Sa taint until Komoko failed us? Will they look at me, who hasn't hesitated to say what I think of the Sa? Will they suspect the person who refused to give them the Sa they demanded?''

''Geema, they can't really believe you'd have anything to do with this.''

''My dear, they won't have a choice but to suspect us. That's why I want to make sure that you're there, so we know what they're saying.''

I spread my right hand in denial, keeping the left cradled on my lap. ''Geema, the Sa aren't going to talk to me. Why should they?''

She stared at me with her too-young eyes. ''Because you'll make them believe that they should,'' she told me. ''Because they'll believe that you're different than the rest of our Family. Because . . .''

She paused, and the cold, undirected animosity on her face made the blood pound in my temples. ''Because, Ishiko, you'll make them think that you like them. You'll make them believe you need them. That you need them as Komoko did.''

CONTEXT:
Firio Allen-Levin of the Rock

AS HE DID NEARLY EVERY TIME HE WORKED IN VeiSaTi's temple on the island of AnglSaiye, Firio decided that the human Sa were definitely . . . well, *strange*. In Firio's opinion, the Sa were too much like the grumblers—no, no, not ''grumblers''; it wouldn't do to call them that, especially here on the island—the Sa were too much like the *Miccail*, then. Not that some of the Sa weren't attractive . . . In fact, Firio had gone to bed with one of them just last year: Agaja, ker name had been. It had been pleasurable enough, but like all his interactions with the midmales, a bit bizarre. They weren't *quite* female, after all, and when Agaja had taken off ker clothes . . .

He'd reminded himself that artists should always be open to new experiences; in the end, it had been a mutually pleasurable one.

Firio lived mostly on the Rock, but he came to AnglSaiye once a month or so because the elderly twins who currently ran the Sa community were both admirers of Firio's work, and because the Sa paid handsomely in raw materials. Four of Fiori's marble statues adorned the Sa temple's main entrance hall, and his mural of Anaïs's life ran the length of the back wall of the temple itself (contrasting sharply, in Firio's opinion, with the whorled, brightly colored and abstract Miccail paintings that covered the other temple walls.)

Now the Sa had been gifted with a massive trunk of ebonyew, and Terri—the intense, strange one of the two— wanted Firio to sculpt an altar out of the dense, black wood. It was bad enough that Firio knew he'd end up spending half his time resharpening his tools after working on the stubborn grain (though he had to admit that it was pretty stuff, with the faint veins of pure white marbling the satin, and ebonyew took oil wonderfully, resulting in a surface that was velvet to the touch), but Terri also had a very specific design in mind. Ke had taken Firio to one of the private rooms within the temple complex and shown him a dingy, scarred altar of plain whitewood.

"It's a Sa altar, over two thousand years old," the old Sa explained. Ker voice was high with excitement as ke showed Firio the ancient piece. "We've been using it because it's so old, and there's such a sense of history to it, but YeiSa assures me that the ancient Sa didn't attach any particular sacredness to the age of an altar. And I have to admit that the poor thing's about ready to fall apart. You need to keep in mind, however, that the basic structure of an altar is important to VeiSaTi. The top must have this shell pattern in it, a reflection of VeiSaTi's shell out in the main temple. Also, the altar must sit on three legs, representing the male, female, and midmale sexes. Do you understand that? The specific design is very important. Very important . . ." Ker eyes, dark and intense, fixed on Firio, and ke sidled up close to him. Ker breath was scented with *kav*.

Firio took a step back from ker intensity, pretending to study the altar. "You want it to look just like this?"

"I've told you what *must* be." Terri shrugged. "Beyond that, I'll leave the design up to your artistic creativity."

Firio wasn't impressed by that: It sounded like his "artistic creativity" was going to be hobbled by chains of tradition in this case. But the ebonyew was so damned beautiful, and the tree from which this block had been cut had yielded three other huge pieces, each of them a man's height tall and an arm span in diameter, and all just as gorgeous. Terri had promised them to Firio in payment for the altar—it was too tempting an offer to turn down.

Firio went over to the old altar and examined it closely. The wood was dry-rotted and brittle, scarred with boreholes from insects and further disfigured by deep cracks in the grain. One leg—he was damned if he could tell from the Miccail swirlies carved in it whether it was supposed to be the male, female, or midmale one—had broken and been badly repaired. The whole structure wobbled dangerously. The top was in the rough outline of the giant shell in the temple, incised lines tracing the pattern with the mouth a hollowed-out depression. The wood was scarred from what looked like a thousand years of knife cuts, and the wood was stained with brown-red. Some of the stains, Firio noted, were recent.

Firio frowned and took a step back from the altar. He knew that the Sa—both human and Miccail—practiced blood sacrifice as part of their rituals, but it was one thing to know it, and another to be confronted with evidence. Terri noted his discomfort, but ker reaction was a smile, as if Firio were a child. "Sacrifice is essential. Once a month or so, we offer a coney we're going to eat for supper anyway," ke said, answering the question Firio wasn't sure he wanted to ask. "It's an old, old rite of sacrifice to VeiSaTi, our *KoPavi*—our religious laws."

As Terri spoke, ke absently picked at the bloodstains on the wood, tiny brittle flecks curling from under the fingernail of ker index finger. Firio stared at the finger as Terri spoke.

It's an old, old grumbler *rite to a grumbler god*, Firio wanted to retort, *and from what I've heard, the grumblers occasionally threw in one of their own for sacrifice, just for variety's sake.* He thought it, but for once was successful in restraining his tongue. His mam Teresa would have been proud, and very surprised. *Three nice blocks of ebonyew to do whatever you want with,* he reminded himself, and managed a nod.

"You can do it, then?" Terri asked eagerly. Ke was still picking at the bloodstains.

"Give me eight weeks, and I want the rest of the ebonyew up front."

"Four weeks, and one of the other logs. You'll get the other two when you deliver the altar."

"Six weeks, two logs now."

"Four weeks. Two extra logs up front, one later."

Firio shrugged. "Agreed."

"Agreed." Terri lifted ker hand from the altar and clapped Firio's shoulder. He tried not to show his revulsion. In his peripheral vision, he could see the brown stains caught under the fingernail. "I'll look forward to seeing you again in a month, then. I'll make sure everything's ready in the morning. We have one of the Sa heading back to the Rock with you, and I'll send along four of our Miccail porters to handle the ebonyew."

Terri left him, then, and Firio retraced his steps back out through the main temple, where sunlight glinted from the huge, iridescent shell sitting on its crystalline altar. The shell was impressive, Firio had to admit. The grumbler mythology said that when the first of the Miccail Sa had come to the great cliff-walled island of AnglSaiye, thousands of years ago, ke had found the untouched shell placed here, hundreds of feet above the bay's waters. When the Sa had disappeared, the shell had remained here in the ruins of their temple, to be rediscovered by the matriarch Gabriela Rusack, and then several decades later by Anaïs herself. The piece dominated the room. As he walked by it, the sounds of his footsteps mingled in the shell's yawning, porcelain mouth with that of the wind and the various sounds of AnglSaiye's life, and the reverberations echoed strangely back to him like the distant hush of a voice, calling in some unknown language.

Firio stopped for a moment to listen—*strange, like all Sa things*—but the voice of the shell was that of a *kami*, mysterious and unknowable, and after a second, he continued walking, thinking of logs of ebonyew and wondering what forms might be hidden within them.

VOICE:
Caitlyn Koda-Schmidt <u>of the Sa</u>

THE *IBN BATTUTA II* WAS CROWDED WITH PEOPLE, which was unusual. Besides myself, my entourage included Linden and YeiSa's SecondHand, RenSa, whom I knew a little from the times ke had taught YeiSa's martial-arts class. I wondered at that, since the SecondHand was behind only YeiSa kerself in the Miccail half of our Community. As a result, RenSa ranked higher than me or Linden within the Community of Sa as a whole, and yet it had been made clear by the SaTu that I was to be in charge of our entire contingent. The SaTu rarely did anything without at least consulting the FirstHand, but I'd yet to decipher the reasoning beneath that decision. RenSa, at least, appeared unperturbed with the decision, though I often found it difficult to decipher the emotions in the Miccail faces.

I was puzzled by the SaTu's declaration. I knew that Linden was puzzled as well, since ke'd worn a perpetual look of amazement since ke'd been told. I was also worried—picking me to head up an investigation made no sense. *Send Rashi*, I'd wanted to say. *Send Linden. Send RenSa. But not me.* No sense at all. But both SaTu had told me that I had to go, and there was no arguing with them.

Between us, we took up three of the four passenger compartments on the craft; the artisan Firio took the other. Four other Miccail—porters employed by the Community—were also along to handle the heavy logs of ebonyew Porfirio had stashed belowdecks. They slept on the deck, under a canvas canopy.

I leaned on the railing as the small stern-wheeler, dipping and bobbing in the swells, maneuvered east out of Crookjaw Bay toward the wide mouth of the Loud River. The steam-powered engine throbbed like a great mechanical heart under our feet, driving the grease-slathered piston which in turn powered the paddles. I watched the red-painted boards slap the gray salt water of the bay, throwing up an eternal cold spray that the wind tossed away. Smoke curled from the twin stacks, sprinkled with glowing embers that gleamed like dying stars in the twilight, and I could smell the sweet scent of burning whitewood. AnglSaiye nestled between the two distant arms of the bay, looming tall and aloof. I could see the faint line of the five hundred steps cut into AnglSaiye's cliffwall, leading from harbor to the plateau far above. Off in the bay, a young sawtooth stooped on the wind, scanning the waves for wavestriders, untroubled by our passage.

"Beats walking, doesn't it?" Linden came up behind me, putting a hand on my shoulder. I touched ker hand with my own, and we interlaced fingers affectionately. Linden had taken me under ker wing early in my life within the Community, had acted as my protector during childhood squabbles, had been my tutor when it was apparent that I was going to fail my studies if I didn't have extra help, had been my mentor when at puberty it was time to learn the essential task of the Sa. I was glad that Linden was going to be along now, even though I suspected ke'd been sent mostly to make sure that I didn't utterly screw things up.

"I don't know," I said. "I've always enjoyed the hike down the highroad. But I'll admit that this definitely beats flying, from what I've seen."

Linden laughed. "Well, my *da* Ely insists that as soon as he gets decent steel out of the ironworks up on Lake Pollux, the engine will work—the cylinders froze up on him. I'm dubious myself, but Ely's not going to give up. He insists that in another year or so the Rock will only be a few hours away instead of a day or more."

"And walking—even though you may spend three or four days on the highroad—will still be the best and safest way to get there."

Linden laughed again and kissed my neck, hugging me from behind, hands lightly cupping my breasts through my *shangaa*, the traditional Miccail robe that the Community of Sa had adopted as our official uniform. I leaned back into ker embrace, enjoying the smell of salt water and smoke, the warmth of the last lingering rays of the sun, and the rhythmic movement of the boat. We were passing Blue Rocks, the steep bluffs that marked the entrance of the Loud River into the bay, and the *Battuta* bucked as she entered the strong freshwater currents; in the pilothouse, I could see the pilot fighting the wheel to keep her nosed into the Loud's mouth. In several hours, I knew, we'd reach the confluence of the Loud and Green Rivers, and we'd turn to follow the smaller Green River to the Rock. I wasn't sure what kind of reception awaited us there, and decided that I couldn't worry about it. Not yet.

I thought about Ghost, about the coming final death of the *Ibn Battuta*, and about the distressing news from the Rock. Ghost I could do nothing about, but I was about to become intimately involved in the other events. I couldn't imagine someone being cruel enough to steal Fianya from her Family and from the Sa. Certainly the Allen-Shimmuras felt they had their reasons to take action against the Sa, or to try to blame the Miccail for the attack. The Miccail themselves had their internal factions like the old QualiKa, and there was an undeniable underlying friction between human and Miccail. Then there were the Shunned—maybe one of them was responsible, taking out a grudge against the Families.

To harm a poor child, to make an innocent a pawn . . . If Fianya was still alive, ke must be terrified and frightened, and that thought made me angry, and the anger made me all the more certain that I was in way over my head.

"What?" Linden asked, ker breath warm against my ear. "Hmm?"

"You just went all tense. What are you thinking?"

"Just going over things in my mind. When's the last time you were at the Rock?"

I could feel the rise and fall of Linden's breath against my back. "Oh, late in the winter. I took the *Battuta* all the way to Warm Water, came back up to the Rock for a few days, then went on to Hannibal."

"I was at the Rock a year ago. I never really feel comfortable there. I always have the feeling that someone's watching me."

"Someone probably is. Not to mention that the Allen-Shimmura family pretends like you're not even there at all. Old Euzhan has them all in line."

"She can't live forever."

Linden chuckled. "Don't bet on it. She's been pickled in her own sourness." I felt ker tongue trace the line of my ear, and I pressed my head down against ker.

"Linden, if they couldn't get Rashi, then you should be in charge of this. Not me. I'm the screwup, the slow one, good for traveling the communities and not much more. Why did the SaTu hand this to me? I know that none of the senior Sa would have recommended me. I understand why RenSa can't be in charge—no one of the Rock's going to accept a Miccail as the spokesperson—but why *me*?"

"Because you can do it," ker voice came, a whisper alongside me. "Because they see what others don't."

"I'm glad you're so confident. I don't know . . ."

"We'll find what we find, Cait," Linden whispered. "In the meantime, we won't solve anything up here on deck, and it's getting colder. My room's warm, and the bed's warmer, if you're so inclined."

On the bluffs, a Miccail howled, a long ululation of inquiry. The Miccail on deck lifted their snouts and howled back: "We are bound to YeiSa FirstHand, and we go to Black Lake," they answered in their own language. "Wish us well."

The Miccail atop Blue Rock barked a blessing to Vei-SaTi, answered in turn by the Miccail on the *Battuta*, who started to sing one of the Miccail LongChants. One of them glanced over at us; when he saw me watching, he closed his mouth, his harmony falling out of the dissonant chant. The others grunted and the LongChant faltered and died in mutters. I glanced up at the bluff; the Miccail there had disappeared. The sun was lost behind the hills, and though the western sky was still awash with orange, the breeze off the water caused me to shiver.

I shivered and turned into Linden's embrace. "Let's go to the cabin, then," I told ker. "It's cold out here."

With the Miccail watching us, we abandoned the deck and my doubts for more hospitable quarters.

VOICE:
RenSa

I HEARD THE CALL OF THE SENTINEL ABOVE ANSUTI, the GodRock that overlooked the bay, the Great River's mouth, and AnglSaiye. I heard the answer of the Workers, and then the beginning of the LongChant. Comforting sounds, those, both familiar and right.

The rest of it I hated without reservation: the sharp smell of the metal beast in its lair within the craft's belly, the oppressive woodsmoke, the oily scent of the lubricants; the din of the engine, hissing steam vents, and the singsong shouting of the crew as they worked. The humans are obsessed: they rip the very stones from the earth, torture them with hammers and fire to extract the ugly, hard graystone they so love—the metal of their machinery. They build loud, noisome machines, all so they can hurry faster from here to there. The Scurrying People, the Impatient Ones: That's how I often think of them, always rushing from one place to another, and then rushing back, without the sense to appreciate the world around them. Even their speech is fast, the syllables flashing by without much inflection, a hurricane of sound.

I know the gods sent them to us to save us, but I don't know why They made them so strangely.

"There's an anger in you I don't understand," YeiSa had said the night ke'd summoned me to tell me the SaTu's decision. "You carry a resentment that colors your soul, and I don't know how to remove it."

"FirstHand, I'm sorry—" I had begun, but YeiSa only raised ker hand, smiling softly.

"You misunderstand me if you think you need to apologize, RenSa," ke said. "I wouldn't have named you SecondHand if I thought that you were unfit. No, I think that what's in you is in many of the CieTiLa, and perhaps that makes you most fit of all of us to understand. And it's why I'm sending you with Caitlyn. Ke will need your help, maybe most of all . . ."

The LongChant, strangely, died in mid-refrain, taking the memory of YeiSa with it. A few minutes later, I heard the door to the human Sa's quarters open and close, and then the LongChant started again. This time I found myself drawn by the sound, and I lifted myself from the bunk and went out of the cabin onto the deck.

The sun was down, though the sky was still touched with fading red. Quali, the smaller of the moons, was visible in the west as a fat crescent, escorted by emerging stars—the waxing crescent of Quali had been the sign of the QualiKa, and I wondered whether the fact that the human Sa had been kidnapped at this particular time had been coincidence or omen. The wind ruffled my spinal mane, and I shielded my *brais* for a moment to let it adjust to the change in light. Through the strong scent of the craft, I could smell brine, mingling with the sweeter tang of the Great River's water, which had traveled all the way from WeiGa, the glacier-riven mountains called the WorldWall. Faintly, the wind bore a trace of roasting paglanut, probably from the sentinel's cooking fire. The Workers, gathered under their canopy, nodded to me as I came near them. Once, we would have called them JeJa, and they would have been indentured to the TeTa of their tribe until they either became XeXa free folk or died. That was the old way—part of the old *KoPavi*—but there are no JeJa anymore. As the humans took up some of the old Sa ways, so the CieTiLa have taken a part of the human ways. O'Sa Anaïs chose what portions of the *KoPavi* would be followed and which would not. The FirstHands have told those who follow VeiSaTi that there are no TeTa, no XeXa, no JeJa (though I know that out in the world, away from the island, almost all CieTiLa still use the old ranks). On AnglSaiye we are defined by what we do, as if identity was the same thing as occupation: Worker; Sage; Healer.

Sa.

I listened to the Workers' song politely, resisting the urge to join in the chorus. An old song, sung by a people who no longer completely follow the tenets of the words they chant. Despite that, the LongChant is still a beautiful thing to hear.

On the pilothouse porch, two of the human crew members were looking down at the Workers, shaking their heads and making comments. I didn't have to hear the words to know what was being said between them. I had heard the same kind of comments when we'd boarded. For too many of the humans, we CieTiLa were just "grumblers": smelly, noisy, stupid, and perhaps dangerous animals. The QualiKa may have gone too far in response, but there was a reason the charismatic rebel NagTe had formed the movement two generations before, and that reason still existed. I listened to the comments marring the LongChant, and my claws emerged unbidden as I gripped the deck railing. I stared out over the wide Great River to the far, steep bank. This was CieTiLa land, all of it, and the land had been ours for *terduva* upon *terduva* through a past that extended back into myth. The human were exiles from the air, their souls not even created here, and yet to watch them you would think they had shat the world into existence and pissed the seas.

I had to admit that I also found galling the fact that all Sa, no matter what their race, are governed by the human Sa. True, it was the human O'Sa Anaïs who had fulfilled the promise of KaiSa's ancient sacrifice and returned the Sa to the Miccail, and for that, they deserved respect. True, it had been the humans who had come to AnglSaiye who rebuilt the temple and re-created the Community of Sa. True, the FirstHand sat with the SaTu at all their meetings, and the FirstHand's vote broke the tie if the twin SaTu did not agree on any decision. Yet . . .

I barked wordless frustration, a jarring note that made the LongChant behind me shiver momentarily, and my claws dug into the polished wood, scratching it. "Hey!" one of the crew shouted in the human tongue. "Watch the damn claws!"

I turned as the LongChant faltered again. I looked up at the humans, making sure that the man was watching me. Then, very deliberately, I raked my claws down the length of the railing, leaving three long gouges as wood curled from the razored tips. "I've watched them," I answered in their own language, "and they work very well, I think."

"*Khudda!*" the man shouted, starting toward the deck stair, but the other crew member, a woman, restrained him. "There are five of them down there, and that one's a Sa," I heard her say, hand on his arm. "Let it go, Garret."

The man shook away from his companion's grip, but he stopped, glaring down at me. One of the Workers laughed softly, and the LongChant started up again. I joined in the chant this time, still watching the crew members. After a minute, they both turned and went back into the pilothouse.

I continued to sing with the Workers, but the Long-Chant's rise and fall failed to comfort me, and a sullen anger burned in my belly like coal.

CONTEXT:
Daniel Allen-Shimmura <u>of the Rock</u>

THE *IBN BATTUTA II* DOCKED, AS ALWAYS, AT OLD Bridge at the foot of the Rock.

Dan, as always, was there to meet it.

The clean scent of whitewood shavings, the sawdust piling in drifts on the floor . . . As a young man thirty years ago, Dan had helped build the stern-wheeler, from plans provided by Ghost. He'd helped plane the whitewood planks for the decking, and had himself carved the great ebonyew wheel up in the pilothouse, now polished from three decades of hands. For several years, he'd worked as dock labor whenever the *Battuta* came in, laden with crops from the fields at Warm Water, or sitting low in the water after picking up Irontown steel from the Hannibal docks on the Loud, or bringing in fish and hard goods from Angl-Saiye. He'd loaded her again with goods from the Rock: faux-wheat, whitebean, peat, bushels of pear-nuts after the harvest, sweetmelons in the fall. He'd even ridden her for three years as a crew member, traveling from Warm Water to the Rock to AnglSaiye to Hannibal and back again. He'd worked the *Battuta* with enthusiasm, at least until his spine had started to curve, bowing him down, hunching his shoulders until what he saw in the mirror was a bent-over, shriveled parody of himself. For the last seven years, he'd been unable to work at all, as his muscles atrophied and his spine deformed even further.

There's nothing we can do about it, Dan. It's a congenital defect, a nasty mutation of scoliosis. All we can do is try to minimize it. I'm sorry. I really am . . .

Yet Dan was there each time the *Battuta* steamed in.

She came in under the wide central span of Old Bridge,

42

the section having been redesigned into a drawbridge to accommodate the *Battuta's* stacks, and she turned sharply just past the bridge to nose in to the dock. Lines were thrown to the dockworkers and secured; the gangplank turned and lowered as the *Battuta* vented steam and water dripped from the now-still paddles. Dan hobbled close to her, clutching the four-legged walker that he had to use now just to walk. Painfully, he raised his head as high as he could and waved to the Garret Koda-Shimmura, the pilot, who waved back—they'd been crewmembers together, back in the eighties.

It's a shame about your back, Dan. You know the rivers and the bay as well as I do. Better, even. You'd have made a great pilot, if only . . .

The passengers were gathered at the railing. Firio he recognized, but at least two of the others were Sa, along with several grumblers, all of the animals wearing *shangaa* like they were civilized—which meant this was the delegation sent from AnglSaiye to investigate the disappearance of the Allen-Shimmuras' little Sa.

The Sa came down the gangplank first, moving into the knot of dockworkers, children and the curious, and striding up the landing's slope toward Dan. They were talking together, all handsome in their grumbler *shangaa*, with long hair and small but distinct breasts, more like women than men.

He'd flirted with the Sa in the AnglSaiye pub even though he knew Geema Euzhan would be furious if she ever found out. He was young, he was very drunk, and the Sa seemed attractive. They even talked over ale for time. No matter what his Family thought, he'd wanted to go to her bed that night—who would know, besides him, after all? He wasn't a woman; he couldn't get pregnant. But not much later, before he could ask, the damn Sa had gone off with someone else, not him, as if he were nothing special, nothing much at all . . .

Dan saw his sib Richard hurrying up from the dock area toward the Rock, and he knew that Richard would be relaying the news of the Sa to Geema Euzhan. Dan envied

Richard's ability to run, even though he was ten years older than Dan. It would be over an hour before Dan could make it up the slope to the Allen-Shimmura compound again, an hour of pain and frustration.

"It's your Family's fault," Garret had said over tart-berry wine up in the pilothouse. *"None of you will breed with the Sa, so you're at the mercy of the Mictlan's kami, who can twist your genes into their own nasty shapes. Hell, if you folks in the Rock would just wake up and realize that you can't keep doing things the old way . . ."*

The Sa were almost next to him now. One of them turned and glanced his way, and ker face . . . ker soft, pretty face shifted with pity as ke looked at him, hunched over his damned walker, bent into Mictlan's painful shape. Then the Sa must have realized ker reaction and tried to smile down at him, but Dan scowled.

Pursing his lips, he spat at ker. The globule hit ker *shangaa* at ker right breast.

"Fuck you," he told ker. "Fuck all of you arrogant bastards."

As they stared at him wordlessly, as the Sa brushed at ker *shangaa* in disgust, Dan turned his back on them and shuffled away toward the *Battuta*.

It was slow progress, but it was the best approximation of a dignified retreat he could manage.

SONG:

"Blue Night": Gather song, composed by Buchi Koda-Shimmura (95–160)

CHORUS:

Amethyst purple, garnet black, or red
Quartz pale yellow, sharp flint brown
We to the dance are led
Gather the stones
Gather the stones
Place them 'round your head
And lest this be a blue night
We may soon be off to bed

VOICE:

Ishiko Allen-Shimmura of the Rock

LIKE MOST WOMEN IN THE ROCK, I REGARD GATHers with a mingling of emotions running the entire gamut from lust to disgust. On the one hand, a Gather is a time of celebration, an opportunity to meet new lovers or reacquaint yourself with old ones, to flirt and feel the electric tingle of attraction, to search the crowd for men wearing the same stone as you, to dance together or alone, to sample a hundred wonderful dishes, to talk, to be close

45

to your Family and everyone else in the Rock and simply enjoy the night.

And yet . . . there were times, especially as a young woman, when I came back to the compound alone and crying, when the man I really wanted to pull into my bed wore a red garnet when I wore yellow quartz and wasn't willing to ignore the custom (originally created by Ghost, in an effort to ensure a random mix of genes in our small pool) that only those with matching stones could sleep together that night; or when someone I'd slept with just a week before now didn't seem interested in me at all; when it was simply the wrong time of month, and I worked the food tables, feeling left out as I watched everyone else dancing the intricate steps of the mating ritual.

Lately, I find that the men I'm interested in are mostly interested in women ten years younger than me. I also notice that the ones who are picked are usually the ones without visible deformities—as too many of my family, like myself, display. Lately, I don't so much hate the Gathers as regret them, because they remind me that I'm almost past the time of childbearing, and all my poor children are dead before me.

It's a reminder Geema Euzhan mentions far too often.

At least this Gather promised to be something unusual.

The Sa had come in that afternoon on the *Battuta*, taking up residence in the old Koda-Levin compound—maintained for Sa visits to the Rock even though the Koda-Levin family had died with Anaïs forty years before. Geema Euzhan had sent them an invitation to come to the night's Gather, and also sent the two human Sa necklaces of yellow quartz to wear.

She'd also made sure that, when she passed out the Gather necklaces to the Family, I was the only one in the Family who had a matching yellow quartz. "What's this supposed to mean, Geema?" I asked her as I looked at the stone, sparking in my palm.

"It gives you an excuse to talk to them," she answered. "That's all. You know how I feel about the rest."

When the moon Longago (which the grumblers call

Chali) peered full and golden above the eastern horizon not long after sunset, the five fires, one for each of the Families, were lit on the ancient cracked concrete of the landing pad below the Rock. That in itself was a small, deliberate insult to our guests, since on AnglSaiye there were always six fires at a Gather, the extra blaze representing the Community of Sa (or, as some believed, the O'Sa's Family Koda-Levin). The stars were bright above the whirling sparks of the fires, and Longago's smaller companion, Faraway, was present also as a crescent that would in a few hours follow the sun over the horizon. I hoped that wasn't an omen. Faraway was called Quali by the grumblers, and its crescent was the sign of the hated QualiKa. A stream of people filled the pathway from the Rock, and among them I noticed the two adult Sa, a grumbler walking with them. Two hundred or more people crowded the area around the pad, all of them quieting as a spotlight plucked the lower gate of the Rock from gloom.

As Eldest, it was Geema Euzhan who walked the traditional caged curltongue from the Rock, each step accompanied by a low, subterranean beat from the great ceremonial drum built by the patriarch Shigetomo Shimmura. Geema looked like a moving carving of a young woman, her long shadow in the spotlight's glare as black as her hair. I felt more than heard each beat, the low, throbbing notes reverberating like low thunder. Alicia Allen-Levin, our current Kiria—the religious leader of all humans who believed in *Njia*, the original faith of the Founders—came forward as Geema reached the pad. She opened the curltongue's metal cage and attached to one foot of the bird a woven string of human hair, the strands coming from each of the Families. Then Kiria Alicia took the cage from Geema and made a circuit of the landing pad, the drum still shivering the air.

At the center of the pad, with all of the gathered Families watching, Kiria Alicia opened the cage fully and released the curltongue as the drum hammered a last heavy stroke. The curltongue arrowed away into the darkening sky chased by the spotlight, bearing away each of us—symbolically—with it. I watched the curltongue until I lost it somewhere over Tlilipan, wishing, as I did every time I watched the ceremony, that I could fly with the creature. There is so much to see on Mictlan that we haven't seen, a hundred sights that Ghost had told us about: the herds of thunderbeasts on the eastern plains, the vast rain forests on the southern edge of the continent, or the Southern continent on the other side of the world where—once—another human colony had been established.

And the stars, and our lost homeworld Earth, that maybe, maybe our great-great-great-grandchildren might one day see again.

I didn't breathe, watching the curltongue flitter away, until the spotlight abruptly shut down and the insistent pulse of *bodhran*, flute, and guitar brought the first couples out onto the pad to dance. I smiled, laughing and applauding as I went over to Geema Euzhan and Kiria Alicia.

"The ceremony was beautiful, as always," I told them. "Every time I watch, I feel like all the *kami* of Mictlan are watching with me."

Alicia smiled and touched my arm. "You'd make a fine Kiria, Ishiko," she said, with Geema smiling in agreement alongside her. "You have a sense of the history of our rites, and I think the *kami* speak to you as they do to me."

"I don't know, Kiria," I answered, laughing nervously. It wasn't the first time Alicia had suggested this, and I still wasn't sure how I felt. To be Kiria . . . "I don't know," I repeated. "That's not something I've considered seriously. I'm happy with my clay and my wheel. Being Kiria is far more responsibility than I've ever considered taking on."

"You've had children," Alicia answered softly. "There's no larger responsibility than that. You've also had to watch them leave you, and there's nothing harder." Her smile was touched with sympathy.

"Ishiko would be an excellent choice," Geema interjected, too loudly. "Meditative, attentive to the rituals, and caring." I noticed that Geema wasn't looking at me or Alicia, but across the pad to where the Sa were standing in a knot of people. Several of the other Elders were with them: Jalon, Theodora, Chung and Futa Allen-Levin, Andrea Koda-Shimmura, Michiko Koda-Schmidt, Shotoku Martinez-Santos. A flock of young men and women all attentively listening to the conversation. We Allen-Shimmuras, of course, were conspicuously absent from the Sa-infatuated crowd. "They fawn over the midmales like they were the Matriarchs and Patriarchs themselves," Geema muttered, thankfully abandoning the topic of the next Kiria. "Look at them—as if being in a Sa's good favor was the most important thing in the world. Well, I suppose the Sa will have no shortage of bedmates to choose from tonight." Her voice radiated disgust.

The Sa must have felt the pressure of Euzhan's gaze—which didn't surprise me, given the intensity of her stare—for the taller of the two suddenly glanced our way. Ke said something to ker companion, then excused kerself from the crowd and walked toward us.

"Kiria," ke said as ke approached, and gave her the sign of the Three: left hand palm down at groin level, palm up at waist, and palm down again at chest. Water, earth, and air—and also symbolizing the three sexes. "I'm Caitlyn Koda-Schmidt. I wanted to tell you how moved I was by the ceremony. Even in the face of this situation, you still show the power of *Njia*. I'm afraid that the AnglSaiye Gathers are only a poor imitation of this. There's so much more history here around the Rock."

Ker voice was androgynous and soft, warm and yet surprisingly tentative. Ker face was the same, perched in that indefinable territory between masculine and feminine, though closer, I thought, to a woman's. I could see the curve of small breasts under the fabric of ker *shangaa*, and ker hips were wide like a female's. For a moment, ker gaze rested on me—ke had those light eyes that are so rare among us, the gray-green of the river on a cloudy day. I put my left hand behind my back and nodded to ker. Ke smiled, ker thin fingers touching the necklace of yellow quartz around ker neck for just a moment, and then ker gaze went to Geema.

"Eldest," ke said, using her title, "I just wanted to tell

you how concerned we all are over Fianya's disappearance, and I hope we can help you find ker. I'm looking forward to meeting with Komoko and your Family first thing tomorrow. I also wanted to thank you for the invitation to attend your Gather tonight. It's a pleasure to finally meet you, and I'm pleased with the cooperation your Family has shown us so far.'' Ke extended ker hand to Euzhan, who simply glanced at it without moving

"I suppose to you I'm more of that 'history' you were referring to a moment ago?'' she said.

To Caitlyn's credit, only the barest hesitation showed in the Sa's answer. ''You are indeed,'' ke agreed, more amicably than I think Geema Euzhan liked. ''I never had the pleasure of knowing O'Sa Anaïs, of course, but SaTu Taira and Terri have told me many times of the special respect the O'Sa had for you, especially since you were Ochiba's daughter.''

I could see the red flush that crept Geema's neck with that. Caitlyn had (deliberately, I suspected, though I wasn't sure) stepped directly on Geema's one sore spot, reminding her that her mam had once been Anaïs's lover, before Anaïs had even realized she was Sa—a relationship which had shamed my entire Family. Not Euzhan's favorite subject, as all of us in the Family knew all too well. I could see her eyes narrowing, and her hand trembling on the head of her cane, but the Sa turned to me before she could speak. ''Do you dance?'' ke asked me. ''I'm afraid I'm not very good, but I love this tune.''

"I don't . . .'' I began, and saw Geema staring at me.

"I'd be honored,'' Caitlyn said. ''Please.''

The band had begun an energetic jig, with Sol Martinez-Santos adding the vocals. ''All right,'' I said, not entirely sure why I was agreeing. The Sa held out ker hand to me, and I took it—a soft hand, a warm hand. ''Excuse us,'' ke said to the Kiria and my fuming Geema, and led me away.

Caitlyn hadn't lied about ker dancing abilities. But while ke wasn't the best partner I'd ever had, ker movements were energetic, and ke laughed as ke tried to twirl through the steps with me, obviously enjoying the music and the dance. When ke took my left hand for the first time, ke hesitated only a moment before curling ker fingers around my unresponsive flesh, without a word and without anything showing in ker eyes. When the last trill of the flute had faded with all of us breathing hard now from the jig, we applauded the band as Sol began "Blue Night," one of my favorite ballads. I started to leave the pad, humming the tune softly, but Caitlyn touched my arm.

"Care to try again?" ke asked. I glanced at the couples around us, dancing close together now as Sol's baritone warmed the evening air. The guitars and flute joined his voice; I looked up at Caitlyn, and ke shrugged, smiling softly. "We have the same stone tonight," ke said.

"So do a few dozen other people. Will you be dancing with them all?"

Again, the smile tugged at ker mouth. Ke had a nice smile, and ker eyes were already dancing, alive with the lights of the bonfires. "I'll promise to restrict myself to you, if you'll make the same promise."

I could feel my breath tightening in my chest, could hear my pulse fighting the slow beat of the *bodhran*. All at once, I wasn't sure of this, wasn't sure what I wanted or what Geema Euzhan wanted or what exactly was being offered, and I suddenly felt like a girl just past her first menses, wearing her first Gather necklace. "My Family . . ." I began, but Caitlyn shook ker head, ker long, dark hair moving.

"Talk to me while we dance," ke said. Caitlyn spread ker arms to me in invitation, and I moved forward. Ker fingers slipped between those of my right hand, and ker other hand behind my back drew me closer but left a gap between us, as if ke knew what I was thinking. There was a scent about ker, a faint perfume. "You do pottery," ker voice said close to my ear.

"Your SaTu definitely gave you an excellent briefing."

I heard an exhalation that might have been laughter. "You have dried clay under your fingernails," ke answered. "Among other things Sa *are* taught to observe. It's one of the few lessons I actually managed to absorb. The

SaTu did give me a briefing, but I'm afraid I've forgotten most of it already. Other than that, I don't even know your name.''

"Ishiko," I told ker. "Ninth generation. My mam is Dana, hers was Isabel, and Isabel's was Geema Euzhan. And yes, I'm a potter.''

"So you're Euzhan's great-granddaughter. Then I'm a little surprised and very flattered that you're dancing with me. That also explains why Euzhan is watching us like I'm a verrechat about to pounce on her dinner." We moved silently together for a few seconds: step, step, turn, step. I found that I was doing the leading. "So I take it I'm wasting my time.''

"That depends on what you're after, I suppose. I'm enjoying dancing with you right now. I don't have expectations past that, and I won't hold you to any promises.''

"Promises are one thing we Sa take very seriously.''

"Then you should be careful who you make them to.'' Sol's voice lifted into the refrain, and I said nothing for a little time, listening. "Would you still be dancing with me if I told you that there's no chance you'll be in my bed tonight?''

"I'd just think that you were following the safest route for you, given your Family name. There's nothing wrong with that. And I'd also say that, yes, I'd still dance with you." Ker fingers pressed slightly against the small of my back, not enough to be insistent but more an invitation. For a moment, I resisted the pressure, then allowed ker to draw me in closer. I could feel the curve of ker body against mine, but the song was ending as Sol reached for the final high notes. Caitlyn didn't release me for a few seconds, and I found that I didn't care to move away. Applause sounded around us, the *bodhran* began a quick, energetic beat, and the band started a gavotte. I finally let my left arm drop from Caitlyn's back; ke allowed me to step back, but ker hand still held my right, good one. "Another dance?" ke asked, ker eyes on mine.

"What about all those other people wearing yellow?''

"Are you really concerned about them?''

"No," I answered truthfully, smiling at ker tentatively. "Besides, your friend's wearing yellow, too." People were already dancing, and the first change of partners had already taken place. "We're in the way here. Are you hungry?"

I led Caitlyn over to the food tables, and handed ker one of *mi* Nobesana's sweetcakes. I felt like half the people at the Gather were watching us; Geema Euzhan definitely was, still talking with Kiria Alicia. Caitlyn noticed as well. "Thanks," ke said, taking the cake. "Is all this attention just because you're an Allen-Shimmura talking to a Sa, or because everyone knows we're here to look into Fianya's disappearance?"

"A little of both," I said.

"After the way I was greeted when I came off the *Battuta* this morning, I have to admit that I worried about the reception I was going to get from your Family tonight."

I blushed at that, since we'd all heard about the spitting incident. "I'm sorry. *Da* Dan . . ."

Caitlyn waved aside my explanation. "It doesn't matter. At the moment, I'm enjoying myself. We don't have to really start work until tomorrow." Ke looked across the pad to where the other Sa was still surrounded. The Elders were no longer with ker, but a good number of the younger men and women were. "It looks like Linden is enjoying kerself, also."

"Isn't that Sa work ke's doing right now?"

Caitlyn laughed at that, gently, without any hint that ke'd taken offense. "That's part of our work, I suppose. *Hai*."

"You know don't have to stay with me. If you want to . . . *work*, also."

"I know. And you don't need to stay with me, either. There are several men wearing yellow." There was just the slightest emphasis on the word "men." Cailtyn didn't seem subtle enough to be much of a diplomat, but I found that I liked ker. There was an empathy to ker, a vulnerability. . . . Another smile, with ker head tilted inquisitively toward me. I took a bite of the sweetcake so that I didn't need to answer, not moving. Not wanting to move.

"Tell me about yourself. You're a potter . . ." Caitlyn

asked, nodding to me. I didn't know what to say. I suddenly felt embarrassed and parochial.

"That's pretty much all there is," I answered, shrugging, and hating myself for sounding so damned apologetic. "I'll bet half the dishes and a quarter of the mugs here tonight are mine. It's what I do."

"I tried that once," ke said. Ker breath curled away white in the night chill. "I loved the feel of it—the slickness of the clay, the way it trickled through your fingers, and there was something magical in the way you could pull form from a ball of gray mud. But . . ." Ke smiled self-deprecatingly. "I, ahh, wasn't much good at it. I could never make with my hands what I could see in my head. That's a true gift, one I'm afraid I don't have. You're lucky to have hands with the talent."

Ke took my hands in ker own as ke spoke, both of them, lifting them lightly so that they lay, palms up, between us. I could see ker gaze on my left hand, looking closely at the way the fingers appeared only as ridges in a wide mitten of flesh. I wanted to pull it away, to hide it from ker examination. "Is it difficult, with your hand?"

"You make accommodations," I told ker. "Actually, I can use it as a tool. Sometimes, it's actually an asset. For pottery, anyway. My Family's known for genetic defects, after all. Don't you use the Allen-Shimmura family as an example of why the Sa are so necessary?"

"Any hands that can make beauty must be beautiful themselves, no matter what anyone says about them. I hope you know that." If someone else had said it, I would have laughed. But there was a self-deprecating lilt in ker voice that made the words sincere. I could feel ker fingers under mine, and I realized how dangerous this Sa was for me. Geema Euzhan was right to fear them, because I could feel myself being pulled to ker, a compelling, emotional tug I hadn't felt in, well, a long time. If this one was like the one Komoko took to bed . . . I found myself scared of Caitlyn, frightened of that face that looked at me so softly, of ker sweet smile and yielding, gentle touch.

Khudda, I told myself, *it isn't supposed to happen this way. This isn't supposed to happen at all.*

Which was when Gaspar Allen-Levin came up to us. He wore a necklace of yellow quartz. I'd thought of Caitlyn as tall; now that Gaspar stood alongside us, a head taller than the Sa, I realized that Caitlyn and I were nearly of equal height. "Hello," Gaspar said to Caitlyn, with a glance at me. "I . . . wondered if you . . . wanted to dance."

Caitlyn looked at me. "Go ahead," I told ker, watching ker eyes. "I'd hate to stop you when you have work to do." Something—I wanted it to be disappointment—flickered in ker light gaze. Then ke smiled up at Gaspar and held out ker hand to him.

"All right," ke said. "Let's dance, then." Gaspar led ker out onto the concrete. I stood there, nibbling on the sweetcake, as they started to dance. Geema Euzhan was staring at me from across the pad. The music was loud, fast, and far too exuberant. Caitlyn, dancing, was laughing at something Gaspar had said, ker head back and ker hair swirling as ke turned and stepped.

I finished the sweetcake as the song careened into the last chorus. I suddenly didn't want to be there when the song ended, didn't want to know what would happen after the last notes echoed from the Rock, didn't want to know if the Sa would dance again with Gaspar or somebody else.

Didn't want to know if, afterward, ke might come back to me.

I left the Gather, sliding back into the shadows of the bonfires and heading back up the road to the Rock's gates.

Somewhere along the way, I took off my necklace of yellow quartz and tossed it away into the night.

JOURNAL ENTRY:
Anaïs Koda-Levin, O'Sa

MAYBE THE BIGGEST DISAPPOINTMENT FOR ME IS that even though it has been several years now since I've settled on the island, the head of Euzhan's family, Dominic, still absolutely refuses to allow me to see her or talk with her. Euz is what, fourteen now? Yes, fourteen—already past her menarche, and I've missed it all, missed being there to give her advice, hear about her first lovers, or talk with her in the soft night about things that woman (and Sa) talk about. I want so much to see how she's changed, what she looks like now that she's no longer a girl but a young woman. Elio's told me, of course, but that's not the same. Not the same as holding her, or stroking her soft hair.

It's not only that Euz is all I have left of her mam Ochiba, but knowing what I know now about the biology of the midmale, I do have to wonder if I might not be partially responsible for Euz's conception. That's certainly possible, given the time frame. I loved Ochiba so much, no matter how forbidden our kind of love was at that time, and Euzhan always seemed to love me also, as if I were one of her *mi* . . .

I'm afraid that Dominic and the rest of Allen-Shimmura family will turn Euzhan against me. They already openly refer to poor, steadfast Elio as "the Betrayer" because he dared to love me—which is just more of Dominic's poison infecting his Family. I've given up hope of ever coming to an understanding with my old nemesis, who will hate me to his Burning (which will be soon, from what I hear of his health). I can only hope that when Dominic's gone, this year or the next, I can finally come to some kind of peace with the new Elders of the Family.

To think that Euzhan could ever come to distrust me or hate me the way her Geeda Dominic does would be a wound in my soul that would never heal. Never.

VOICE:
RenSa

FROM THE SUMMIT, I COULD SEE THE FIRES OF THE humans and the crowd of them far below, gathered around the huge square of flatstone they'd laid at the base of the hill sacred to the CieTiLa. Faintly, the distant sound of their music, so dissonant and harsh to my ears, drifted up on the night air. Human music jumps all over, with too many notes all frantically jumbled together. Their music lacks the slow patient slide of the LongChant from one tone to the next, and thus is, to my mind, too much like the humans themselves.

I didn't know why I'd come up here. I was supposed to be down there with Caitlyn and Linden, meeting the various Elders of the Families, but somehow the light and the noise had seemed intolerable, and I'd slipped away from the crowds, eventually finding the old path to the summit of the great rock. As I'd ascended, I'd felt a strange pull, the same feeling of rightness I felt when I entered the temple at AnglSaiye and looked upon VeiSaTi's great shell.

Somehow, I knew I was supposed to be here. Something had called me here.

The light of the moon Chali suddenly dimmed in my *brais*; I shivered and glanced up, ready to cover or attack if a wingclaw were stooping above to attack. But it was only a cloud passing in front of the moon, and I relaxed, my claws curling back into their padded sheaths. In a moment, the silvered cloud had moved on, and in the creamy moonlight, I could see the *nasituda* set at the edge of the cliff. I walked over to them, stooping down to look at the ancient glyphs carved on them.

I could still read some of them: *I, MepTe, declare Black Lake free* ... the nearest and oldest of them said. MepTe, I knew from the histories we'd been taught on AnglSaiye, had been the first of the Great TeTa. SayaTa, MepTe's mate, had given birth to the very first Sa, near this rock. MepTe and SayaTa had declared the area around the Black Lake a sanctuary for all CieTiLa, and so it had remained for more *terduva* than anyone could count, until the Sa-Death that followed the ravages of the infamous DekTe and CaraTa.

I sighed. *All the names ... all the long, long turnings of the seasons* ... The vast history of the CieTiLa had unfolded here. Yet now the great Black Lake was gone to marsh and peat, the CieTiLa had plunged into a long slumber from which we'd awakened only a few generations ago, and our sacred hill was now the home of the humans, hollowed and scarred by their technology. Four of the seven *nasituda* here were shattered, stumps leaning in the ground like broken teeth—

The laughter of the humans came to me as the music ended. I crouched in front of the *nasituda*, letting my fingertips run affectionately over the ancient carvings and musing on how the Black Lake must have looked then, covering most of the valley spread before me.

Shadows moved on the hilltop as another song started, the darkness more felt than seen in my *brais*. I held my breath, peering from behind the stone. There was the sound of a footfall, then another CieTiLa stepped into moonlight. She was female, I noticed, but was no one I recognized from the tribes I had visited over the years. The stranger's *shangaa* wasn't made of the human cloth, but was woven from yellowgrass dyed a deep red. Her attention was all on the humans below. I wondered whether I should make my presence known, but then the stranger shifted to get a better view, and her *shangaa* opened slightly.

In the moonlight, I could see the sign of the crescent moon on the upper swell of her breast.

The mark of QualiKa! So that's why VeiSaTi brought me here, to show me that the rumors are true. The QualiKa are active again.

Cautiously, I rose to my feet. My hands were shaking, and I took a deep, calming breath as YeiSa had taught me, shifting my feet carefully into a defensive stance. *The QualiKa killed more CieTiLa than humans, two generations ago.* "I wouldn't think a QualiKa would like the human music any more than I do," I said loudly

The QualiKa spun around with a clatter of stones, daggered claws sliding from wide pads of her fingertips and the great ripping claws on her feet rising. Her lips were drawn up in a grimace of challenge, and her nasal vents flared. I didn't move, didn't react. Though I trembled inside, I kept an outward semblance of calm. *VeiSaTi brought me here. Ke will protect me.* "Their songs sound like two whining padfeet in heat," I continued, stepping out from behind the *nasituda*.

The QualiKa's stance relaxed slightly as she saw me, though the claws remained out and threatening. Her gaze skittered nervously past me, scanning the summit of the peak, and she moved smoothly to block the entrance to the path down the steep hill, cutting off any chance I had to retreat. She had strange eyes, pale eyes that were piercing and deep, and her face was extraordinary. While she stared at me, I found myself holding my breath again. I forced myself to exhale. "I'm alone and no threat to you," I told her. "Or have the QualiKa lost their respect for Sa, also?"

"*I* trust the Sa as much as they deserve to be trusted," she answered, but the scythelike claws of her feet lowered, and all but the tips of her handclaws retracted back into their fleshy sheaths. She tugged at her *shangaa*, pulling the knitted mesh of yellowgrass over the mark on her chest. "And there are no QualiKa. Not since your human O'Sa died stopping their last battle. Not since NagTe was killed by the flatfaces."

I gave the quick shiver of a shrug. "Yet that's not what

the CieTiLa who come to AnglSaiye from outside tell us. I've heard the tales that come to the Sa from the tribes. They say that the QualiKa have come together again. We even hear that their leader has called herself a Ta: Cos is her name. the grandpup of old Nag himself. We hear that she has claimed to be the Cha'akMongTi.''

The silver-shot eyes narrowed slightly, but beyond that there was no reaction to my words. ''The JeJa believe all the old myths,'' she said. ''That's their nature—isn't that what the TeTa believe? The JeJa don't have your education, your breeding, or your luck, Sa.''

''There are no JeJa or TeTa. Or have you forgotten what seven generations of FirstHands have said?''

''No one has forgotten that the FirstHands try to pretend we are human, or that you follow a *KoPavi* that is not the *KoPavi* our people once followed.''

''The QualiKa have forgotten that the humans brought the Sa back to us and saved us from losing what was left of our culture.'' To that, the stranger only shrugged. ''The humans think the QualiKa have returned, also,'' I persisted. ''Some of them believe that the QualiKa stole a human Sa from here, just a few hands of days ago.''

She laughed at that—a bitter, short sound that made her face briefly harsh. ''Then you must think that CosTa and these mythical QualiKa are very stupid as well. Why would they do that? Why would they want the flatfaces aroused? Why would they deliberately antagonize the Sa, who they need as much as any CieTiLa? What would the QualiKa *gain* by taking a human Sa?''

''I thought those were things a QualiKa might know,'' I said carefully. ''My name is RenSa.'' I waited, but the other made no move to give her name. ''I have the honor to be the SecondHand to YeiSa,'' I continued. ''The fact that the FirstHand would dispatch ker Second here should tell you how seriously the Community of Sa considers this. I was sent here to ask the very questions you asked.''

''None of those questions have answers. At least not from me.''

''And you are . . . ?''

The QualiKa—if that was indeed what she was—ignored my query. Instead, she turned back to glance again at the bonfires far below them, and the brightly colored, milling crowd. She still blocked the path, and I could see the tension in her back, in the way her spinal mane lifted. In the moonlight, I saw her face twist with distaste.

"The human SaTu have sent their own Hands to look into this," I said to the CieTiLa's back. "They wonder about the QualiKa, too, but they also look at their own kind." Again I waited, but the other didn't respond. "I know CaitlynSa and LindenSa, and I believe they will be fair. If the QualiKa knew what had happened to the child, and if they helped the Sa find ker—"

"Then what?" She spat out the words angrily, still staring down at the Gather. "What would change? Would the flatfaces leave the Black Lake? Would they abandon AnglSaiye? Would they stop tearing at the earth everywhere they go? Would they hate us less? Would the CieTiLa magically go back to following the *KoPavi*—the *full KoPavi*—as they should?" Now she turned, and a sardonic smile twisted at her lips. Her eyes, bright as the moon, seemed to impale my soul. I had rarely seen anyone so compelling just in her presence. "*If* the QualiKa existed," she said.

I took another slow breath. *I can feel the danger in her. I can feel the anger, like a smoldering fire, and I want to join with it . . .* "Those humans who are frightened of us might be less frightened," I told her. "I think that's possible, but not all humans hate us, no matter what you might want to believe. Will they leave? No, but I remind you that it was a human who did VeiSaTi's bidding and brought the CieTiLa back from our long sleep. Without the humans, the CieTiLa would still be a frightened shadow of what we had been, most fighting like animals in the wild, and a few of us clinging to old ways we barely understand. No one knows what the true *KoPavi* once was, not even the QualiKa. Maybe we will know, when we finish translating the *nasituda* under the temple. But not until then. What the QualiKa call the *KoPavi* is a collection of myths twisted by time and shaped by NagTe's ambition. They are not the real *KoPavi*.'' I lifted my chin slightly, my spinal mane rising as I spoke the words I wasn't sure I really believed, but that were the creed of the Sa. "The QualiKa would do well to remember that. *If* they exist," I added.

The music from below sounded louder now, and several human voices from below joined the song. I sighed. "I must go back," I said, more to myself than the other. "They'll be concerned if I'm missing for too long." I glanced at the QualiKa, at the odd, light eyes that seemed to see all the way through me. I shivered, and pulled my *shangaa* tight around me. "If you would meet one of these mythical QualiKa, I'd ask a favor," I told her.

"And what would that be, RenSa SecondHand?"

"Get word to Cos, the one who would call herself the new Cha'akMongTi, and tell her that I'd like to speak with her. Tell her that our interests—at least as far as the disappearance of the human Sa are concerned—aren't so different as she might think."

"An interesting notion, that. But not particularly believable."

I shrugged, wishing she would stop staring at me, wishing that her presence didn't so visibly bother me. *Remember your training* . . . But the words did nothing to dispel the stranger's perilous aura. "YeiSa told me once that knowing the truth is finding sweet water. You can't tell the sweet from the salt by the look or the sound—you have to taste it."

"And if I would taste you, RenSa, which would you be?" The QualiKa took a step toward me, and I instinctively dropped into a martial stance, the tips of my hand-claws emerging. The QualiKa saw, and that crooked smile tugged at her lips again as her eyes gleamed.

"I must leave now," I said, hating the tremble in my voice. *Calm yourself. Breathe, and be ready, because she may attack.*

"Then go." She took a step away from the entrance to the stone stairs, but only a step, so that I had to nearly touch her to get by. I tried to ignore the crawling of my spinal mane as I passed her. I could smell her, could almost feel the heat of her body, and I half expected her to lash out at me.

But she did not, and the moment passed. I started down to the long, winding trail. "RenSa," she called after me, and I stopped, not looking back at her, not daring to do so. "You have me curious to know if your water is truly sweet. I'll offer you one truth in return—my name. I am called CosTa."

Startled, I finally turned, but the summit was empty now. Only the *nasituda* stood there, alone in the moonlight and awash in the alien sound of the human music.

CONTEXT:
Eris Allen-Levin of the Rock

ERIS DIDN'T KNOW WHY HE WAS HEADING BACK TOward the Rock from the settlement at Warm Water. There was nothing for him at either place, of course, not for another month: No one who would talk to him, no one who would offer him a meal or a place to stay for the night.

That's what it meant to be shunned.

Hai, Eris had admitted to Andrea Koda-Shimmura as she sat before the Elder Council as judge, he'd stolen the paglanut cakes from the Family food stores. *Nei*, it was not the first time he'd stolen from Family stores. *Hai*, he'd also taken various things from other Families. *Hai*, he'd been warned by Geeda Jalon the last time he'd been caught that a repeat offense would cause the Family to bring him before the Elder Council. Eris admitted it all. He'd been caught in the midst of his last theft; there was no sense in denying what was obvious.

When Elder Andrea had pronounced him shunned for six

months, when Eris had looked at the impassive faces of the
Elder Council staring at him (especially the Elders of his
own family), he'd almost been tempted to shrug. How bad
could it be, having to live outside the community for half
a year? He'd have time to think, time to see some of the
places he hadn't had the chance to visit, not while working
the fields and helping run the woodshop under *da* Caril's
sharp eyes and sharper tongue. Hell, it was damn near a
vacation. A pack with a tent, bedroll, rifle, and supplies
waited for him at the entrance to the Rock, and no one
spoke to him from the moment the sentence was pronounced.

Eris told himself that he didn't care, that it didn't matter.
For several days, it hadn't. The weather was unseasonably
warm, and the autumnal snows that would normally have
covered the ground by now were late. The jaunecerf had
just finished their migration back to the area, so there was
game enough to hunt, and though most of the fruit and nut-
bearing trees had already dropped their bounty, there were
still the remnants to forage.

Then, a week later, the snows came snarling in from
Crookjaw Bay, howling and shrieking. The jaunecerf-skin
tent trembled and shook in the fury of the storm, and the
small fire Eris had started guttered and went out, and all
the wood Eris could find was soaked.

He thought he was going to die that night. He thought
of the warm and dry Family compound back home, and the
full import of what he'd done to himself came rushing over
him, as cold and furious as the storm outside.

For the next six months, he would be alone. Shunned.
For six months, the tent and the few possessions in it were
all he would have between himself and the harsh, cold reality of Mictlan.

He wept, then. On many nights.

He thought, several times in the next few weeks, that if
he didn't actually die, he might go crazy. It was the lone-
liness that was worse than the storms, worse than the cold,
worse than the hunger. He decided that he had to leave the
vicinity of the Rock, because all of the sudden he'd top a

ridge and see the tall flank of bare stone standing in the distance, the river winding around it, and the pain would clench his chest so hard he could barely breathe. He turned his back on the Rock and headed south and east toward Warm Water.

Eris knew it would be no better there. A message would have been sent to AnglSaiye, to Warm Water, to Ironworks, and to Hannibal, alerting them as to who was shunned, and when the sentence was to be lifted. There would be no welcome for him anywhere. Erin avoided the roads for that reason, not wanting to meet anyone because he couldn't stand the knowledge that they would look through him, that they would pretend not to see him, that they would not talk to him or offer him food.

But traveling to Warm Water was something he'd always wanted to do, and if nothing else, it would be something to do with his time. It took him a month and a half to get to the lake, wallowing through the snow-wrapped woods, up and down the tangled hills. He stayed there for another month, in the woods near the settlement, until the smell of woodsmoke and the sound of distant voices made the pain return, and then he turned back toward the Rock.

It was full winter then, and the trek back took much longer. Five full months of Eris's sentence had passed before he saw the Rock again, from a hilltop several kilometers away.

Like many of the hilltops in the region, this one was adorned with several old *nasituda*, the Speaking Stones of the Miccail. These seemed to have been restored, the old carvings cleaned and the stones set upright. One of the stones appeared to be newer, with recent carvings on the milky face of the soft crystalline rock. There were grumbler tracks in the snow, as well—it had last snowed three days ago, so Eris couldn't tell if the tracks were new or days old. Still, he'd killed two grumblers two months ago, a mated pair who had suddenly appeared in front of him one morning. His warning shot hadn't frightened them at all, and the male had started toward him, claws extended. He'd dropped him with two quick shots, and then, when the female came rushing at him, killed her also. Eris unslung his rifle and made sure that there were shells in the clip. The hillside was suddenly decidedly unpastoral. There were a hundred hiding places, behind the *nasituda*, in the trees behind him, in the folded rocks to his right, where there might be caves.

Eris decided to move down into the valley below for the night. The grumblers could have the peak if they wanted it. Eris shrugged his pack back onto his shoulders, checked the rifle once more, and headed down to where a grove of bubble-trees shivered around a small iced-over pond. There was no path, and, as he walked, the hillside steepened rapidly, seeming to end abruptly in a sheer drop-off. Eris stopped, squinting into the sun. Someone had tumbled down this slope recently—just here, the person had slipped, and a flailing step further on, had gone down, plunging down, the snow disturbed where the poor unfortunate had tried to grab at rocks and shrubs to stop the freefall. It hadn't worked, Eris saw suddenly, for where the wind had formed the snow into a graceful ledge at the cliff's lip, there was a hole. Whoever it was had gone over.

Moving carefully, Eris worked his way down, sitting on his rear and half-sliding. A meter from the cliff, he turned and lay prone, crawling forward until he could see over the cliff edge.

"*Khudda!*" he uttered as he saw what lay crumpled at the bottom, atop a scree of black rocks. "By the blood of Buddha . . ." He didn't even notice that he'd spoken aloud, for the first time in months.

Eris knew then that, shunned or not, there was something he needed to tell the Families in the Rock.

VOICE:
Caitlyn Koda-Schmidt of the Sa

KOMOKO ALLEN-SHIMMURA WAS A THIN WOMAN IN her early twenties, and her grief and worry wore her like a veil. They darkened her features, painted circles under her eyes, and wreathed her in melancholy that even the touch of Edzná, her older sib sitting alongside her and clutching her hand, couldn't lift. Tears started in my eyes just looking at her, an empathetic pain that cut through the cold of the Allen-Shimmura compound and the weariness I felt from staying up far too long at the Gather the night before. The fire crackling in the massive hearth of their Common Room promised warmth and delivered none, and the twisting flames kept dragging Komoko's eyes away from me.

I could feel a sense of incompetence nagging at me, a voice that kept muttering: *You can't help her. You should never have been sent here.*

"Fianya is a sweet child," she told us, as Edzná stroked her arm. Out in the adjoining kitchen, I could hear the voices of several other family members, and some of the little ones kept looking in to be chased away by their *mi* and *da*'s scoldings. I could smell river grouper broiling for the Family lunch. I'd also noticed the way they looked at Komoku, that odd commingling of sympathy and disappointment. "Ke is a joy, just a joy, and I was hoping to convince Geema Euzhan to let me go to AnglSaiye for a few months, just so I could be near to ker even after ke was in the Sa community. I know that might not have been the best thing for ker or me, but . . ." Komoko glanced up at me, snaring me with her shadowed eyes.

I nodded, even though we both knew it for a convenient

67

lie. Even if Komoko had asked, Euzhan wouldn't have permitted her to bring Fianya to AnglSaiye. Euzhan had made it plain Fianya was *never* going to AnglSaiye.

Komoko sniffed and nodded to me. "I imagine it was just as hard for your mam to think about giving you up," she said. "It's the curse of birthing a Sa, knowing that you only have ker for a few years, that you have to lose . . . lose . . ." A soft cry came from her trembling lip, and Edzná glared at me as if I were entirely responsible for her sib's sorrow. Komoko took a deep, shuddering breath, her eyes closing, and then smiled softly at me. Her pain tugged at me, made me want to hold her myself. "I'm . . . I'm sorry. It's just that every once in a while . . ."

"You don't have anything to apologize for," Edzná told her fiercely.

"No, you don't," I agreed, quickly. "And I'm sorry to have to ask you these questions, since I know they hurt you. But I must ask. I hope you understand that."

Komoko nodded; Edzná glared, as she had through most of the interview. "I promise you that I'm nearly done," I told them. "And I appreciate your going over what I know has been very painful ground for you." I glanced at the notes I'd been taking, letting my breath out in a long sigh. The paper was covered with my scrawling handwriting, all the details of that horrible morning from Komoko's viewpoint, and all the details swirled confusedly in my mind. "So you spent the entire night out looking for Fianya, is that correct?"

"It was so cold that night. I didn't want ker to freeze to death. None of us did. Most of the Family was out there with us, even Geema Euzhan. Geema loves Fianya. She really does. I kept hearing them calling ker name, and I hoped I'd hear ker suddenly answer, that ke'd see the lights of our torches and come out of some hiding place. We combed the entire area within a kilometer of the Rock that night."

"And you didn't see any sign of ker."

"Nothing." Komoko's voice was bleak and empty. "There were grumbler tracks all around, though."

I nodded. "My companion Linden is talking to Matsu now. What about other signs, other footprints?"

"No one could tell. Matsu had already walked all over the immediate area looking for ker, and then when we got out there . . ." Komoku shrugged. "There were footprints everywhere, of all kinds." She looked up at me, and I hated the dullness of her gaze. "I haven't been much help to you."

"That's not true," I assured her, though she was right—I hadn't learned much that I didn't already know. Maybe buried somewhere in my notes was a clue that could move us forward, but I had no idea where. "You've been a great help," I said, echoing the words I knew she wanted to hear, the meaningless comfort. The lie. "I want you to know that we'll do everything we can to help your Family find ker. Fianya is part of the Community of Sa, even if ke never came to the island, and that makes ker my sibling. I will do for ker what I would do for any of my sibs."

Komoko smiled uncertainly at that. Edzná only scowled, which was expected. I knew what I'd just said wasn't what the Allen-Shimmuras wanted to hear. "Just one last thing," I told them. "Can you think of anyone here who might have had reason to want to do this—perhaps someone with a grudge against your Family, or Fianya, or even the Sa?"

"You think someone *here* is responsible?"

I heard the raw disbelief in her voice, and I shook my head quickly. "I'm not saying that at all. I'm just trying to make sure that we haven't missed any possibility."

Edzná grunted, answering before Komoko. "Our Family didn't have anything to do with this."

"I never mentioned the Family."

"But that's who you meant, isn't it?"

I'd have been a fool *not* to be thinking of their Family, given the long history of animosity between their Family and the Sa, going all the way back to O'Sa Anaïs, but I wasn't going to admit it. I gazed into Edzná's skepticism with what I hoped was neutrality. "I had no one in particular in mind," I said. "All I'm trying to determine is if there is someone here who might have reason to abduct

Fianya, for any reason. There's been no contact from any-one, no demands?''

"No," Komoko answered. "That's what makes me most afraid that Fianya's . . ." She couldn't say the word, though we all knew what it was. Neither Edzná or I were going to say it, either, although I was already fairly certain that we weren't going to find Fianya alive.

"There are currently five individuals shunned from the Rock?" I asked, hoping to deflect Komoko's thoughts from the grim landscape in which they were wandering. "Maybe one of them?"

Komoko glanced at Edzná. "Could Eris . . . ?" she be-gan, then looked back to me. "Eris Allen-Levin was shunned almost six months ago for repeatedly stealing from common supplies. I was the one who caught him, the last time, and I told his Geeda Jalon, who ordered him brought before the Elder Council to be sentenced. But I don't think—"

"Has anyone seen Eris recently?"

Komoko shrugged. "He went south. One of the Martinez-Santos family said they saw him in the woods on the way to Warm Water. But his shunning is over in just a month. Why would he do something like this now?"

"Maybe he can answer that for us." I made a note to try to contact Rashi, who should now be in Warm Water, to see if Eris had been seen in the vicinity. I stood then, and Komoko and Edzná stood with me. I went over to them, tucking my notes into my pouch, and hugged Komoko.

"I know how you must feel," I told her softly. "I'm so sorry for you. We'll find Fianya. I know we will." More lies, but they were all I had to give her. I hugged her once more. "Take care of your sib," I told Edzná, and left the room.

The Common Room gave way to a long, wide alcove with immense wooden doors, open to the main room of the Rock, sliced from the stone by the lasers of our ancestors' shuttlecraft. The twin doors of the Rock were pulled back; sunlight and a cool wind streamed into the cavern. The crystalline rock caught the sunlight and threw it back, and the tracks of the lasers had molded the stone into cascading waves on the wall, extending over fifty feet high here, and dwarfing anyone who stood in the room. Echoes chased themselves along the room as people meandered in and out on various errands, and I could see more than one of them glance at me with curious eyes. I just stood there, watching them watching me, and thinking over all I'd learned this morning. It was all a muddle in my head, and I wondered whether the best thing I could do would be to hand over the investigation to Linden and go back to AnglSaiye in defeat.

"So . . . were you asking Komoko whether Geema Euzhan kidnapped the baby herself?" I turned, and found Ishiko Allen-Shimmura standing behind me. She was holding a slatted wooden box stuffed with straw on one hip, the misshapen left hand hidden behind the box. I saw the glaze of pottery tucked in the padding. As I had been last night, I was struck by her. She had a rare presence, and eyes that defied and invited at the same time. "Geema did it, you know," Ishiko continued, those eyes holding me. "In fact, I helped her put on her cloak of invisibility, and Geema ran out, snatched up the little Sa all by herself and then walked all over the marsh making those grumbler tracks. Pretty spry for someone who's a hundred and six, don't you think?"

I decided I wasn't going to get anywhere down that particular conversational path, and ignored it. "Last night, I came back to the table after I danced with Gaspar, and you were gone. I was disappointed, since I was enjoying our conversation so much."

"I'm sure Gaspar didn't mind." The tilt of her head challenged me, the long fall of dark hair over one shoulder swaying.

"I kept hoping you'd come back, but eventually one of your sibs told me that you'd gone back up to the compound."

Something shifted in her face. Her mouth twisted. "I suddenly wasn't feeling well. I'm sure my absence didn't . . ."

She hesitated, then caught my gaze again. ". . . spoil your evening."

"The truth is that it made the evening less than it might have been."

"Ahh. I'll let Gaspar know."

"That would be terribly cruel."

A wisp of smile traced her lips. "I'm an Allen-Shimmura. All of us are cruel. Especially where the Sa are concerned."

"I can hardly believe that the creator of something so lovely—" I reached toward her. Ishiko's eyes widened, and she started to take a step back until she realized that my target was the box she carried. I stroked the cool glaze of one of her pots. "—could be cruel," I finished.

Ishiko didn't look at me, but at my hand. "You're easily deceived by decoration—" she began, but an echoing shout interrupted.

"*Caitlyn!*"

We both turned to find Linden hurrying toward us. Ke was out of breath, ker face ruddy with exertion, and there was a careful neutrality in ker face, covering ker features like a mask. Ke glanced at Ishiko, then at me.

"Fianya's been found," Linden said, and the tone of ker voice told me all I needed to know.

INCLINATIONS

"I said that the state of Israel has not had peace and will not have peace because there can be no peace structured on injustice, lying, thievery, murder and using God's name as a shield for your dirty religion."

—MINISTER LOUIS FARRAKHAN,
quoted in the *Washington Times*,
February 27, 1990

VOICE:
Ishiko Allen-Shimmura of the Rock

THE ELDER COUNCIL, WITH GEEMA EUZHAN'S INsistence, firmly limited the number of people who went to investigate Eris Allen-Levin's discovery of Fianya's body. A wise move, since half the Rock would have gone otherwise, and that would have been chaos. The Sa contingent were all included, with Geema's grudging acceptance. Komoko had insisted on going; surprisingly, Geema Euzhan had agreed to that. William Allen-Levin also petitioned to be one of the party. Even his Family referred to William as "Grim Bill" for his sober, humorless demeanor. The lack of a smile wasn't Bill's fault—it was another of the hundreds of small mutations in our population. He lacked the fine facial muscles that lend animation to a face; maybe his psyche was so doleful simply because he couldn't smile. Bill had been Komoko's most consistent lover; at one time, they had talked of entering into a covenant. Bill, I knew, firmly believed that Fianya was his child, despite the fact that Sa biology meant that was a physical impossibility. The Sa Komoko had slept with would have ejaculated into her the culled, revitalized seed of whatever man ke'd last made love to, and that hadn't been Bill. Despite that, Bill had always treated Fianya like Family, and he and Komoko were still lovers.

And somehow, I was one of the party as well. To be Geema's eyes and ears.

"I don't understand, Geema," I told her. "There's absolutely no reason for me to go with them. If anyone, you ought to send *da* Cuauh—a doctor makes more sense than a potter. And with my hand . . ."

75

Geema Euzhan turned her china-doll face toward me, her body moving stiffly as she came away from her study window. Patriarch Shigetomo's cane tapped on the stone floor with each step. "The Sa called Linden has had extensive medical training, evidently," she told me. "And Caitlyn has had a bit as well. But that hardly matters. Fianya's dead; there's no need for a doctor except to examine the body, and the Elder Council appointed Cuauh to perform the autopsy back here." Her voice brimmed with satisfaction at that, and I knew who had made that suggestion. "Hands don't matter. What I do need are unbiased eyes and ears. You know the kinds of questions they've been asking, and the Family needs to make sure that we aren't implicated in this. This Caitlyn's investigation seems to be totally unfocused, from what I've heard."

"I still don't understand—"

Frown lines appeared around her eyes, like cracks in the glaze of her perfect face. Geema's infamous anger looked so out of place in that perfect, youthful doll's face, and her occasional rages always appeared more sinister and disturbing to me because of that. "*You*," she barked, "don't *need* to understand. I've asked you to go. Are you refusing?"

No one ever refused Geema, not if they wanted to stay on the Rock. The few Allen-Shimmuras who consistently defied her were now all on AnglSaiye, because Geema had made their lives too miserable to remain here. "No, Geema," I began, and she waved off the rest of the explanation. The frown lines remained, though.

"And what happened with you last night? Caitlyn seemed to be well taken by you, but you left. Why? That fit perfectly into my plans for you."

Because I found I was well taken by ker also, Geema. Because I found myself drawn to ker in a way I haven't been drawn to someone in far too long, and I got scared. That's it, Geema. Because I didn't know what I'd do if I stayed.

I didn't say any of that. Geema would have scoffed at that, or become truly furious, or simply wouldn't have understood. So I shrugged. "I thought that if I stayed with ker too long, it would be suspicious. Our Family and the Sa, after all . . ."

The frown lines faded, slowly, as if drawn in thick batter. "Hmm," Geema grunted, but the disapproval was mild. "I don't think a few more dances would have mattered, and you might have learned more about their intentions. But no matter; it's done now." She sat behind her desk, lowering herself carefully and leaning the cane against the dark-grained wood. She picked up a memorandum from the pile of papers there. "You will leave within the hour. I have Porfiera packing your things for you. She said she can handle the studio for you for a few days. You're an artist; so use your artist's eyes. I need to know everything you see."

It was my turn to frown. I knew I should have simply nodded and left; Geema's gaze had already left me in dismissal, as her attention went to a Council memorandum on her desk. "Geema, why are you so worried about this? Our Family's *not* involved, is it?"

The blush rose slowly from her neck to her cheeks, but for once the anger didn't overflow. "Don't be foolish, Ishiko," she snapped. "The QualiKa took Fianya, in all likelihood."

"Then the Family has nothing to fear."

"No? Our Family's fought the influence of the Sa ever since Anaïs Koda-Levin started the colony on AnglSaiye, ever since that bitch stopped us from destroying the QualiKa once and forever at Hannibal. Look at them: On the island, the Elder Council is a toothless anachronism; it's the Sa who are the arbiters of disputes. It's the Sa who provide the majority of the medical care. It's the Sa to whom everyone runs when there's a problem. It's the Sa who corrupt us with grumbler ways and their *KoPavi* corruption of *Njia*. No one on AnglSaiye has children in the human way anymore. The Sa want us to be like the grumblers. They want us to live their way, they want us to believe in their gods."

Geema Euzhan spat out the words, as if they were bitter in her mouth. Her dark eyes glittered with bright fury.

"Without our Family, it would be the same here," she continued. "You don't think that the Sa would love an opportunity to damage my influence with the Elder Council here on the Rock? They don't even need to prove anything, just put enough doubts in the other Families' minds, and the damage will be done. 'If everyone would breed the Sa way, there'd be almost no mutations, there'd be fewer still-births and infant deaths.' That's the poison they whisper now, and each whisper is an axe blade to the root of our society here, to the system the Matriarchs and Patriarchs created and that has kept us alive. Well, that's *khudda*. I know it. Our Family knows it, even if others are deceived."

Geema's hand had crumpled the memo into a ball, her fingers fisted deep in the paper folds. She looked from her hand to me, and her gaze was sharp-edged flint. "You *will* go," she told me. "I expect to know everything. Everything. Do you understand, Ishiko?"

There was only one thing I could say to that. "*Hai*, Geema," I told her. "I understand."

With that, Geema's hand relaxed, and the ball of paper fell to the desk. She didn't seem to notice. The scarlet flush receded like a slow tide, and the lines that anger had carved around her eyes smoothed once again. "Come here, then, child," she said to me, gesturing. She was smiling now. Why not?—she'd gotten her way, as always. As I approached the desk, she tilted her cheek toward me for a kiss.

I kissed her. It was like kissing a piece of my pottery.

TRANSLATION:
From the AnglSaiye <u>KoPavi</u>, <u>Nasituda</u> 27, Grouping A: "The Threes"

THERE ARE THREE:
The air
  The earth
    The water

THERE ARE THREE:
The male
  The female
    The Sa

THERE ARE THREE:
The child
  The adult
    The elder

THERE ARE THREE:
The JeJa
  The XeXa
    The TeTa

THERE ARE THREE:
The life of conflict
  The life of peace
    The life of honor

THERE ARE THREE:
The death of accident or intent

79

The death of age or disease
  The death of sacrifice

THERE ARE THREE:
Those who seek nothing
  Those who know not what they seek
    Those who have found it

THERE ARE THREE.

VOICE:
Ishiko Allen-Shimmura <u>of the Rock</u>

ERIS, HIS SHUNNING REVOKED BY THE COUNCIL, LED the way back. While Eris served as our guide, the expedition had no clear leader. I had actually thought that, if anyone, it would be the older Sa, Linden, who would head the Sa contingent. But Linden always waited for Caitlyn to speak when questions were asked of the Sa. Caitlyn tried to take command, and though RenSa and Linden seemed to defer to ker, William and Eris ignored everything ke said, while Komoko was lost in her own dark thoughts, and the grumbler porters listened only to RenSa.

The sun had set by the time we came within sight of the cliffside where Eris had found the body, though twilight lingered wearily on the horizon and wizards were squabbling noisily in the amberdrops. We could see the rocks, and the ragged notch in the snow above, but globe-trees and vines hid the rest. "Komoko," Caitlyn said softly, ker hand resting lightly on the woman's shoulder. "I think you should stay back here with the porters. This is nothing you need to see."

"*Nei!*" Komoko shouted, shrugging ker hand away.

"That is *my* child out there, and I *am* going to see ker. You can't stop me."

"Komoko..." Caitlyn had drawn back a step. Ke looked at Linden as if for help, then at me. "Komoko, I'm not trying to keep you from ker. Ishiko and William can identify the body"—I saw Komoko flinch at the word— "and then we'll bring ker back here to you. I promise."

Komoko had begun shaking her head before Caitlyn had finished. She started to walk toward the base of the cliff, as if daring Caitlyn to stop her. It was Bill who stepped forward then.

"The Sa's right," he said with his slurred voice. "I'm sorry, Komoko, but ke's right. You should wait. I'll take care of ker. You know I will. I always have."

Komoko's mouth opened as if she were going to object, but then she slumped and nodded. Caitlyn's posture relaxed in visible relief. "RenSa," ke said, "would you tell the other Miccail to set up a camp here for the night? Linden, you stay with Komoko." I thought I saw disdain in the way the grumbler Sa's snouth wrinkled, and Linden simply nodded, grim-faced. The rest of us followed Eris into the tangle of vines.

I wish I hadn't. It was far worse than anything I'd expected, and I knew that the vision would prowl my nightmares for months to come.

The foot of the cliff was littered with rocks and boulders, and the tiny body lay atop them sprawled on ker back, the head turned violently around at an impossible angle. As I saw it for the first time, the body shivered for a moment, my nervous gaze lending the body a life it no longer held. The child's eyes were open, ker mouth wide with a final, silent scream, one bloodstained hand outflung as if ke were reaching for us. Ker skin was the white of pale stone, though orangish snow had drifted over ker hair and clothing.

Someone was cursing, and I suddenly realized that it was my voice. Then Bill and Caitlyn stepped between, hiding the appalling display.

"It's ker," Bill said in his slurred voice. In the dusk, his voice was loud. "It's Fianya." Frowning as always, he turned away, looking up toward where she'd fallen, his throat pulsing with emotion. Caitlyn crouched in front of the body, giving the sign of the Three and staring as if ke could cause Fianya to rise up again by the sheer force of ker gaze. Geema had demanded a full description; holding my breath, I went and stood behind Caitlyn.

"Such a waste," ke said without looking at me. "Such an awful, awful waste." Ke reached out and softly brushed the snow from Fianya's face, then gently closed ker eyes. I saw then that scavengers had found the body before we did, and suddenly Fianya's face shimmered and I saw my poor Timon's face as it had looked when he was lying feverish with the Bloody Cough in my bed, and then my little Euzhan's face as well, and the other three unnamed children I'd birthed and held and cuddled and who, despite all the love I gave them, died before their Naming Day.

They were all there, lying dead on the rocks with Fianya.

I had to turn away myself as my stomach roiled and protested. I found myself on all fours, throwing up into the snow as helpless spasms rolled through me. "It's okay, Ishiko," Caitlyn said, ker voice close to my ear. "It's all right." I felt ker arm around my shoulder. I wanted to shrug it away as Komoko had, but couldn't. I wanted ker there. I wanted ker comfort, and hated myself for it. I spat once and wiped my mouth, standing and taking in a deep mouthful of the cold air. Caitlyn's arm fell away, and I was looking into ker seafoam eyes. I could feel the presence of Fianya's corpse behind me, and I didn't dare turn away.

"For about a year, I was apprenticed to the AnglSaiye clinic. I remember that the first few times I had to work with the dead, I did the same thing," ke told me. "I never, ever got used to it."

I felt a strange disappointment that Caitlyn had misread my reaction, that ke didn't understand why I'd responded as I had. I just nodded. "I'm fine," I told ker. I took another long breath, which shivered as I released it. "Something's been at ker . . ." I couldn't say it, as tears gathered in my eyes, and my throat clenched. I wiped at my eyes angrily with the back of my coat sleeve. *All their faces. My poor lost ones . . .*

"I know," Caitlyn said. "Eris told me, and that's why I didn't want Komoko to see. Why don't you go back with her?"

Another breath. My stomach muscles still ached, but everything had settled again. "No," I grunted. "I'll be fine." I could see the doubt in ker eyes, and the resulting irritation banished the last of the nausea. I turned around to look at the body again. This time everything stayed down, and Fianya's face was just Fianya's. "What do we do now?"

Caitlyn crouched again close to the body. "We should all take a close look around, in case there's something we're overlooking, but I don't think there's much here. Fianya fell or was thrown from up there; it looks like the fall broke ker neck. Those are snarlripper tracks in the snow—that's what was at the body. Eris, the bootprints around the body are yours from earlier today, is that right?" Eris grunted—he was staying well away from the body, and he still didn't seem comfortable conversing with people again. "My best guess is that the body's been here a day, maybe two," Caitlyn said, more to himself than any of us. Except for me, nobody was paying much attention to ker.

"Is that what a year in an AnglSaiye clinic teaches you, Sa?" Bill said drily. "I'm impressed."

Caitlyn ignored the comment. "We'll know more when we do an autopsy back at the Rock clinic. If there's more here to learn , it's up there"—Caitlyn nodded toward the top of the cliff—"and that will have to wait until tomorrow. We should wrap the body and bring ker back to the camp. If Komoko wants to see Fianya's face then, just to know, she can. William, do you agree?"

Bill grunted something I couldn't hear. Caitlyn swung ker pack off ker shoulders and opened it, pulling out a long length of heavy cloth and laying it on the ground.

I moved forward to take the cloth from ker, as did Bill. "You don't need to," Caitlyn told us. "I can do this."

"We knew ker," I told ker. "We hadn't given ker to the Sa yet. Ke was still of the Rock."

"Ishiko's right," Bill grumbled in agreement. "Fianya is our responsibility, not yours."

Caitlyn held the cloth for a moment, then nodded, stepping away. Bill and I placed Fianya's tiny, broken body on the cloth and wrapped ker. When it was done, Bill lifted ker in his arms, as he must have done a thousand times when Fianya was alive, and carried ker back to the camp.

VOICE:

RenSa

THE HILLTOP WAS MUCH AS THE HUMAN ERIS HAD described it, with the track of the toddler Sa's fatal tumble poignantly visible. I wondered how it must have felt for ker, falling head over heels down the steep incline, and then all of a sudden plunging over the lip of the cliff into cold air.

I hope the poor child never realized it.

"Just like I said," Eris pointed out. "See—grumbler tracks."

He glanced at me as he said it, realizing that he'd used the animal word. I could have told him that it didn't matter, that calling us "Miccail" was as much an insult since that was just another of their human words, too, and meant nothing more than noise to us.

But I didn't say it. I could taste the man's fear and dislike of me on the wind, and the same scent came from the one they called Bill, and from Komoko and Ishiko as well, though not quite as strongly. Caitlyn and Linden alone didn't carry the scent. I marveled again at the blindness of the human nose, which could not notice the fear-scent, or the faint challenge I gave in return.

SPEAKING STONES 85

I was glad that Caitlyn had ordered the Workers to stay back at the encampment, so they didn't have to smell the humans' dislike and listen to this ignorance.

"It has snowed since the child fell," I pointed out. "The CieTiLa tracks"—I used our own word for ourselves—"are newer."

Eris's face twisted, as if I'd caught him in a lie. "Maybe, but they're still *grumbler* tracks, aren't they?" This time he used the word harshly, deliberately, and his chin lifted in defiance. "And I don't see any other tracks around except mine."

"Then perhaps we should suspect you," I told him, and turned away from the protest I knew would follow.

"*Hakuchi!*" Eris bellowed, and I heard him take a step through the snow toward me. I turned, ready to defend myself, but Bill grabbed Eris, while Linden stepped in front of me.

Caitlyn looked bewildered. "That's enough!" ke shouted. "Enough! RenSa's right. The Miccail tracks were made *after* Fianya fell. So were yours, Eris, and RenSa knows that also. We're up here to see if we can figure out what happened. So let's do that."

Eris shrugged himself away from Bill with a glare back to me. Linden patted my shoulders. At Caitlyn's insistence, the group grudgingly broke into two to explore the area: Linden and Komoko with me, the others with Caitlyn.

I followed the path of the Sa-child back upslope. Where the rut of her fatal tumble began, there was a large rock tilted up from the ground. Ker footprints upslope were softened and blurred by the snow that had fallen since, but I could tell that ke had been running, for the toes were deeper than the heels. Evidently Fianya had stumbled over the rock in ker flight. It had flurried two nights ago for a short time, when we were still on the boat to the Black Lake, so the child died sometime before then—maybe even during that brief storm, since ker prints weren't totally obliterated. Near the *nasituda* set on the hilltop, the stones thrust upward in folded columns, and the line of footprints led to a shallow, tall cave nestled in the lips of the rock.

Linden and Komoko caught up with me there. "Wait a moment," I told Linden. "Take a look . . ." The snow in front of the cave, and also that leading away down the other side of the hill toward a heavy stand of globe-trees and bramble, had been disturbed. A few needlelike leaves from a pricklespice branch lay in the wide, back-and-forth sweeping lines in the snow. "It appears that someone didn't want us to see what their prints looked like," I said.

Linden nodded. "Let's see if they left anything inside."

We crowded into the narrow space. The cave was dry, and a small fire of peat and pagla-nut husks had been built in the center. I held my hands over the ashes—they were as cold as the ground. Near the fire, there were three indentations pressed into the ground and spaced equally apart—something had been set there once. I had just bent down to look at the marks more closely when Komoko gave a small cry and rushed past me, going to the back of the cave, where she picked up a small, red-and-yellow-checked scarf.

"This was kers," she said, holding it up to her face. "This was Fianya's." She was crying, the tears falling in glistening lines down her cheeks. Her sadness throbbed in the confined space, so powerful that I could feel it tugging at me. *I know sadness, too,* I wanted to tell her. *I know the pain of having someone who is close to you ripped away too early. I've knelt by the body of my sister, killed by a human's weapon—"an accident" they said—her blood staining the snow a deeper red* . . . I wanted to hold Komoko as I held my own mother that night, sharing our misery and grief. But I didn't. I only watched her, burying her face in the cloth that once warmed her child. "I can . . . I can still smell ker on it."

So perhaps humans are not as scent-blind as I believed.

"Ke was held here, at least for a time," Linden said. Ke glanced at the remnants of the fire. "Pagla-nut," ke said, looking at me. I knew the rest of ker thought without it being said: *like the CieTiLa.*

"And peat," I answered. *Like the humans.*

Linden nodded and gave the shoulder lift that is the human shrug. There was nothing else in the cave, and the dirt was too hard-packed and frozen to have left footprints. Near the entrance, however, there was the print of a CieTiLa, and it was not mine. I decided not to point it out—we knew that there had been CieTiLa here after Fianya's death. Any of my people could well have checked out the cave as we were doing now, since the Sa-child's tracks led back to it. "Whoever was here cleaned up after themselves," Linden said.

"With the amount of ash and the way the husks are almost gone, I'd say the fire was going for several days," I said. "Probably Fianya was brought here right after ke was taken."

"But why?"

I could feel the hair of my spine bristle with the question. *I should know because you've already decided that CieTiLa were responsible, is that it*? "You don't expect an answer from me, do you?"

Linden gave me a rueful smile, and I caught the scent of ker embarrassment. "No. I'm sorry, RenSa. That was entirely rhetorical."

YeiSa taught me well. I know that human etiquette would have been to smile in return and tell ker "that's all right." I know it, though I don't understand it—when someone apologizes and that satisfies you, the incident is ended. I gave Linden the CieTiLa response instead, which was to ignore the apology and not embarrass ker further with ker mistake. I looked at Komoko, still lost in the memory of her child. "We should go tell the others what we've found," I said. "Caitlyn should see this, if ke's to give the final report to the SaTu."

Linden frowned, as if wanting to say more, but ke finally shrugged again and went to Komoko, touching her arm and telling her that we were leaving. I went outside, shielding my *brais* from the light until the brightness settled in my vision. I could see Caitlyn and the others by the *nasituda*.

"Good. We need you, RenSa," Caitlyn said as I approached. The female with the deformed hand, Ishiko, was standing near ker. I wondered if either of them sensed the strong pheromones around Caitlyn and Ishiko, or remarked on the way they often looked at each other. I'd noticed; I think Linden had as well. This was not a good thing, this attraction between them. Caitlyn had enough difficulty handling the responsibilities the SaTu had given ker without the additional burden of a relationship. "A few of these carvings on the *nasituda* look new," Caitlyn continued. "Can you translate them?"

I noticed that there were no footprints in the snow around the *nasituda* except our own; someone had swept the snow here, too. I crouched down in front of the Speaking Stone. Caitlyn was right—the chiseled marks in the soft, milky crystal were new-cut, the edges sharp, and the marks in the pale rock had been stained a bright yellow-orange with urine. Pale flecks of the translucent stone were still lying on the snow. The rune-signs were recognizable: a hollow circle pierced with a phallus which was the Sa-sign, and then the ascending triangle that represents triumph or victory, and what might have been glyph of ending, but it leaned right, not left as it should have. "These could be CieTiLa glyphs, but there's nothing to read. The syntax is wrong, there's no identifier, and I'm not certain about the last symbol. I don't know who carved this or what they might have been trying to say."

"I don't need a translation of *this*." The voice was angry: William, standing alongside one of the other stones. I could smell the fear-scent on him again, stronger than ever before. William pointed—a new symbol had been cut into that Telling Stone as well, incised over ancient marks: a crescent moon. "The fucking QualiKa did this. That's what the hell this says."

CONTEXT:
William Allen-Levin of the Rock

"THE FUCKING QUALIKA DID THIS. THAT'S WHAT the hell this says," Bill said.

Bill had already made up his mind, even if the damn Sa were prancing around trying to pretend that there were still questions to be answered. Bill *had* the answer: It was fucking grumblers who had killed little Fianya. It was the goddamn QualiKa, and yet this pissant Sa grumbler stared at him like he was a turd, ker mouth in a tight little line and ker snout all scrunched up like ke was sucking on unripe tartberries.

"Anyone can carve anything they want into a *nasituda*," ke said, ker words slurred even more than his own. Bill hated the way grumblers talked worse than the way they stank or the way they looked. They couldn't get their twin tongues around the human language; they always sounded like they were about to spit. "If I carved your name there, William, would that make *you* guilty?"

Afterward, Bill would agree that he should never have let the grumbler get to him like that. It was circumstances, he'd say: finding poor Fianya's broken corpse, seeing the grumbler tracks all around, knowing that they'd snatched Fianya up and killed her simply because ke was a human, sacrificing ker like an offering, an offering to their damn cause and alien gods. And when the Sa stood there in front of the evidence, looking down at the QualiKa sign ker kind had put on the stone to boast about it, well, it was more than he could stand.

The rage filled him suddenly, explosively. Bill shouted, a wordless roar, and charged at the grumbler Sa, wanting to knock ker down to the ground, wanting nothing more than the satisfaction of feeling his fist hitting ker face, of seeing ker blood on his knuckles. It wouldn't bring Fianya back, no, but it take away some of the aching frustration and anger that was building up inside him, inside all of the Families.

He lunged at RenSa, striking for the grumbler's face, but the Sa suddenly wasn't there. Ke had pivoted smoothly on ker front foot, and in one rushing second, as Bill started to turn toward ker, he felt his hand grabbed as RenSa's claws dug into the skin of his wrist, and a cry of pain was wrenched from Bill as the grumbler torqued the wrist with a twisting motion. Bill crumpled, snow flying as he went down hard, then the Sa's huge, ripping footclaw was out and at his throat, curling and pressing down just enough that Bill had to struggle to breathe.

"I said nothing that wasn't true, William Allen-Levin," RenSa said slowly. Ke was still holding Bill's wrist, pinning him with both hand and foot, and ker dark eyes staring down at him. "Calm yourself, and I'll accept your apology."

Even though he knew that the footclaw could rip open his throat in a moment, Bill started to struggle, and RenSa increased the pressure on his wrist and throat. Finally, Bill nodded. The footclaw relaxed, lifting away from his throat, and RenSa let go of the hand, taking a step back. Bill coughed and rolled away from the grumbler before getting to his feet. His wrist throbbed, and there were four bleeding pinpricks where the claws had broken the skin. Snow piled cold under his collar. Everyone was staring at him: Komoko, Caitlyn, Linden, Ishiko, Erin.

RenSa.

The grumbler's placid face had no anger in it at all. Ke just stared blandly at Bill, like ke was daring him to attack ker again, and RenSa's calm fueled Bill's anger and shame even more. But he wasn't stupid. No. Let the fucking grumbler have ker little victory now. But Bill would remember. *Hai.* He'd remember very well. And he'd be damned before he'd tell the goddamn grumbler that he was sorry.

"All right, that's enough of this," Caitlyn said, like ke'd

actually had something to do with ending the incident. "We all need to stay calm out here."

Bill brushed snow from his pants and coat. "Bill, are you okay?" Komoko asked. She was glaring at the grumbler herself, and Eris had moved alongside her. The two human Sa had each stepped between RenSa and Bill; Ishiko watched, silent, her face troubled.

"I'm fine," Bill mumbled. "And I've seen enough here. I'm going back to the camp. Fianya needs to be brought back to the Rock."

Bill stalked off down the slope. After a moment, Komoko and Eris followed him.

"I love my Family," Linden said. "I really do. We're all so reasonable. Especially cousin Bill."

"I said nothing that was not true," RenSa repeated to the others as they watched the others leave. "And he did not apologize as he promised he would."

Caitlyn stroked the Miccail's spinal mane, smoothing the fine, braided strands. "The truth isn't what they wanted to hear," ke told ker.

"Maybe that's because some people can't accept it when it's staring them in the face." Ishiko shook back her long, dark hair, her chin raised. RenSa noticed that her gaze was on Caitlyn; when their eyes met, her mouth tightened. There was a strange scent about her, too complex to unravel.

"I want to know what happened here as much as anyone," Caitlyn answered softly. "We all do." Ke exhaled loudly, a sigh of frustration, and glanced at the receding backs of the Allen-Levins. "We'd better go with them. In William's mood, the poor Miccail porters back at the camp aren't likely to be safe."

JOURNAL ENTRY:
Anaïs Koda-Levin, O'Sa

I MET NAG—WHO INSISTED ON THE HONORIFIC
"Te" being attached to his name, despite the
fact (or perhaps because of it) that FirstHand NefSa and I
had ruled that the old titles were no longer to be used—
not long after the first fatal incident involving the QualiKa,
at the new settlement at Warm Water. Such a senseless
waste of life, and over nothing more than the placement of
a tent that the QualiKa felt was too close to the ruins of an
ancient Miccail village. One of the QualiKa had asked or
demanded (the verb depended on who was telling the tale)
that the tent be moved, and an argument had started. Two
humans and four Miccail died before it ended.

I'd already heard a dozen variations on the incident from
the eyewitnesses, both human and Miccail. Most of the ac-
counts were mutually incompatible, and I'd already given
up hope of ever really understanding what had happened.
The best I hoped for was to negotiate a quick peace with
the QualiKa's leader, since I'd known him and his parents
well.

"How is it that your QualiKa can claim to hate us humans so much?" I asked him. "Surely this animosity was
nothing you learned as a child. Dottó saved my life when
I was wounded, and Whitetuft carried me to safety afterward."

Nag laughed bitterly. The black crescent moon tattooed
on his naked chest leaped with his scornful amusement.
"Who are those people, Anaïs Sa? My mother was FasTa,
and my father SefiTe. Those are their *real* names, yet you
sit there and call them 'Dottó' and 'Whitetuft' as if they

were things you owned and could name yourself. Look at your own arrogance, and then ask me that question again.''

I remember that I sat there, my cheeks burning with mingled embarrassment and irritation, and I couldn't answer. For I did look inside myself and saw the dark flaw there, and inside a part of me cursed Nag for illuminating that unthinking prejudice for me.

CONTEXT:
William Allen-Levin of the Rock

WHEN THEY'D RETURNED TO THE ROCK, POOR KO-moko had fled to her Family's compound and what little comfort her kin could or would offer. Bill had carried Fianya's body to the clinic, then had stoically watched Fianya's autopsy, as if the child were of his own Family. It was not easy, seeing the infant he'd held and cuddled being dissected and examined as if ke were a hunk of meat, especially since the Sa Linden was doing most of the cutting, and Caitlyn stood alongside Bill the entire time. More than once, he'd wanted to turn away, but he'd used the seething rage in his *hara* to support an iron shell of apparent calm. He'd watched, and he'd felt the anger and passion grow with each cut of the scalpel, with each emotionless comment by Linden or *dottore* Cuauh. Ghost had arrived as they were finishing, and afterward Caitlyn had taken the projector and gone off with the AI.

The stink of chemicals and corruption lingering in his nostrils, Bill had returned to the Allen-Levin compound. On the way, he saw the grumbler RenSa just coming out of the main entrance of the Rock in ker orange *shangaa*. The grumbler had noticed Bill as well, and ke stopped, staring at Bill with ker large, dark eyes, perhaps expecting Bill to speak to ker. Ker snout wrinkled, as if ke could smell the stench of the clinic clinging to him. ''I understand the pain of your loss," ke said at last. "I know how you felt about Komoko, and I know you treated Fianya well. I want you to know that."

The slurred words ignited the sour pain smoldering in Bill's gut. He had no words in him; they were all consumed by the white fire inside. When Bill didn't respond, the grumbler had given a little shiver and continued on, ker *shangaa* moving in the cold wind as ke walked down the path away from the Rock. Bill had watched ker go for long minutes, until he saw ker crossing Old Bridge.

He'd gone back into the Rock to the compound and snatched a rifle from the stand in the Common Room. Bill calmly loaded the weapon, enjoying the metallic clatter of the metal shells as they dropped into the cartridge, each sharp *t-chink* resonating with the emotions inside him.

After the weapon was loaded, Bill headed out from the compound and the Rock. At the entrance to the Rock, the frost-laden open air embraced him. Bill took a deep breath of the comforting cold, settling the fire and staring at the forested, snowy hills on the farside of the river.

He strode purposefully down the lane toward Old Bridge.

It was easy to see where the grumbler Sa had left the path leading to the ancient Miccail highroad. The underbrush was just beginning to spring back up, the snow was disturbed, and a branch had snapped on an overhanging amberdrop. Bill followed the trail into the shadow of the trees.

The grumbler was heading upslope, toward the glade where Bill knew there was another grouping of *nasituda*. If it had been possible for him, Bill might have smiled at that. He hurried forward, moving as silently as possible. As he moved through the pale blue shadows of the dying day, the woods seemed haunted, filled with a sense of watching eyes, and more than once Bill spun around to look, but there was never anyone there. The soul-heat within him drove him forward, and he wondered that the trees didn't catch fire as he passed.

Not long after, his breath steaming in front of him, Bill crouched in the brush at the edge of the small clearing at the hill's summit. RenSa was there, standing in front of the *nasituda* as if ke were waiting for someone. As Bill took a step into the high winter grass, the foliage rustling with his movement, RenSa started to turn. "CosTa . . . ?" ke called softly, and the white fire Bill held flared. He'd heard that name once before in the last month—a visitor to the Rock from AnglSaiye had mentioned that someone named CosTa was supposed to be the new leader of the QualiKa. Hearing RenSa call for CosTa confirmed the responsibility of the grumblers for the attack on Fianya.

"I'm no goddamn QualiKa," Bill spat out as the grumbler turned. "I'm your fucking death." Ker chest was centered in the sights of Bill's rifle, and the shock on ker face as ke realized who had spoken to ker was sweeter than he'd imagined. He saw the claws slide quickly from ker finger-pads, and the great ripping claws of ker feet rise, but he didn't care. He wanted the fucking grumbler to know who had killed ker. He wanted ker to understand who had done this. He wanted ker to take the image of his vengeance with ker to VeiSaTi or whatever god claimed ker soul.

As Bill squeezed the trigger, the sharp report of his rifle mingled with the cracking of a branch behind him.

VOICE:
RenSa

I KNEW COS (OR COSTA, AS SHE PREFERRED TO BE called) was out there. I could sense her presence, watching us, and I wanted desperately to talk with her. I needed to know, needed the confirmation that I was right about what I'd said on the hill where the little human Sa had died. I needed to know that the QualiKa had not done this.

The Black Lake region has been sacred to all CieTiLa

since the days of the gods, and I'd seen the path marked by a pale wingclaw feather twined in a branch, leading to the hill just across the river. I knew the feather had been left for me, so I would know how to find CosTa again. I suspected that if I left the Rock, alone, she would come to me.

The *nasituda* on the hilltop above the river dated from DekTe's reign, to just before the Long Night of the Cie-TiLa—the *terduva* when we were Sa-less and lost, when what culture we managed to retain was passed down by word of mouth from sage to sage, inexorably changing each time the ancient rites and customs were relayed. During those long *terduva* of darkness, we changed as well, because there were no Sa to keep the line pure, to hold at bay the mutations that reshaped each succeeding generation. Like the *KoPavi*, we emerged from the darkness changed. Different. That's why the FirstHands have always rejected the beliefs of the QualiKa. The *KoPavi* the QualiKa claim to follow, the supposed ancient path of the CieTiLa, is undoubtedly far different from the rites our ancestors followed.

I'd read the *nasituda* on previous visits to the Black Lake, and found them incredibly sad, especially knowing the history behind them.

MarKe here pledges his fealty to DekTe.

MerTa, by whose hand DekTe died, comes for the blessing of VeiSaTi and the Sa Beneath The Water.

HarKa, whose five children were all born deformed, has come to Black Lake to ask VeiSaTi and the Sa Beneath The Water to give her children who are whole.

JaiKa, childless, comes to the Black Lake to seek the blessing of the Sa Beneath The Water.

The tribe of BerTe and SadiTa comes to give sacrifice and beseech the Sa Beneath The Water to bring the Sa back to the CieTiLa.

But the Sa Beneath The Water would not come back, not until the humans rode their fireships down from the clouds and O'Sa Anaïs returned the body of KaiSa back to AnglSaiye. Not even the QualiKa could deny that.

The gods chose the humans to fulfill the promise of the Sa Beneath The Water, whose sacrifice before the onslaught of DekTe and CaraTa had wiped the Sa from the lands, and brought down the long darkness of CieTiLa. The humans brought back the Sa to us. The humans set us on the path that led from the darkness of our fall. The humans were the instruments of the gods.

I know how the knowledge galls the QualiKa. I know, because I feel the gnawing unease myself. The land itself cries out at the presence of these crude people of the air, but those same people that some CieTiLa would mockingly call "flatfaces" have brought back the CieTiLa. Such an awful irony, that.

I stood in front of the *nasituda* again, brushing away the snow clinging to their windward sides and looking at the carved signs in the stones without reading them. I felt the last light of the day on my back. The hill was imbued with a presence, as if a *kahina* lived here—what the humans would have called a *kami*. I could almost hear it whispering to me and trying to call to me, but when I held my breath to listen, other sounds intruded.

I heard a branch snap, and the rustle of foliage. Something moved under the trees downslope from me, and I started to turn. "CosTa?" I said, but then the wind changed, and I caught the scent of a human and the oil they use on their graystone implements.

It was the one they call William who stepped forward into the light, and the blackened mouth of his weapon was aimed at me.

"I'm no (expletive meaning 'cursed-by-the-gods') QualiKa," he said in their harsh speech. "I'm your (expletive meaning 'sex-without-love') death."

I heard the truth in his words, and I extended claws, intending to leap at him, to try to take him to VeiSaTi with me. As I gathered myself, I saw CosTa behind William, and I saw the death-gleam in the QualiKa's eyes.

Everything happened at once then.

—I saw CosTa's left foot slash forward in a quick kick, her ripping claw gouging a fountaining red canyon in William's side. The human screamed, a shuddering wail that held terror and fear and agony . . .

—I saw the flash of the muzzle of William's weapon, and before I heard any sound at all, a great blow struck me, turning me sideways and knocking me to the ground. I may have screamed also, though I felt no pain. Not immediately. I tried to rise, tried to push myself up with my arms, and I heard the grating of shattered bone and saw the hot blood that turned my *shangaa* nearly black, and then . . . then the pain came, and with it a rushing darkness that swallowed me like an ocean wave, bearing me down and away.

SONG:
Miccail DeathChant

Kahina, *we give your ashes back to earth*
We give our tears to water
Our song we sing to air
  We sing, kahina
  We cry, kahina
  We give you to the flames
Kahina, *you are stone*
You are stream, you are cloud
Three times then we ask you
Give us life
Give us life
Give us life

VOICE:
Ishiko Allen-Shimmura of the Rock

FINDING SOMEONE OUT HERE—TWO PEOPLE, SINCE I could hear a faint conversation—was startling enough that I nearly dropped the bucket I was carrying. Instead, I placed the bucket carefully, and quietly, on the ground. The wooden-slatted container was full of the blue-gray clay from the riverbank on the east flank of the Rock, and the handle had already worn a groove in the unresponsive flesh of my left hand.

Caitlyn was sitting on a boulder a meter or so off the river path, cross-legged and staring out over the shallow river bluff. The susurrus of the river thrashing its way past the pilings of Old Bridge was a steady white noise in the background. Being low on clay had seemed like a good excuse to get away from the Rock and everyone's questions about Fianya; it seemed Caitlyn had the same idea.

I heard a voice I didn't recognize. Through the tartberry vines between us, I could see a woman who looked like pictures of Matriarch Gabriela Rusack when she was young, standing in the snow at the foot of Caitlyn's boulder and looking up at ker. A faint heat-waver surrounded her, and I realized it was Ghost's voice I'd heard.

". . . listened to the recording from the autopsy, and I'd have to conclude that Fianya's death was accidental."

"That's what Linden thinks, also." Caitlyn's voice seemed heavy, darker than I remembered.

"That's not going to be what Euzhan and most of the Elder Council want to hear." Through the vines, I saw Ghost shake her head. As hated as Gabriela had been, I still had to admit that I found her avatar interesting. Gabriela had been wrong in most of what she'd done and said, and had been rightly shunned for that, but it had taken an incredible will to have defied every other last human on the world, to have remained firm in the face of universal disagreement. I don't know that I would have been able to maintain the same unaltered conviction had I been in her situation. "They want a nice, clean—well, actually, *dirty*—scapegoat. They want a devil to blame."

"There isn't one. Nothing about this is going to be clean, black-and-white."

"That's not going to be the popular opinion," Ghost answered.

"It's the right one."

"You know, in the past, messengers bearing bad news have been pretty regularly killed."

Caitlyn gave a quick, bitter-sounding laugh. "History again, Ghost? You don't have to tell me that this is a tough job the SaTus handed me. I've already figured that out, and I wish like hell it wasn't mine. I'm really not good at it, that's pretty fucking obvious. I'm not much in the mood for history lessons."

"There's a quote I could give you regarding those who fail to learn from history."

"I'm sure there is. Please keep it to yourself."

Gabriela's face twisted into almost comic disappointment, then just as abruptly cleared again. A flurry of sparks shimmered through her body. "I only have a minute or so left this orbit. I'll look at the autopsy material I uploaded and give you anything I can glean next time—I'll put the file under your password. Talk to Ishiko, too."

Caitlyn visibly started. "Ishiko?"

Ghost grinned at the Sa and pointed right at me. "Of course. She's been listening, after all, and . . ." Another flurry of sparks, and Ghost's body disappeared for a moment before returning. ". . . she's actually quite . . ."

But then another storm of sparks roiled through her, and she was gone entirely, and I was looking at Caitlyn through the screen of frosted tartberry leaves. "I honestly didn't intend to eavesdrop," I told ker. "It was accidental."

"You don't need to apologize. I . . ." Ker voice drifted

off, and I thought for a moment that ke was going to stay silent. "Actually, I just needed to go somewhere and sit by myself for a while," ke said at last. "And Ghost is a good confidant."

"I wouldn't know. It's usually the Elders who talk with Ghost. I'm too much of a peon to be allowed such a privilege."

"Until a week ago, I wasn't one who had that privilege either. I tell you . . ." Ker voice trailed off and started again. "I don't know that I'd ever get used to it," ke said, and it took me a moment to realize that ke'd changed the subject, not looking at me but staring out over the tops of the bubble-trees into the green-purple distance. Wizards called from their nests in the trees below, punctuating ker words with their strident calls. "Not with a little one like Fianya. They're supposed to *live*, damn it, and yet their whole life is snatched away before they even have a chance to experience it. It's not fair. Not right."

Ker head turned, and I saw the glistening of a tear curving down ker cheek. "Have you ever . . . ?" ke began, then stopped.

"Five of them," I answered ker unasked question. "Two Named, three not. And more miscarriages than I care to remember." I bit my lower lip, forcing myself not to see their faces again. "I understand. Believe me, I understand."

"I'm so sorry, Ishiko," ke said, and ker eyes glistened. "Really I am. It's different for Sa. We so rarely even see the children we help bring into the world. Sometimes we don't even know who they are." Ke stared out over the valley again. "Tell me, when you've held them, when you've fed them at your breast and cuddled them and cared for them, does the pain ever go away?"

"No," I told ker simply. "It doesn't. I think of them every day, each of them."

Caitlyn nodded. After a few minutes, watching ker watching nothing at all, I climbed up on the boulder alongside ker. Caitlyn never acknowledged my presence, though I could feel ker warmth along my side. We didn't quite touch, couldn't reach through the barrier of emotions between us.

"Fianya died of injuries from the fall," Caitlyn said at last. "That's what Linden believes, anyway. There's nothing to indicate she'd been hurt otherwise—no bruises, no marks on ker body that didn't appear to have been caused by ker fall. Ke hadn't been sexually molested, as far as they could tell. Ker spine was broken in two places, the neck completely snapped. Fianya was running away from whoever had taken ker, and ke fell. That's all. Whoever took ker didn't intend to kill ker."

"At least not then." That brought ker head around to me, but I wasn't looking at ker. I rubbed my clay-streaked hands on my pants.

"So you've made up your mind already—like William, like your Geema. You think it's the QualiKa."

"Do I suspect the QualiKa? *Hai*," I answered. "Am I convinced yet that they *must* be responsible? *Nei*." I sniffed; the cold air held the scent of the river and mud, or perhaps it was just the dirt on my clothes. "A Family is a powerful influence, CaitlynSa, but it doesn't mean we all think with the same mind."

"I didn't mean—"

"*Hai*. You did."

Ke stopped, ker mouth open at my interruption, and ke shook ker head before spreading ker hands wide. "You're right. I did. Because you're an Allen-Shimmura, I assumed you'd mouth the Family line. I'm sorry. I should have realized you wouldn't."

"And why is that?" I asked ker. The sunlight was just behind ker, falling into the west and turning ker hair into molten flax. I squinted into the brilliance. "And I hope you're not planning to tell me that it's by the way I danced at the Gather."

Caitlyn smiled finally at that, and I realized how pleasant ker smile was. "No," ke said, and then the smile was gone again. "I realized it out there." Ke nodded toward the southwest, where we'd found Fianya's body. "You were the only one who wasn't ready to lynch poor RenSa. You were the only one who kept her head." Ker hand brushed against mine, the left one. When I didn't move away, ker touch lingered. "I want to thank you for that."

I finally brought my hand back and slid down from the rock. Caitlyn watched me as I made my way back through the tartberries. I picked up the bucket again. The weight couldn't obliterate the soft memory of Caitlyn's touch, and couldn't hide how—suddenly—I hadn't wanted it to end there. I put the bucket down again, the decision forming in my mind.

"Caitlyn—" I started to say.

It was then, from across the river, that we heard the echoing clap of a rifle shot, and a scream.

JOURNAL ENTRY:
Anaïs Koda-Levin, O'Sa

WHILE I WAS SEXUALLY ACTIVE, I MUST HAVE GONE to bed with, oh, almost two-thirds of the population. It was my job, what I had to do as Sa, and for almost all of them, it was just sex—sometimes good, sometimes not. I know that many children were born of my encounters; that was, after all, why I had them. For the survival of our kind, those nights were necessary, and I certainly don't begrudge them, but they were not usually necessary for *me*.

It's interesting to have experienced the evolution of our little society during my lifetime. On the Rock, things have changed little, but on AnglSaiye, everything's evolved. We live alongside the Miccail here and have learned from them, even to the point of adopting many of the old Sa customs for ourselves. The Families still form the core and backbone of our society, but they look more and more to the Community of Sa for guidance and direction. The Elder Council still deals with minor inter-Family squabbles and the day-to-day direction of the community, but on AnglSaiye major conflicts come to the Sa. If you are homosexual, a *rezu* or a *culear*, you no longer have to hide your sexual preference, even though it's still not something most Families wish to acknowledge. While people have always paired off before, now there are formal "covenants" where a male may live with a female's Family for the duration of the covenant's agreement. A few of the covenants have even been monogamous, though it's rare for those to be long-term. A few of the new Sa have also formed covenants (though the rules of my Community of Sa forbid any exclusivity of sexual relations—there are too few of us, and we have our work to do), and their lovers have come to live on AnglSaiye.

I know, because I was the first to have such a covenant, even though we didn't have the term then. I performed my duty as Sa faithfully, but it was only when I was with Elio or Máire that I could truly use the term "lovemaking" for sex. With the two of them, sex remained a special kind of sharing, and there was a joy in just being with them, in talking and touching and listening. After I left the Rock, I lived with one or the other or both of them most of the time. I loved them, and I've missed them every day since I gave their bodies to the flames at their Burnings. Elio and Máire, this old, old Sa misses the two of you terribly. You were my friends, which always means more than being just another lover. The two of you completed me, fitted the jagged edges of my soul, and I'll be forever grateful for the wholeness you gave me.

Rest well, and I hope to see you again one day, in the Shadow World where the gods of Mictlan live.

VOICE:
RenSa

I DON'T THINK I WAS UNCONSCIOUS FOR LONG. The next memory I have is of CosTa's face filling my vision, and the sweet smell of kalava root. My shoulder burned, as if someone had placed a burning coal there, and I groaned, trying to sit up.

"No," CosTa said. "You'll start the bleeding again. Please lie still, RenSa."

"How ... bad ... ?" My mouth was dry, and my tongues did not want to move. My *brais* was tilted to the sun, and the inner glare nearly blinded me.

"You'll live. The kalava's stopped the bleeding, and I've already set your shoulder. I promise that by GhazTi."

"GhazTi's not ... my god."

"Then I promise by your Sa Beneath The Water. Lie still and let me bandage you."

I heard the ripping of cloth and felt the soft brush of nanta wool around my shoulder. "What ... about William?"

"The human? Dead," CosTa grunted.

I closed my eyes with a deep intake of breath. "No ..." I whispered. "You didn't ..." But I knew she had. I could still see it, William's eyes widening in shock, the sound of his scream ...

CosTa had straightened, and I saw her glancing away downhill, toward the human settlement. "They're coming," she said. "Listen! They make so much noise." I heard them as well: voices calling from below, the thrashing as they struggled through the thick underbrush. "I'll

105

get you up, and you'll come with me. We have a haven nearby where they won't find us.''

"No," I told him. "I can't go with you."

"They'll blame you for the human's death, SecondHand RenSa.''

"They won't. I know you don't believe this, CosTa, but they are a fair people in their way. Most of them.''

"Fair?'' CosTa laughed. She crouched in front of me, her shadow easing the glare on my *brais*. "You call the flatfaces *fair*? How many of us did they kill when they came down from their home in the clouds, calling us dangerous animals? They killed my grandfather, the last Cha'akMongTi; they killed O'Sa Anaïs. They care nothing for the *KoPavi*.''

"This is not . . .'' I sank back, gathering the strength to finish the thought. ". . . the time to debate, Cos.''

"I am Cos*Ta*.'' She made the correction gently, with a soft smile that belied the vanity of the title.

"CosTa, then. Go on, before they come.''

"Why did you come here looking for me, then?'' CosTa asked. I could hear the humans, very near now, calling as they struggled up the rise.

"I don't know," I told her. It was simple honesty. "Please, go.''

She crouched down first, showing me her hand with claws withdrawn, then stroking my face. "When I saw you the first time, I felt the same fire inside that I felt when GhazTi first called me to be Cha'akMongTi. I wish I could come to know you better, RenSa. I wish . . .'' Then the warmth of her hand vanished, and her shadow passed over my *brais*. A few breaths later, I heard CaitlynSa and Ishiko enter the clearing. "By the blood of Buddha—'' Ishiko cried. Rising up a bit, I saw the two of them standing in front of William's body, staring down as if they could not believe what they saw. Ishiko was hugging herself, as if she were cold, and Caitlyn's face was set in an eerie calm, as if ke were viewing a drawing of the scene and not the reality. Then ke saw me, and ker pretense of calm dissolved.

"RenSa!'' Ke was there in a moment. Ker hands touched

my face where CosTa's hands had been but moments before, and then ke lightly touched the dressing on my shoulder. "What happened here?" ke asked.

"William . . . shot me. CosTa tried to . . . stop him."

"Cos? The new Cha'akMongTi is *here*?"

I nodded. It was all I had strength for.

"Lie back, Ren," Caitlyn said, and ker voice trembled. Ke was looking around, as if ke expected to see QualiKa come shouting out from the under the trees, and Ishiko had drawn close to ker. "Others are coming, and we'll get you back to the Rock. Just lie still . . ."

Ker voice seemed to be growing fainter, and the sky was darkening. I lay on the grass, and for a time, the world went away again.

VOICE:
Caitlyn Koda-Schmidt of the Sa

KNOWING EUZHAN, OR AT LEAST HER REPUTATION, I should have realized how she'd react to William's death. I should have known she'd grasp the opportunity and use it like a stick. By the time we'd made a stretcher pallet to carry RenSa back, other runners had arrived from the Rock. A few immediately headed back with word of what they'd seen on the hilltop, and when we reached the Rock ourselves, Euzhan was waiting. She stood like a grim statue at the entrance to the caverns, with several members of her family and William's behind her. Komoko saw us and wailed, trying to rush forward and being restrained by her sibs. Ishiko, holding the other side of the stretcher, muttered a soft "*Khudda*" under her breath at the sight. I wondered at that, wondered exactly where Ishiko's sympathies lay, but didn't have time to pursue the question. As we came up to the great doors, Euzhan's gaze flicked once over RenSa, still unconscious in ker litter, then back to me.

"Is it true?" she said, with her strangely young voice. "William is dead?"

"*Hai*, Eldest," I nodded. "I'm sorry to have to be the one to say it, but yes. Evidently he attempted to kill RenSa before he was killed himself."

A wail went up from the Allen-Levins at that. Jalon, the Eldest of the Family, standing next to Euzhan, grunted as if he'd been shot himself. William's *mi*, Mirsada, sank back into the arms of comforting relatives.

"Is that what the grumbler tells you?"

"It is," I said, "and right now I need to get ker to the clinic."

Euzhan didn't move. "Cuauh has no medical knowledge of grumblers. Neither do any of his assistants. We don't treat grumblers here, Sa. You should have brought back William's body, not this."

I could feel my hands knotting around the rough wood of the makeshift stretcher. If I were Taira or Terri, if I were YeiSa, I would simply have kept walking, knowing that they'd have moved out of my way, pushed aside by sheer force of personality. Everyone was staring at me, and Linden was nowhere to be seen. "Eldest, I need for you to move," I said, not knowing how else to express it.

She laughed, a quick, bitter trill. I could feel the anger rising up, and I knew Euzhan could see it as well. "We don't treat grumblers here," she said again. "Take it to the QualiKa, perhaps. Or back to AnglSaiye."

She started to turn away, as if she'd dismissed me entirely, and the shame of it drove away everything but the anger. "Euzhan!" I shouted at her back. "*I* know the Miccail," I told her. "And I *will* treat RenSa here, whether Cuauh wants to help or not. Now, we need to get through."

She had looked back with the shout. She stared at me with something almost like amusement on her face for several seconds, her glance occasionally straying to Ishiko. Finally, she took a step back, gesturing to the others. We made our way through the knot of people, and I could hear the murmurs and feel the animosity that radiated from them like heat from a fire.

Evidently word had gotten to Cuauh, as well. The older man was sitting at his desk marking patient charts in the clinic's front room when we entered, and he made no move to get up. His skin was covered with pale splotches, as if someone had spattered him with white paint—another common and minor genetic mutation in the Allen-Shimmura family line. "I don't know grumbler anatomy much at all," he said, glancing at the litter. "And my people are all too busy with patients. Besides, from what I can see, someone else has already done the first aid."

"You won't help me?"

"Paperwork," he told me. The pencil tapped at the stack of folders in front of him. He seemed embarrassed at having to say it, his cheeks flushing around the white patches. "The charts, for my patients. You know how it is."

"I think I do," I told him. "At least, I'm beginning to get a good idea. Do you at least have an available operating room we can use?"

Cuauh shrugged, his eyes down on the chart in front of him.

"All right, let's take ker in then." Linden came rushing into the clinic as we started to move, and I nodded to ker with rief. "Linden! By VeiSaTi, I'm really glad to see you. Scrub up and get ready—you're going to have to do the surgery on RenSa. Tell me what I need to do, and I'll assist as best I can, since our *dottore* here won't help."

"*I'll* help," Ishiko said softly, and Cuauh's gaze came up at that, sharp and angry. "I don't have any paperwork right now," she told him. "And I've always been curious about Miccail anatomy."

"Ishiko, you can't—" Cuauh started to say, then abruptly shut his mouth with a grimace.

"Don't worry, cousin," she told him. "Geema Euzhan won't hold you responsible for me, will she?" The flush crept further up Cuauh's cheeks at that as his lips pursed, brightening the contrast on his blotched, half-albino face, and his fingers clenched tighter around the pencil.

Ishiko looked at me. "We're a passionate Family," she said. "When we believe something, we tend to believe it all the way. That's as much as virtue as a fault. I have one good hand to offer you, if you want it."

"You have two," I told her gratefully. "And we can use them both."

It took a few hours—I didn't really keep track of time. The work also took all of Linden's skill and my clumsy aid, and I was glad that Cos had been there to do the field dressing. My apprenticeship with the AnglSaiye clinic had been, as *all* of my apprenticeships had been, a disaster. Medicine, like everything else I tried, was not a skill I seemed to possess. If it weren't by virtue of the fact that I was a midmale, and thus was gifted by simple biology with a needed commodity, I would have probably ended up shoveling *khudda* from the middens.

Linden, by contrast, had been offered the position of clinic resident several years ago, though ke'd turned it down to travel as a Sa. With Linden directing the operation, we managed to clean and close the wound. The slug had bounced off a rib, breaking it, and had torn through the webbing of muscles and ligaments just below RenSa's shoulder, finally lodging itself deep in the thick muscles of the upper back. CosTa had already set the rib, and most of the bleeding had been staunched with powdered kalava root. Linden cleaned up the clotted kalava, pried out the slug, and repaired the torn muscles and ligaments while we handed ker instruments and kept the wound clean.

It wasn't as pretty a job as Cuauh might have done, maybe, but it sufficed.

Every so often, we saw one of Cuauh's assistants peer into the room, and once Euzhan herself glanced in—Ishiko waved her bloody, thorn-vine-sap-covered left hand toward her Geema, and Euzhan frowned and vanished. "You can always come and live on AnglSaiye," Linden told her, and Ishiko laughed. I think it was the first time I'd heard her laugh freely. She has a lovely laugh, infectious enough that we all laughed with her. "I don't think it'll be quite that bad," Ishiko said. "But I may need to rely on you two for supper tonight."

Afterward, as we washed up, Linden clapped me on the back. "I'll stay with RenSa until ke wakes up and make sure ke's comfortable," ke said. "You'd better go check on how things are out there. I'll send for you if there's a problem here."

"Linden, maybe you—" I began, but saw the hardness starting to form in Linden's eyes. "No, you're right. The SaTu gave this to me, for whatever reason they had. I'll go."

"I'll come with you," Ishiko told me. "Geema Euzhan will be waiting for us."

She was right. Euzhan was in the clinic's waiting room, along with Cuauh and Jalon, William's Geeda. Cuauh mumbled something about rounds and immediately left, leaving the four of us alone. Euzhan turned toward us with that awkward stiffness, a cane in her hand and her too-young face settled into a sour scowl that aged her considerably. Euzhan stared at Ishiko with an intensity that made me uncomfortable, and I was aware that Ishiko was standing very close to me. "Is the grumbler Sa awake?" Euzhan asked. Though her gaze was still on Ishiko, I assumed the question was directed toward me.

"RenSa's still asleep, Eldest," I told her. "However, I'm sure you'll be pleased to know that ke'll be fine."

She snorted at that, a sound at odds with her doll's face, and her gaze finally came to me. "Is that supposed to make me feel guilty, CaitlynSa, that I didn't immediately ask after the grumbler's welfare? Well, it doesn't. Frankly, I don't much care. One of our own is dead tonight, and that bothers me a hell of a lot more. Your RenSa has questions to answer."

"For what? For being attacked?"

"For killing my *William!*" Jalon thundered. He ran anguished fingers through his thin white hair. Jalon's eyes . . . the pale ghost of catacracts dimmed the pupils, and he squinted, as if confronting a specter he couldn't quite see.

I felt sorry for the man, with his grief and pain so obvious. "The animal *killed* him."

And suddenly I didn't feel quite so empathetic. "RenSa is not an animal, and ke killed no one," I told him. "Ke told us what happened: William ambushed ker, threatened to shoot ker, and was in turn killed by Cos of the QualiKa, who RenSa didn't even know was watching."

"That satisfies you, Sa?" Euzhan asked, the irony set like iron in her tone. "Your precious grumbler Sa is conspiring with the QualiKa, who are responsible for Fianya's death, and not with just any QualiKa, but the reputed Cha'akMongTi herself. William—out hunting, according to his sib Mohandas—stumbled across the two of them conspiring, was attacked, and managed to shoot one of them before he was killed himself. And this is just fine with you. This satisfies you. You feel *sorry* for the poor grumbler."

"That's not what RenSa says happened, Eldest."

"And we're supposed to believe it? It's just a pity William didn't manage to shoot the Cha'akMongTi also."

"You can't mean that, Elder Euzhan. You've been on the Elder Council too long and served as judge yourself too many times to take that attitude. You've already decided who's guilty without knowing any of the facts."

There was nothing pleasant in the smile she gave me then, or the way her gaze held mine. "And you haven't done the same? Listen to yourself, Sa. As to the facts, we'll get them, and we know what to do once we have them. You're not needed here anymore, Sa. Go back to Angl-Saiye."

"I also believe that RenSa is telling the truth, Geema." Ishiko broke in softly, firmly. Euzhan's smile traveled from me to her.

"Stay out of this, great-granddaughter. This isn't your fight, and there's no sense in getting your nose bloodied for nothing."

"If the Family is involved, it *is* my fight, Geema, as much as yours."

"If the Family is involved, then you will listen to me. You've made your point by helping the Sa with ker grumbler friend. Fine; consider the point made with me. But that's done now—go back to the compound and we'll talk later, after I've settled things with the Sa."

"I won't do that, Geema."

Euzhan's head drew up stiffly at that, and she clutched the cane in her hand tightly. "So . . ." she said, the word a long, slow exhalation. "A Sa is for a night. A Family is for life." The way Euzhan said it, I suspected she'd said the same thing many times to those in her family—a little aphorism of her own. I wager she said it to Komoko, too. Probably many times, both before and after. "Do you really want to make that trade?"

"Is that the only choice you're giving me, Geema?"

Her lips pressed together into a thin line, like a knife cut in a sweetmelon's skin. For several seconds, the loudest sound in the room was Jalon's breathing. I hurried into the silence. "Elder Euzhan, this isn't a good time for anyone to make critical decisions. It's been a truly awful day, for all of us, and we're all exhausted."

Euzhan and Ishiko were still glaring at each other, Euzhan leaning heavily on her cane, Ishiko with her left hand half-hidden behind her hip. "I know grumblers," Euzhan told me, or maybe it was both of us she was talking to. "I'll always carry the scar from an attack when I was a little girl, from here to here." She touched herself from above her navel to her right hip. "I nearly died that day—a child, who was doing nothing but walking through a field."

"That was before we knew that they were the Miccail," I reminded her. "Before we could even speak with them. We hunted and killed them, too—just as ruthlessly as they attacked us."

"*Phaah!*" Euzhan spat out in derision. "And there were thousands of grumblers out there then, as there are now. Remember that we started out with *nine*, and we were still no more than a hundred when I was attacked as a child. A couple of grumblers dead made no difference to them. Had a few more *humans* died in those times, you wouldn't be standing here handing me empty platitudes like they were wisdom. Remember that, Sa. Our very existence hung in the balance back then, and it's still an extremely fragile thing." Euzhan took a long breath. "But I'll give you your rest, since you've asked for it. There are other people I need to talk with. In the morning, Sa..." She nodded to me, leaving me feeling as if I'd just been dismissed, and she glanced at Ishiko.

"I'm not coming with you, Geema. Not right now."

Euzhan's left shoulder lifted. "Do what you will. You're mistaken if you think I still care." The cane tapped as she turned away. Jalon rose to his feet, swaying a bit, and glared at me as well before leaving behind Euzhan.

The sound of the door closing after them was strangely soft and anticlimactic.

CONTEXT:
Blake Allen-Levin of the Rock

BLAKE HOVERED OVER JULIUS KODA-SHIMMURA'S shoulder as her apprentice swung the body tray holding William's corpse over the infusor tank. Chains rattled and squealed in protest from the ceiling tracks, and the tray rocked sideways a meter over the open tank. With a frantic glance back at Blake, the boy quickly reached out to stop the tray's motion, then as quickly released it, as if he hated to have his hand remain that close to the body.

Yesterday, Fianya's body had come in, and handling the tiny corpse had visibly upset the boy, and tonight he'd been almost useless with William. Blake remembered how she'd been herself, when she'd first been apprenticed. Tending to the bodies of the old people had been easier—they were supposed to die, after all. But the first few children who'd died of the Bloody Cough or some hereditary defect had been harder to take.

But no more. No more. Blake had seen too many of them

over the decades to have one more bother her. It didn't even much matter that William was Family, that only just the other night they'd sat in the same room, watching the fire in the hearth turn to ash. Blake set her thin mouth and slapped Julius's shoulder.

"I want those tracks greased this evening, boy. That's sloppy work. Sloppy work." Blake's voice was sharp and high, even through the muffling fabric of the mask she wore.

"Yes, ma'am. I'm sorry, ma'am." The boy's eyes darted sideways over his own mask, and Blake sniffed in satisfaction, taking in the mingled odors of the fragrant oils and the faint scent of rotten meat that never seemed to leave the mortuary.

The clinic had held its own smell, also: heavy disinfectant covering a miasma of illness. Blake still remembered it, and she remembered the way that ancient old hag of a doctor Ama Martinez-Santos had ridden her, hounding her every moment, always there to criticize. Blake had never been good enough for Ama, no matter how hard she tried, no matter how much effort she put into her medical study. Ama had finally sent her away, telling Blake's Geema Ranan "I'm sorry, but she's just not bright or quick enough for medicine. . . ." The memory still stung.

"Did you check the temperature of the oil, Julius? Are you sure it's not too cold?"

"I checked it twice, ma'am. Honest."

The trembling subservience was adequate, and Blake backed off a step from the roiling, thick liquid in the infusor, nodding to the boy. Julius loosened the chains on the block and tackle and slowly lowered the tray toward the tank. The naked body's midsection was covered with thick, black stitching, where Blake had sewn together the jagged wound that had been William's death.

Blake's cousins, not Blake, had been the stars of the family: Firio with his talent for art, Ely with his mechanical inventiveness. Geema Ranan was still alive then, and she had sentenced Blake to apprenticeship with Buchi Koda-Shimmura, then the head undertaker for the Rock. No glory for Blake, no art, no inventions. No, Blake's world would be corruption and death. To the others went the praise; Blake would have the worms.

Blake reached out and patted William's stomach, causing Julius to start at the drumlike resonance. "Nasty-looking, wasn't it, boy? That's what the damn grumblers can do, with just one kick. You'd best remember it, and make sure that you shoot first when one looks like it's about to go for you. Disemboweled poor William back and front, it did. I had to stuff half of his intestines back inside before I sewed him up. Next time, I show you how to use the needle, eh?" That gained her an apprehensive, frightened nod from Julius, and Blake tried not to let her gratification at the display show.

"Good. Now, lower him in. Slowly . . . slowly."

The oils bubbled and lapped over the tray, splashing over the body, leaving behind a coppery, thick residue. As Julius continued to play out the chains and submerge the body, Blake nodded. "That's it. Now Poor William will burn like a torch in his gravepit. This is an art, boy, an art, as hard to do well as any sculpture of Profirio's, and a hell of a lot more necessary. Everyone dies, boy. Everyone will have their turn in our little bath. Learn this now, boy: they'll be damned polite to your face, because they know that one day their precious bodies end up in your hands, but you watch. Watch how they avoid sitting next to you at the table. Watch how they make sure they don't eat after you. Watch how most of them will give you polite excuses when you ask them to go to bed. Watch, and remember."

Blake sighed, then clapped her hands loudly. "*Enough!* Get him up now. Slowly again—I don't want him dripping over the floor, or I'll have you clean it up with your toothbrush."

William's body emerged from the infusor gleaming and brown, as if dipped in wax. The ugly stitch marks were gone now, blurred with thick oil, and his features were smoothed and no longer recognizable. Blake watched as Julius used the overhead tracks to move the tray to the wrapping table. There, sticky, oil-saturated cloths would be wound over the body, which would be taken tomorrow morning to the gravepit already prepared for it—Blake's two other younger apprentices were there now, digging the grave and placing in it the whitewood for the pyre. "Now, bring it down. Carefully still, boy—I don't want a mess on my table." Blake watched as Julius lowered the corpse and opened the tray so that the body slid out onto the wrapping table. "That's adequate. Now let's see how well you've remembered the proper way to wrap. That's it—start at the feet. Carefully now. Do it sloppily, and you'll be doing it over again."

She had turned to rack up the chains and infusing tray, and caught Julius's angry pout from the corner of her eye and a muttering under his breath. Pointing a crooked index finger at the youth, she fixed him with a scowl. "If you think that's an idle threat, just test me, boy. I'll have you here all night if that's what it takes. All I need to do is tell your Geema that I've no use for you, and you'll be doing nothing but mucking out the *konja* stables the rest of your life."

A gratifying widening of eyes followed that pronouncement. "I'm sorry, ma'am. I meant nothing."

Blake sniffed. "Oh, you meant it. And if you had half a spine, you'd admit it, as well. But you don't. That's why you're here. You're just grumbler meat."

He didn't answer. Blake knew he wouldn't; the boy was just too timid to protest, as she had once been herself. *Too timid. Too afraid, and because of that, I ended up here.* She gave him another scowl, then tossed him a roll of bandages. She watched as he began to wrap William's body. "Just grumbler meat," she repeated, softer this time.

Blake poked an inquisitive finger at William's chest, then examined the brown residue on her fingertip. "He'll burn nicely," she said. "Quite nicely."

Ishiko Allen-Shimmura <u>of the Rock</u>

"YOU DIDN'T HAVE TO DO THAT, YOU KNOW."

I looked at Caitlyn. Something between smile and frown tugged at ker soft lips, the muscles twitching at the corners of ker mouth. Ker eyes were somber, and I could see myself in them, a distorted figure in the clinic's eterna-lamps. "I think I did," I told ker. "She'll get over it."

Ke glanced at the door through which Geema and Jalon had gone. "It didn't sound like something she'll get over anytime soon."

"We've had arguments before. I just need to give her a few days to cool down."

Ke shrugged finally. "You know her better than I."

The surgery, followed by our confrontation with my Geema, seemed to have exhausted Caitlyn. I could see how ker shoulders sagged, ker hand fluttered restlessly over ker *shangaa*, and ker eyes fought to stay open. "You're worn-out," I told ker. "Why don't you go to bed?"

The fact that ke didn't protest told me just how weary ke was. Caitlyn nodded in mute acceptance. "What about you?" ke asked. "It looks like you burned your bridges, at least for tonight."

"I'll just sleep in one of the clinic's rooms. Cuauh won't mind."

Caitlyn half nodded, half shook ker head. "Why don't you come with me? We have the old Koda-Levin compound all to ourselves." When I hesitated, ke continued with a soft smile. "There are plenty of rooms and beds

118

there. You'll be more comfortable there, and you won't have Cuauh glowering at you."

I laughed at the image, enjoying the way Caitlyn's face lightened in return, and I knew I'd made a decision. "All right," I told ker. "That sounds good."

Ker smile widened, and I was sure the decision was the right one. "Just let me tell Linden . . ."

We didn't say anything on the walk to the compound, and no one said anything to us, though I saw several people trying to appear as if they weren't watching us. The fact that I accompanied Cailtyn to the Koda-Levin compound would no doubt be the new gossip all over the Rock by tomorrow morning, and no doubt embellished with juicy details. I told myself that I didn't care and halfway managed to believe it.

The Koda-Levin compound is the smallest in the Rock, since the Koda-Levins had never been a large or fertile family. O'Sa Anaïs had in fact been the final person to carry the Koda-Levin name. The compound had in her lifetime become the *de facto* residence for any Sa staying at the Rock, a tradition that had continued after ker death. I'd never been in the compound myself—we Allen-Shimmuras have as little to do with the Sa as possible, so it was left to the other four Families to keep the old compound clean for the occasional Sa visitor.

Their Common Room was much smaller than ours, with several pieces of Jason Koda-Levin's extravagant chairs arrayed around the hearth like dark, brooding sentinels. The air was scented with *kav* leaves and nutspice. Caitlyn prodded the ashes with a poker to uncover the coals, and coaxed the sullen orange into flame with whitewood kindling. After ke'd put a few peat bricks onto the fire, ke gestured to one of the chairs. "Have a seat," ke said. "Get comfortable. I'll be back in a moment."

I sat, enjoying the fire and the way Jason's chair seemed to cradle me. Crockery rattled in the kitchen, and Caitlyn came out a few minutes later with a bowl of sweetmelon, some bread and butter, and a pot of *kav*. Ke poured the kav into two mugs from the mantel. Ke took the sweetmelon and bread over to a small plate set on a tripod. Ke touched the food quickly with a stone axe, a garrote, and a flagon of water. I watched the ritual blessing—a sublimated sacrifice, and another grumbler rite the human Sa have picked up. "Is it true that the Sa grumblers used to sacrifice their own kind?"

Caitlyn set the food down on a table in front of me and put the bowl of sweetmelon in my lap. "It happened two or three times in their history," Cailtyn answered. "When VeiSaTi demanded it."

"Would you do it? Allow yourself to be killed that way?"

One corner of ker mouth lifted, and ke brushed ker hair back from ker face. "*Hai*," ke answered, then shook ker head. "I answered that too easily, didn't I? I really don't know. I haven't thought about it that much. Maybe. If I was certain that it was necessary. But I can't know. I don't think anyone can ever answer that kind of question truthfully until the choice is forced on ker." Ke didn't say anything for several seconds then, sipping at ker *kav*, ker regard turned inward and far away. Then ker gaze focused with a visible start. "Is that one of yours?" ke asked as I nibbled at the melon. I looked at the bowl in my lap.

"No. We . . . umm, don't generally barter much with the Sa. Only when we have to. It's probably one of Tulùm Martinez-Santos's. Looks like his glazing."

Caitlyn nodded. "I didn't think it was yours—too plain. I like what I've seen of your work much better."

"You haven't seen very much of it."

"Sometimes you just know," ke answered, and I had the sense that the subject had now drifted from pottery. Caitlyn handed me one of the mugs of *kav*; ker hand stayed on the warm handle for a long breath, both of us holding the mug, our fingers touching. When ke let go, ke took a piece of melon from the bowl in my lap. I watched ker hand, watched the way the long fingers curled, the delicate touch. We didn't talk much as we ate, though I was always aware of ker, sitting in the chair next to mine. When we were done, Caitlyn took the dishes back to the kitchen, then returned. Standing in front of my chair, ke held out ker hand. "Come on," ke said. "I'll show you your room."

My stomach suddenly knotted. I ignored ker hand and stood. Ke looked at me strangely, and after a moment, led me out into a hall.

The room to which ke led me was tiny and windowless, and the bed there took up most of the space. "This was O'Sa Anaïs's room, a century ago," Caitlyn said. "The furniture's not kers—that was moved to AnglSaiye after ke left the Rock for good, but this was where ke lived before. Anaïs never came back to the Rock kerself, but we keep ker room ready for guests."

"Where are you sleeping?"

Ker eyes held me, unblinking. "Just down the hall."

I nodded. I wanted ker to go away. I wanted ker to stay. I had nothing more to say to ker except inanities, and yet I didn't want us to stop talking. An awful ambivalence filled me: a cold, gray fog.

Caitlyn was still watching me, quietly, ker head tilted slightly to one side. Ker face, caught in the netherland between male and female, pulled at me, and I wanted to reach out with my good hand and stroke ker skin, to see if it was really as soft and warm as it appeared to be.

And I did reach out. It was nothing I thought about, nothing I did consciously. As my hand stroked ker (*hai*) soft and warm cheek, ker own hand came up and trapped mine. Ker eyes closed briefly, and ker lips touched my palm with the lightest of kisses, ker eyes opening again to search my face. Ke kissed my palm again, then lowered my hand. Still holding me, ke closed the distance between us, so that I felt ker breasts brush mine as ke reached behind me to take my other, deformed hand. I hadn't realized that I'd placed it there.

"You don't need to hide anything, Ishiko," Caitlyn said, ker voice a whisper. "Not from me. Not from anyone." Ker fingers pressed against my own.

"I don't know . . ." I began, then faltered, not knowing for certain what I wanted to say. A smile of sympathy, tinged with sadness, played with the corners of ker mouth.

"I know," ke said. "I understand. I can tell you that it's very . . . *different*, being with a Sa." Ke hesitated, seeming to be as unsure of kerself here as ke had been at the cliffside where Fianya had died. "Ishiko, you and I, we don't . . . if this isn't what you want . . ." Ker shoulders lifted, but ker eyes would not release me.

"I don't *know* what I want," I told ker.

"Then let's wait until—" Caitlyn said, but I knew that if we waited, I would find excuses to avoid ker, that we might never be alone together again and that moment would never be there for us and I would never know. Instead, I would always wonder, as I knew others in my Family wondered.

Caitlyn had released my hands, and I reached up to ker and pulled ker head down to mine. Ker lips were soft and moist and yielding against mine, and ke pulled away again after a breath, looking at me with the questions still in ker eyes before pulling me toward ker. This time, the kiss was demanding, long and deep, and I found myself responding. When ke looked at me again, I said only one word— "*Hai*"—before we allowed ourselves to fall onto the bed . . .

Different? In that Caitlyn was right.

It was very different.

CONTEXT:
Gerald Allen-Shimmura
of the Rock

GERALD GESTURED TO JOMO, USING THE HAND SIGnals they'd agreed upon before they'd started out. *To your left. Twenty meters. Wait.* Jomo nodded and moved away, and Gerald then sent a similar message to Sergio: *To your right. Ten meters. Wait.* As Sergio slid away, Gerald grimaced at the cracking of brush in his wake. *That fucker's going to get us killed if he doesn't learn to*

*move quietly, and he's going to goddamn hear about it
once we're done . . .*

They were within fifty meters of the grumbler encampment. Since the Sa grumbler back at the Rock had been
talking to CosTa when William tried to kill ker, Gerald had
figured that the Cha'akMongTi would still be in the area,
and Gerald knew the grumblers and the terrain well enough
to guess that the QualiKa would have sheltered at the cave
under the old highroad. Gerald had seen grumbler signs
there often in the last few months—QualiKa passing
through, he'd be willing to bet, after what had happened.
It seemed he'd guessed right. He could smell them on the
cold evening breeze, and he could hear their mumbled,
slurred speech. Which meant that there'd be a guard posted
close by. Gerald eased himself forward a few meters, then
peered out through a screen of tartberry bushes. *Hai*, there
he was, a big male crouched down by a globe-tree with a
spear across his lap.

This would make things right with Euzhan. This would
put him back in her good graces.

William had been an amateur, and that's what had gotten
him killed. Gerald had killed several grumblers over the
last few years, and he knew how to do it with the least risk
to his own precious skin. Grumblers were damned dangerous, fast and intelligent, and their claws were weapon
enough in close quarters. If you gave them half a chance,
you'd end up like poor Grim Bill with your guts hanging
out in front of you while you bled to death. As far as Gerald
was concerned, it was too damn bad Bill hadn't managed
to kill the grumbler Sa before Cos got to him.

That wasn't going to happen here. Not if things went
according to plan. As did many of the Allen-Shimmuras,
Gerald bore the stamp of Mictlan. His genetic twist, however, was more asset than liability. Like a few others in his
Family, his skin was a mottled patchwork of every color
from albino snow to African ebony, a crazy quilt. But out
here, that merely served as camouflage, making him more
difficult to see as he passed among the twisting shadows of
the forest. Gerald moved quietly and slowly through the

cover until he was behind the guard, making sure that he
stayed downwind, since the grumblers had a better sense
of smell than humans. He slid the garrote from his pocket,
grinning to himself as he did so—he thought it fitting to
kill grumblers with a garrote, since the Sa used the same
device in the sacrificial rituals they'd borrowed from the
old grumbler society. For the guard, the garrote was Gerald's weapon of choice, since Gerald didn't want a com-
motion that would alarm the other grumblers.

He took a slow, deep breath, then leaped forward. The
garrote looped around the grumbler's neck, and Gerald
pulled the thin rope instantly tight, his knee against the
grumbler's spine as the ligature collapsed the grumbler's
prominent windpipe. The dying grumbler clawed at the
loop around his throat in a flailing panic, and then did
something Gerald hadn't expected—the grumbler lurched
forward, bending at the waist as if he were bowing, bringing his head quickly down to the ground. The motion and
the grumbler's superior strength flung Gerald, still holding
the wooden handles of the garrote, up and over the grumbler's body, and he lost his grip as he fell hard to the
ground. The impact stunned him for a second, but then he
rolled, snatching his rifle from where it had fallen alongside
him. The grumbler was still clawing at the noose, coughing
violently as he ripped it from his throat and tried to take a
breath.

Cursing inwardly, knowing that the grumbler would be
on him next, screaming alarm, Gerald brought his rifle up
and shot the creature, which went down in a heap. "Now!"
he shouted to his companions. "Go! Go!"

Everything was confusion. Grumblers seemed to boil out
of the cavern entrance. "Quickly! Get the Cha'akMongTi
out of here!" one of them shouted in the grumbler language. Jomo and Sergio emerged from the trees, firing
madly in the dim twilight. Three grumblers were charging
Gerald, and his next shot sent the closest one sprawling on
the ground. He saw CosTa stumble from the cave as she
stared wildly around at the carnage. Gerald brought his rifle
up to fire at the Cha'akMongTi, but one of the other two

grumblers was nearly on him, screeching and howling. Gerald tried to spin away from the grumbler's kick and felt heat on his side as the footclaw tore cloth and opened a long cut along Gerald's hip. The grumbler barked in triumph, almost on top of him. He slammed the butt of his rifle into the grumbler's snout, then shot the beast as it backed away a step in distress. Gerald tried to take a step and stumbled, blood running down his side.

The Cha'akMongTi was gone, and there was a haze of blue gun smoke in the last light of the sun. The other grumblers seemed to have fled; Jomo was standing over a prone grumbler, the muzzle of his rifle nearly on the creature's skull. There was a percussive cough, and the grumbler twitched once and went still. No one else was moving.

"You okay?" Gerald called.

"*Hai*," Jomo replied. "Scratched up a bit, but otherwise fine. You?"

"One of them cut me pretty good, but I'm still mobile. Where's Sergio?"

"Dead. Over by the cave. He was trying to stop the Cha'akMongTi, and she ran him down."

"*Hakuchi!*" Gerald spat. Sergio was a fool; he wasn't surprised the man had gotten himself stupidly killed. There were at least a half dozen dead QualiKa, but *she* had escaped.

Gerald grimaced at the pain in his side and spat. "*Khudda!* Damn it!"

Euzhan wasn't going to be pleased. She wasn't going to be pleased at all. This was the second time in the last month Gerald had been unable to do what she'd asked, and she wasn't going to like it one bit.

Caitlyn Koda-Schmidt <u>of the Sa</u>

I SHOULD HAVE KNOWN THAT THE ROCK WOULD be no different than the island of AnglSaiye: In both places, rumors are like lightning on summer tinder, producing flames that dance in flickering brilliance from person to person, sometimes flaring in great conflagrations of exaggeration before finally extinguishing themselves in the cold waters of fact.

Ishiko and I slept together that night. Our lovemaking was tentative at first, but she was a loving, tender partner, and she patiently learned my body as I learned hers, and then there was a fierceness to her passion, an urgency that surprised me. Afterward, she cried: deep, racking sobs that frightened me. I held her, her distress a throbbing hurt deep in my own stomach. "Why?" I asked her, touching the tears that tracked down her cheek, wiping them away with my thumb.

"This wasn't . . ." she began. "I mean, all my life, I've been told how wrong this was, making love to a midmale, to someone who is both woman and man at once. That was the grumbler way, not the human way, and it was wrong. This wasn't supposed to happen."

"Ishiko . . ." I kissed her forehead, her neck, her mouth, and tasted the salt of her tears. "I'm sorry. I shouldn't—"

She stopped me with a finger to my mouth, shaking her head. "No," she said. "Hush. Don't misunderstand. I'm glad. I enjoyed it, and I'm not sorry. I'm not."

"Do you want me to go now?" In the candlelit darkness, I watched the way the light played on the lines of her face, the way it shimmered in her eyes. I started to get up from the bed, but her hand, her left hand, touched my shoulder.

"Stay with me, Caitlyn," she said. "Please."

I stayed. We spooned together under the covers, whispering to each other, and she told me about her life here, and growing up in her Family, and about her Geema and how she both loved and feared the woman. In turn, I told her of AnglSaiye and the Community of Sa, and what it was like to be a Sa. I told her . . . I told her things that I had never said to another lover before. We're taught to be private, we Sa, since a lover is someone we most often stay with but once, and may never sleep with again. I could hear the ghost of all my teachers scolding me, telling me that I didn't know this woman, that by the blood of Buddha she was an Allen-Shimmura, and because of that I especially needed to keep that emotional distance I'd been taught to maintain.

I ignored the specters. We talked until we both drifted into sleep, and I woke with her still cradled into me. I kissed her hair, her neck, and she turned her head to kiss me, and we began again, slowly this time.

"Is it this way with all your lovers?" she asked me, her cheeks still flushed with her climax.

"No," I told her, whispering the word into her body. "No, it's not often like this at all," I said, and it was the truth, and I wondered if she knew how different it usually was. I wondered if she knew what I was really feeling for her.

I wondered myself. Attachment, infatuation, love: Those are all dangerous emotions for Sa, and we reserve those feelings for our own kind. I'd always told myself they were feelings I would never have for a man or woman.

"Thank you," she said to me as we dressed.

"Why?"

"For . . ." She shrugged, her hands on the buttons of her blouse, the sweet curve of her breasts half-hidden under soft cloth. "For being with me. I think Geema Euzhan is wrong about the Sa. About you, at least."

She smiled, and didn't know how dangerous that smile was for me.

When we'd dressed and eaten, Ishiko and I went back to

the clinic to check on RenSa. On the way, we both noticed groups of people talking together. I'd (perhaps egotistically) thought that Ishiko's night in the Koda-Levin compound with me would have ignited the obvious gossip being passed around, but despite a few open, appraising stares, we didn't seem to be the main topic of conversation.

We quickly found out why. The clinic staff was alight with wildfire chatter about a "massacre" on the other side of the river. The details were difficult to pin down: Gerald Allen-Shimmura and Jomo Allen-Levin had returned bloody and hurt to the Rock, and had immediately gone to the Allen-Shimmura compound and Euzhan. Other Elders had either been summoned or had not, depending on who was telling the story. According to most sources, a hunting party had been ambushed by the QualiKa and a dozen grumblers and several humans were killed, or maybe it was only one human, but the Cha'akMongTi herself had led the ambushing party and had personally killed poor Sergio, and the rest of the hunting party was in bad shape, but definitely Sergio had managed to mortally wound the Cha'akMongTi before being killed himself, and Cos had been carried away from the site by the QualiKa . . .

After the first few versions, I gave up listening. I knew with a sickening certainty that we didn't have long to wonder about the truth.

I wasn't disappointed.

When one of the Allen-Shimmura children came running into the clinic with the "request" that we come immediately to the Family compound, none of us were surprised. Linden grimaced. "Go. You can fill me in later," ke said. "You can deal with Euzhan—I haven't been able to get any of the staff to help me with RenSa, and ke should be waking up soon. One of us should be here."

My stomach was knotted. My chest burned. "Linden, I'm not ready for this kind of crisis. *None* of us are prepared for this. Everything's falling apart. I don't know what to do, what to expect, what to say. We need to contact the SaTu, get someone here who's experienced. Maybe Rashi . . ."

"Caitlyn, it's at least four days to AnglSaiye and four days back. There isn't time. You have to handle this."

"But you—"

Linden was shaking ker head. "I'm the only one who can help RenSa if ke needs it. You can do this, Caitlyn. You can. And you don't have a choice. You know that." Ke nodded to Ishiko, who stood listening to us. "She'll go with you. Won't you, Ishiko?"

She nodded. Watching me.

I looked over at RenSa, looking frail and dark against the white sheets of ker bed, and touched ker forehead, stroking the fine hair of ker mane. Ker skin felt warm, and I didn't know if that was normal or not, or whether the coldness in my gut had spread to my hands.

"All right," I told Linden. I took a long, slow calming breath. *"Breathe,"* YeiSa had told me once. *"If you can do nothing else in a situation, if you can remember to breathe, you are already halfway to getting through it."* "Tell ker we'll be back, and that ke's going to be fine."

As we started from the room, Linden called out to us. "Be careful, Caitlyn," ke said.

I waved back at ker, pretending nonchalance, but I knew what ke was feeling. I was feeling it myself.

The child who escorted us to Euzhan's room (with several half-frightened looks at his *mi* Ishiko) had simply knocked on the door and vanished down the stairs as if being chased by an invisible monster. A muffled "Enter" was heard from beyond the thick wood. Ishiko pushed the door open.

I expected, actually, there to be more people in the room. Euzhan's private study was bigger than the common hall in the Koda-Levin compound and could have accommodated most of the Elder Council. But the room was occupied only by Euzhan, who stood at one of the windows surveying the long, steep slope of the Rock, and Ghost, who waved at me from the chair nearest the projector. Ghost wore the appearance of an old man, no one I knew or recognized, though there was similarity to Euzhan in the features. I wondered if he was a Family ancestor. *"Komban wa*, Caitlyn, Ishiko," he said. His gaze passed over me to Ishiko, and he tilted his head appraisingly. "Did the two of you enjoy yourselves last night?"

"Shut up, Ghost," we said in unison, and Ghost grinned comically.

"Now if you two did *everything* together like that last night—"

"Shut up, Ghost." That was Euzhan. She had turned as we entered, stiffly, as if it pained her to shift her weight. Her chin lifted, giving that eerily youthful face the look of a pouting child, and she came toward us, the ancient family cane tapping on the wood floor. She ignored Ishiko as if she weren't there, looking only at me.

"Good morning, Geema," Ishiko said, loudly. "I'm just fine, thank you."

Dark eyebrows lifted on Euzhan's head, and her lips pursed as if she'd been eating unripe tartberries. "I don't need or appreciate your sarcasm, girl," she said. "Nor did I ask *you* to come prancing in here with your Sa lover."

Ishiko's face colored as if she'd been slapped. "You have no idea—"

Euzhan's hand waved at Ishiko, slicing her words. "I know all I need to know. I have more important things to worry about at the moment."

Ghost chuckled, crossing his legs in his chair and leaning back as if waiting to view a performance. I wasn't sure I wanted to be Ghost's primary entertainment.

"I take it you've already heard the news," Euzhan said to me.

"*We*"—I overstressed the word, touching Ishiko's shoulder with my hand, just because I knew it would irritate Euzhan; so much for any pretense I had of being a diplomat—"heard the rumors this morning. I take it you have the real story, Eldest?"

She was staring at my hand, still on Ishiko's shoulder, with the same expression she might have on seeing a bug on her food. She suddenly seemed to realize it, and her attention snapped back to me. "I do," she said. She went to her desk, a massive thing of ebonyew that must have taken a half dozen people to haul up here. She looked frail and tiny behind it. ''My greatgrandnephew Gerald came to me immediately upon his return. In brief, he and two others were attacked late last evening, a cowardly ambush by the QualiKa. The Cha'akMongTi was there, and she directed the attack. Gerald and Jomo Allen-Levin escaped with their lives, but Sergio Koda-Shimmura is dead.''

Despite the fact that I'd been expecting it, my stomach roiled at her words, a twisting unease. Another death laid at the feet of the QualiKa . . . I wanted nothing more than to run back to AnglSaiye, to give all the responsibility back to the SaTu. I wanted Linden and RenSa to be here with me as well. ''Eldest, this is horrible news. What about the Miccail and Cos?''

The polished surface of the desk threw her frown back at us. ''Seven grumblers were killed, but Cos escaped.''

Ghost, in his chair, barked a dry laugh that brought all of our heads around to him. He held up his hands in false apology, still chuckling to himself. ''Sorry. I just couldn't help it. Let me see if I have this right: The QualiKa ambushed Gerald. You know, you have to admit it's a damned poor ambush when the QualiKa lose seven of their own and only kill one of those they were after. And here I thought that Cos was supposed to be as brilliant as her grandfather.'' Then all the amusement drained from Ghost's face and he tilted his head toward Euzhan. ''Now that just doesn't make sense to me. Wouldn't you agree, Eldest?''

She glared at him, and came close to hissing. ''Are you accusing Gerald of lying to me, Ghost?''

''Oh, not at all. No, no. I'm just saying that I could drive the *Ibn Battuta* sideways through some of the holes in his story, that's all.'' He favored Euzhan with an innocent smile. I heard Ishiko chuckle once under her breath, and I was suddenly glad that Ghost was here.

''You weren't here when I spoke with him,'' Euzhan retorted. ''You didn't see him, didn't see how badly hurt he and Jomo were. You didn't see poor Sergio's body.''

Ghost shrugged. ''It's not like I can time my visits to

coincide with your crises. But I did listen to the recording you made with Gerald, and the one Jalon made with Jomo. Funny how they don't quite agree on what happened, or even why they were out hunting nik-niks so late in the day."

"I'd like a transcript of those recordings," I said to Ghost.

Ghost nodded. "No problem. I just downloaded it to the terminal in the Koda-Levin compound, and sent a copy to the SaTu as well. In fact, I'm talking to them as well at the moment."

I felt a sudden relief. "Wonderful," I said. "Tell them—"

"Those were private conversations," Euzhan half shouted, interrupting me. She slammed the cane on the floor to accent her words. "Ghost, you had no right to broadcast them to anyone else, and *you* have no right to them at all, CaitlynSa."

Her arrogance and naked prejudice drew defiance from disbelief. "Eldest, I was sent here to investigate Fianya's death. Your own council voted to allow the Community of Sa that right, and I'm still pursuing the investigation."

"This has nothing to do with Fianya. Not anymore."

She waved a hand at me as if in dismissal, and I took a step forward, leaning my hands on her desk. "Eldest, you seem to feel that Cos and the QualiKa were responsible for Fianya's death, and I agree that's a possibility. William was killed by Cos, either in self-defense or not, and now Gerald is claiming to have been ambushed by the Cha'akMongTi. I would say that there's a good possibility these are all interconnected events, wouldn't you?"

"*Nei!*" she exclaimed, tapping the cane again. "I would not. I resent this Sa interference into my Family's affairs, and I know the other Families will feel the same way." She pointed the tip of the cane toward me. I could see the worn brass tip, dimpled with hard use. I felt the urge to snatch the old stick away from her. "We have lost three of our people to the QualiKa in the last few days," she said. "Three. And I don't see that anything you two Sa or your grumbler companion have done has stopped that. Have I missed something that you've accomplished, CaitlynSa, some grand achievement? I thought not. It's time that we of the Rock take care of our own problems. We don't need the Sa.''

"What are you saying, Eldest?" I asked her. "Are you condoning vigilante action against the Miccail?"

"I'm saying that I *will* do what I need to do to protect my Family, and the other Families here.''

"What you're saying is that you'll take us back to the days of the Hannibal Massacre, back to when we fought the QualiKa openly.''

Euzhan laughed suddenly, an amusement that sent cold shivers through my gut. "You forget, CaitlynSa, that I remember Hannibal. I may look young still, but I'm the *only* one still living who remembers.''

"Not the only one," Ghost interjected. He waved a hand to her, still leaning back in his chair. "As I recall, I was the one who broadcast the news to your Family, Eldest. Though I probably didn't have the right to do that, did I?''

Euzhan ignored him. I could see static beginning to touch the edges of Ghost's avatar, which probably meant that he'd be out of range of the projector in a few minutes. I wasn't quite sure of Ghost's agenda here, but at least he seemed to be mostly on "my" side, and I didn't want him to leave. "Eldest," I said quickly, "why did you ask for me to come here? Was it just to tell me about this attack?''

"No," she said, and a decided smugness crept into her tone. Her chin lifted, her hand gripped the cane more tightly. "I sent for you to tell you that I've met with the members of the Elder Council. We've called for the capture of Cos and have sent runners to Hannibal, Irontown, Warm Water, and AnglSaiye with the declaration that when she is taken, she is to be returned here to the Rock, to be tried for the murders of Fianya, William, and Sergio.''

"Eldest, we are still inves—''

"And you may stop immediately," she said, interrupting with a clash of cane on floor. "There is enough evidence already.''

"You mean that you've already made up your mind. In

any case, Eldest, Cos is Miccail, not human. She's not
yours to try. As a Miccail, she falls under the FirstHand's
jurisdiction.''

"She's killed humans. She'll meet human justice.''

Ghost chuckled. Static was rippling down his chest.
"Are you going to *shun* her, Eldest? Are you going to tell
her that no human will talk to her for the next twenty years?
I'm sure that will be utterly devastating to the
Cha'akMongTi.''

Euzhan turned slowly toward Ghost, her whole body
swiveling. "Shunning is for humans,'' she said. "Not animals.''

"Geema!'' Ishiko shouted, and the cane slammed the
floor again as Euzhan rose from her chair.

"*Hai*, an animal!'' she shouted back. "And it will be
hunted down like one.''

"You can't,'' I said into her rage. "The Community of
Sa won't allow it.''

"Won't *allow* it?'' she flung back to us. "What will you
do, Sa? Will the Sa refuse to give their damned services to
my Family? We don't want them anyway. Will AnglSaiye
refuse to trade with us here in the Rock? It's the Rock that
supports you, not the other way around. Will the Families
there rally around you, when it's their sibs, the *mi* and *da*,
their Elders whom they must oppose? *Nei*. So tell me,
CaitlynSa: Just what is it that you Sa will do that will prevent us from doing what is right and what justice
demands?''

"Eldest,'' I began, and realized that I was empty, too
astounded by this assault even to think of how to respond.
I realized that I'd been looking at the world with eyes colored by AnglSaiye, with my own prejudices. I knew I
needed to speak, needed to find the words that would make
her understand that going after CosTa would almost certainly escalate the situation, make it far worse than it already was. Ghost might scoff at my lack of historical
learning, but I remembered enough of what I'd been taught
to know the ravages caused by NagTe's QualiKa decades

ago. I didn't want to be the cause of another outbreak of violence from his granddaughter.

But I was empty. I had no answer, because Euzhan was right.

There was nothing we could do. Nothing. Just as there was nothing we could do when Euzhan refused to send Fianya to us in the first place. There were whirling, chaotic wisps in my head, the husks of a dozen futile arguments. I looked to Ghost for help, and saw that he had vanished, the snout of the projector dead and cold. Ishiko was looking at me, waiting, and all I could do was open my mouth in astonishment and spread my hands.

"Go back to AnglSaiye and tell your SaTu," Euzhan said, and I saw the triumph in her eyes, those ancient orbs set in a youth's face. "Tell them what's happened here, and tell them that we of the Rock will deal with it."

I stood there: still fuming, still empty, still hating my ineptitude. "Eldest," I began again, then dropped my hands to my side. "Please. Think about what this means."

Her face was smooth stone. Her voice was flint. "I have, and that's why I do it. You may leave me now, CaitlynSa. Ishiko, stay here. We need to talk."

I looked at Ishiko. Her face was pale, but she nodded to me, faintly. "Go on," she said. "You should tell Linden and RenSa. Go on."

Feeling that I'd just been dismissed like a misbehaving child, I went.

CONTEXT:
Euzhan Allen-Shimmura
of the Rock

"GEEMA—" ISHIKO BEGAN, BUT EUZHAN SHOOK HER head and the word died in a whisper.

"Hush, girl," she said. "There's no need for you to say anything. You played your part perfectly. I'm very pleased. You did exactly what was needed . . ."

PASSAGES

"When the struggle propels to a higher degree
of hostility, we will slay all enemies of the
white race. This is the call of our ancestors!!"

> —GRAND DRAGON,
> Realm of Delaware,
> American Knights of the Ku Klux Klan,
> from their web site, September 1997

JOURNAL ENTRY:
Anaïs Koda-Levin, O'Sa

EVEN THOUGH I SENT NAGTE AND HIS QUALIKA away from AnglSaiye, I knew that this would not be the end of it. I knew it, and it was probably equal parts cowardice and stupidity on my part to declare the Cha'akMongTi and his followers shunned. I can appreciate NagTe's point of view, even while deploring his methods.

We *are* the intruders here. We *did* come down here and set up our houses and fields and industries as if we owned the planet. We *did* trample on their sacred places, tunneling caverns into the Rock without knowing that it was sacred to them, and settling on AnglSaiye before we realized its place in their history. NagTe's anger is understandable. I would tell him (again) that we did all that in ignorance, not knowing that the Miccail were still alive. I would tell him that if we had *not* come here, then the Sa Beneath The Water would still be waiting to fulfill ker promise, and all the ancient and wonderful Miccail customs and society would still be lost except in the oral history of a very few. I would tell him that what's done can't be undone, that neither Miccail nor human will go away and leave this land to the other, so we must find a way—somehow—to share it.

I *have* told him all that, many times. It's not a concept he will accept. Just as the Miccail—who have only a rudimentary grasp of astronomy—either don't believe or can't understand that we came from another world, they don't understand why we can't simply leave again. The gods sent us down from the clouds; why can't we just ascend back into them again?

Like all our problems, they can't be so easily solved.

If I could, I would give AnglSaiye back to the Miccail, but the Families here don't want that, nor do most of the Miccail who live here. I would give back the Rock, but the Elder Council would never allow it. I would even call Nag "Te" and myself "Ju" if it meant that we could come to an agreement.

So I banished the problem from the island, unsolved, and left it to the rest of the world to deal with. I knew in my heart, had I bothered to look there, that more and greater violence must follow—and it has, worse than I'd feared.

Now it's up to me to do what I should have done in the first place. I just pray that it's not too late.

CONTEXT:
YeiSa

AFTER THE HUMAN *KAHINA* GHOST HAD GONE TO snow and static after telling them of Caitlyn's conversation with Euzhan, Terri had rushed from the SaTu's office obviously upset, leaving Taira and YeiSa to gape after ker. YeiSa would have followed, but Taira gave a quick shake of ker head. They'd waited, had the acolytes bring them a cold lunch, then gone to Terri's apartment, high on the seaward tower of the Sa temple.

As expected, ke was there.

YeiSa could smell the bitter tang of *jitu* before Terri opened the door, and the dilated pupils that regarded the two of them told the rest. Terri's ancient face was furrowed even deeper with distress, and ker hands were streaked with blood. An altar was set near a window in the first room. YeiSa could see the limp body of a guffin lying on it, the feathered head crushed by the stone axe, the neck broken by the garrote, and its wings dappled with water droplets.

"VeiSaTi won't speak to me," Terri said, ker quavering voice flat, hardly more than a hoarse whisper. "I sacrificed, and I took *jitu*, but all I get are confused images. Nothing is clear, nothing shows us the way."

YeiSa glanced up from the sacrifice of the guffin. Storm clouds were rising on the horizon. Ke took a deep breath, savoring the clean scent of a squall coming in off the ocean.

"Terri, this is something we need to solve ourselves," Taira said. "We should have realized that the situation had the potential to explode as it has, and we should have assigned someone stronger to oversee it. We should have sent Rashi. Maybe we should have gone ourselves."

"*No!*" Terri half shouted. "The visions I had—"

Humans spend too much time looking backward, YeiSa decided. "Either way, the point is moot," ke said, interrupting the two humans. YeiSa's voice was gently chiding, causing Terri to close ker mouth on ker retort. YeiSa rubbed ker *brais*, the lens irritated by the cold wind through the open window, as ke spoke. "There is an old CieTiLa saying: 'The past has but one path, the present has many and the future none.' The decision was made, and it can't be changed. The question becomes 'what can we do now?' Which path do we take?"

YeiSa truly loved the two human SaTu, as much as any CieTiLa could be said to love a human. The SaTu seemed to genuinely care about the CieTiLa within the Community, and they included their FirstHand in most of their decisions regarding the Community of Sa. But they *were* human, and because of that, would never truly understand the CieTiLa their decisions touched. Most of the human Sa and even some of the other humans might be able to speak the CieTiLa language (though they spoke it badly; as badly, YeiSa had to admit, as ke spoke their tongue), but their genetics, their behaviors, their cultural background, and their history were all entirely different. There would always be a gulf between them, one that might be bridged, perhaps, but into which there would always be the danger of falling: into misunderstandings, into conflict.

Into violence and death.

It didn't surprise YeiSa that the situation in the Rock had escalated. Ke would have been more astonished if it had not.

Taira had settled Terri into a seat at ker dining table and gestured to YeiSa. YeiSa fitted kerself carefully into one of the chairs, the human shape of it pressing uncomfortably against ker hips and pelvis. Taira reached over and patted YeiSa's hand: a human gesture, and one that made YeiSa see again the distance between them. To the CieTiLa, hands are always potential weapons. To touch someone else without first showing your own hand to display that the claws were hidden was at best poor manners, if not an outright insult. Yet after seventy turnings, the SaTu still did not realize it. YeiSa found kerself consciously holding back the inclination to raise claws.

"You're right, as usual, YeiSa," Taira said, a self-deprecating grimace on ker old, lined face. Ke glanced at ker twin, who nodded. "In one sense, we've been gifted. Euzhan has made her agenda obvious, and that's to our advantage. Unfortunately, she's also right in what she said to Caitlyn: our real influence on the Rock is small, and since Ghost won't return for several days, any decision we make now will take at least four days to relay to Caitlyn, Linden, and RenSa—if they even remain at the Rock after tomorrow."

"We may know what Euzhan is intending, but we don't know CosTa's mind," Terri added. "For all we know, Euzhan is right, and CosTa is directly responsible for all the deaths." Ke shook ker head, the last of the *jitu* trance giving ker stare an unfocused intensity. "This wasn't supposed to happen this way," ke said. "This was not the vision VeiSaTi gave me."

"Then perhaps you saw wrongly," YeiSa answered, more sternly than ke would usually be with the SaTu, but Terri had been so distant in the last few months. "And if Cos was responsible for the murders, would that justify Euzhan's actions?" YeiSa asked.

"No, certainly not," Terri answered, ker tone almost as sharp as YeiSa's.

"But do you think it possible, YeiSa?" Taira asked. "Could Cos have kidnapped Fianya, then deliberately attacked and killed the others?"

YeiSa heard the implicit, unvoiced addendum to Taira's question: *because after all you're one of them and therefore you must think alike.* YeiSa was watching Terri's face as Taira spoke, and something flickered over ker features with Taira's conjecture, and the *jitu*-wide eyes went to the body of the guffin on the altar. *Why? Has ke seen something in the visions that ke's not telling us?* "It's certainly possible, Taira," YeiSa answered, keeping ker voice carefully neutral. "Is it likely? No. We've already read RenSa's report on ker meeting with Cos, and she denied involvement then."

"She could have been lying."

Lying is much more a human trait than a CieTiLa one, YeiSa wanted to say. "A CieTiLa is more likely to evade than to lie directly," YeiSa answered. "Cos went out of her way to insist that the QualiKa hadn't been involved. That indicates to me that she was telling the truth."

Taira nodded, but YeiSa could see that ke wasn't convinced. *Ke finds it difficult to believe, because that's not the human pattern.* Terri seemed to be paying no attention to the conversation, still staring at the altar. "No matter who precipitated this," Taira continued, "we need to show a strong response, both to this self-styled Cha'akMongTi and Euzhan. And I think all three of us need to be there, to demonstrate the depth of our concern. I'm sorry, Terri, but I believe this is beyond Caitlyn's abilities, actual or potential."

Terri shivered under ker *shangaa,* and ker gaze came slowly back to the others. Still, ke said nothing.

"The *Ibn Battuta*'s down in Warm Water by now," Taira said as Terri continued to stare, frowning into some unseen distance. "We'll have to go overland. YeiSa, we'll need a Miccail runner you can trust who can leave the island this evening. We'll prepare a message for Euzhan to let her know we're coming."

"And what is it we'll do when we get there?" YeiSa asked Taira.

"I don't know." They glanced at each other, and Taira gave the lift of ker shoulders that in a CieTiLa would mean irritation, but in a human was only a shrug.

"We'll figure that out on the way," Taira said. "And we'll pray to VeiSaTi for inspiration."

YeiSa glanced back to the window once more. Beyond the stiffening body of the guffin on the altar, the storm clouds had spread anviled thunderheads, gleaming ironically bright in sunlight. YeiSa could smell the distant rain now. On the horizon, in the purple darkness under the hood of the thunderclouds, lightning flickered silently.

Certainly, YeiSa decided, it was too obvious to be an omen.

TRANSLATION:

From the AnglSaiye KoPavi, Nasituda 5–6, Grouping A: "The Senses"

Listen . . . for the words of VeiSaTi are echoed in the sounds around you, and in the smaller voices of the kahina, who remain after their body has died.

See . . . for the works of VeiSaTi surround you, even in the placement of the stones, and there is within them the ancient tales, if you use the eyes of KoPavi.

See with the brais . . . for the movement of light across the world is the chisel with which VeiSaTi carves your destiny on the inner nasituda of your soul.

Touch . . . for it is in the feel of things that VeiSaTi has placed Ker most secret messages—in the cold silk of water through your finger, in the prickle of the burrs, in the smooth roundness of a river pebble.

Smell . . . for in the scent of life is the lingering odor of
  VeiSaTi's passage through the ShadowWorld beyond
  this one, and in the scent of life is life.
Taste . . . for the tongues know the whispers of VeiSaTi.
  They see what the eyes cannot, hear what is silent in
  the ears, smell what the nose misses, feel the subtleties
  that the fingers miss.

VOICE:
Caitlyn Koda-Schmidt of the Sa

"I COULDN'T HAVE DONE ANY BETTER WITH HER."
        Cold comfort, Linden's words. They did nothing to the disappointment inside me.

I'd spent the rest of the morning listening to the transcripts Ghost had recorded—Gerald and Jomo's separate versions of the QualiKa "ambush"—and mulling over my meeting with Euzhan. I thought of a hundred sparkling responses I could have made: glittering gems of metaphor and startling verbal ripostes. I imagined it ending with understanding and agreement, but none of the fantasy changed reality. None of that assuaged the dull ache inside me.

I'd expected Ishiko to return from her Family's compound, but she didn't. Then word had come from Linden that ke wanted to move RenSa from the clinic to the Koda-Levin compound, and that had taken the afternoon. By the time we'd eaten and I'd told the two of them about the morning's encounter with Euzhan, the sun had vanished behind thunderheads piling up on the western hills. I closed the shutters of the Common Room windows and stared at the detritus of our meal.

Linden hugged me, pulling me close. I resisted, then let myself fall into ker embrace. "The *Ibn Battuta* should be back from Warm Water in a few days," ke said, stroking my hair. "RenSa should be able to travel by then."

"I can move now, if we need to," RenSa said. Ker voice was hoarse and barely more than a whisper, and from the way the wrinkles in ker leathery face folded and deepened as ke shifted weight in ker cushion-layered chair, the pain was still bad.

"*Nei*," Linden told ker. "There's no need for that. We'll take the ship back to AnglSaiye. There's nothing we can do here, and the SaTu need to know." Then ke seemed to realize how that sounded. "It's your decision, of course, Caitlyn," ke added, but the addendum was halfhearted and too late.

"The SaTu already know," I told ker, pulling away from ker arms. I felt chilled, goose bumps down my arms. "Ghost will have told them. What we don't know is what they'll do in response. And if they manage to capture Cos . . ."

"They won't," RenSa said. Ker eyes closed, and ker *brais* looked cloudy and discolored. I thought for a moment that ke'd drifted back to sleep again, but then ker eyelids flickered, and ke licked ker lip ridges with double tongues. "She knows the land, better than any human." Ke blinked. "I'm sorry. I don't mean to insult either of you, but it's the truth."

"No offense taken," I told ker. "What we have to worry about is how Cos will respond. I listened to the recordings Ghost made of Gerald and Jomo before I came here, and their versions of the incident don't match well at all. It's pretty obvious to me to Gerald tried to ambush Cos, not the other way around." I sat on the arm of RenSa's chair. "I suppose we'll find out what Cos will do when she does it. Maybe Ishiko can give us some idea which way Euzhan will jump next. Anyone seen her, by the way? I left her with Euzhan this morning, and haven't seen her since."

Linden shook ker head. "Can you trust her, Caitlyn? Are you certain?"

"*Hai*," I answered, and the thought of Ishiko brought

her face into my mind. I found myself smiling, unconsciously. "*Hai*," I said again, emphatically, nodding with the word. "I trust her."

"There's a strange air about her," RenSa said. "She keeps her emotions shrouded. I can see that she's attracted to you, Caitlyn, but part of her is hidden away. You should be careful. Her Family—"

"Ishiko isn't like the rest of her Family," I said heatedly, getting to my feet again. Linden and RenSa were both staring at me. "Neither of you knows her."

"Neither do you," Linden answered. "Not really. If you think one night with her . . ."

Ke was interrupted by a gust of cold wind that snapped the shutters back against the stone walls. I hurried to shut and latch them. Outside, the storm was coming in. The low clouds just to the north were lit from underneath by an orange glow that seemed to emanate from the next valley over: a large fire of some sort, probably set by lightning, I thought—the rain would take care of that soon enough. I closed the shutters on the gale and snugged the latch bolts tight.

The cold, clean air had at least cooled the heat in me. "I'm sorry. You're both right, and I should remember what we've all been taught as Sa. I'll be careful with Ishiko. As for the rest, we should stay here. Maybe we can convince Euzhan that aggression is the wrong strategy with Cos and the QualiKa; at the worst, we'll be here to report on what happens. In any case, the SaTu will be sending us what help they can. If we leave, we may miss it. So we stay."

I looked at Linden and RenSa, both of whom watched me. I wasn't sure what I saw in their eyes, but for once the decision felt right.

"We stay," I told them again.

CONTEXT:
CosTa

THE FUNERAL PYRES BURNED LIKE BALEFUL EYES IN the darkness. They burned fury into CosTa's soul. Even as the hungry flames licked the blackened flesh from her slain companions, CosTa could hear their *kahina* calling to her from the ShadowWorld, their ghostly wails spiraling from the bright sparks wafting skyward.

Revenge! they called to her in crackling tongues of flames. *Death for death!*

CosTa huddled on her knees in the center of the circle of seven pyres, rocking back and forth while sweat streamed down her body and the heat battered at her like a living thing. Her *shangaa* was soaked with perspiration and grimy with ash, and the other QualiKa stayed back outside the fiery circle.

CosTa was in the mad grip of GhazTi tonight, they saw. Only her god and the voices of the dead spoke to her. She did not hear the living.

A storm wind off AnglSaiye Bay whipped the flames, driving them higher and threatening to spread the fires to the grass of the high clearing and the forest beyond. Ominous lightning flickered in the distance.

"We should leave," JairXe, CosTa's FirstHand and her lover, shouted to the other members of CosTa's personal guard. The wind made his words sound thin and weak. His *shangaa* thrashed against his muscular body, the yellow-grass cloth snapping. "The fires will bring the flatfaces."

No one answered him, and he could see a fear on their faces, ruddy in the firelight—a fear not of the humans, but of CosTa. With an inarticulate growl, he raked open claws

148

in their direction and stalked into the ring of fire himself, bringing his arm up to shield his face and *brais* from the searing heat.

"CosTa!" Her arms were wrapped around herself in a fierce hug. The clawtips had emerged from her wide fingerpads, raking bloody furrows down her shoulders and forearms. Her face was lifted to the roiling clouds, where sparks were torn away by the rising wind; her mouth was open in a soundless cry. Her *brais* glittered, tossing firelight back to JairXe. "CosTa!" he called again, and still she didn't answer. Taking a step forward, his firelit shadow fell across her *brais*.

CosTa whirled as if struck, leaping to her feet and turning, her footclaws lifting. JairXe backed away, his own arms spread wide to show her that there was no threat. Against the backdrop of flame, CosTa looked like an apparition, a god-vision. "Who are you?!" she shouted, then her manic gaze seemed to clear, as if she'd returned from some far interior distance. "JairXe," she said, and her voice was freighted with weariness. The wind riffled her spinal mane. "Leave me."

"My Cha'akMongTi, we should go from here. The fire will lead the humans to where we are, and this storm . . ."

She answered as if she'd heard nothing he'd said. "Can you hear them, JairXe?" she cried, and he shook his head, almost sobbing at seeing her in such obvious pain. "No? Their voices are so loud to me, so insistent, and I can feel in my heart that they're right. The land belongs to itself and we should exist within it through the *KoPavi*. Yet the humans treat the land like they were TeTa and the very stones JeJa. Tonight I can hear the voices of all the *kahina* from the WorldWall *WeiGa* to the sea, all calling me as one, and they scream in my head so loudly that I can't even feel my grief."

She looked wildly at the pyres that ringed them, her arms spreading wide as she spun about, kicking up dust from the ground. "I can't mourn you!" she shouted to the burning bodies. "Not while you roar in my heart. Be silent! Be silent so I can give you my tears!"

CosTa kicked at the nearest pyre, and her footclaw

snagged one of the logs. The pyre collapsed with a thunderclap and a cyclone of sparks, the last remnants of the corpse it held falling into the coals. CosTa was momentarily surrounded by embers and flame. JairXe cried out in alarm, but though CosTa's *shangaa* was singed and blackened, the Cha'akMongTi herself seemed unharmed. "Take up our *lansa*, you say, *kahina?* Once taken up, they won't be easily put away again . . ."

CosTa collapsed, as if struck by an invisible fist. When she didn't move, JairXe started to go to her, but CosTa shook her head and staggered to her feet. "Come with me," she told JairXe, and together they walked out of the circle, the Cha'akMongTi seeming to grow stronger with each step. CosTa called to the others in the wind-tossed night, and her voice was louder than the storm.

"GhazTi has called me," she shouted. "The *kahina* of our dead companions have called me also." CosTa drew herself up, her claws raised. "For a hand of days, if you come upon a human outside their towns, kill it without offering *xeshai*, for they have shown they do not deserve honorable combat. For a hand of days, let the flatface lives pay for the lives of the CieTiLa they've killed. For a hand of days, take up the spear my grandsire NagTe cast down."

The Cha'akMongTi's eyes were bloodshot, though her *brais* glimmered bright in firelight. She glared at them: dirty, filthy, and yet god-touched. "Do you hear me, QualiKa?" she shouted to them, and they shouted back affirmation. "Will you do this?" she roared, and the answer shook the first rain from the clouds. Cold sleet hissed on the fires.

"For a hand of days, then," CosTa said, her voice softening. Water pearled her hair. "Then we will meet again at *TeNon*, where I will go to be with the *kahina* of NagTe." She gestured to them. "Now go!" she told them. "Go and show the *lansa* of the QualiKa to the world again."

SONG:

"KoPavi (Open Door)"—QualiKa LongChant (call and response refrain)

the rock under my foot calls
    KoPavi *(loudly)*
the wind breathes my name
    KoPavi *(whispered)*
the sea beckons endlessly
    KoPavi *(bass voices only)*
as we become you
you become we
look, the open door
the light!
    the sound! (tenor voices, loudly)
the rock, the wind, the sea
and we
    KoPavi *(all)*

CONTEXT:

Josslyn Allen-Levin of AnglSaiye

IT WAS AS MISERABLE A TRIP AS JOSSLYN HAD EVER taken.

She had been employed by the Community of Sa since she was nine, and after many years and many varied re-

151

sponsibilities, she was now the executive administrator for the SaTu. She traveled with them whenever they left the island, but those trips were almost always on the *Ibn Battuta*, where she would have her own cabin and maybe even one of her children along to keep her company.

Not this time. Taira had insisted on leaving even though it had stormed all night and a persistent rain was still falling in the morning, with a gusty wind frothing the bay with whitecaps and finding all the seams in their thorn-vine-sap-protected slicks. The boat ride to the highroad terminus had nearly made her lose her breakfast over the rail, and what the rain hadn't already soaked, the waves crashing over the open-sided craft had found. The rain had persisted all that first day, a steady, soaking downpour that at times drifted into a sleet mixture and during the evening occasionally became thick-flaked snow. The highroad was slick with the flagstones glazed in dark ice, and the *konja*-pulled passenger coaches slid and shuddered as they made their way up and down the steep hills around the bay. They kept the side panels shut against the weather, not that Josslyn could have seen the spectacular views from the ridges anyway, wrapped in fog and hidden by curtains of mist and snow. Lunch was a disaster, with no wood dry enough to burn. Everyone had to be content with cold meat and fruit.

They came hours later than expected to the first way-house, and decided to stay there for the night, everyone in the party too soaked and miserable to do more than fall into bed and sleep. They awoke to a fresh layer of ankle-deep, wet snow on the ground. A freezing gale had swung around from the northwest, rendering the surface of the snowfall crusty and hard. Travel was even more uncomfortable and slow the next day, with the *konja* whickering and complaining as they slogged through the heavy drifts.

The coaches were cold and drafty, their progress glacial. Josslyn was riding in the first vehicle with the two SaTu, who sat in the facing seat and spent most of their time arguing with each other in their verbal shorthand, and another Community retainer, Joáo Martinez-Santos, who seemed bored by both the scenery and the company, and snored loudly in his corner of Josslyn's seat. YeiSa, the Miccail FirstHand of the Community, was in the rear wagon with two of the Community's Miccail workers, and the FirstHand's own secretary.

Josslyn found herself longing for home, where a roaring fire would keep out the cold sea winds, and where her son Samuel would be cooking dinner, with the scent of warm bread and stripers basted on a bed of salty kelp, with a heavy mug of pale ale to sip. Sam and her eldest daughter Idina would be looking after the littlest of Josslyn's eight children, Sadda and Crista. Eight children, Josslyn had birthed, all of them Sa-conceived, and only one of them—poor little Hakan—had died young.

Sadda and Crista had cried when Josslyn had informed them she would be gone for several days, and both had insisted on sleeping in her bed that night. "Take me with you, mam," they'd said, with their wide, pleading eyes shimmering with tears, their chins puckered and trembling. "Please, mam. We don't want you to go . . ."

She might have taken them, and Idina to watch them, had they been traveling by steamer. She even considered taking them overland—the SaTu would have been willing to hire another coach—but the weather had been so bad. It had been difficult prying their clinging hands away from her clothes when she'd left, and the good-byes had been tearful and anguished for all of the Family, but she was glad that she'd left them behind.

"Here, mam, take this," Crista had said at the last moment, handing Josslyn a piece of paper covered with her two-year-old's penciled scrawl, attached to a blue ribbon. "It's a necklace I made for you last night, mam. See, that's you holding me, and the sun is shining on us." Josslyn had smiled and cried again, and placed the necklace around her neck.

Josslyn decided that they could not get to the Rock and then back to AnglSaiye soon enough. She was still wearing the necklace under her coat. She touched the satin ribbon and grinned at the memory it brought.

They passed the cutoff that led to Hannibal around midday, then moved on into the rolling, forested hills through which the Loud River cut its winding bed. Josslyn had always thought this part of the country particularly beautiful and peaceful, with tendrils of fog threading through the dense groves of amberdrops and bubble-trees clinging to the hillsides, with the occasional stand of tree ferns lending their blue-tinged color. Wizards flew loudly through the trees, nik-niks bounded alongside the highroad, and jaune-cerf gazed wide-eyed from their grazing. It was a lush land, a gorgeous, pastoral landscape, and Josslyn understood why this part of Mictlan had called to the original settlers from the old starship, far more enticing than the desert beyond the mountains the Miccail called the WorldWall, the flat plains that dominated the southeast of the continent, or the rain forests along its southern edges. This panorama seemed vast, kilometers upon kilometers of unsettled land, untilled land rolling out to the horizon—enough land and more for two races, she decided.

The coach lurched to a sudden halt that shook Josslyn from her reverie. The SaTu shouted in alarm, and João awoke with a snort. "What's going on?" the twins asked together, and the driver called down from his seat.

"The road's blocked, SaTu." Josslyn heard the distinct, frightening click of a rifle bolt. She leaned out through the opened windows as Taira clambered down.

A massive tree trunk straddled the stones of the high-road—not a natural fall, for Josslyn could see the marks of an axe in both the log and the stump a few meters off the road. A Miccail male stood on top of the tree trunk, wearing a bright red *shangaa* and holding a spear. His spinal mane was braided, and his long arms and shoulders diplayed distinct, molded musculature. His *brais* was covered with a woven band, and on that band was a prominent crescent moon.

QualiKa ...

Josslyn felt adrenaline buzz in her ears, her hands white as they gripped the roof supports. Taira stepped slowly away from the vehicle, taking a few dignified steps toward the fallen tree. The *konja* reined to the coaches flared wide nostrils and stamped their feet as ke came near them; the driver kept his rifle discreetly down but ready. "I'm SaTu Taira of the Community of Sa," Taira said to the grumbler. Behind him, YeiSa and the JeJa were just opening the door to their coach. "Why have you blocked the highroad?"

The male's lips drew back in the lipless smile of the Miccail, that Josslyn had always found unsettling in its alien-ness. "I am JairXe, FirstHand of the QualiKa," the grumbler declared, his breath a white cloud before him. "I blocked the road for one purpose only."

"And what is that?" Taira asked.

The answer was sudden and unexpected.

With a hoarse shout, the QualiKa hefted and threw his spear all in one motion. The weapon's aim was terribly accurate. Josslyn heard an awful sound, a dreadful soft tearing like nothing she'd ever heard before, as the spearhead ripped into Taira's stomach. The old SaTu collapsed to ker knees with a strangled, high cry, ker hands clutching the thick wood of the shaft: as Josslyn screamed, as Terri gave an anguished wail behind her, as the driver stood gazing down in shocked, wide-eyed horror.

Then there was no time to react at all. Josslyn experienced the next minute only as a disconnected jumble.

. . . with a massed cry, at least half a dozen Miccail burst from cover alongside the highroad, charging toward the wagons. "QualiKa!" they shouted, the sun glinting on spear tips, the earth gouged by raised footclaws as they ran. "For the Cha'akMongTi and *KoPavi* . . ."

. . . Terri still wailing behind her, as if ke'd been struck by the same spear that had impaled ker twin. Through the sound came the bark of a gunshot and a yell that died too quickly . . .

. . . clawed four-fingered hands reaching inside the wagon as Josslyn, Terri, and Joáo cowered away from them, the daggered fingertips of a Miccail tearing the cloth of her coat, scoring deep, jagged cuts in her arm, gouging deep into her shoulders and neck as they dragged all of them out onto the snowy, cold ground. Josslyn screamed, her throat ragged, pleading with them not to kill, please don't hurt her any more, please . . .

. . . and Joáo's guttural cursing from somewhere to her left, and SaTu Terri's wail behind, and blood—bright blood—everywhere. Through a red-tinged vision, she saw two of the Miccail around Taira's crumpled form, kicking ker over and over with their deadly feet, and scarlet dappling the snow everywhere, and the FirstHand, still on ker feet and fighting the attackers with a spear . . .

. . . the paper Crista had drawn for her, the ribbon torn, lying on the ground in front of her. Josslyn reached for it desperately, her fingers trembling and streaked with blood, and a Miccail foot stamped hard on her outstretched hand, the footclaw stained with dark, thick blood, and she looked up to see the other foot drawn back, and Josslyn knew that it would be the last thing she saw, the very last thing. "Please . . . my children . . ." she said, only a whisper . . .

. . . and then pain exploded in her gut, a searing agony. When she brought her hands down to cover her stomach, she felt only a wet, steaming ruin, and the world was growing smaller and smaller and brighter and brighter and . . .

CONTEXT:
JairXe

THE ATTACK HADN'T GONE THE WAY JAIRXE HAD expected. They'd spied the two passenger coaches struggling up the steep hills of the highroad, heading toward Black Lake. Flatface drivers held the reins of the plodding *konja*—that was as good an indication as any that more flatfaces were sitting in the compartments, since only on the rarest of occasions would a human driver be employed by CieTiLa.

The ambush had been planned so well: the tree across

the highroad, JairXe's companions hidden just off the road. He'd been startled, admittedly, when it was one of the SaTu twins who stepped from the coach, but CosTa's vision had been very clear and made no distinction between humans: young or old; male, female, or Sa. Then—just as he started the attack—he'd seen the Sa FirstHand disembark from the second coach, and suddenly everything was confusion. The CieTiLa attending the FirstHand were not a problem: they all fled as soon as they saw the ambush, jumping from their seats and running. JairXe let them go untouched—they would find them later, and they would become JeJa for the Cha'akMongTi.

But the FirstHand had waded into the fray like a cyclone. JairXe knew, as all CieTiLa knew, that the Sa were taught their own secret fighting art. The art had been preserved in the oral histories passed down by the keepers of history on AnglSaiye, and the CieTiLa Sa had revived it again. But JairXe had never seen that skill in action before. YeiSa stepped toward WiriXa, the nearest of the QualiKa. "Stay out of this, FirstHand," WiriXa said loudly, thrusting his *lansa* halfheartedly at ker, and YeiSa . . . well, ke *moved*. WiriXa had gone tumbling away with a screech, and YeiSa was holding his spear, which ke quickly reversed and smashed into the side of WiriXe's head. He went down in a silent heap.

Two other QualiKa now attacked the FirstHand in earnest. With the shaft of WiriXa's spear, YeiSa took the legs out from under one, whirled around in a tight half circle, and thrust the butt end of the spear hard into the other's stomach.

Three QualiKa were down, and YeiSa had a weapon.

JairXe shouted to alert the others—the flatfaces had been dragged from the first coach and were already dead or dying, all but the other SaTu, but then YeiSa gave a cry and moved toward the QualiKa holding the remaining SaTu, the *lansa* flashing in ker hands. JairXe's companions let go of the SaTu as YeiSa bore down on them—the SaTu went stumbling away into the tangle of tartberry vines along the highroad. Another QualiKa went down as JairXe ran toward the body of one of the drivers. He plucked the rifle from the flatface's dead grasp, the cold graystone feeling strange in his hand. As he'd seen the humans do, he slipped a finger into the guard, put the wooden end against his shoulder. But the weapon, made for flatface hands and flatface strength, betrayed him. His fingers were too large, too strong . . .

The unexpected recoil of the rifle against his body nearly made him drop the ugly device, and it wasn't until he heard the moan of pain and surprise from the FirstHand that he knew what had happened. A patch of sodden, dark red had appeared on the chest of ker orange *shangaa*, a stain that welled and spread as the FirstHand clapped a hand over kerself and stared down in disbelief at ker gore-stained fingers.

YeiSa looked at JairXe with strange calmness while the QualiKa crowded around ker. "Is this the Cha'akMongTi's *KoPavi*?" ke said mockingly. "Do the QualiKa use human weapons now?"

"I use what I must," JairXe answered ker, but his voice shook now after the FirstHand's rebuke, and he hated the weight of the flatface thing in his hands, the mingled smells of acrid gunpowder and sharp oil, the bitter *power* of the thing. *I didn't intend for this to happen*, he wanted to tell ker. *I only thought to use it as a bluff. I wasn't going to shoot you, only stop you from hurting my people.* "I ask for *xeshai*," ke said. "Single combat, with you or your Cha'akMongTi. Let us settle this. If you follow the old ways, then you must grant me that."

"Put down your *lansa*, FirstHand," JairXe said shakily. The rifle seemed to burn his hands, and he flung the detestable thing away from himself. It thudded heavily to the ground near the coaches. "You're badly hurt, and there is no *xeshai* for you here. The QualiKa have no quarrel with the CieTiLa Sa. Put down your spear and let us stop the bleeding. We can help you."

"Help me?" YeiSa mocked her bitterly. Bloody foam flecked the corners of ker mouth. Ke coughed suddenly and violently, ker breath wheezing between spasms as ke nearly doubled over in pain. One of the QualiKa started to approach ker, but YeiSa's spear snapped back up, threateningly. "I think I've had quite enough of your help." Ke took a wobbling, uncertain step toward the bodies of the humans. "Get out of my way if you want to help. Fei! Kelli and Aynat! I need you!" ke called to the JeJa, but ker voice only echoed unanswered from the hills. YeiSa took another step and nearly fell.

JairXe hurried forward, grasping the FirstHand's arm before ke toppled. The touch of ker wrinkled flesh burned like the flatface's rifle barrel, accusingly. The FirstHand shouted gutturally and ker spear jabbed quickly under JairXe's chin, the flaked blackstone point breaking skin at his throat.

"Go ahead," JairXe whispered to the FirstHand, his head lifted and his hand still holding ker arm. "If this will help you, go ahead. Take my soul to accompany yours. I give you my life freely." He could feel the warm trickle of blood running down to stain the collar of his *shangaa*. He closed his eyes, wondering what death would feel like.

YeiSa howled, a wordless cry of rage and pain and grief all blended together, a sound that shredded JairXe's soul and shivered the air around them. The FirstHand's legs collapsed under ker; the spear tip was gone from JairXe's throat. He bent over the FirstHand's huddled form. YeiSa's eyes were open, but ker *brais* was clouded and opaque. "It hurts," ke said simply. "It hurts so much."

"I'm sorry, FirstHand," JairXe told ker. "I'm sorry."

YeiSa licked ker lips, smearing blood. "Tell the Cha'-akMongTi that she has only guaranteed her own death now," ke said. "Your way isn't open, but closed." Ker left hand grasped JairXe's right, claws extended slightly so that the tips dimpled his skin. He felt ker press the shaft of ker spear into his hand. "Take it," ke commanded hoarsely. "At least finish what you've started, QualiKa. By your *KoPavi* . . ."

The Sa closed ker eyes and JairXe realized what ke was asking of him. "No," he told ker, but YeiSa simply breathed the words. "Finish it . . ."

JairXe stared at the spear in his hand, at the faces of his companions. They stood around him, watching silently; behind them, he could see the stiffening bodies of the humans. "As you wish, FirstHand," he said. "By the *KoPavi*."

He put the spear tip to ker chest and leaned against it hard.

VOICE:

Caitlyn Koda-Schmidt of the Sa

"HAI, THAT'S TAIRA. I DON'T SEE SATU TERRI'S body or YeiSa's, though."

It was all I could say. I couldn't believe the carnage, could never have imagined a scene as gory or awful as this.

An exhausted Miccail runner from YeiSa's staff had arrived from AnglSaiye two days after I'd met with Euzhan, telling us that both of the SaTu and the Miccail FirstHand were on their way to the Rock. Two days later, they'd yet to arrive, and the first reports were coming to the Rock of attacks on human travelers by the QualiKa. When a third day had gone by without the SaTu arriving, I'd gone to Euzhan and the Elder Council and asked for an escort to search the highroad; reluctantly, they'd agreed to help, giving us an escort of a half dozen volunteers. Ishiko was among them, surprisingly. I hadn't seen or spoken to her since the morning we'd talked with Euzhan. We managed to find some time to talk as we rode our *konja* from the Rock, but she kept the conversation distant and safe, and during the first night, she spread out her bedroll with the others, away from Linden and me. When I started to come over to her with my supper, her eyes widened as if she were afraid of me. I stopped and turned to sit next to Linden.

She didn't come over to me, then or later. And I didn't go to her.

At noon the next day, at the end of one of those rare Mictlan mornings, with a vault of sapphire fleeced with pristine white clouds, and the sun dancing warm on the shoulders of the hills and shimmering on the last remnants of the fog on the slopes below us, we'd found . . . *this*.

The attack must have been quick and savage; if any QualiKa had been killed, the bodies had been taken away for burning elsewhere. The SaTu Taira and the Sa entourage had been dragged from the two wagons and murdered—their bodies had been left for the scavengers. By the time we arrived, they'd pretty well had their fill. Arms and legs had been carried off, the bodies were partially skeletonized. Buzzflies whined in moving clouds around what was left, and the sickening scent of rotten carrion forced us all to put perfumed scarves over our nostrils and mouths.

The SaTu Taira was among the remains we could identify, as well as our administrator Josslyn, and Joáo, another employee of the Community. There were two other human bodies we couldn't put a name to, probably the drivers of the wagons but definitely not SaTu Terri. The Miccail runner had said that the FirstHand YeiSa was with the SaTu, but we never found ker body or those of any of the Miccail who would have been attending ker. The seats of the second cart had been modified for Miccail, so the FirstHand had almost certainly been there. There was blood splattered around that carriage as well, but whose we couldn't tell. The QualiKa had left all the belongings and goods, and we found the *konja* not far off with broken traces—the attack had been intended to kill, nothing more.

We burned the bodies in a common pyre that night, and the noxious black smoke stained the sky. Like most of the others, I burned the clothes I wore that day, and tossed my gloves into the flames with the bodies. I must have washed my hands four times that night, scrubbing at them wildly, and I thought I could still smell death on them. . . .

The day was a nightmare I will never forget. Never.

The others set a guard schedule for the night, and both Linden and I made certain that a rifle was within reach for each of us, as well. At the moment, I didn't intend to ask questions of any Miccail who wandered into the camp that night, and I was glad that RenSa had been too weak to travel with us—I didn't want ker to see my prejudice and my fear. In fact, the depth of my reaction surprised me as well, and I knew that Linden was feeling much the same. We huddled around the campfire like its heat and light were the air itself, and tried not to hear QualiKa in the rustling of the amberdrops or see ghosts in the flickering of shadows at the edge of the light.

The folk who had come with us watched the shadows also, and sometimes they watched us, and I wondered whom they blamed for this atrocity. I could see Ishiko staring at me from across the fire; when she saw that I had noticed, she looked away again quickly. I wondered what she was thinking, and why she wouldn't let me come near her.

I wanted her then, for the comfort her presence would give me.

"By all the *kami*," I whispered to Linden, and could get no further than the simple curse. All the words had drained from me.

"I know," ke said. "I know. SaTu Taira and almost certainly Terri and the FirstHand as well . . . May VeiSaTi be kind to their poor *kami*."

I rubbed my hands together, rubbing away imaginary grime. "We started this, Linden: William attacking RenSa, then Gerald with CosTa . . . We started this, and it's going to get worse."

"Caitlyn—"

"*Nei*! I can feel it, feel it here." I touched myself in my *hara*, my center. "We can both guess how the Rock is going to respond to the attacks, and then the QualiKa will give us back the same redoubled, and then . . ." I took a breath. "The Community will vote Rashi to be the next SaTu, I suppose. And RenSa—ke's now the FirstHand for the Miccail."

"Maybe," Linden agreed, "but RenSa doesn't even know about this yet, and AnglSaiye won't know for several days more. We should still confirm the deaths before we do anything. No matter what Rashi might want us to do, we're at least a week away from hearing about it, and RenSa's still recovering. This is our problem, Caitlyn. That hasn't changed."

There was nothing I could say to that. Ke was right. For the time being, this was our problem, *my* problem. I just wished I knew what to do about it. I glanced at Ishiko, across the fire. She'd been watching us, but when she saw me look to her, she turned her head away to the glowing ashes of the funeral pyre, settling her rifle across her lap. When I looked back, Linden shrugged.

I don't know that we slept much that night. We jumped at every sound, never quite falling into deep sleep. The *kamis* of all the dead ones seemed to move around us, whispering in the trees and howling in the winds. In the morning, exhausted, we started the long trek back to the Rock.

VOICE:
Ishiko Allen-Shimmura of the Rock

I KNEW I COULDN'T AVOID KER FOREVER. I KNEW that ke would ask the questions I didn't dare answer truthfully. Not now.

I watched ker, most of that awful day. I saw ker weeping over the bodies of ker SaTu, I saw the horror and grief in ker eyes and the frightened guilt that tempered it. I knew Cailtyn blamed kerself at least partially for this, thinking that if ke had been able to deal with my Geema, then the SaTu twins would never have decided to come to the Rock, and thus would still be alive.

I wanted to tell ker that I shared that guilt.

But I couldn't.

So I ignored ker, knowing that my coldness and silence made the pain worse for ker, and hating myself for having to do it. Hating Geema for making it necessary. At the scene of the carnage, after the bodies had been burned on the pyres, I sat across the fire from Caitlyn and Linden, watching them talk even though I couldn't hear their words, and wanting more than anything to walk over to Caitlyn and simply hug ker, to be next to ker. When they finally crawled into their rolls to sleep, I did the same, remembering the feel of ker body next to me, the strange mingling of male and female that, after all I'd been told, was neither awful nor so strange once I became used to it. I remembered the gentleness of ker lovemaking, of how ke moved with me, laughed with me, kissed me.

The memory of ker taste clung to my mouth, even now.

We broke camp before the sun was fully up the next morning, without anyone actually ordering it, and we rode the *konja* hard for the Rock, none of us wanting to stay out here for another night, all of us bursting with the news of the attack and on edge because we felt that at any moment the QualiKa could leap from the shelter of the thorn-vines or out from under the drooping limbs of the amberdrops. We hadn't gone far before I felt Caitlyn's presence at my side.

"What's happened between us?" ke asked simply. After my first glance at ker, I didn't dare look in ker direction again. We rode along in silence except for the jangling of the *konja*'s harnesses, the creaking of saddles, and the steady thud of hooves on the ground.

"Nothing's happened, Caitlyn. Nothing's changed. It's always been this way, and we just didn't want to admit it." The words tasted like the ashes of the pyres we'd left behind. "Our relationship can't work, Caitlyn," I said finally.

"Just like that? 'Our relationship can't work.' What did she say to you, Ishiko?"

"I can't tell you," I said, which was only the truth.

"Ishiko—"

"*Nei!*" I told ker sharply before ke could say more, before ke could say something that would make the pain even worse. "You fucked me, like you've no doubt fucked half a hundred other men and woman. You did your job like a good Sa, and now it's over." I saw ker face harden with that, the muscles knotting at ker jaw, ker nostrils flaring with a sudden intake of breath, and the highlights in those lovely light eyes turning as cold as yesterday's snow.

"That's the way it has to play, is it?" ke asked.

I nodded. "That's the way."

"She's that good at twisting people, your Geema?"

"This has nothing to do with Geema. It has everything to do with me. Or don't you believe I'm capable of thinking for myself?"

"I think I saw you do exactly that, for a little bit, anyway. Now I see you hiding yourself again, the way you did when I met you." Ke glanced pointedly at my left hand—in my coat pocket. Hidden. I could only stare at ker, not daring to bring the hand back out. I thought I saw the ice in ker eyes melt then, just a little. "Ishiko, I didn't hold anything back with you. I still would not, if it were what you wanted."

I felt tears gathering in my eyes, and I turned my head so ke wouldn't see them. I wasn't sure how to answer. "Caitlyn—" I began, but then a ragged voice called from alongside the road, the voice quavering and weak despite the urgency of the words:

"Help me!"

A figure staggered out from the brush alongside the High Road, dressed in a tattered orange *shangaa*, with blood clotted in thin white hair and a palsy shaking the bony hand that lifted toward us.

"SaTu Terri!" Caitlyn shouted, leaping from ker *konja* and hurrying over to the old Sa, who sagged into ker arms.

JOURNAL ENTRY:
Anaïs Koda-Levin, O'Sa

I MET AGAIN WITH NAGTE THIS SUMMER, KNOWing that if I didn't take some action, the Elders of the Rock would do something on their own, something more drastic than I'd like.

He was much changed from the years when I knew him in AnglSaiye: gaunter, more restless, as if his passion had burned away any extra flesh on his body, leaving behind only wiry muscles and that searing, commanding presence that had always been his. When we finished with the polite nothings, I decided that I would simply ask him the questions I had, without dissembling or courteous padding. Since NagTe refused to speak the human language (though he knows it very well) and my Miccail has never been very good, I could hardly be anything more than direct.

"What will it take, NagTe?" I asked him in my halting Miccail. "What will make your QualiKa put down their *lansa* and end this violence between us?"

He grinned at me, as if he found the question amusing. "You have been gifted by VeiSaTi with many wonderful qualities, and we owe you much, O'Sa," he told me. "The gods sent you humans down to bring back the CieTiLa and the Sa. They chose *you* for the task, and you accomplished it. Now your work is done—you don't need to stay here any longer. You don't have the power to end this struggle."

"Pretend that I do and would use it, NagTe. What is it you'd ask?"

The grin remained on his face, deepening the wrinkles in his cheeks and along his thin snout. The triple slits of his nasal vents widened. "Leave," he said. "Go back to the clouds. Give us back AnglSaiye. Give us back the Black Lake. Fill in the tunnels you carved in our sacred rock and destroy the buildings that deface it. Go away, and return the land to us. The gods did not send you here to destroy us after you returned the Sa to us.''

I sighed at the impossibility of what he asked. ''You're right, I can't do what you ask. But why does it have to be that way? There must be some middle path. Be reasonable.''

NagTe was shaking his head before I finished. '' 'Be reasonable'—that's what your people always tell us. 'Yes, we've defiled your most sacred places without so much as a thought to you, but *be reasonable*. Yes, we built our homes where CieTiLa once worshiped their gods in peace, but *be reasonable*. Yes, this land, over here was also the CieTiLa's, but it has the rocks we need to make our gray-stone, so *be reasonable*. Yes, our furnaces soil the air, land, and water, but *be reasonable*. Yes, we insist that all you ''grumblers'' follow our *KoPavi* rather than your own, but *be reasonable*. Yes, we've killed uncounted numbers of you since we came here, but *be reasonable*.' ''

He grinned at me again, but the smile was humorless and hard. ''Tell me, O'Sa. Is this simply a translation problem? Does 'be reasonable' mean 'stop complaining because we are going to do whatever we want anyway' in your language?''

''No,'' I told him. ''NagTe, I know the history of our respective people's relationships have been tarnished by violence, and I know that we humans made many mistakes because we initially believed the Miccail to be extinct. But that history doesn't need to repeat itself.''

Now NagTe gave the barking, percussive cough that is Miccail laughter. ''Those are very brave words, O'Sa,'' he told me. ''I applaud you. I've learned some of the long, long history of your own world in the clouds. A very *reasonable* people you've always been, even with your own kind, all *through* that history. Sharing the same land with others, understanding cultural differences, tolerating another person's religion: Those are really your people's great talents, aren't they? You tell us that you lost contact with the cloud world when you came here, and most of your ancestors believed that was because your 'reasonable' species had yet another dispute. Knowing your history, I have great confidence that violence is inevitable between us. We both covet the same land, but we would do different things with it.''

Boers and Zulus, Palestinians and Jews, Irish and English, Native American tribes and European settlers, Angles and Saxons, Gauls and Romans, Serbs and Croatians, Aztec and Spanish, Chinese and Japanese, Hindu and Moslem, Catholic and Protestant, Christianity and damn near *any* other religion, Earthers and Outworlders . . . NagTe's words brought up an endless list to my mind. For all I knew, it might go back to Neanderthal and Cro-Magnon. He looked at me for long moments, and a sadness touched his features, softening them. ''And I think that when you listen to the song of your heart, you believe the same thing.''

He was right. He was terribly right. ''What I think,'' I told him finally, ''is that your people are not so different from us at all. And that's what frightens me.''

CONTEXT:
Ama Martinez-Santos

AMA WATCHED HER MAM AS SHE CLEANED THE kitchen of the Sa's compound, sniffing as she always did when she came into this strange old place. The compound smelled funny, full of a faint mustiness that made her nose wrinkle. Sometimes, when she poked into the old, long-unused closets there, she would sneeze, suddenly, as fine dust trickled down from disturbed shelves and filled her nostrils.

The place smelled even stranger now, with the old grumbler Sa in there. Ama didn't really think that was the way grumblers smelled all the time, because she'd smelled the same nose-wrinkling odor on *da* Donni when he'd hurt himself last year and he was in bed with bandages all wrapped around his leg and his face pale. He didn't get up for a long time, and he still limped, sometimes.

Ama's mam Galadrielle had always gone over to the Sa house every week or so to dust, just in case a Sa might come, and now that the Sa were there, she came every day. Ama came with her, usually. The Sa fascinated her. Agaja, her mam's sib, was a Sa, and ke lived on AnglSaiye. Ama thought she would like to meet ker, one day, and she imagined ker looking like one of the Sa who were staying here now, more like the younger one than the older one, she thought, but more beautiful and with long, black, and straight hair like her mam.

Her mam was scrubbing the sink now, her back bent over the porcelain. Ama swung her legs on the kitchen chair, bored. "Mam, I want to go home," she said, as she had every few minutes since they'd arrived.

"Not *now*, Ama," her mam said, not even turning around. "I'll be finished here soon."

"But I want to go *now*."

"Ama—" Her mam gave the sigh that meant Ama had gone as far as she could go without getting her angry. "Just sit there and be a good girl for a few more minutes, would you, please?"

Ama sighed herself. Her mam was still scrubbing. Ama let herself down from the chair and padded quietly from the kitchen. She went into the Common Room, but there was nothing there that she hadn't seen many times before, and after a moment, she turned down the hallway to the sleeping rooms.

The two human Sa were away for a few days, her mam had said, but the grumbler Sa was still here. Ama could hear the sound of ker slow, deep breathing in the next room. The door was opened slightly, and Ama slipped through to stand at the foot of the bed. The grumbler was sleeping on ker side, the covers over ker bandaged body. Ama had never been this close to a grumbler before. She'd seen pic-

tures of them, seen them at a distance when they traveled
through the area or came to trade with the Families. Once
she'd even glimpsed what her *da* Abui had said was a pack
of wild ones, off across Tlilipan. She'd heard all about
them, but actually seeing one was much different and much
better.

Carefully, Ama lifted the quilt covering the grumbler's
foot—*hai*, there it was, the great claw she'd heard Abui
talk about, the one that could rip you open with one kick.
The footclaw was folded up, lying against the top of the
leathery skin of the grumbler's foot. Ama reached out with
a quivering forefinger and touched it, snatching her hand
back as soon as she made contact as if it might burn her.
It had felt . . . cool, smooth, and hard. The color was the
ivory yellow of Geeda Shotoku's remaining teeth, with an
earthy brown in the creviced lines running through it. Ama
reached out again, braver this time, and touched the very
tip. It wasn't as sharp as she had expected, more like the
end of her mam's letter opener that she'd found while rum-
maging around in her dresser drawer, but the thought of it
tearing into her stomach made her suddenly shiver, and she
pulled the ribbed diamonds of the quilt back over the foot.

The grumbler was still sleeping. Ama tiptoed around the
side of the bed to look at the grumbler's face. It was
strange, the skin darker than her own, with more wrinkles
than Geeda, and leathery. Ke didn't have ears, just big,
drumlike ovals low on the side of ker neck. The triple slits
on the end of ker snout were opening and closing with each
breath, and the pupil-less, lidless eye in the middle of ker
bony forehead was a blue-white like the moon Faraway.
The seeing eyes were closed, the lids fluttering in a dream.
Ama wondered what grumblers dreamed about.

The hair that started high up on ker foreheard attracted
Ama, and she stretched out over the bed to touch it. The
hair was surprisingly soft, softer than even her mam's, and
reddish-colored. The grumbler shifted in ker sleep as she
stroked the mane, and Ama drew her hand back quickly,
stepping away from the bed and ready to dart out of the
room if ker eyes opened.

One of the grumbler's hands had come out from beneath the quilt, and Ama crept forward again to look at it. The three fingers and thumb were impossibly long, with wide pads at the tip in which the handclaws were nestled. There was webbing between the three primary fingers, almost all the way up to the knuckles. The thumb was strangest, far too long to look like her own, and with an extra joint that made it curl in almost to the center of the grumbler's palm. The hand reminded Ama a little of the paws of the Family's verrechat. If you pressed just the right way on the verrechat's pads, the claws would come out—her mam did that when she wanted to trim the verrechat's claws. Ama wondered if the grumbler's claws would come out if she pressed on its fingertip pads the same way. The curiosity drove her forward.

The grumbler's hand was warm. That was the first thing she noticed. She could feel the thin muscles just under the skin, and the bones. She took the pad of ker index finger between her thumb and forefinger and pressed.

Ama smiled in delight. Just like the verrechat—the curved dagged of a claw rose from the pad. She let go of the finger . . .

. . . and the fingers of the hand closed. Ama glanced up to see the grumbler staring at her. She screamed in shrill surprise and fright, jumping backward away from the bed. From the kitchen came the clattering of crockery, and then the sounds of her mam's running footsteps—"Ama! What's wrong?"—as the grumbler stretched ker arm out toward her. Twin tongues moved behind its lipless mouth. "Don't be scared," ke said, or something like that. It was hard to tell, the way ke slurred the words, and with her blood pounding in her head.

Her mam came hurtling into the room. She saw the grumbler and ker outstretched arm, and snatched up Ama with a cry. "You stay away from her! Ama, are you hurt, darling?"

"She's fine," the grumbler said, as Ama burrowed her head, sobbing, into her mam's shoulder. "Just frightened."

"What did you do to her?" mam Galadrielle accused the grumbler.

Through her sniffling, Ama thought the grumbler sounded tired. "Nothing at all," ke said. "She was just curious and woke me, and that scared her. That's all."

Her mam pressed her head down protectively, arm tight around her. "Are you all right, Ama?" she asked, ignoring the grumbler. Ama choked down a last sob and nodded. "I was playing with ker claws," she said.

"Oh, Ama . . ." Ama could hear the quick intake of breath, the quickening of her mam's heartbeat. Galadrielle carried her to the door. "You stay out of ker room," she said to Ama, but Ama knew that her mam was staring at the grumbler, giving ker the same ultimatum she was giving to her daughter. "Just stay away from ker, do you hear?"

"*Hai*, mam." Ama sniffed. "I will."

As her mam carried her out of the room, Ama lifted her head to look back at the grumbler. Ke was watching her, ker alien eyes following her.

As her mam hurried her back to the kitchen, Ama stuck out her tongue at the grumbler, silently, her face screwed up and her chin lifted. Ama held the pose until the doorjamb cut off sight of the strange creature.

VOICE:
Caitlyn Koda-Schmidt of the Sa

REALITY CAN SHIFT UNDERNEATH YOU IN A MATTER of days. In a few days, the grass slug goes from papery chrysalis to mating adult and an inevitable messy death in the jaws of the coitus blossoms. In a few days, the snow can come screaming in from off the bay to blanket the ground in a meter of orangish drifts, then melt completely to feed the icy streams while leaving the hills bare.

In a few days, you can find affection and love in someone you expected to be an enemy and lose it again.

You can discover that there is more inside you than you had ever believed . . .

SaTu Terri was suffering from exposure, shock, dehydration, and loss of blood. Ke'd been wounded: There were Miccail claw marks along ker back, down her arms, and across the top of ker head, along with minor abrasions and scratches from the vines and underbrush in which ke'd been hiding. Ke wasn't completely coherent, but we gathered from ker rambling, breathless commentary that the SaTu had seen ker companions slaughtered, including YeiSa, and had barely escaped the same fate kerself. Linden took the fastest *konja* and two of the other riders, and headed back to the Rock and the clinic there with the SaTu. The rest of us continued onward at a slower pace, camping that evening near the ruins of Gabriela Rusack's cabin.

The Matriarch Rusack had built the cabin in the last decade of her life, when she'd been shunned by the Rock for being a *rezu* and corrupting Adari Koda-Shimmura—over two hundred years ago, not long after we humans had first arrived on Mictlan. Very little remained of the structure: A chimney fire and the normal ravages of time had seen to that. A hearthstone, a tumbled corner of knee-high stones, and a jumble of rotten beams were about all that were left now. In another fifty years, the land will have reclaimed it entirely.

Sometimes things take more than a few days, I suppose.

We set up camp alongside the cabin as the sun touched the humpback crests of the surrounding hills. I was unrolling my bedroll in my tent when I heard the uproar over by the road.

Adrenaline surged with the noise level, snapping my head up and shifting my body into a defensive stance—I suppose the lessons with YeiSa had their effect after all. I expected a swarm of QualiKa to come hurtling toward us from the woods, but the shouting had already stopped. I slowly relaxed again. I could see Radulf Allen-Levin over near the amberdrops across the highroad, with half of our party gathered around him and the other half (Ishiko among them) heading there at a trot.

I followed.

"... found it hiding over there," Radulf was saying. "Probably waiting for us to go to sleep."

"It" was a Miccail, a very frightened-looking male trapped inside the ring of humans. A gash from just above his right eye nearly to his *brais* had fanned blood across his face. His claws were out, on both hands and feet, and he turned slowly in the center of our wary circle, hissing and sputtering as he glared at each of us in turn.

"*Khudda!*" muttered someone. "Look at it, just waiting for one of us to get too close. Just kill the bastard and be done with it." A general murmur of agreement swelled around me.

"Who are you?" I asked the Miccail in the CieTiLa tongue. That brought his head swiveling around to me. "Hey!" Radulf shouted to my left. "What the fuck did you say to him, Sa?"

I glanced at Radulf. Ishiko was standing near him, a rifle in her own hands. I looked more at her than Radulf. "I asked his name, that's all," I said. "You're talking about killing him, and you don't know whether he's QualiKa or not."

"I know he was hiding here, watching us. That's all I need to know," Radulf answered. Again, the swell of agreement surrounded him.

"What's your name?" I asked the Miccail again, trying to ignore the crawling unease that seemed to settle in my shoulder blades. The Miccail brushed at the blood in his right eye with the back of his hand; ivory claws clashed with the motion.

"AracXe," he answered. "Of the tribe of MalcTe and NaorTa. We live over there." He pointed to the hill behind Gabriela's cabin. "You're a Sa?"

"I am," I told him, giving him the sign of the Three, which he echoed back to me. "We ... you must understand. Several humans were killed, not far up the highroad."

"I know," Arac said, grimacing. "The QualiKa."

Saying the word was a mistake, and I knew it . I heard the click of Radulf's weapon as he brought it up to fire. "*No!*" I shouted. "Wait! You can't!"

"I heard him, Sa. 'QualiKa.' That's all I need." Radulf sighted down the barrel. His finger curled on the trigger, and Arac growled, ready to leap.

"He's not QualiKa," I told Radulf. "He didn't say anything of the sort."

"Then he's lying. Let him go, and he'll come back later with a few dozen of his friends to murder us. Well, I'm not going to let that happen."

"Let me talk to him, Radulf," I told him. "This is insanity."

He didn't answer. He settled his cheek against the rifle's butt, closed one eye.

At another, earlier, time, I might have backed away then, still protesting but feeling I couldn't control the situation. Unwilling to try. I don't know what had changed in me, but something had. I didn't think about it, didn't consider at all what I was going to do. I simply stepped in front of the Miccail. "No," I told Radulf, again.

None of the others had moved. I could feel Arac at my back, wanting to attack, and the black-singed muzzle of the rifle held steady at my chest. "Step away, Sa," Radulf said. I shook my head. "Or this will take two shots, that's all." When I still didn't respond, he shook his head. "I'm not letting it go, Sa. I'm not letting any more of us get killed."

I turned around to Arac, feeling the rifle barrel at my back. "Listen to me," I said in his language. "You are not QualiKa yourself?"

"No. That is the truth."

I nodded. "You're frightening my companions. You need to pull your claws in, AracXe. I can't do anything for you if you won't do that."

"They'll kill me."

"No," I told him, hoping I wasn't lying. "They won't. I promise you that."

His twin tongues slithered over his lips. He blinked blood

away from his eye. Slowly, the handclaws began to slide back into their fingerpads, his footclaws lowered. I went to him, then. I patted the Miccail's shoulder, looking at Radulf. At Ishiko, who stared at me. "Come with me," I told Arac, and then switched back to my own language. "Radulf, back away."

I started walking out of the circle. I wondered how far we'd get, whether Radulf would simply fire and end it that way. I walked directly toward him, and the Miccail followed me. At the last moment, Radulf let the rifle drop to his side and slid to his left, letting us pass. I took Arac across the highroad to the ruins of Gabriela's cabin, feeling everyone's gaze on the two of us. There, I gestured toward the hills. "Go on," I told Arac. "Get out of here. Go quickly."

"Thank you, Sa," he told me.

"Go," I said.

He went, moving quickly into the darkening shadows of the amberdrops. Within a few seconds, I'd lost sight of him.

It was only then that I began to shake, and wondered what kind of idiot I'd turned into.

CONTEXT:
CosTa

COSTA'S GRANDSIRE, NAGTE, HAD BEEN CARRIED DY-
ing from the field of KariVal, or Waters Meeting, which the humans called Hannibal. In a tent at the rear of the QualiKa force, he had succumbed to his grievous wounds, surrounded by the stricken faces of the innermost circle of his followers. Before the O'Sa Anaïs had even arrived at Hannibal in ker attempt to end the confrontation, NagTe's corpse had been borne away to the steep, rocky hills to the east.

There, where GhazTi had first spoken to him of the *KoPavi* and the QualiKa, NagTe had been laid to rest, his body burned on a great pyre that—tradition said—had turned the clouds above a deep, sorrowing blood red that was visible from AnglSaiye to WeiGa. Later that year, though the QualiKa were leaderless, scattered, and fighting among themselves, the loyal core of the QualiKa came to the hills and built a resting place for NagTe's ashes.

CosTa stood there now, at the mouth of TeNon.

TeNon was a passage grave, a long, arrow-straight tunnel that was part natural cavern and part artifact. The entrance, formed from three great menhirs of polished granite that had once been part of DekTe's temple to GhazTi, was built low and narrow, so that CieTiLa entering TeNon must bow their heads and go to their knees in respect. This CosTa did now, with a quick supplication to NagTe's *kahina*, whose presence was felt in the chill that welled from the black, lightless mouth of the grave. Once past the constriction of the imposing entrance, the passage beyond opened so that CosTa could stand upright, though she could touch either side of the passageway with her outstretched hands. The tunnel walls were decorated with images from NagTe's life, she knew, but except for the mural visible here at the entrance, where a little reflected daylight lingered, they were lost in darkness. A torch rested in a stone ring on the north wall. CosTa pulled it down and rummaged in her pouch for her firebox. From the small container, she took one of several finger-length, slender pieces of wood and moistened the tip with her tongue before dipping it into a vial wrapped in moss, which contained a pungent resin. She blew on the nodule of black tar as it dried quickly on the stick, then struck the stick sharply on a nearby stone. The stick crackled and hissed, then burst into sputtering flame. The end of the torch was coated with a similar unguent, and CosTa set it alight.

From the end of the passage, sixty-four steps away, three hands of torches glittered back at her. CosTa headed toward them.

At the end of the passageway, the narrow corridor suddenly opened out into a large chamber. Like the interior of some huge geode, the hollow was lined with crystals, the smooth faces of which threw firelight back at CosTa in dizzying, flaring reflections. Shards of CosTas clutching at fragments of torches flickered and danced all around her, and the light they carried illuminated an obsidian pillar in the center of the room, atop which was set a simple wooden box holding ashes: the remains of NagTe.

Once a year, TeNon blazed with its full brilliance and grandeur—on sunset of the anniversary of NagTe's death. The grave entrance faced west: On that day and that day only, the light of the dying sun struck full on the menhirs and flooded the passageway, shattering on the crystalline interior in a dazzling, aching glory for a few brief minutes before fading once again.

CosTa had witnessed the startling celestial display nearly every year, as had many of the QualiKa, her breath caught in her heart as searing light played around the box which held her grandsire's remains, the shimmering glow making her cover her *brais* in defense. But she preferred to come here at other times, when she could be alone with NagTe's *kahina*, alone in the echoing quiet of the tomb, alone in the twilight of torchlight, alone with her own self.

"Father of my mother," she said, and though she whispered it, the words seemed impossibly loud. In the torchlight, the box seemed to shudder, as if awakened by the noise. "It's begun. I have taken up GhazTi's *lansa* and your legacy. I've set my people on the path you once followed." CosTa ran a hand through her spinal mane. "I . . . I want to know that what I've done is right. Father of my mother, I know that even though I never met you in life, I've asked much of your *kahina*. Now I've come to ask again, because I find that I'm frightened of what I feel. I would ask you if this was how you felt, when you were Cha'akMongTi. Sometimes I am so consumed by GhazTi's fire that I can barely contain it, and at those times there is never any doubt in me at all. And yet afterward, when GhazTi's presence is gone, I'm so empty and so cold and so . . . uncertain of my path. Was it that way for you? Was your *KoPavi* like mine, all shrouded in my own doubts?"

CosTa set the torch on the stone floor of the tomb and

went to the pillar. She lifted the lid to the box and plunged her fingers into the dark granules inside, letting the gray ashes and bits of charred bone sift back through her fingers as she raised them. "NagTe, I wish I could have known you. I wish I could have asked these questions of you when you were alive. I can feel your *kahina*. I know you watch, and yet I can't hear your voice."

Sighing, she let the last of the ashes fall back into the box and closed the lid once again. She slumped down, her back against the pillar, hand over her *brais*. She sat that way for a long time, not thinking but simply breathing slowly in and out, taking in the *kahina* of NagTe as she sat there.

"CosTa?" Someone called from the entrance of the tomb. CosTa could see the shape of him outlined against the sky. "JairXe," she called to him. "I'm here."

"I must speak with you, Cha'akMongTi." She heard the throbbing of anxiety in his voice, the deep emotion caught in his breath.

"My lover, what's wrong?" she asked, suddenly troubled as quick fear lanced through her heart. In silhouette, she saw JairXe's head go down, then lift again. When he spoke this time, his voice was clearer, almost defiant.

"I have done as you asked," he said. His voice struck crystal and echoed, reverberant. The torch on the chamber floor guttered and flared, sending light crashing around CosTa as JairXe spoke his next words. "I have slain one of the SaTu, and I have slain the FirstHandYeiSa."

"Gods . . ." CosTa felt the breath go out of her, as if someone had struck her in the stomach. Yes, she had ordered the QualiKa to kill humans, but she never thought that it would mean the death of someone like the SaTu, and the FirstHand as well . . . She wondered what her anger might have brought them.

JairXe's bravado had collapsed with CosTa's exhalation. "My Ta, I only thought to follow your command—"

She held her hands out to him, claws withdrawn, and touched his face. "Hush," she said softly, willing herself to be calm, not to show him the apprehension inside. "You did as I asked, and I am pleased. This is what GhazTi desired. It must be."

She hoped she was right. She feared she was not.

VOICE:
RenSa

THE MEMORY OF THE LITTLE HUMAN GIRL STICKING her tongue out at me remained in my mind for a long time. It was such an instinctive gesture for her, something she did without thinking. A reflex. I know it was derisive, and I know it was meant to hurt me, yet . . .

There is such a gulf between us.

I heard the door close. I rested for a while longer, then forced myself out of the bed. I went to the Common Room, searching for . . . I didn't know what. All I felt was an emptiness, a sense that there was something I must do and yet I couldn't remember what it was. A fire—fueled by peat and not pagla-nut husks—smoldered in the hearth, and I stood before it, enjoying the warmth on my body, naked except for the bandages around my shoulder. The firelight glittered against the polished ebonyew of the sacrificial shell, set on its tripod of carved whitewood legs. I stared at the altar for a time, then went over to it. From the compartment in the Water leg, I took the vial of *jitu* and Black Lake water; from the Earth leg, the small stone axe; from the Air leg, the garotte. I poured a small amount of the *jitu* into the palm of my hand, then lapped it up quickly. The air seemed to shiver before me, and I knew that I needed no sacrifice to bring VeiSaTi's vision to me, not this day. Instead, I lifted the implements and touched them to my own head, whispering the words: for earth, for air, for water.

The altar melted before me, like dharwood sap in the spring. I melted with it, my body flowing down and merging with the stones beneath me. I became the Rock. The sun warmed my steep flanks, the *nasituda* burned on my crown, and the humans moved within me like insects boring into a tree trunk, and there was the dull pain of the caverns they had cut into my stony flesh. I could feel the wind, like the world breathing through and within me, and my roots were snuggled deep in the blanket of the earth. Grasses clung to my flanks with tiny roots, birds alighted on me and flew off again. Though the cycles stretched before me in an endless line, I knew that with each day, the rain and sun and ice and wind stole away infinitesimal frangments of me: thousands of *terduva* from now, I would be nothing more than a stone a CieTiLa could hold in her hand, an incredibly ancient and wise stone, having seen the far larger cycle of the world's life.

"So . . . you've come to realize that we fail to see the other, much longer lives around us. Because of that blindness, we mistake our own individual lives as being important. Is that something you can understand, RenSa?"

A stone can hear. A stone can feel. A stone can see, if it chooses. I opened my eyes, and saw the colors of YeiSa's *kahina* standing before me. I saw the purple strand of ker that should have tied ker to earth and it was waving free, dancing in the wind. "You've died," I said, and felt no sadness for ker passing, since I knew that death had only changed ker, not ended ker.

The *kahina* that had been YeiSa extended a wave of rich umber toward me. "The burden of my life is yours now," the earth tones told me. "You are the FirstHand."

"I don't want the title."

I sensed the *kahina*'s amusement. Ker laughter was a swirling, cool gust. "You lie without knowing it. You do want the burden, or you would not be here."

I could not argue with truth. There were a hundred things that I wanted to ask the *kahina*, but I couldn't put the words together. They swirled inside me, disobedient and mocking. The *kahina* laughed again, seeing that.

"RenSa, you can't form the question until you understand what it is you want to know," ke told me, and the *kahina* dissolved before me, all ker bright colors fading. For a moment, I thought I saw the image of a male, a *lansa* in his hand, standing before YeiSa's spirit, his weapon striking at the fading image. "Wait!" I called after ker.

"I am always here," the wind called to me, faintly. "Always here."

Always here. I closed my eyes and when I opened then again, I was only RenSa in the Common Room, still standing before the shell altar with the last of the *jitu* shivering in my head.

But I knew what I wanted to know, and I knew whom I needed to ask.

TRANSLATION:

From the AnglSaiye <u>KoPavi</u>, <u>Nasituda</u> 23–26, Grouping B: "The Hearkens"

Hearken to the voice of Ke Who Dwells In The Wind.
  Hear me in the rustling of the dead leaves in
  midwinter, for I am there.
  Hear me in the wailing of the storm gale, for I am
  there, too. Look for me above you, for I write with the
  ephemeral clouds on the nasituda *of the sky, releasing*
  them within you through your brais, *though you know*
  it not.
Hearken to the voice of Ke Who Dwells In the Water.
  Hear me in the soft clatter of the stream, for I am
  there. Hear me in the patter of the rain, for I am
  there, too. Look for me within you, for I write on your

*kahina with your own blood, and I sing in your body,
though you know it not.*

*Hearken to the voice of Ke Who Dwells In Stone.
Hear me in clatter of a pebble falling from a high
cliff, for I am there. Hear me in the sound of crisp
snow under your feet, for I am there, too. Look for me
below you, always, for on me is written the signs of
everything that has crawled or walked or grown within
me, and they are part of you, though you know it not.*

*Hearken, Sa, to the KoPavi of male and female, of TeTa,
XaXe, JeJa. Their voices fail without you, and without
the chorus of their song, your own voice will be silent
on the earth.*

CONTEXT:
Linden of the Sa

CAITLYN HAD CHANGED IN THE SINGLE DAY THEY'D
been apart. The signs were subtle, easy to miss,
but Linden immediately sensed the alteration. Ke was confident, sure of ker decisions now, all the doubts in ker
wiped away.

Caitlyn strode into the Koda-Levin compound with a
rush, shedding ker coat on the way. Though ke embraced
Linden as warmly as ke always had, there was a distance
in ker gaze, a new timbre in ker voice, and an iron calmness
to ker, as if ke had passed through some rite of passage
and come out the other side. "How's SaTu Terri?" ke
asked Linden. "I overheard some of the talk on the way
up. The Families are saying that Terri's addled and strange.
And where's RenSa?"

"I don't know where RenSa is," Linden answered. "Ke
was gone when I got here with the SaTu. One of the Allen-

Levins said they saw ker walking out by the river yesterday afternoon, and ke hasn't returned. I'm worried about ker, Caitlyn, especially given the mood around here.'' Linden lifted ker shoulder and exhaled loudly. The rest came out in one long rush, as if ke were glad to be rid of the burden of holding it in. ''As for what's been said about the SaTu, well, it's true enough. Terri would barely let me dress ker wounds on the way back. Ke was acting . . . oddly, at one moment grim and dour, in the other laughing as if everything were an enormous joke that only ke could understand. Ke insisted on being taken immediately here—ke wouldn't see Euzhan or anyone in the Elder Council. I had to deal with them and let them know what had happened. They're understandably upset and angry. Some of them— and not just the Allen-Shimmuras—were talking seriously of 'cleaning out' any of the Miccail settlements near the Rock. I argued with them, but they mostly ignored me and finally had me escorted from the chamber when I wouldn't keep quiet. By the time I finally got back here, I learned that Terri had sent one of the Martinez-Santos children for three live goathens—when they got back with the animals, Terri locked kerself in one of the studies. I could smell *jitu* through the door, and I've heard ker crying out now and again. For the last few hours, ke's been quiet. I don't know if ke's asleep or still lost in the *jitu*. Ke won't unlock the door.''

Caitlyn sighed. ''Then we'll get one of the Family smiths to come over and unlock it for us, or we'll break it down. Come on. . . .''

They didn't need force. Caitlyn called to SaTu Terri, knocking hard on the door, and after a few seconds, they heard the click of the lock. Caitlyn pushed the door open, and Linden followed.

They could both smell the coppery blood-scent. Terri had dragged the altar with its three-legged stand from the Common Room; the bodies of the goathens—skulls crushed by a single axe blow, strangled with gut cords knotted three times, and furred feathers damp with water—were heaped at the altar's base. Terri stood there as well, the sleeves and chest of ker shangaa dappled with thick smears of reddish brown.

Ke smiled: an eerie, calm smile. "Caitlyn, Linden," ke said, as if greeting someone ke'd passed in the halls of the temple.

"SaTu, how are you feeling?" Caitlyn asked, and Linden heard that new sense of command in ker voice again. Terri felt it as well; ker eyes blinked and seemed to focus suddenly.

"I'm . . . perturbed," the old Sa answered. Ke dipped a forefinger in the shallow bowl of the altar, stirring the liquid there. Ker finger emerged dripping red. "VeiSaTi is so elusive. Maybe it's the goathens; their *kami* just aren't strong enough to call Ker and bring Ker here from the ShadowWorld . . ." Terri looked at the goathens, then back to them again. "My twin is dead, you know," ke said in a conversational, light tone. "The big QualiKa male killed ker."

"We know, SaTu," Linden said, glancing at Caitlyn. "And the FirstHand's dead also."

"*Hai.* That's really too bad. I had wanted them both to see the promise of the *KoPavi* brought to fulfillment. The QualiKa are actually right in that, you know. The Elder *KoPavi* is so powerful, so strong . . ." Terri shook ker head, strings of white hair swaying over a face creased like old leather. "I asked who should go to the Rock, and VeiSaTi said it should be you, Caitlyn. In the *jitu* vision, I asked Ker because I knew that if we sent the wrong person, questions would be asked that shouldn't be asked, and your name was called. But then things went wrong, all wrong, and I thought perhaps I had misheard Ker. I wanted to ask Ker again, but . . ." With the same unchanging smile, the SaTu spread ker hands wide over the carnage in the room. "I don't hear the answer. Nothing in the *jitu* spoke to me. If only I'd given Ker the sacrifice for which ke asked, none of this would have happened. None of it . . ."

The SaTu's knees buckled, suddenly, and the two Sa rushed forward to catch ker. Terri's head lolled, and Linden felt the heat on ker forehead before ke even touched ker.

"Ke's really feverish," Linden said. "I need some cloth, and water . . ."

Together, they put the SaTu to bed, and Linden soaked away the worst of the fever with cool washcloths and an infusion of *sali* bark. It was EighthHour before ke left the SaTu. Ke went looking for Caitlyn; passing the study, ke saw the younger Sa standing by the altar where Terri had sacrificed the goathens. "Is RenSa back?" Caitlyn asked softly, without glancing up at Linden.

"No. And no one's seen ker."

A nod, as if Caitlyn had expected that answer. "How's the SaTu?"

"Sleeping. The fever's down."

Another nod. Caitlyn had disposed of the goathen bodies and cleaned the floor, Linden noticed. Caitlyn was staring down into the incised shell-form of the altar plate, as if ke could read something in the whorls and brown stains there. "Why was I supposed to come here?" Caitlyn said, as quietly as before. "Why did VeiSaTi speak my name to the SaTu?"

"Maybe Ke didn't. Maybe all the SaTu heard were just dreams and nothing more."

Caitlyn's head lifted with that, ker light eyes regarding Linden from under the falling sweep of dark hair. "Terri's been obsessed with the translation of the *KoPavi*, trying to resurrect old rites that have nothing to do with us or what O'Sa Anaïs created for the Sa," Linden continued. "We've all been worried about ker for months now. I know Taira was. And you know how much *jitu* Terri drank. I know I don't always see clear visions with *jitu*—do *you*, Caitlyn? Usually the visions are just that: images that mean nothing or that reflect back at you what's inside your own head. VeiSaTi isn't a human god, after all, even if Ke is our Protector."

Caitlyn hadn't really heard ker. Linden knew it even though ke shook ker head. Ker attention had gone back to the shell of the altar. "What questions weren't supposed to be asked?" ke said. "What sacrifice was to be made?"

"The SaTu's fever was speaking, Caitlyn. That and too much *jitu*. That's all."

Even as ke said it, Linden knew ke didn't believe it. Nor did Caitlyn. Linden could see it in the way ke gripped the edge of the sacrificial bowl, in the seafoam hollows of ker eyes.

VOICE:

Ishiko Allen-Shimmura of the Rock

THE CLAY REFUSED TO WORK WITH ME. OH, I know that it was only my own clumsiness, my own preoccupations, but that's what it felt like. Each time I tried to throw a pot, something would abruptly go wrong: A kick of my foot to the turntable would send it lopsided, or my left hand would spasm and I'd tear a hole in the clay, or I just wouldn't like the way it looked. By the time Porfiera and I were called to supper, I was covered in slip from forehead to ankles and had nothing to show for the effort but a mountain of slick, gray lumps in the discard bin. Porfiera glanced at me as I washed the worst of the clay from my hands.

"Bad day," she commented.

"Awful," I agreed.

"Was it as terrible as it sounds, what you saw out there? I heard . . . well, I heard that Radulf caught one of the grumblers that did it, but that CailtynSa made him let the thing go. Geema was furious when she heard that, I'll bet."

I shook my head, drying my hands on a towel. I'd spent most of the day trying not to think of the last few days, and not succeeding. "Radulf's an ass."

Porfiera looked at me with the same appraising tilt of her head she has when she's trying to decide how to decorate

a bowl. "You actually like ker, don't you?—that Sa, I
mean. Ish, you didn't actually—"

I scowled away her inquiry. "I'm hungry," I said.
"Let's go upstairs."

Geema Euzhan was already seated at the head of the
table, with half of the Family arrayed around her. Despite
our lateness, she actually favored me with a smile when we
came in, waving to an empty seat to her right, next to Gerald. I sat, and Gerald passed me the bread. I cut a slice and
passed it on, reaching for the goathen butter. "I will speak
to the SaTu tomorrow," Geema said, satisfaction pulling
her mouth into a taut simulacrum of a smile. "It's obvious
enough now who killed our Fianya: The QualiKa were responsible. There's no reason to suspect our own Family
anymore. It was absurd to consider it in the first place. I
wasn't about to hand our Fianya over to the Sa, but I had
no need to try to hide her away. The Sa can all go back to
AnglSaiye."

There were general murmurs of agreement around the table. Of course, Geema could have said that the Rock was going to dissolve in tomorrow's rain, and everyone would have
nodded sagely and concurred. Disagreeing with Geema at
the table led to general indigestion all around. "And the
QualiKa can all go to hell," Gerald added. "I'll be happy to
help send them there." He handed me the bowl of mashed
meatroot. I set it down in front of me and put my left hand in
my lap under the table. "What do you mean?" I asked Gerald. I looked from my sib's self-satisfied grin to Geema
Euzhan.

"The Elder Council's decided that we need to clean out
the QualiKa around here, for our own safety," Geema answered. Her smooth forehead crinkled slightly. "Certainly
that makes sense to you, of all people. You've just witnessed the atrocities they're capable of committing. For our
own survival, we need to make sure that the grumbler settlements around the Rock are free of the QualiKa taint."

"And so we kill more of them, and they'll try to kill
even more of us in turn, and this will keep going on until
there are either no more humans or no more Miccail."

"Sounds good to me," Gerald said with a dark chuckle that subsided under Geema's glare.

"Don't try to make it sound like we're oversimplifying the problem or that I'm not aware of the implications, Ishiko," Geema said. "I am. But I also can't let my Family be threatened this way."

"This isn't a solution."

"Have you heard any other plan that sounds better, or is more likely to succeed?" Geema persisted. "Maybe the Sa have a strategy other than hurling words?"

The bite of bread I'd had was a rock in my stomach. The food on the table had turned to ashes and dust. I pushed my chair back and stood. "I'm not hungry right now," I said, and left the room, feeling Geema's black stare on my back.

"What the hell's the matter with *her*?" Gerald said loudly, as I turned down the corridor and left the compound. I walked from the echoing main cavern out into the frigid, clear air of the night, and the chill felt warm against the aching cold in my stomach.

I went to the railing along the cliff edge and looked down and over the tops of the amberdrops to where Old Bridge arced over the moonlit river—Longago's light, the moon the Miccail called Chali. Faraway—Quali—was hidden, either already set or yet to rise. I didn't know which, didn't care, but I was glad not to see it.

I could see the laser-cut windows of the Koda-Levin compound shining bright against the dark rock, just upslope from me. Somewhere behind there was Caitlyn.

My right hand gripped the railing tightly. My left simply lay atop the freezing steel. I looked out across the river to the night-wrapped mounds of the hills. Somewhere out there were CosTa and the QualiKa.

I pushed away from the railing. I went to the Koda-Levin compound and knocked on the door. Caitlyn answered. Ke was in ker *shangaa*, ker hair disheveled and ker eyes bruised with weariness. "I . . ." I began. Stopped. "There's something you should know," I finished.

Ke held the door wide and stepped aside. "Come in," ke said.

TRANSLATION:

From the AnglSaiye KoPavi, Nasituda 23–26, Grouping B: "The Sexes"

KNOW THAT THE MALE IS MOST LIKE THE AIR
*for like the air, the male is ephemeral. Like the wind,
they can be first here, then there. Like the clouds, they
are ever-changing, and will go wherever they are
blown, gathering sometimes into great angry masses
that shriek and thunder and spark. The male is breath,
coming in and out, essential yet not always noticed.
This is why GhazTi was born within the storm, why
SahfiTi is seen in the shimmering arc of the rainbow,
why TilikTi is the voice of the wind and VarlaTi
emerged from the first light of the sun.*

KNOW THAT THE FEMALE IS MOST LIKE THE EARTH
*for like the earth, the female is the fertile field from
which all CieTiLa spring. Like the stones, they are the
foundations in which we build. Like the world, they
change slowly but always, giving forth to new vistas at
each turn and holding both air and water within them.
The female is rock and soil, plant and animal, each
different and yet each the same. This is why YlekTi
stepped forth from the molten rock of the volcano, why
OhinomTi is present in the flowering herbs, why
NodhiTi scratched Her name in the earth to make
rivers and VerdTi gave color to the bright gems.*

KNOW THAT THE SA IS MOST LIKE THE WATER
for like the water, the Sa is substance. Like the seed of

*air which is rain, they contain male. Like the lakes
and rivers which gather in the womb of the land, they
contain female. The Sa is the blood within us, which
when spilled releases our* kahina *to the ShadowWorld.
This is why VeiSaTi came from the sea, which is held
by earth and nurtured by air; why VeiSaTi gave the
Sa the great shell of AnglSaiye, which has the solidity
of the earth and the shimmering glow of the air. This
is why VeiSaTi was created from the tears of all the
other gods, male and female, when they found that
they could not easily conceive and that the children
formed of their unions were fey and strange.*

JOURNAL ENTRY:
Anaïs Koda-Levin, O'Sa

GHOST WAS SO CASUAL ABOUT IT THAT I ALMOST
missed it: "And our new settlement at Hannibal's had a few minor problems. The Elders of the Rock
are complaining that AnglSaiye's not giving them the support they need, they're out of milled and cured lumber, and,
oh, NagTe killed Mahesh Allen-Shimmura."

"Ghost!"

She gave me a look of faux amazement. "What?" she
answered in kind, wearing Gabriela Rusack's face as if it
were a mask she could use to hide her own despair. "You
expected everything to go smoothly with Hannibal, even
after NagTe warned us that the QualiKa would protest any
settlement placed there?"

"When did this happen?"

"Two days ago," Ghost said. "A runner relayed the
news to the Rock yesterday. The Elders have dispatched a
runner to AnglSaiye to tell you, since they weren't sure if

I'd get the news to you first. I'm talking to Elder Micah Allen-Shimmura at the moment, but he's not telling me how they're planning to react beyond saying that 'we'll take care of the problem.' "

"Tell Micah for me that Elders had better not consider force as the way to take care of the problem."

Ghost blinked, held up an index finger for a moment, and then gave me a taut smile. "Micah said to inform the O'Sa that AnglSaiye does not dictate to the Rock how to deal with internal issues, especially when it concerns the death of one of their Family." Ghost grinned at me. "My, he *does* sound like old Dominic, doesn't he? Must run in the Family."

Even though the sun was streaming in off the bay and warming the room, I felt cold. Sometime you feel destiny clutch you, and her touch is ice. It was almost as if I'd taken *jitu*. My vision shuddered for a moment, and I knew. I knew I had to go to Hannibal *now*, even though it might already be too late. I called for my NefSa, my FirstHand, and told ker to make things ready.

VOICE:
RenSa

GO TO COSTA.
        That's what the *jitu* vision had told me. So I went. I thought of leaving a message for Cailtyn and Linden because I knew that's what they would have done, but that was a human thing. A CieTiLa called by ker god *went*. Ke did not pause to give explanations.

I had heard of the tomb of NagTe—the TeNon—and I knew that the QualiKa considered it a holy place. Why there?—I was simply following what my inner *kahina* told me. CosTa would be there, or not. She might find me on the road. I didn't know, didn't question. The thought came to me, and I acted on the impulse, trusting it.

That was also something few humans would do.

Because it was on the way and because it seemed to be right, I stopped again at the place where Fianya had died. Blood still dappled the stones where the poor child had died. Up above, the cave where ke'd been held looked the same. I went inside once more, looking at the fire: peat and pagla-nut. Someone trying to hide their identity, or perhaps only someone who knew both ways. I looked again around the cave and again saw little evidence of who had been there. I crouched down, and saw once again on the floor the trio of indentations where something had been set . . .

. . . and this time, I wondered, and what I wondered, I didn't dare say aloud.

I left then, and continued east, moving slowly because my shoulder still ached from the gunshot wound, and I didn't know if I could trust the arm if I fell. I came down the other side of the hill, crossing the road that went south and west to TiMur, God's Piss, the lake fed by thermal springs. Not a human name at all—I remember I once translated it for one of the human Sa pupils, and ke shud-dered at the thought. Warm Water, they call it, instead. I stood on the road, hesitating for a second, and then crossed over it and into the forest again, still moving east.

I'd not gone a dozen paces when I heard the squabbling of tree-leapers just ahead. Their querulous voices went si-lent as I approached, and I heard them skittering away into the cover of the foliage above. While they made their rus-tling retreat, I stepped into a small clearing; as the wind shifted slightly, I caught the scent of corruption an instant before I saw the cause.

The earth under me shivered, and I felt every hair on my spinal mane stand up. My claws came out, unbidden. My shoulder throbbed.

A human body swayed sickeningly three strides from me, one end of a *shangaa* sash knotted around the neck, the other end secured to a thick, overhanging branch. By the smell, the body had been there several days, though being suspended well above the ground it had been out of the reach of most of the scavengers. The tree-leapers had been nibbling at the exposed flesh: The eyes were gone, the lips and nose were gnawed back to the skull, and the fingers were nothing but white bone. Even without the face, I knew who it was. The orange *shangaa* told me it was a Sa, and the rotund shape told me it was Rashi.

After the first shock, I forced myself into calm, trying to take in the details of the scene before me, forcing myself to disengage my emotions and just be an observer. It wasn't easy—I knew Rashi well, had spent hours working with ker on the mat. Ke was the favorite of the human SaTu Terri, and helped ker with the translations of the *KoPavi nasituda* found under the temple, sharing Terri's fanaticism regarding the ancient text. Ke'd left AnglSaiye for Warm Water only a few days before we'd left ourselves; it appeared ke'd never arrived there.

Ker death wasn't the result of theft. Rashi's pouch lay on the ground beneath ker body, undisturbed. Nor did Rashi appear to have been murdered. There were no signs of struggle anywhere around the area, and ker *shangaa* wasn't torn or bloodied.

Rashi had killed kerself: I knew it. Another human thing—to take one's own life that way, to feel so depressed or so ashamed that you can no longer bear living.

A CieTiLa would commit suicide only if VeiSaTi asked it. I doubted that VeiSaTi had called to Rashi.

I moved around the clearing, avoiding looking at the body. The thorn-vine patch at the southern end of the clearing looked as if something had been thrown into it—I picked my way carefully through the prickly snarl of vines, stopping when I saw something dark a few arms away from me. I hunkered down, feeling that crawling sensation along my spine once more: A sacrificial shell-altar, its tripod stand broken and lying a few hands away, was caught in the nest of vines ahead of me.

I knew then why VeiSaTi had brought me this way.

I knew, and I was frightened at what that meant.

MOVEMENTS

"If anyone thinks the murder of little girls will bring this people to its knees ... break our spirit or that we will relinquish our birthright, holy land and our eternal capital, he does not know the strength that exists in each person standing here around me today and in the entire nation."

—BENJAMIN NETANYAHU
in the *Jerusalem Post*, March 14, 1997

TRANSLATION:

From the AnglSaiye <u>KoPavi</u>, <u>Nasituda</u> 11–12, Grouping D: "The Admonitions"

Sa!
When you hear the voice of VeiSaTi
  listen and obey, for with your God you are as JeJa is
  to TeTa
When you see the vision of VeiSaTi
  watch and believe, for it is a rare and true gift to
  glimpse the ShadowWorld
When the light of VeiSaTi moves over your brais
  do not crouch down in fear, for it is your duty to go
  where VeiSaTi takes you
When the taste of VeiSaTi is in your mouth
  swallow it gladly, for you will be both nourished and
  strengthened for what is before you
Sacrifice!
  for by the gift of earth, air, and water the boundaries
  of the ShadowWorld are shattered and VeiSaTi's
  presence is released
Give to VeiSaTi what Ke asks
  By earth
  By air
  By water

JOURNAL ENTRY:
Anaïs Koda-Levin, O'Sa

JUST BEFORE I LEFT FOR HANNIBAL, I TOOK *JITU*, which is something I do rarely, and sacrificed a guffin before the Great Shell in the temple. I placed my sacrificial altar directly over the flagstone under which the Sa Beneath The Water now rests. Through the eyes of *jitu*, I saw the flagstone rise and the *kahina* of KaiSa came out to stand before me. Ke was lovely, with deep brown eyes, a golden *brais*, and a soft, embracing smile. Ke held out a hand to me, and I took it as I had many times during the weeks ker bog-preserved body had rested in my clinic back at the Rock—only now ker hands were warm and supple and alive, and they pressed back against my fingers. "O'Sa," Kai said, and though ke spoke in the language of the Miccail which I speak only badly, I understood ker perfectly. Ker smile held the warmth of the sun. "Thank you for returning me to AnglSaiye. Thank you for bringing the Sa back to us."

"That was VeiSaTi's will. All I had to do was listen to Ker and do as Ke asked," I answered, and ke laughed at that, gently.

"VeiSaTi isn't your god."

"Not then," I agreed. "But Ke has become so, over the years. Ke is the god of all Sa, and many of my people."

"Then you will listen to what Ke asks and do it, as I did?"

I could not lie to KaiSa, who was now a demingod to ker people. "I don't know. I do what I think is best, and I trust that VeiSaTi will approve. I trust that VeiSaTi wants me to help my people."

Again the smile. "VeiSaTi's intentions aren't ours to

know, O'Sa." Ker voice chided me, softly. "We either obey or not, without understanding. We must trust Ker. Do you trust Ker, O'Sa?"

I started to answer, and KaiSa held up ker hand, ker head tilting. "You answer with your mind, not your heart," ke told me. "Look deeper."

I looked, and I could see within my body as if it were glass, and what was within me was not blood and organs, but lights and shades, and each meant something to me. Far within me, I saw the core of my beliefs, glowing softly green and gold. "*Hai*," I told ker. "I do trust Ker."

KaiSa's gaze went sad, and I could feel the empathy welling from ker, enveloping me like the shimmering pearl radiance of VeiSaTi's Great Shell. "What Ke asks of you now will require courage," ke told me. "Do you have that courage?"

I looked within me again, at the darting blue, the sweeping red. "I have so little left here on Mictlan," I told ker. "I am old, and all my lovers are dead, and I have done what I set out to do. What is there for me to be afraid of?"

Ke nodded, and fell into sparkling dust before me. VeiSaTi came to me then, in Ker full glory, and I saw the future Ke gave to me.

CONTEXT:
SaTu Terri of AnglSaiye

TERRI COULD HEAR THE WOMAN IN THE OTHER room, talking her poison. ". . . everything you knew and planned, Caitlyn, everything you told me, I was supposed to tell her. But I didn't. Not everything. I swear it . . ." The Allen-Shimmura whore was pleading, but it was like the annoying whine of a snarl-fly in the SaTu's ears, and ke walked into the room, knowing that ker presence would at least make her shut her mouth.

"Why do you bother to listen to this garbage, Caitlyn?"
Terri demanded. Ke leaned against the archway leading into
the Common Room, ker *shangaa* disheveled, ker white hair
wild and stiff. "She's an Allen-Shimmura. You can't trust
her. Everything she says about me is a lie."

"She is not talking about you, SaTu," Caitlyn said, but
the expression of ker face told Terri that the bitch had already seduced ker. The Allen-Shimmura woman stared: a
cold, unsympathetic face, Terri thought. The tears in her
eyes were as false as her soul. There were accusations in
her gaze: ke could see them, crawling around her like mag-
gots.

"It's all lies, I tell you!" Terri shouted at Caitlyn. "She
doesn't understand me. None of them can understand me."

"SaTu, let's get you to bed . . ." Caitlyn said it the way
ke might have spoken to an acolyte who was having bad
dreams.

"Damn it, don't you be condescending to me!" Terri
thundered. "I'm still the SaTu. VeiSaTi chose me to show
Ker vision, and I *will* follow through with it. I tell you that
I will make Ker vision real, and it doesn't matter what lies
they're saying about me. I know I failed before, but they
don't understand. They can't understand."

"SaTu . . ." Caitlyn put ker hand around Terri's arm,
and Terri pulled away angrily.

"Don't patronize me, and don't think I can't see what
happened here." Ke pointed at the Allen-Shimmura
woman. "Just because you've fucked her doesn't mean that
she's on your side. Didn't you listen to any of your lessons,
CaitlynSa? Are you so naive?"

"SaTu," Caitlyn persisted, and Terri saw an anger in ker
eyes now. Ker hand on Terri's arm was insistent. "You're
tired, you've been through a terrible experience, and you
need to rest some more. Please . . ."

Terri didn't have the strength to resist. Ke allowed Caitlyn to guide ker back to ker room, and lay down on ker
bed until Caitlyn shut the door. Then ke sat up again, the
turmoil of thoughts in ker head not allowing ker to sleep.

In the mirror on the dresser, ke could see kerself—an old, old Sa sitting on the edge of the bed, ker face still flushed with anger. Ke hardly recognized kerself—ke might as well have been looking at Taira.

Taira. The thought brought back images of ker death, of seeing ker eviscerated and dead on the ground, the blood pooling around ker, the earth drinking the thick redness like rain . . .

They would be telling Caitlyn about ker, all of the apostates here. They knew, and they would tell ker. But they didn't understand. They didn't believe in VeiSaTi. Not really. Not in the way Terri did. Terri had heard the voice of the god, but ke hadn't fulfilled Ker vision yet. Because ke had failed, VeiSaTi had taken Taira and the FirstHand, had sent the QualiKa to kill them in front of Terri. *This is the terror that awaits if you do not obey soon,* VeiSaTi was saying to Terri. *You've already failed me once, and this is your punishment.*

Ke would not fail VeiSaTi. Not again. Ke thought ke had found the way, but it had all fallen apart somehow, even though ke'd entrusted Rashi with the truth. Somehow, Terri would find a new way to give Ker what Ke asked.

Terri hammered ker fists on ker thighs. "I will do it," ke said aloud. "I will."

The face in the mirror nodded back to ker.

VOICE:
RenSa

I SUPPOSE THAT I WAS LUCKY I WASN'T SIMPLY killed outright.

The QualiKa were as nervous and touchy as wingclaw parents guarding their nest. The two guards at the entrance to TeNon held their *lansa* pointed at my chest, and I could sense bows nocked and drawn, aimed at me from the heights to either side.

"I am RenSa, the FirstHand of AnglSaiye," I told the guards again, for the fourth time. "I have come here to see CosTa."

"CosTa is seeing no one," they told me, also for the fourth time, with less patience than before. "Are you deaf or just stupid, Sa? Turn around and be glad that we let you leave with your life."

"Ask *her* if she wishes to see me or not," I persisted. "Don't answer for your Ta. I am the FirstHand of the Sa, and I wouldn't have come here unless my seeing her weren't vital." I took another step toward the guards, as I'd been doing, slowly, since I'd first been confronted. The tip of the nearest *lansa* was now within an arm's length.

"She is *not* seeing anyone," the guard answered again, exasperated.

"She *is* inside TeNon, though," I persisted, gesturing toward the dark opening of the tomb and using the gesture to mask another shuffling half step.

His hesitation and the glance from the other guard told me that I was right, but they both tried to shrug simultaneously. "CosTa is wherever CosTa is," one of them said. "And we're finished talking with you, Sa."

"I would agree with that," I said. This time, I took a deliberate step toward the nearest guard. As I expected, he halfheartedly thrust his *lansa* in my direction, but I had already taken another, final deep step to the side of him, leading with my good arm. In one motion, I grasped the *lansa* shaft with my hands and used the energy of his thrust—twisting the *lansa* in his hands and stepping back across his front at the same time. My injured arm screamed at the sudden abuse, but the guard, toppled by his own momentum, went flying into his companion. As both of them went down, I quickly slid back into TeNon as arrows hissed and clattered against the carved stone columns flanking the entrance. I slammed the door shut and jammed the guard's *lansa* between the columns to bar them, trying to ignore the pain in my shoulder. I turned toward the torchlit, long passage leading into the tomb.

A male was standing three strides away, his *lansa* back in throwing position. I spoke with what I hoped was calm. "Never throw your weapon," I told him. "If you miss, your enemy will use it against you."

"I don't miss. Ever," he answered, but he didn't throw, though the long muscles of his arm quivered.

"JairTe," a deep, familiar voice came from the darkness beyond him. "Let ker pass."

I hadn't known that CosTa had named anyone as Te, but I bowed my head to him. *There are no more TeTa*, the O'Sa had said, but the titles are ingrained deeply in the CieTiLa, and if AnglSaiye Sa didn't use them, we were the exception. Equality in rank was a nice pretense, but it was still just a pretense—even among the humans, from what I'd seen. "I'm sorry, Te," I said to the ground, hoping he wouldn't strike. "Forgive me for coming to you this way, but the guards left me no choice."

JairTe didn't turn away from me, but he lowered the spear. Behind me, the doors crashed open and clawed hands grabbed me; JairTe shook his head at the guards, who reluctantly let me go. The Te stood aside in the narrow corridor and gestured toward the interior. At the end of the passage, set deep in the heart of the hillside, I could see the column where NagTe's remains rested, the room lit by what seemed to be hundreds of glittering torches. I walked toward the room, hearing JairTe fall into step behind me. The tomb was gorgeous, brilliant with crystalline mirrors, and atop the column I'd glimpsed from the entrance, a plain wooden box sat. CosTa sat to the left, the remnants of a meal on a low tray before her. Seeing her brought back the night I'd met her above Black Lake, and how equally frightening and attractive she had been. I felt that duality again now, as I stood before her.

"I can only imagine how this must look on NagTe's deathday, with the sunset shining here," I said. "It must be as splendid a sight as rumors have said."

She smiled at that, a gentle smile. "It is," CosTa answered, looking at the box holding her grandsire's remains. Behind me, JairTe slipped into the room. He moved to stand to the right and just behind CosTa, protectively, almost jealously, and his hand went to her shoulder as he gave me a strange glance. CosTa glanced at me, appraisingly, her handsome face tilted. "RenSa," she said, nodding, "I'm pleased to see you again. But why does the SecondHand of the Sa seek me out?"

"I'm the FirstHand now," I answered. Something—a flicker of emotion—moved across JairTe's face, and I knew something else, remembering the male with a *lansa* in YeiSa's vision. I pointed to JairTe. "He knows. He killed YeiSa."

JairTe tried, but he could not disguise the intake of breath or the way his claws emerged to grip CosTa's shoulder, or the anguish in his face. He had done the murder, yes, but I could see that guilt stained his *kahina* because of it, a guilt that wouldn't let him rest easily. "Be calm, Jair," CosTa told him. "You only did as I asked. It wasn't your fault—you know that I would not have called you my Te if I felt differently." She took a sip of her *kav* and then set the cup back on the tray. The click of pottery against lacquer was loud in the room. "YeiSa's death wasn't something we looked for, nor was that of the SaTu," she said to me. "VeiSaTi has given you Sight, but I hope Ke has also shown you that their deaths were . . . unfortunate. The QualiKa do not look to kill CieTiLa unless they directly oppose us, and we do not look to hurt the Sa, whom we need as much as anyone."

I could see the trembling in JairTe's face and hands, and I knew that what CosTa had said was the truth. YeiSa would have tried to protect the SaTu, and I could well imagine that JairTe had little choice but to kill ker or be killed himself. "I know that," I said. "I also know that the QualiKa did not kill Fianya, our little human Sa."

A glimmer almost of amusement passed over CosTa's face. "That is something we've always known, RenSa. As I recall, I told you that myself above Black Lake, a turning of Chali ago."

"And do you know who was responsible?"

CosTa nodded sadly, a motion almost too small to see. "I do. I knew it then."

"You could have said so. You could have come forward with that information and maybe none of this recent bloodshed would have happened."

A shiver. "The act was nothing that involved the QualiKa, FirstHand. It was a human matter. A Sa matter. Tell me, would I have been believed had I gone to them, or would the humans have instead held me for their own idea of justice?"

"I don't know," I answered honestly. "I thought Vei-SaTi was asking me to come here to find who had killed Fianya, but Ke showed it to me on the way. Now, I'm not certain why Ke sent me here. All I know is that this is where Ke wants me to be."

"Then stay, FirstHand," CosTa answered, and I saw JairTe, from behind, fix CosTa with a glance of surprise and irritation. "Stay as long as VeiSaTi wills it, under my protection."

"CosTa, ke is here only to report back to the flatfaces," JairTe said heatedly. "The FirstHand is nothing but a tongue to lick the SaTu's ass."

"If you believed what you just said, JairTe," I answered carefully, "you wouldn't be concerned with my presence. And you are. I know it. CosTa knows it."

The Te bared his handclaws, but didn't move. Lines curled around his seeing eyes, his mane bristling.

And CosTa laughed.

It was a melancholy laugh, laden with doubt and despair and guilt, and the sheer weight of the sound broke the tension between JairTe and me. JairTe turned to her, forgetting me for a moment in his concern for his lover. And I did the same.

"Jair, my sweetness," CosTa said, "the Sa knows you as well as I do. A hand of *terduva* ago, DekTe and CaraTa were mad enough to think that they could control the Sa, and the Sa were mad enough to kill themselves rather than be controlled." CosTa looked at me then. "I have the same

madness," she told me then, and what little amusement her
voice still held drained from her. "I am Cha'akMongTi. I
am QualiKaTa. And I would rather all CieTiLa die than
have us live to be controlled by the humans."

"I understand your feelings, Cha'akMongTi," I told her,
and I knew again that it was the truth, something I felt more
deeply than I had believed possible. Every insult, spoken
and unspoken, from the humans seemed to burn in me,
every act of ignorance or blind superiority, every sideways
glance of unreasoned fear or distaste. "I understand them
very well."

"Then let us sit down and talk, FirstHand Sa," CosTa
said to me, and waved toward the ground before her. "Be
as a Sa who came to our lands on ker travels." She showed
me ker hands, claws hidden, and gave me the Sign of the
Three. She smiled again, and I knew that I wanted to stay,
wanted to be with her, wanted to be with her as a Sa.

I sat, and listened to the echoes her voice raised in my
heart.

CONTEXT:
Gaspar Allen-Levin <u>of the Rock</u>

HIS STOMACH RUMBLED, SO LOUDLY THAT GASPAR
thought that they'd alert the grumblers in the
settlement ahead, and acid burned in the back of his throat.
Gaspar swallowed the bile and checked the clip on his rifle,
trying to ignore for a moment what might be about to happen.

The day had not started well. The two Sa had been standing in front of Old Bridge when Gaspar's group had tried
to cross the river. Caitlyn had held up ker hand, and Gerald
Allen-Shimmura, at their head, laughed in response.

"Well, you Sa have better sources of information than

I thought,'' Gerald said. His piebald face glistened in the sunlight, arrogant. "I'll give you that. But it doesn't matter. This isn't your business. Go back and nurse your SaTu, Caitlyn."

"I know what you've been asked to do,'' Caitlyn said. "And I know how you're likely to interpret that request, Gerald. But your way of handling the problem isn't going to solve it. All you're going to do is raise the stakes."

"Frankly, Sa, I think the stakes *should* be raised. We should wipe out the whole fucking lot of them. You know what?—doing that would actually 'solve the problem.' But Geema and the Elder Council won't let me do it. This is the next best thing."

"On AnglSaiye, we've managed to live together with the Miccail for decades now."

"This isn't AnglSaiye, is it? And your SaTu may have changed ker mind now about how peaceful and idyllic things are. In any case, you've already argued all this with the Council, and they've made their ruling. Now, move out of the way. We've got work to do."

Gaspar thought that Gerald's angry little speech had ended things. The Sa called Linden, with a sigh, stepped to one side of the bridge, touching Caitlyn's arm. But Caitlyn didn't move. Instead, ke looked at all of them. At Gaspar. "This is *wrong*," ke persisted, ker gaze stopping at Gaspar's face. "Council ruling or not, you know it's wrong." Ke continued to look at him, and Gaspar felt everyone's else's scrutiny on him as well.

"It's survival," Gerald answered for everyone, and Gaspar felt a strange relief as Caitlyn's gaze moved back to Gerald. "Pure and simple. Now, move aside, Sa—or I'll have you moved."

"What about you, Gaspar?" Caitlyn called out to him, and Gaspar felt a flush rising to his cheeks as the others in the group turned looked again at him. "Do *you* agree with Gerald here? Don't give me the goddamn rhetoric. Answer me with what you're feeling. Is this right?"

"I . . ." Gaspar stammered, feeling the heat on his face. He was angry with Caitlyn for singling him out and placing him at the center of this, but he remembered the Gather night with ker, and ker sweet, soft lips . . . He shrugged. "I don't really know. Don't put this on me, Caitlyn. It wasn't my decision to make."

"It is," ke insisted. "It *is* your decision. For each one of you."

"All we're doing is making sure there's no QualiKa around here. That makes sense to me, after what they've done to us. After what they did to your SaTu, I'd think it would to you, too."

"Do you really think that's all that's intended with this— 'making sure there's no QualiKa around'? Even if it were, do you think the Miccail are going to tell you who the QualiKa are, just because you ask politely?"

Had he been alone, Gaspar might have wavered, might have turned back to the Rock. As it was, he hesitated, hunching his shoulders under the pressure of everyone's eyes. "I do what the Elders say, Caitlyn," he answered, knowing he said the words because they were the easiest ones to parrot, because they shifted the blame away. "That's all any of us can do."

Caitlyn was shaking ker head, but they both knew that there were no more arguments to be made, and Linden was plucking at the sleeve of Caitlyn's *shangaa* again. "I ask you, all of you: Don't go," Caitlyn persisted, but ker voice was fragile with hopelessness, and ker hand dropped to ker side. Gerald pushed past ker, and ke let him pass without protest.

"Let's move," Gerald called to the rest. "We'll need all the sun we can get, and we've wasted enough time already."

They went. Gaspar noticed that all the others avoided looking at the two Sa, but they all went. Gaspar was the last to move. As he passed Caitlyn, he lifted his face. "You understand?" he asked. "You don't have to agree, don't have to like it. But do you *understand*?"

Mutely, Caitlyn shook ker head in denial. The wind tossed ker hair in front of ker eyes, and ke lifted a hand to push it away again, not blinking as ke stared at him.

"I'm sorry," Gaspar said, finally pulling himself away from that silent accusation. "I really am, Caitlyn."

He shifted the weight of rifle and pack on his shoulders and hurried to catch up with the others.

The rest of the day had not gone any better. The wind was cold, and spatters of frigid sleet raked them the entire morning before the clouds thinned in the afternoon to allow through a few rays of wan sunlight. Lunch and dinner were cold meat and bread eaten while huddled around a small fire, and not enough time to rest. Gerald had them up again as the sun laid a rose tint on the clouds to the east. By midday, they marched into a small grumbler village.

The Te and Ta came out to meet them as faces peered from the doorways of the six or seven wooden dwellings. The Te was a small grumbler, his spinal mane gray with age; the Ta looked to be his daughter, and she stepped forward as spokesperson, speaking haltingly in the human language. "Welcome," she said, but the skittish movement of her eyes and the way the tips of her claws were exposed belied the word. "I am HarTa; this is my . . ." She seemed to look for the word at her feet before finding it. ". . . father, LiriTe." She glanced at each of them, and Gaspar felt like hiding from the apprehensive query of her gaze. "You are from Black Lake—I comprehend . . . no, recognize some of you. You are . . . passing through? Hunting? We can offer you, ahh, water, and the XeXa can describe . . . no, show you where nik-niks . . ."

"We're hunting, *hai*," Gerald said, interrupting her as he hefted his rifle. "But not nik-niks. QualiKa."

Something changed in her eyes then, Gaspar saw. They grew hard and suspicious and distant, and the Sun's Eye, the *brais*, went dull. "There are no QualiKa here," she said, but her voice was harsher now and harder to understand, her tongues slurring the consonants. Gerald laughed, and others around Gaspar did the same.

"Right," Gerald said. "And the sun won't be coming up tomorrow."

"The sun . . . ?" the grumbler Ta said, confused. "I don't understand."

"You don't need to understand. All you need to do is point out the QualiKa you have staying here."

She was shaking her head now, holding both hands to her temples. "You speak . . . too fast for me. Can't understand . . ."

There was a burst of grumbler-talk from the Te then, and the Ta turned to answer him, speaking rapidly and gesticulating back toward the group of humans. It sounded like verrechats hissing at each other to Gaspar.

"What are they saying?" Gaspar asked Gerald.

Gerald shrugged. "Anyone here know grumbler?" When no one answered, Gerald swung back around and fired his rifle once in the air. The Te and Ta went silent in midyammer. "Hey!" Gerald shouted. "You can fucking talk to us. No more of this grumbler *khudda*. Understand?"

There was fright in the Ta's gaze now, and anger. "I was . . . explaining my father . . . how you said . . ."

"Shut up!" Gerald roared. "We want the QualiKa you're holding. We want them *now*."

Again the stubborn head shake. "No QualiKa," the Ta repeated. "Not here."

Gerald snorted. "I doubt that. Maybe you're even one yourself, eh? Maybe you have one of those moon tattoos. Let's just see . . ." He reached toward her, the fingers of his free left hand curling around the collar of her *shangaa*. The Te howled in outrage that needed no words or no language to understand and started to move. With a strange, calm look on his face, Gerald lifted his rifle with other hand, held it out at arm's length, and shot the Te in the face. Before the sound even registered, Gaspar saw the Te reel backward one step and collapse, his features a bloody ruin. Gerald hadn't even looked. He tugged the Ta's *shangaa* down, ripping the cloth and revealing her small breasts. "Well," he said, chuckling. "I guess I was wro—"

Which was when it all went to hell. The Ta raked her claws down Gerald's face, ripping three great furrows from scalp to chin. "Fuck! *Khudda!* You goddamn *bitch*!" Gerald screamed, the words sibilant with blood and the open flaps torn from his cheeks. He staggered away from her, blood streaming over the fingers holding the raw strips of flesh to his face.

His mouth open in a soundless scream, Gerald lifted his rifle and pressed the trigger once, then again and again and again. The Ta was dead with the first shot, but Gerald continued to fire into her body. A grumbler started to rush from one of the houses with a spear—another one of the group killed him before he'd moved two steps. Someone else fired to Gaspar's right, and then another, the concussions hammering at him. Adrenaline surged; Gaspar had to fight the impulse to simply turn and run from the carnage, and he felt his bowels turn to water. Grumblers were howling and squealing all around them, Gerald was still emptying his rifle into the body of the Ta, the rest of the group was shouting and cursing as they fired wildly. The smell of gunpowder and death was overpowering.

Gaspar heard a sound behind him: running footsteps. He turned swiftly, shouting some wordless alarm as he brought his rifle up to his shoulder and fired at the blur of movement. Something . . . some form . . . dropped to the ground two steps in front of him. Gaspar leaned forward, still cursing, as he squinted at it.

It was a grumbler child, no more than a few years old, no older than his nephew Abbie or most of his sib Arlin's children back at the Rock. Its life was pumping out of a red hole in its chest onto the cold, dusty earth, and its open eyes stared: a dead gaze, focused on the stones in front of it, but the eyes transfixed him with a silent accusation. Behind him, half-heard, there were more shouts, more shots being fired and screams both human and grumbler, but Gaspar reacted to none of it. He was still holding the rifle up to his shoulder, sighting down the barrel at the child. Little details came to him: the tendrils of gray-white steam curling gently off the suddenly heated barrel of his weapon, the sullen ache in his shoulder from the kick of the gun, the ringing in his ears from the report, the tiny hands of the grumbler child, empty, outflung on the dirt.

The eyes. The child's eyes.

Ishiko Allen-Shimmura <u>of the Rock</u>

NOT LONG AFTER GERALD AND HIS GROUP LEFT the Rock, Aleppo Martinez-Santos arrived breathless from Warm Water with the tale of finding a smoldering funeral pyre just off the highroad, a pyre that indicated that the person who had been cremated was a Sa. Aleppo hadn't disturbed the site—from what I was told, the sight spooked Aleppo and he was afraid of lurking *kami*. Instead, he'd hurried on to the Rock. From there, things happened rapidly: Shotoku Martinez-Santos, that Family's Eldest on the Rock, had immediately sent word to Caitlyn and Linden at the Koda-Levin compound. I think that they would have preferred to investigate on their own, but there are no secrets in the Rock, as their O'Sa Anaïs would have once told them.

Word had also come to our Family compound, through one of the younger sib's lovers. When Geema Euzhan learned that the two Sa were making plans to leave the Rock and investigate, she had sent word to them that she would "give" them a contingent from the Rock Families to accompany them "for their protection.'

Caitlyn's answer surprised her, I think. It surprised me, certainly. While declining the "protection" offered them, ke suggested that I accompany them instead, as the Rock's representative. I was called to Geema Euzhan's rooms immediately. "Why does ke want *you*?" she asked me immediately, without any preamble.

It was very nearly the first thing she'd said to me since our argument two nights before. I assumed she knew—through her usual grapevine—that I'd gone to the Koda-Levin compound afterward. But though she'd ignored me since then, she also hadn't asked me what had happened in the several hours I'd been there or what I'd said.

That was good. I wasn't sure how I would have answered. *Geema, I told Caitlyn everything—told ker how I was supposed to report back to you what the Sa were thinking and doing and what they knew, and how I didn't do it. Hai, you heard me right, Geema—I wasn't quite the fount of information you'd thought. And Geema, no, I didn't go to bed with ker again, but not because ke's a Sa and you don't want our Family "contaminated" with Sa seed. It was because I don't know if that's something ke wants anymore. That's all. If Caitlyn had asked or if ke had indicated any interest . . . well, I might have. I don't know. Geema, I think I may love ker more than I love you, and I hate you for having ruined that possibility for me.*

"Have you gone deaf, girl? I asked you a question."

"I heard you, Geema. And I don't know. Why don't you ask Caitlyn?"

"I thought you said ke suspected what you'd done and wasn't speaking to you anymore."

I shrugged.

"That's changed since you went and saw ker the other night?"

Hai. The grapevine at work. Geema knew. Geema always knew. Still, in the end, she grudgingly agreed to let me go with them. I suppose she figured that this was nothing really important—which translates to "nothing that would directly affect her or the Rock." That was Geema's sole definition of "important."

It didn't matter who else things might hurt.

So I went . . .

"This is it," Caitlyn said. "Through here."

Ke held aside the thorn-vines so that Linden and I could pass through. We could see the blackened area a few meters beyond. The odor of woodsmoke still hung in the drooping amberdrops, their trunks streaked with sticky yellow where the heat had melted the sap.

As I stepped off the highroad, I glanced back at the rising land behind me. We'd all noticed that the hillside where

Fianya had died was only a few minutes' walk off the other side of the road, though none of us had bothered to mention the fact aloud. I ducked under the thorn-vines and Cailtyn's arm, following Linden.

The smell of old smoke was stronger in the clearing just beyond, and it was mingled with another scent, one I knew well from the funerary burnings I'd witnessed over the years. In the pile of ash at the glade's center, there were sprinklings of charred bone.

"Over here," Linden said. Ke was standing next to a large shallow bowl shaped like a shell that was placed atop a tripod of carved wooden legs. Linden had lifted a *shangaa* from the bowl. "Gods, this thing *reeks*!" The *shangaa* was orange—the Sa color—and large. I saw that much before Linden dropped it back with a scowl, ker nose wrinkled with disgust.

"Rashi," Caitlyn said. "This was poor Rashi. Damn . . ." Ke glanced around the clearing. A *shangaa*'s cloth belt hung from a stout tree limb above ker, the end of it knotted into a noose. The Sa's pouch was lying near the tripod. Caitlyn crouched down, looking at the patches of open ground. I saw what ke was searching for: The prints of a naked foot were pressed in the ice-glazed earth—a grumbler's foot.

Caitlyn glanced at Linden. "RenSa?" Linden shrugged. "By the smell of ker *shangaa*, Rashi had been dead for a long time. The pyre was built no more than two days ago. The timing's about right for RenSa to have done it. If ke came across the body, ke would have performed the Burning for ker."

"Why wouldn't RenSa have come back and told us?" Linden asked. "And did Rashi kill kerself, or was ke murdered? Did RenSa *know* ke was out here? And why would Rashi be lugging around one of the big altars? Ke was supposed to be in Warm Water, and should have taken one of the small traveling ones."

"Too many questions, and none of them have answers. At least not at the moment." Caitlyn was looking at the noose again. "Rashi was always SaTu Terri's favorite," ke said, softly. "What *happened* here?"

I barely heard ker. Through the tops of the trees, I could see the crown of the hill where Fianya had died, still patchy with snow, and I remembered RenSa and Linden afterward describing the cave in which the Sa child had been kept. I went over to where Linden was standing by the altar. Linden watched me curiously while I lifted the shell-bowl from the stand, set it aside, and moved the stand. Where it had been, three shallow indentations pocked the ground. Linden looked at me, then down.

"*Khudda!*" He breathed the curse, looking at me again. "No . . ." he moaned, as Caitlyn came over.

"Linden?" ke asked, ker hand on the other Sa's shoulder. I noticed that ke stood well away from me, so we couldn't accidentally touch. Linden glanced at me again, then picked up the tripod, collapsing the wooden legs, which fell together with a harsh *clack*.

"Let's walk a bit," Linden said. "We've seen enough here." Carrying the tripod mechanism, ke started walking back out of the clearing. Caitlyn cocked ker head, brushing ker hair behind ker ear with ker left hand. I watched ker fingers, graceful as mine could never be.

"What did you show ker?" ke asked.

"Nothing," I answered. "Or maybe everything. Caitlyn, I . . ." I wasn't sure what I wanted to say, but there was too much. "Just . . ." I took a breath. ". . . follow ker," I finished.

We went across the road and up the hill. Linden strode ahead, almost angrily, not looking back. Caitlyn said nothing as we went up the long hill, and turned to where the small cave opened dark in the tumble of rocks at the summit. When Caitlyn and I entered, Linden was already there, unfolding the legs of the tripod next to the remains of the fire. Ke pointed at three small marks in the ground.

"These were here when RenSa and I first entered the cave," ke said. Unfolding the tripod again, he lowered it gently to the dirt floor.

The legs of the tripod snuggled perfectly into the hollows.

"Whoever kidnapped Fianya couldn't return ker," I said

slowly, looking at the tripod rather than either of the two Sa with me. "They didn't *want* to return ker. That was never their intention. Fianya ran away because ke was scared—ke tripped and fell to ker death. But ke would have been dead anyway. Whoever brought ker here did so to kill ker." I looked again at the tripod sitting in front of us; at the two Sa who stood there, not wanting to understand the import of what they were seeing. I could see the pain in Caitlyn's face, and I wanted to go to ker. Instead, I said the words in all of our minds.

"After all, what would the Cha'akMongTi have done with Fianya, if she was the one who ordered Fianya to be taken? What would it gain the QualiKa to kidnap a human Sa child? Nothing. For that matter, why would Geema Euzhan or someone in my Family have done it, since Geema had already refused the SaTu's demands to send Fianya to AnglSaiye?"

I looked again at the tripod, and I shuddered.

"It's the Sa who perform sacrifices," I said. "It's the Sa who have even sacrificed their own." I could imagine the scene: the altar set up here by the small fire, poor Fianya looking at the axe, the garrote, and the water as Rashi reached for ker . . .

Linden moaned. I saw Caitlyn shudder with the words and clutch kerself, hands to shoulders. "Why would Rashi . . . ?" ke began.

"I don't know," I answered. "But I know how I would have felt after Fianya died, accidentally or not. I might have been tempted to hang myself, too."

Caitlyn whirled around to face me, ker face suffused with anger. "This is all still wild speculation," ke said heatedly.

I nodded. "*Hai*. But it's what you're both thinking, too, isn't it?"

Caitlyn didn't answer. Ke brushed past me, going out of the cave into the chill air. Linden was leaning against the rock wall, ker gaze still on the tripod. "Go to ker," ke said without looking at me. "Ke needs you right now."

"Linden . . ."

"Go on. I'm fine. Well, not fine, actually, but . . ." Ke gave me a wan smile. "Go on."

I went, blinking into the sunlight. I saw Caitlyn well down the slope, standing at the edge of the precipice over which Fianya had fallen. I approached ker, moving carefully over the loose rocks and patches of ice. The wind was tossing ker hair and pressing ker *shangaa* tight against ker body. "Caitlyn?"

"It's true," ke said, without turning around. "I know it's true. Everything you said."

"Caitlyn, would you please step back a little? You're making me very nervous."

Ke ignored me. Ker booted feet, shifting, sent small rocks tumbling over the edge of the cliff. I could hear them bounding down to the rocks where Fianya had died. "Caitlyn, please . . ." I could hear panic beginning to shiver in my voice.

"We started this. All the bloodshed. A Sa started it. Why? By VeiSaTi Kerself, why?" The wind nearly tore ker words away. I wondered whether I should make a grab for ker. I wondered whether ker *shangaa* would hold if ke fell, or if I would fall with ker. I wondered whether I could move at all.

Caitlyn turned, and took a step toward me, away from the cliff. A single tear was tracking down ker cheek, glistening.

"I'm sorry," ke said to me. "Ishiko, I'm so sorry."

CONTEXT:
Ghost

"YOU DON'T THINK ANY OF THIS PREJUDICE YOU carry around with you stems from being attacked by a Miccail when you were a child?"

Ghost wore the shape of Sigmund Freud, and he'd even

projected a couch on which "he" reclined as he spoke, a long, fat cigar snared between his fingers. He doubted that Euzhan would understand the visual reference, or particularly appreciate it if she did. No one much seemed to comprehend the shapes he wore, but Ghost wore them anyway, because doing so amused him. Being a construct, "amusement" wasn't precisely the right term, but it was a close approximation for the exhilarating openness of the neural web, the crackle of new pathways and unexpected interconnections.

Ghost/Sigmund stretched his legs on the couch, looked up at the ceiling and exhaled a cloud of holographic smoke. "All that happened over a century ago, Euzhan. You're the only one alive who even remembers it."

"This psychological *khudda* is wasting our limited time, Ghost," Euzhan snapped. Her exhalation made a fog on the windowpane of her study. She wasn't looking at him, but out to the wide pathway leading from the Rock to the river.

He ignored her rebuke—Ghost's programming could make him maddeningly obstinate with the people with whom he interacted, but experience had taught Ghost that this was a way to extract the maximum amount of information from recalcitrant subjects.

"Ahh, but psychology is what underlies everything with humans, where we find meaning and insight into the way we think. Take my cigar—such an obvious phallic symbol." What Ghost twirled between his fingers was no longer a cigar but an erect penis, with curls of bluish smoke emerging from the mushroom-headed tip.

"Damn it, Ghost . . ." Euzhan's voice was shrill with exasperation as she turned to regard him. "You are making far more of this than you need to. It's very simple: My job is to do what I must to ensure the survival of the Families. The grumblers are a threat to that, and I am dealing with them as such. I don't like it, don't like it at all, but I think it's the best choice to ensure that the Families live and thrive. Beyond that, there's no hidden agendas here."

"If that's your intent, then why do you persist in keeping

your Family away from the Sa?'' Ghost grinned at her, deliberately, knowing the smile would be an additional goad. He let the couch and Freud's image dissolve, morphing into the shape of an elderly man he knew Euzhan would recognize all too well: her long-dead Geeda Dominic.

Ghost/Dominic addressed the glowing tip of his cigar. ''Don't you just love inconsistencies? Personally, I think it has to do with the fact that the child Euzhan regarded Anaïs as a mother-substitute, and she subconsciously has never forgiven Anaïs for not taking her to Ang!Saiye even though she knows it was her Geeda Dominic who refused to let—''

''Shut *up*, Ghost!'' Euzhan's voice nearly broke with the half shout. The cheeks of her too-smooth face burned red, and hard lines frowned over and around her eyes. She banged the end of her cane—Dominic's cane, Ghost noticed with something akin to pleasure—on the floor. ''My feelings toward the Sa have nothing to do with Anaïs, and I don't need to defend myself to you.''

Dominic's image shifted, becoming those of Anaïs Koda-Levin, as she'd looked before she'd been exiled from the Rock by Dominic and the other Elders of the time. The cigar still smoked in ker fingers. ''When you breed with the Sa, you dramatically increase the chance of pregnancy and lessen the incidence of genetic defects. That seems like a good strategy to—how did you just put it?—'ensure the survival of the Families.' ''

''When we breed with the Sa, we are no longer human.''

''So the Miccail and the Sa are pretty much one and the same for you: not human.''

''I don't have time for this, Ghost. I've made my decisions, and I'm as comfortable as I can be with them. As to what's happening with the grumblers . . .'' Euzhan shook her head, her whole upper body moving with the motion. ''I've lived longer in this world than anyone except you, Ghost, so give me credit for some understanding of how things work. Anaïs gave the grumblers back their Sa and helped them rediscover their culture, and she died trying to mediate between our two species. We both want the same land.''

"It's a damn big world."

"And we know we can survive *here* in it. Here. We don't know whether that would be true anywhere else. In fact, the evidence is to the contrary. Let the grumblers leave if they can't stand being here with us." Euzhan sighed. "Ghost, I know how this sounds. I honestly do, and I don't like what I'm saying any more than do you or the Sa. But I don't have any confidence that we can share the land together. We're a few hundred; they are thousands. The one truth is that there are enough grumblers out there that if they decided to kill us all, no matter how well and better armed we are, they could overrun us with sheer force of numbers. If CosTa has her way, that's exactly what *will* happen. I don't condone genocide, but if I have to choose between the survival of my people or theirs . . ." She inhaled: slowly, deeply. "Well, I know where my loyalties lie."

"In that, your loyalties are the same as mine," Ghost answered. "My one imperative, my own pursuit, is your survival. Period." All the humor was gone from ker voice now. Ghost let the image of Anaïs fall from ker. The cigar fell from ker fingers and vanished before it hit the floor She became a mirror of Euzhan herself.

"Then why are you wasting my time with this nonsense?"

"Because I don't *have* much time," Ghost answered in Euzhan's own voice. Deep in the neural web, there was a throbbing as pathways opened and closed. Possibilities, none of them pleasant, surged before her. "And I have my own decisions to ma—"

"*Geema*!" Nawal Allen-Shimmura burst into the room without knocking, then pulled up short, looking from Ghost/Euzhan to the real Euzhan. "It's *da* Gerald," the young woman said frantically to both of them. "The group you sent out just came back, and he's hurt badly . . ."

JOURNAL ENTRY:
Anaïs Koda-Levin, O'Sa

‏‏OUR LITTLE DELEGATION—HALF-HUMAN, HALF-Miccail—stayed the night at a wayhouse a half day's *konja*-ride from Hannibal. While the others fixed supper, my FirstHand NefSa came from the wayhouse and found me, sitting on a rock near a creek rushing to its confluence with the Loud River. The sound of the water was soothing, a lovely white noise that made meditation easy.

"O'Sa," NefSa said softly. "Supper's nearly ready."

"Thanks, NefSa. I'll be there." As ke started to turn, I called to ker without turning around, still watching the foaming cascade in front of me. "I've come to a decision. I would like you to be the next SaTu."

I heard NefSa pause, heard ker feet scuffle on the fallen leaves. NefSa was the youngest of that first spurt of Miccail Sa I'd helped birth in those first years on AnglSaiye, and ke was now the oldest of the Miccail Sa. A half dozen Miccail Sa had been born within as many years, as if they'd just been waiting for the right time after long centuries of slumber. At fifty-three, NefSa was old for a Miccail, ker spinal mane stark white, ker skin wrinkled into deep folds on ker long face. Ke had been with me for all that time, helping build the Community of Sa, forging our new *KoPavi*. I thought I knew ker well, but ke surprised me then. *"You are not going to die,"* I thought ke might say. *"You will be SaTu for years yet, O'Sa."* I expected platitudes.

Pleasant lies. Ones that I would have made to someone else without thought.

"It's good for you to think about who will come after you, especially now," NefSa answered. "But no Miccail can ever be SaTu.'' Ker voice chided me gently. "Surely you realize that."

"Why not?" I said it with genuine bewilderment. I turned away from the creek, looking into ker quiet regard.

"For the same reason that you did not put yourself under the direction of the CieTiLa sages on AnglSaiye. For the same reason those sages named you SaTu when the Temple was reopened." NefSa touched ker *brais*, ker face, and held out ker hands to me. "Because we CieTiLa are different than you humans, and your people do not like 'different' well enough to follow it. Because—" ke continued, holding up ker hand to stop the protest I was about to make— "we both want our Community to thrive and become strong, and if you name me as SaTu, you will have undone all the progress you've made, whether you want to believe that or not. The only reason we CieTiLa did not kill all the humans when you first came was because most of us were half-wild, with no organization. That is why your people survived. Then you, O'Sa, brought back the Sa to us and fulfilled the promise of the Sa Beneath The Water, and we could not harm those who had done that. On AnglSaiye, we even lived together, and you and those of the Families who came brought us back from our long darkness, so when some whispered that we should rid the land of humans and take back what was ours, the TeTa said 'no.' ''

"That seems to me to be all the more reason for you to be SaTu, to show the trust between our people."

NefSa shivered. "O'Sa . . .'' Ke took a breath. "Name me as SaTu, and your Families will stop listening to the Sa. They will mock the Community, they will stop welcoming the Sa when they come. A few humans will leave AnglSaiye because the island is now run by 'grumblers,' and then the rest will follow. Your Families will attack the Community of Sa with their words and perhaps with their actions, and when they do *that*, to us it will be an attack on all CieTiLa and our customs. Eventually, the TeTa will begin to wonder if the QualiKa are not right, and then . . .'' NefSa stopped. "There are so many of us, O'Sa, no matter how powerful your weapons and your machines may be."

"NefSa . . ." I truly didn't know what to say. "I think you're exaggerating."

"I know some of your people's history, O'Sa," NefSa answered. "It would seem that 'differences'—in religion, in political beliefs, in skin color—have fueled most of your conflicts."

"Once that may have been true. But we came here in a ship built by *all* countries, crewed by all races and religions." *And I know from Ghost how difficult that was to accomplish, and I know that when we arrived here, after decades of travel, the crew could never recontact Earth, and many of them worried that another war might have broken out there . . .* But I didn't say any of that.

"Then look at more recent examples. Tell me, then, O'Sa—how did your own people react to *you*?"

To that, I had no answer: I carried the scars, both physical and emotional, of the treatment I'd received from the Families. I know I sat there for a moment, mouth open, without answering. Then I shook my head stubbornly. "We change, NefSa. We grow."

Platitudes.

Ke bared ker lips in the Miccail smile that I always thought looked more like a grimace. "Then wait until your people have changed enough. That is not now. Maybe it will be never. Name Gonzalo of the Allen-Levins as the next SaTu; I will be ker FirstHand, as I am yours." Ke held out a hand to help me up. "O'Sa, supper is waiting, and tomorrow will be a difficult day."

Perhaps I should have continued the argument. Perhaps I should have insisted. I didn't.

I reached out for NefSa's hand and let ker help me to my feet.

VOICE:
Caitlyn Koda-Schmidt of the Sa

"RASHI IS *DEAD*?"

SaTu Terri kept repeating that over and over as if ker wondering mantra could force reality to take a new shape. "*Hai*, SaTu," I said again. "Rashi is dead. SaTu, please listen to me. I also told you that Linden and I believe Rashi was responsible for taking Fianya from the Allen-Shimmuras. We need to discuss that."

"Rashi is *dead*?" Terri looked like an acolyte puzzling over homework given to ker by ker teachers, ker white hair curtaining ker face as ke shook ker head. Terri's lone order to the runner we'd dispatched to AnglSaiye after finding ker was to bring back the translations of the *KoPavi* on which ke'd been working. They'd arrived yesterday. The sheets of parchment were spread out in front of ker now, drifted across ker desk like great piles of dry leaves, scattered over the coverlet of ker bed. Ke was holding one of the sheets as we spoke, the paper trembling in ker fingers.

The paper slipped from ker grasp, careening from side to side until it came to rest on the desktop.

"*Hai*, SaTu," I tried again. "But we need to know what you want said to Euzhan about Fianya. She's already upset over what's happened with Gerald, and we have to assume that word has gone out to the QualiKa as well. I'm afraid—"

"Rashi was obedient to VeiSaTi and to me," Terri said. A gnarled, long finger tapped the papers in front of ker. "Ke believed in this *KoPavi* as I did—the proper *KoPavi*. Ke sacrificed, and VeiSaTi spoke to and through ker. I would have named ker SaTu after me." Terri glanced up

224

at me, ker eyes narrowed and ker thin mouth tight. "Ker obedience to me was unquestioned."

"No doubt, SaTu," I said wearily. "But Rashi's dead, and we need to deal with the repercussions."

"When we last spoke, Rashi said that ke would do what VeiSaTi asked. VeiSaTi wouldn't have allowed ker to die. We need to follow the *KoPavi*. We need to sacrifice. The visions I have been granted . . ." Terri was breathing fast and shallow, and ker eyes flicked wildly around the room. "The time that is on us is as dangerous as that of the Sa Beneath The Water, and we must give no less than ke did."

I was tired of arguing, of going around in useless circles with someone whose grip on reality—never particularly strong, in my opinion—was now rather tenuous. I could see that we needed to get SaTu Terri back to AnglSaiye; we needed to convene the Advisory Council, who could make a judgment as to Terri's competency as SaTu.

Another crisis among the others piling up around us. "*Hai*, SaTu," I said, unwilling to stay any longer. "SaTu, we need to leave now. We need to go back to AnglSaiye."

"We can't leave yet. We must sacrifice. VeiSaTi will tell us what we must do."

"We don't have time for that, SaTu."

"That's the only way. That's the *KoPavi*. We must give Ker the sacrifice she has asked for, what I failed to give Ker."

"SaTu—"

Terri waved me away, ker head on ker forehead as ke stared blankly at the translations on ker desk. I left the room, pulling the door closed, and went to the Common Room. Linden was there with Ishiko, who was just taking off her coat in front of the fireplace. "Any luck?" Linden asked.

I gave them both a shrug. "No," I told ker. "Ke just keeps saying ke can't believe Rashi's dead. I can't get anything more from ker. How were things with the Families, Ishiko?"

"Bad," she said. "Evidently Gerald's wounds are serious. Da Cuauh's told Euzhan that even if Gerald makes it, he's going to be badly disfigured. The grumbler nearly tore his face off. Geema's already had the entire Elder Council up to her rooms, one at a time, and my sibs are saying that she's trying to convince them that the Miccail are too dangerous to tolerate. I don't know how much support she's been able to drum up, but other Families have had people injured, too. I think there's more sympathy for Geema's view than is comfortable for us."

For us. I heard that and wondered if she really meant the words. I wanted to believe she did. "What did you tell her about Rashi?"

Ishiko shrugged. She lifted her right hand; her left, as usual, stayed hidden in her jacket pocket. "I told her that the cremated body was almost certainly Rashi, and that it looked to be suicide."

"And the rest?"

Ishiko gave another shrug. "We don't know any of it for certain, do we? To tell you the truth, Geema hardly listened to me at all. She hasn't any time for anything but Gerald right now and doesn't think the suicide of a Sa is worth her consideration. 'You can tell them that I'm sorry, if you think they'll believe it of me' is what she said. As for the speculation about Fianya . . ." Ishiko gave a shrug that mirrored my own of a moment ago. "That's all it is, anyway: speculation."

"Is that what *you* think?"

Ishiko lifted her chin, staring at me. "No," she said. "I think Rashi was planning kill Fianya, even if ke hadn't died trying to get away. I don't know why, but I think all three of us believe that's what ke intended."

"That must make you hate the Sa."

Small muscles knotted her eyebrows. "It would if I were like some in my Family, Caitlyn. But I'm not. I don't make the mistake of blaming an entire group for the acts of one." She was still holding my gaze. Behind her, Linden slid silently out of the room, leaving us alone. The fire discovered a moist pocket in the peat bricks; they hissed, then popped in a flurry of sparks. I used the excuse to break

Ishiko's stare, going over to the massive fireplace and prodding the coals with the poker. I could feel her watching me, her gaze a palpable pressure on my back. "So what about me, Caitlyn," she asked. "Are you going to hate me for the sins of my Family?"

I impaled coals on the lance of my poker. "I don't hate you, Ishiko. You've done nothing to make me feel that way about you. But you were avoiding me, up until a few days ago. You were clear about how you felt." I still hadn't looked at her. I couldn't look at her. I put the poker back into the holder, listening to the harsh clatter of iron on iron.

"When I came here after we found the SaTu, Caitlyn, when I told you how I'd been supposed to be Geema's conduit to you and Linden, I saw your face. I saw you close yourself off to me."

"You saw me dealing with SaTu Terri. That was all."

Ishiko shook her head into my denial. "My interest in you was supposed to be a lie, Caitlyn, but it wasn't. Not completely, and not at all when we made love. Not even from the first night at the Gather—I knew that quickly that I couldn't pretend with you, that I didn't want to. I'm sorry that *any* of it was a deception, but I thought you deserved to know the truth. I didn't want to hurt you, Caitlyn, and I did. I thought . . . after I told you what I'd done . . ." She'd stopped speaking. I turned and saw her silently crying, her eyes closed. When they opened again, twin glistening pearls fell from her lashes.

"Ishiko—" I started toward her, but she held up her right hand.

"Don't," she said. She rubbed at her eyes angrily with her jacket sleeve and shook her head. "Please don't," she said again. "It's late, and I need to get back to my Family." She pulled her coat from the wall hook and put it on. "Caitlyn, I . . ."

I don't know what she intended to say. Ishiko grimaced and turned before I could react, striding quickly toward the corridor that led to the compound's entrance. She was gone before I could think of words that might make her stay.

Before I realized that was what I most wanted.

I heard the door open and then close. A few seconds later, a cold draft welled from the corridor to shiver the flames in the fireplace.

VOICE:

RenSa

IT WAS A BRUTAL DAY. A COLD WIND BLEW RE-lentlessly from the north, tearing strings of pale orange snow from the massed clouds overhead. The cold flakes slapped at my face, hissing past my ears as they fell and making me cover my *brais* with one hand in defense. I shivered, even with a meatfur cloak over my *shangaa*, and I could feel the insistent earth-chill through the soles of my feet.

CosTa didn't seem to be touched by any of it. She stood before the entrance to TeNon, at the top of the stairs leading to the tomb, the wind whipping her *shangaa* and flakes of snow caught in her spinal mane. Hands at her sides, she surveyed the ranks of CieTiLa before her. Many, probably most, were QualiKa, but not all. In the three days since news had come to us of the carnage at LiriTe and HarTa's village near Black Lake, they'd been coming here, a hand or so of them at a time. The valley of TeNon was filled with tents and makeshift shelters, and the pall of campfires drifted like morning fog among the trees.

They were waiting, all of them. Waiting for CosTa to make her appearance.

I'd gone out among them, these new disciples, and felt the tension, like the uneasy anticipation that comes just be-fore the breaking of a storm. "Have the Sa joined the QualiKa, then?" they asked me. "Are you with us?" "No," I would reply, and that simple, unadorned answer seemed to satisfy them, though I wasn't sure it satisfied *me*. In three days, I'd come to know CosTa better.

I'd come, I think, to know her *too* well. *"Be as a Sa who came to our lands on ker travels,"* she'd said to me, and I had known what she asked, and I had given that gift to her: gladly, willingly.

It's difficult unreservedly to hate a person with whom you've made love, to detest them even when they say things you find completely wrong, when their actions tear at your soul and beliefs. In passion, pretenses are ripped away, and the mask of distance can never be completely put on again. You've seen their naked vulnerabilities displayed and they, in turn, have seen yours. However faint, that remembrance blunts your anger.

You can't demonize someone you understand.

We Sa are taught that painful lesson over and over again, first by our teachers on AnglSaiye, then by our own experience. Our sacred duty compels us to share intimacy with those we might prefer to avoid, and that is painful enough. But duty also can compel us to leave those with whom we might wish to remain, and that . . . that is true agony.

I thought, when that first night CosTa asked if I would perform the Sa duty with her and JairTe, that it would be simply duty, nothing more—another night where I lay between two people and felt the seed pass through me without being touched or affected by the intercourse. Not this time. Sometime during that first night, all the barriers of title and duty vanished unasked, and we found that the people behind those walls responded to each other with a hunger that was almost frightening in its intensity.

I hadn't known I desired intimacy—it's something that Sa are taught to avoid. I hadn't known I was holding back so much of myself. If I could, I would stay here with CosTa and JairTe. I might hate the Cha'akMongTi and what the QualiKa represent, but not the person who wields that title. No.

On this cold morning, JairTe came from the TeNon and stood beside me. He shivered, also. I was fairly certain that

I'd given CosTa a child through JairTe in these last few days. He gave me a brief smile, almost as cold as the wind. "I don't know how she can stand there so composed, with this wind," I whispered to him.

"The affection of her people keeps her warm," he answered stiffly, and I knew it was true. CosTa basked in the heat of their gazes as the multitude gathered at the base of TeNon. "And she has the fire of GhazTi inside her."

That may also have been true. When the messenger had come with word of the incident near Black Lake, CosTa had left us and gone into solitude in the main chamber of the TeNon. I had smelled the bitter odor of *jitu* brewing, and I had heard her call out her grandfather's name . . . I wondered what it would feel like to be one with GhazTi. Where VeiSaTi was warmth, GhazTi was a burning conflagration. Where Ker touch was gentle, His was reputed to be harsh and cruel.

It was no wonder that DekTe and CaraTa, who had together destroyed the Sa and thus nearly all the CieTiLa *terduva* ago, had worshiped GhazTi.

A chant began somewhere at the front of the crowd— "Cha'akMongTi, Che'Veyo!" The chant swelled rhythmically, until they were all shouting the words, the roar shaking more snow from the clouds and causing me to shudder. "Warrior of our Spirit" they named her, and I knew that any hope of peace had faded. Part of me yearned to shout it as well, to join in the booming thunder of the chant. "Cha'akMongTi, Che'Veyo!"—the words slammed against our chests, pummeled the doors of TeNon, but through the assault of noise CosTa stood, impassive, her face betraying no emotion at all.

CosTa suddenly raised her hands and the chant died in an instant, its absence leaving the echoes even louder in our ears. "QualiKa!" she shouted to them, and they shouted back: "Aabi!" *We hear!*

"We of the QualiKa began in silence, but even in our silence, the humans feared us. We heard the name of QualiKa used when they need something to blame for events they could not explain. Even in our silence and solitude, we found ourselves attacked.''

"*Aabi!*" they shouted back at CosTa, a roar of affirmation.

CosTa waited until the last echoes had died, leaning forward as if supported by their voices. "While the fires sent the *kahina* of our companions back to GhazTi, I heard His voice, and I listened, sending out the QualiKa to take vengeance for the honorless killing, to repay life for life and violence for violence.''

"*Aabi!*"

I could see CosTa take in a great breath, as if she breathed in their adoration. Alongside me, JairTe had shouted as one with them. CosTa closed her pale eyes, then opened them again. "The scales of fate were balanced. Did that satisfy the humans?'' She paused, and the next word was a deep roar: "No!''

"*Aabi!*" they roared back to her, and the chant began once more: "Cha'akMongTi, Che'Veyo! Cha'akMongTi, Che'Veyo!'' CosTa let it continue for a few moments, her head bowed. When she covered her *brais* with her hand, they went silent again.

"They attacked us, again and again,'' she continued. The heat of her words, the fire of her presence, banished the cold. Now her voice softened, so that we all leaned forward, straining to hear CosTa against the wind and snow. "Without honor, they killed us. Without regard to the *KoPavi*, they used their weapons. And I say: *ENOUGH!*''

The single word cracked, sharper than two rocks clashing together. We all jumped, as if the shadows of a wingclaw had passed over our *brais*, and CosTa continued before we could react further. "Because they are without honor does not mean that we must be the same. Because they ignore the *KoPavi* does not mean that we will also. I will do as the path dictates: I will send to the humans my *xeshai*, and ask them to place their own champion against ours. I will send them the terms of the *xeshai* and ask them to abide by them. I will do that because the *KoPavi* demands it, but

GhazTi has already told me the answer I will receive. They will refuse *xeshai*. They will refuse honor.''

CosTa waited and the massed voices responded: "*Aabi!*"

I found myself wanting to scream the word with them.

"We will go to Black Lake," CosTa shouted. "That is what GhazTi tells me. When the humans refuse *xeshai*, we will go to Black Lake. When we know that the *KoPavi* has been broken, we will go to Black Lake. When words have failed, we will go to Black Lake. There, at Black Lake, we will fulfill my grandfather's vision. At Black Lake, we will take back what has always been ours. At Black Lake, we will take back our *land*!"

This time, the clamor shook the very ground: "*Aabi! Cha'akMongTi, Che'Veyo! Aabi! Cha'akMongTi, Che'-Veyo!*" They would not stop. The tumult continued—an avalanche of noise—as CosTa stood there before them. They were all shouting: the QualiKa in the valley, the guards on the TeNon, JairTe alongside me. They screamed their covenant.

All but me.

Like seeing a scratch in the finish of a fine bowl, my silence drew her. CosTa, her arms wide to them, turned her head slowly to look at me. She frowned. "FirstHand," she said softly, her call audible only to me and JairTe. "You disappoint me."

CosTa's gaze held me, sad but already distant, already turning from me. Beside me, JairTe had gone silent also, listening. "*Aabi! Cha'akMongTi, Che'Veyo!*" The chant hammered at my chest, dinned in my ears, and in it I heard death, like the eternal grin of a skull.

"This is not why I came to you," I told her. I looked out at the mass of CieTiLa, mouths open as they faced CosTa and the TeNon, the bright points of *lansa* jabbing at the dark, snow-filled clouds above. "This is not why I came," I repeated. "I'm sorry," I told her.

And with that bare apology, I let the insistent beat— "*Aabi! Cha'akMongTi, Che'Veyo!*"—chase me back into TeNon.

VOICE:
Ishiko Allen-Shimmura <u>of the Rock</u>

❧ "I'M SORRY," CAITLYN SAID.

Behind me, Porfiera cleared her throat, tossed her tools into the bucket of water alongside her wheel, and mumbled something unintelligible as she went upstairs, leaving us alone. Caitlyn watched her go, ker strange light eyes glittering in torchlight and the ghost of a smile tugging at the corner of ker mouth. "Off to tell Geema that the awful Sa's here again?"

"Geema already knows," I told ker. "Trust me on that."

"I do," ke said. "It's about time I *did* trust you, I suppose."

I'd been working on a bowl when Caitlyn had entered the studio, a bare few seconds after my niece Nawal's breathless announcement that "one of those awful Sa is here to see you, *mi* Ishi." I let the wheel spin down, the unfinished piece thick-walled and wet at its center. I wiped gray slip from my right hand onto the landscape of caked, half-dried mud on my apron; my left I left obscured in ridges of wet clay. I used the back of my right hand to push a curl of wayward hair back under my headscarf. I could feel a smear of clay drying on my left cheek.

I was a lovely sight. I hated that ke saw me spattered and filthy, and hated even more that it mattered.

"I'm an ass and an idiot," Caitlyn said, then grinned when I simply looked at ker in stupefaction. "Don't be in such a hurry to correct me on that," ke said.

"You don't need to apologize to me," I said, which just proves that sometimes we say things we don't mean, simply because we don't know what else to say.

"I think I do. I don't have many allies here on the Rock.

233

In fact, right now I think it's down to Linden and you, since I'm not exactly a favorite of the Families and SaTu Terri's living in ker own fantasy world since Taira was killed, and I don't need to alienate half of my support group." Ke grinned again, shifting ker weight from hip to hip. "Gods, that sounded awful," ke said, then the grin faded, and ker lips tightened. "Look, Ishiko, I'm scared, I don't know what's going to happen next, and I can use all the friendship and good advice I can find. You told me the truth when you didn't need to, and I haven't repaid you very well. I certainly don't need to hurt you, Ishiko. I'm sorry."

I just stared at ker. My left hand twitched under its glove of clay. Ke must have seen the motion, taking a step forward until ker finger just touched the rim of the bowl above my left hand. "You know, the Miccail believe that a good potter is also a shaman, linked with the *KoPavi*. The act of working the clay connects the potter with the ShadowWorld and places a *kahina* in their work. They say that the sound of a bowl can tell you that: While the spirit lives within the piece, tapping it produces a nice ring. When a bowl cracks or chips, the spirit's released immediately, and all you get is a dull thunk." Ker finger dropped and touched my hand, smearing ker fingertip with gray. "You produce magic."

"Caitlyn, why are you here?"

A half smile tugged at ker mouth. "I came to talk with your Geema and Komoko, actually," ke said. "I thought they deserved to know the truth, too—about Fianya and how she died. Linden and I feel we need to tell them."

"What about the SaTu?" Now that we were off the subject of ourselves and magic, I could trust myself to talk.

Caitlyn shrugged. "Whenever we bring up the subject, ke goes into one of ker fugues. And by the time we take ker back to AnglSaiye and settle the question of whether the SaTu's fit to continue to run the Community . . ." A deep exhalation, and a spreading of hands. "Your Family deserves to know what happened, or what we think happened. Komoko certainly deserves to know what happened to her child, so she can have some peace. I'm not looking forward to telling them about Rashi, but it has to be done."

"You've changed, CaitlynSa."

The grin came and went: a flash. I wanted to smile in response. "That's what Linden said, too, just a few minutes ago. 'A month ago, you wouldn't have been able to handle this.' That's probably right, but it doesn't make it any easier."

"I'll go with you," I said.

"You don't need to," ke said, but ker voice betrayed ker.

"I know. But Geema sent me with you, and I can verify what I saw. It'll help—to have one of the Family on your side."

A flash of teeth, a turn of ker head, then a nod. "Give me a moment to wash up," I told ker. "Then we'll go."

POEM:
"A Moment"—scrawled in the margins of the last journal of Anaïs Koda-Levin

The island's cliffs do not grasp the cloud's shadow
The amberdrop cannot hold the wind's sigh
Like the cloud, like the wind
Your breath takes the moment in
Your breath sends it away again

CONTEXT:
Gentle Koda-Schmidt of the Rock

IN HER SIXTY-EIGHT YEARS OF LIFE, GENTLE HAD seen many things she thought odd. But the male grumbler who stood before the Elder Council was among the strangest. Despite the cold northern air which had descended on them in the last few days, the creature was entirely naked save for white lines swirling over its chest and—more intricately and delicately—about its face.

The grumbler had appeared at Old Bridge, frightening the people gathered at the dock waiting for the *Ibn Battuta II* to arrive from Hannibal and AnglSaiye. It had no *lansa*, no weapon except for the dangerous claws on its hands and feet. The grumbler had made no resistance, remaining calm as several of the Rock inhabitants armed themselves and surrounded it. The grumbler seemed unwilling or unable to understand human speech; when questioned by one of the young Allen-Levins who knew grumbler, it claimed to have been sent by CosTa of the QualiKa to offer *xeshai*, and it requested to speak with the Elder Council.

Xesahi, it was hurriedly explained to Gentle and the other Elders as they gathered in the chamber, was single, unarmed combat used to settle disputes between grumbler tribes.

"That's absolutely wonderful," Euzhan sniffed when she was told. Yellow-tinged light from the everlamps sparked glistening reflections from the crystal-studded walls of the chamber. A geodelike fissure within the rock, the curving, tall walls of the chamber were crowded with calcite growths, ranging in color from a deep, throbbing yellow to startling white. Gentle had always found it ironic that such a beautiful space had been home to so many petty

236

and angry exchanges over the last two centuries. Such ire should have shattered the crystals and left the walls dark and bare. "And does CosTa expect that we're going to accept that kind of challenge?"

"Of course we won't," Jalon Allen-Levin retorted, his craggy face as sharp as stone. "That's utter nonsense."

"I think we should send for the Sa," Gentle suggested, seeing the obvious sentiments around her. She didn't know why she suddenly worried about the hostility. Something shivered deep inside her, a portent, a *kami*'s voice. "I know both Caitlyn and Linden know the grumbler language, and they know their customs. We may need their input."

"Absolutely not." Euzhan, her far-too-young face entirely out of place in this gathering of aged women and men, slashed into Gentle's suggestion before it was even finished. "We will leave the Sa out of it. I never did trust them, and I trust them even less now."

The news that a Sa had been responsible for Fianya Allen-Shimmura's death had flashed through the Rock like a fire through summer's dry tinder, the story growing more interesting with each retelling. Most of Families seemed to be convinced that Rashi hadn't acted alone, that the kidnapping of Fianya had been a deliberate act concocted by the SaTu as retaliation against Family Allen-Shimmura's refusal to willingly send Fianya to AnglSaiye. Gentle had heard speculation that Rashi's "suicide" had simply been the Sa's attempt to hush up the botched kidnapping. Wilder and more exotic theories abounded: that Fianya was going to be sacrificed to VeiSaTi, that ke had indeed been sacrificed and the body thrown over the cliff to hide the evidence, that the QualiKa had been involved in helping the Sa snatch the child.

Gentle believed none of that. She'd grown up on AnglSaiye—her mam was Anaïs (named for the O'Sa herself); her grandmam was Gabriela, the first child born from a human-Sa relationship; her great-grandmam had been Máire, the woman for whom O'Sa Anaïs had been shunned. Despite her lineage, Gentle didn't feel particularly close to the Sa. Terri and Taira had been given to the Community

of Sa two years before Gentle had been born—she'd never
had a chance to know the twin Sa since they were usually
at the Sa temple rather than the Family's AnglSaiye compound. Not long after her menarche, Gentle had fallen in
lust with Jorge Allen-Levin, Jalon's brother, and followed
him back to the Rock. The lust had lasted only a month or
so before they drifted apart, but Gentle had stayed at the
Rock, in her Family's compound there, ever since. She really didn't know the Sa or the SaTu much better than Euzhan did herself. Still, Euzhan's reaction to her suggestion
to consult the Sa was understandable.

"I know how you feel, Euzhan," Gentle said. "I'm only
thinking of the good of our Families."

Euzhan scowled at that, lines marring her perfect face.
Gentle had always expected that one day all that bitter acid
Euzhan carried around inside her would corrode that youthful shell of a body from the inside and come spilling out,
her body shriveling into a wrinkled puddle like the husk of
a spring peeper in autumn. It hadn't happened yet. It probably never would, but the image was pleasant to contem-
plate when Euzhan was ranting. "Nothing that comes of
the Sa is good for the Families, Gentle, and what's happened recently has only given further illustration to that.
Any of the Families who can't see the Sa poison now are
hopelessly blind."

Gentle let that comment pass—Euzhan knew perfectly
well that SaTu Terri and Taira were Gentle's elder sibs and
that the Sa—especially Linden—had spent many a night
recently with members of the Koda-Schmidt Family. The
barb had been well placed, but Gentle was determined not
to let Euzhan see that it hurt. "Blindness is not using all
the resources available," Gentle answered. "I say we need
them here. I doubt that I'm the only one who feels that
way."

She hadn't been—except for the Allen-Shimuras, every
Family had relatives living on AnglSaiye, and even on the
Rock there were a few Elders whose sympathies lay with
AnglSaiye. It had ended up going to a vote, at Gentle's
insistence. She knew she'd lose in the end: Her tenacity in

pushing the issue had been more to annoy Euzhan than anything else. As usual, Euzhan's opinion was upheld by the majority of the Elders. As usual. Euzhan's great age and history gave her power within the Elder Council far beyond the size of her Family.

The grumbler was brought before the Council with the doors to the hall shut to keep out the curious.

The grumbler was defiance personified. That was the first impression Gentle had. It shrugged away the hands that guided it to a chair before the curved rows of the Council seats. It did not sit; it stood, legs spread wide. For a moment—a moment only—its stoic face softened as it gazed at the brilliant, dazzling walls around it, then the sour expression solidified once more as its gaze found the humans. Its hands fisted and the tip of its footclaws lifted, causing the two armed guards at either side of the Elder's dais to bring their weapons up. It glared at them disdainfully, lifted its chin and spoke. A moment later, over the stream of low-pitched grunts and growls, Gavrilo Allen-Levin translated.

"I am FayiXe, and I have been sent to offer *xeshai* to the Elders of the Rock. CosTa of the QualiKa declares that the Rock and land of the Black Lake belong to the CieTiLa, as a free place and refuge for all the people. The CieTiLa have been generous in letting the humans remain here as if you were CieTiLa, but you have betrayed that trust. You prevent the CieTiLa from coming here. You kill CieTiLa and drive them away. You despoil the sacred rocks and change the land. You do not respect the *kahina* who live here also, and you do not listen to our gods. Because you will not talk with us, because you will not listen to our grievances, CosTa now asks for formal *xeshai* to settle this dispute. Send your chosen *xeshai* champion with me. Let us come together to the shores of Black Lake, where both human and CieTiLa can witness *xeshai*. Let us struggle with the blessings of our gods, so that we may see who is stronger."

"And if you win, we're supposed to leave the Rock, is that what you're suggesting?" Henrik Allen-Levin, to Gentle's left, shouted it with a laugh. "And I suppose that if our champion wins, the QualiKa will disband and CosTa will surrender herself for the murders he's caused. I certainly believe *that* will happen.''

Euzhan was shaking her head. "Don't even give it the dignity of talking about this *xeshai*, Henrik. That's not even an option. Let's not pretend that it is.''

"Ask it what happens if we refuse, Gavrilo," Gentle said. To Euzhan's glance, she added: "I don't disagree with you, Euz, but we need to know the answer to that so we can plan, *nei*? Go on, Gavrilo.''

Euzhan shrugged; Gavrilo translated the question. "I don't know," the grumbler answered. "I am only *xeshai*. No more. Ask CosTa.''

"Tell us where we can find her, and we will," Euzhan responded.

The grumbler gave an audible snort when that was translated, the triple nasal slits flexing. Muscles rippled along its body as it shifted weight from one foot to another. It glanced casually from face to face of the nineteen Elders, as if memorizing their features. "CosTa may come to you, instead," FayiXe told them. "But if she does, it won't be to answer your questions. Do we have *xeshai* or not?—that is all I'm here to ask.''

"You do not," Euzhan answered, and the murmur of agreement that followed her statement told Gentle that there was no need for discussion or to call a vote on the issue. FayiXe received the answer with no change in its expression. The grumbler's body seemed to shiver, the white lines painted on it shifting with the motion, then FayiXe turned and began walking toward the doors. The two guards— both from Family Allen-Shimmura—started to go after it, but Euzhan shook her head. "Go with it to make sure it doesn't cause any trouble leaving the Rock, but otherwise leave it alone," she told them.

FayiXe opened the doors and walked out of the chamber without so much as a backward glance.

"I hope we didn't just make a mistake," Gentle said, as the doors boomed shut behind the grumbler.

"Mistake?" Euzhan loosed a short, bitter laugh. "Call

it back then, and let it know that you'll hand over your Family's compound to the grumblers. Are you willing to do that, Gentle? *I'm* not. Not while there's still breath in my body. This is our *home*. We built it from nothing, and generations of our Families have died here guaranteeing that we could survive here. That's all I need to know.''

''I know that too, Euz. It's just . . .''

''Just what?'' The other Elders watched the two of them, and Gentle saw no sympathy in their faces at all.

''Nothing,'' she sighed. ''Nothing.''

Or simply so much that there was no way to say it all.

With a shadow over her soul, Gentle said good-bye to the rest of the Elders and left the chamber.

DECISIONS

"The Israelis are mistaken if they think we do not have an alternative to negotiations. By Allah I swear they are wrong. The Palestinian people are prepared to sacrifice the last boy and the last girl so that the Palestinian flag will be flown over the walls, the churches and the mosques of Jerusalem."

—YASSER ARAFAT
Ha'aretz, September 6, 1995

JOURNAL ENTRY:
Anaïs Koda-Levin, O'Sa

THE FOLLOWING IS THE FINAL ENTRY IN THE JOUR-
nal of Anaïs Koda-Levin, dated the day before
ker arrival at Hannibal in September of 164:

I didn't start out being a particularly religious person.
Oh, I participated in the rites like most everyone else on
the Rock as I was growing up, but without any particular
fervor. Just as the religions of Earth had seemed somehow
wrong and misplaced once the inhabitants of the *Ibn Battuta* left Earth (and so they created the religion called *Njia*,
or The Way), *Njia* seemed wrong to me on Mictlan. It
wasn't until later in life, as Whitetuft and WiseOne explained to me the intricacies of their beliefs—the *KoPavi*—
that I started feeling something, a stirring down inside me
that cried out to me that this, *this* was part of me. This was
the link between myself and this land. The *KoPavi* was old,
as old as most of the Earth-based religions, and it belonged
here. The *KoPavi* was Mictlan, and I could sense the *kami*
and *kahina* who were the gods of this world.

Maybe that was just my age and a desire to feel that
there was something else beyond this all-too-finite life.
While I could feel the pull of *KoPavi*, I have always been
a skeptic. "Real" answers to questions were found through
scientific method, not through a belief system which demanded no rigorous proof. But I also knew that we needed
something, those of us who had come to AnglSaiye. We
wanted something in which to believe, as many people on
Earth once believed in demons, or in sunken lost continents,
in a face on Mars, crop circles, visitations from being on
other planets, or God, Buddha, Christ, Allah, and so on.

245

The fact that all of the above were total nonsense didn't change the *desire* to believe that there was Something Else out there, something that could make sense of chaotic lives and events.

Too much had changed for us here on Mictlan: We needed a belief system that blended with the new race we were becoming, that linked us to the Miccail with whom we shared our island and who were teaching us so much about this world. So selfishly and deliberately, I took the *KoPavi* of the Miccail and grafted it onto *Njia*, and called it *our* religion, the religion of the human Sa.

I was the prophet, who knew the truth and thus couldn't believe. I knew that this new and improved *KoPavi* was a charade—not divine, but something I (who was definitely not divine) had made up. I was still a skeptic. The first time I took *jitu* (all unknowingly, when WiseOne gave it to me to drink after I'd delivered the first Miccail Sa), I'd had a prescient dream. But dreams like that are full of symbols and images, and it's easy to link them afterward with *whatever* events happen, and it's also true that subconscious free association—a state enhanced by meditation or exhaustion or drugs—can lead you to an epiphany that you wouldn't otherwise experience. Occam's Razor: The simplest explanation is also the most likely one. Jitu *simply allows the unconscious mind to break through all the barriers that normally limit our thinking*, I said to myself. *This is no different than what Native American tribes did with peyote, but the truth is that everything you see with* jitu *is already inside you. There is nothing mystical here.*

I rarely took *jitu* afterward except when ceremony demanded it, because I think that it would be easy to become lost in the visions, confused by them. I didn't want my actions based on hallucinations and dreams. A religion and its rites are simply tools, another way of seeing the world— they are not existence themselves . . .

And I wander. Rambling . . .

There was so much I wanted to put down here tonight . . . Tomorrow we'll reach Hannibal and the crisis awaiting us there. We've had three runners come to us today, two human and one Miccail, and the news is not good. The fighting's already begun between the QualiKa and the Families, and I'm beginning to worry that I may already be too late.

And I feel . . . I don't know how to describe it. Tonight I feel religious. I feel as though VeiSaTi were right along-side me, so close that Ker presence is like a heat around me so that I don't even notice the cold. NefSa asked me if I wanted to sacrifice tonight. *No*, I told ker, *the sacrifice comes tomorrow*. I don't know where those words came from—I didn't consciously say them, but I knew they were true as soon as I uttered them.

And I'm afraid. I'm afraid that I know exactly what those words mean. *Hai*, I've known all along and thought that I was comfortable with it, but now that the actual moment is upon me . . .

I'm afraid.

I am the prophet, the O'Sa, the creator of a belief system which half the humans and a fair number of the Miccail believe and in whose rituals they take comfort . . . but I don't believe. I can't.

And I'm afraid.

VOICE:
Caitlyn Koda-Schmidt of the Sa

". . . CosTa is following the *KoPavi* as she un-derstands it," Ghost was saying as we entered the room, and I saw the SaTu nodding ker head vigorously in agreement.

"*Hai, hai*," Terri said. "We all should. We all must."

Ghost seemed to ignore that. Instead, he looked at me, Ishiko, and Linden. This time around, Ghost appeared to be some comic general, with an outlandish khaki uniform and medals sprouting like bright weeds over his chest. A brimmed hat was pulled down low over his forehead, mirrored sunglasses shimmered in the room lights, and a corncob pipe was clenched between his teeth. He took the pipe from his mouth and jabbed the stem toward us. "And now that *xeshai* has been refused, she is free to do whatever she wishes."

The projector belonging to AnglSaiye had been carried down from the island by the *Ibn Battuta II*, since the SaTu seemed to have no inclination to return to AnglSaiye despite Linden's and my feeling that we must. We knew that Ghost was also talking with Euzhan and the Elder Council at the same time, not far away. I wondered what that conversation was like.

"Why didn't CosTa ask for *xeshai* a month ago?" Linden asked. "Why now?"

Ghost took a long pull on the pipe and sent a cloud of blue-white smoke through pursed lips that vanished a few centimeters from his mouth as it reached the limits of the holographic field. "There was no need for *xeshai* a month ago. In CosTa's point of view, the latest round of violence was started by humans when William tried to shoot RenSa. CosTa saw her killing of William as simple self-defense— of another Miccail, and of herself since William probably would have tried to kill CosTa as well. Had nothing else happened, that would have ended it. But Gerald ambushed CosTa's group—without asking for *xeshai*, without any warning, and in CosTa's eyes, entirely unprovoked. So she retaliated in kind, both as revenge and as a warning. Unfortunately, both the FirstHand and SaTu Taira were caught in that. Again, had nothing further happened, I suspect CosTa might have been satisfied to end the violence—at least that's my take on it. RenSa would be able to give us better insight into CosTa's thinking."

"But we didn't let it stop there," I said, glancing at Ishiko. She was hugging herself, her head down as she listened to Ghost. "Again. Gerald and his group attacked the Miccail village."

Ghost shrugged. "CosTa's now making this an open

conflict, declaring war, if you will, because that what she thinks she *must* do. In her mind, you've backed her into a corner. The *KoPavi* demanded this last action.''

''*Hai*,'' SaTu Terri said again, ker head lifting up at the mention of the *KoPavi*. ''That's right. The *KoPavi* says 'those who ignore *xesahi* lack the soul of a *kahina*. Do not respect them.' I know this. I read it on the *nasituda*. That's why my Work is so important. VeiSaTi told me I must do it.'' Terri looked at all of us, and I thought I saw insanity lurking behind ker eyes. ''You understand, don't you? That's why we have to do it—I saw it in VeiSaTi's vision.''

''*Hai*, SaTu. We understand,'' Linden said. ''But Ghost doesn't have much time, and we need to talk with him before he goes. Ghost, what happens now?''

''I don't know,'' Ghost answered. ''But I can tell you what I've seen. I don't have the resolution I'd like on the orbital cameras that are left, but I've seen a gathering of Miccail close by, maybe twenty kilometers northeast of the Rock, at the place where NagTe was buried. From the images, there could be over a thousand Miccail there. I think CosTa has an army.''

I heard Ishiko's intake of breath. ''We couldn't stop that many of them, '' she said. ''Even if we killed them three or four to one . . .'' She stopped. ''I'm scared. For the first time, I'm really scared.''

''A gathering isn't an army,'' I said. ''For all we know, there's some kind of ceremony going on, some ritual. It doesn't mean there's going to be more violence.''

''There won't be,'' Ghost said, and the ominous finality in his voice brought all of our heads around. Ghost heaved an overdramatic sigh. ''I am dead in less than a month. Nothing can keep the poor *Ibn Battuta* in orbit any longer than that. But I have retained enough fuel so that I can direct when and where I land within that time frame. This is what you have to understand.'' In all the centuries of Ghost's existence, I had never heard of the AI doing what he did now.

He cried. From behind the sunglasses, tears trickled

down the rugged, old-man cheeks. "My entire task, the entire purpose of my programming, has been to keep this colony alive. If I must, I will make certain that my death has meaning in the context of that purpose. There's no other decision I can make, as repugnant as it seems. I *will* do what Gabriela asked of me; I have no choice."

"What do you mean, Ghost?" Linden asked, but I had already begun to have a glimmering of what he intended. Ishiko must have as well, for I felt her right hand grasp my arm and tighten.

" 'When the Trumpet sounds a single blast; when Earth with all its mountains is raised high and with one mighty crash is shattered into dust—on that day the Dread Event will come to pass.' "

"What's that?"

"It's from the Koran, the chapter called "The Inevitable." Most religions have the apocalyptic passages in their sacred texts. When the *KoPavi* is translated, I don't doubt it will be the same."

"It's true!" the SaTu shouted suddenly, leaping to ker feet as if ke were seventeen rather than seventy. "I have it here, in the papers upstairs. Let me get it for you—"

I could see the mad glimmer in ker skittering gaze, in the twitching fingers of ker hands. "*SaTu*," I said sharply, and ker mouth snapped shut with an angry glare. "Ghost, please be more specific. What decision have you made?"

Ghost's image shimmered and changed. He was featureless, sexless, the body shimmering like molten steel. "Do you know how much energy is expended when something, oh, the size of the *Ibn Battuta* slams into the ground from high orbit? If I come in at the right angle, at the right velocity, I can ensure that nothing within kilometers of where I land will be living afterward." Ghost's head thinned and melted into his body, the legs contracted into his hips while the torso smoothed out. Now Ghost was just a round, thick gray metal cylinder two meters tall and tapering to a point. Mouthless, the cylinder spoke.

"My last act would be my final effort to keep humankind safe here. I can wipe out any force CosTa might raise. If I see her moving toward the Rock, I will do just that."

TRANSLATION:

From the AnglSaiye <u>KoPavi</u>, <u>Nasituda</u> 52, Grouping G: "The Ending"

The wild beast will come from the sky
  its breath the cold fire of the stars
  its seeing eyes the moons
  its brais *the sun.*
Three horns it will have upon its head, three mouths will
    open and in a voice louder than thunder it will speak
    of the Void and the life that awaits for the people
    but the people will be deaf to the beast's voice.
The beast, angry, will speak again the words of the Great
    Void and again the people will not hear
    for their ears will be full of their own voices.
    Furious, the beast will speak again, and again its
    voice will be as silence.
Then three times the beast will stamp its hooves on the
    land. With the first, the clouds will turn to smoke and
    the air to fire with the second, the rocks will crumble
    to ash and dust.
    With the third, the waters will rise and crash down on
    the earth.
Then the beast will devour the gods
    it will breathe all the kahina *into itself*
    and spit them out again, broken
    And the stones, the seas and the air will scream in
    agony.
And the people will finally hear
    They will hear the wail of the beast
    the weeping of their dead kahina
    the scream of emptiness

VOICE:
Ishiko Allen-Shimmura of the Rock

After Ghost vanished, Linden took the SaTu back to ker room. Caitlyn and I stayed in the Common Room. I sat in the ornate chair that had been carved by one of the Koda-Levins, long ago, and watched ker as ke stood in front of the fireplace, trying to find solace in the small blue flames of the peat. I could see the form of ker body, backlit through the cloth of ker *shangaa,* the slope of ker small breasts, the curve of ker hips. We could both hear the SaTu shouting something at Linden, ker voice muffled by the walls between us. Caitlyn turned, ker mouth twisted in a grimace, and put ker long hair behind ker ear with a fingertip.

"I don't know what to do," ke said, looking everywhere but at me. Finally ker pale eyes found me, and ke shrugged. "I'll send a runner back to AnglSaiye, but the SaTu's here, and they won't act without ker."

I curled into the worn, satiny recesses of the chair, tucking my legs under me, my left hand warm between them. I scraped with a fingernail at a splotch of clay on my pants. "When I'm working, I have to pay attention to the clay. There's a point where you and the wheel and clay all become one. Try to force that moment early, and the walls are thick or you've botched the curve . . ." I glanced up; Caitlyn's gaze was on me, intense and piercing, and I tried to smile into it. "I'm sorry. Analogies are never . . ."

"I'm listening," ke said. "Go on."

"I'm just saying that you can't wave a magic wand and have CosTa change her mind. I know damn well that won't work with Euzhan, either, though the *kami* know I've

252

wished for it often enough. Right now, there *is* nothing you can do. Wait. Pay attention. When the time comes, you'll know it.''

''I wish I knew that were true.''

''You can't change the world, Caitlyn. All you can do is work on the pieces of it you can touch.'' The piece of clay came loose from my pants. I tossed it into the fireplace and wiped the dust from my fingers. ''I guess I should head for the compound. It's late,'' I said it, but I didn't move. I was comfortable in the chair, with the heat of the fire warming the front of me.

''Ishiko.''

I looked up at ker.

''Where are we?'' ke asked. ''What about you and me? If we can't solve the big issues, maybe we can at least do something about a smaller one.''

I felt strangely calm, as if I'd been expecting the words. And at the same time, I had no answer for ker. I could feel myself pulling in all directions at once, a part of me wanting to do nothing more than reach for ker hand and pull her down to me, and another part still resonating with the decades-long prejudices lent me by Geema and my Family, and still another internal voice telling me that it was just simple lust I felt for ker, that a few days or weeks or months from now the attraction I felt now would fade and I would still be empty, still alone.

And something else . . . My period was almost a week late now. Maybe that was nothing. *Probably* that was nothing. I've certainly been late before and found it to be a false alarm. But I wasn't feeling any of the symptoms that go along with my menses. If it were true, if I were pregnant . . .

A child conceived through a Sa. I remembered how Geema Euzhan had been with Komoko, Fianya's mam, screaming at Komo that she was a whore and an abomination and a traitor to her Family. Geema railed at her for soiling herself with a Sa. For weeks, she refused to come see the baby in the creche, and the Family wondered whether—if the child survived the childhood diseases and accidents and made it to ker Naming Day—Geema would participate in the celebration. Yet a few months later I walked past Geema's door, and I saw her cradling the baby in her arms, rocking ker and crooning nonsense words, and it wasn't hatred or anger or pity I saw in Geema's eyes then, but a grudging love. If Geema never quite forgot what Komo had done, at least she eventually came to forgive her. I think, I hope, that it would be the same for me, if . . .

"Ishiko?"

"I'm sorry, Caitlyn. I was just . . . thinking." I sighed, curling deeper into the womb of the chair. Caitlyn knelt on the floor alongside the chair, ker hands resting on my legs. Ker face looked so soft, so open, and ker hair had escaped from behind ker ears again, curling lightly over ker face. I reached out to brush the hair away with my right hand; as I did, Caitlyn turned ker face to kiss my palm—as ke had once before, the night we'd made love.

Ker lips were gentle and very warm. "Stay here tonight," ke said. "Stay with me."

I wanted that. I did. I wanted to sleep with ker again, wanted to feel ker heat along my body, wanted to kiss ker and explore the strange curves of ker body, wanted to hold ker afterward and feel that I was loved again. I wanted to sleep with ker and stay with ker, to spend hours and days and weeks . . .

"No," I told ker. I said it as softly as I could, not more than a trembling breath. I don't think I could have said more.

Caitlyn caught ker lower lip between ker teeth for a moment, ker eyes glancing away. I saw ker shoulders lift under ker *shangaa*, then drop again. "It's that one-sided?" ke asked. "I thought . . ."

I touched ker lips, shushing ker like a child. "It's not that," I said. "It's just . . ." I took a long breath, sitting up in the chair. "I'm not so different than anyone else here. I've had several lovers over the years. With one of them— Anjiro Allen-Levin—we even talked a bit about pledging a covenant. What I realized was that even if my relationship with Anji had worked out that way, he would never have been happy living with my Family. He had a wonderful relationship with his own Family, and that would always have been pulling him back. Eventually it would have broken any covenant we might have made, and that was with the best of conditions, with Geema's blessing of the relationship." I gave Caitlyn a weak, uncertain smile. "How likely do you think it is that Geema would welcome *you* into the Family? Caitlyn, we had our night. Maybe we could have another or even several of them, but in the end you're going back to AnglSaiye, and I'm staying here. The closer I get to you, the harder that's going to be."

"Then come with me to AnglSaiye. The Community of Sa would welcome you, and you'd be away from Euzhan."

I was shaking my head before ke finished. "I don't doubt that the Community of Sa would treat me well. But none of my Family are on AnglSaiye. Caitlyn, I might not like all of what Geema says and does. I may disagree with her most of the time. But I don't hate her. I can't. I've seen the parts of her you've never had the chance to see. I've watched her stay up all night nursing one of the sick children. I've watched her cry at the Burnings, watched her laugh with sheer joy when someone announced she was pregnant, or joke and tease with one of the boys when he found a new lover. I've been alongside her working in the faux-wheat fields or carding wool or making paper. She was the one I'd run to when I fell. She was the one who was at my bedside when I went into labor with Timon, and she was at Timon's bed with me when he died of the Bloody Cough three years later, and she held me all that night when I couldn't stop crying just from the pain of his loss."

I could have talked forever that way, once I'd started, recalling shared moments. I felt tears starting, remembering, and I didn't care. Caitlyn listened, silent. "She helped me through the miscarriages in the years following, through the three little ones who died unnamed and the birth of my daughter, and when my little one reached her Naming Day, I was proud to call her Euzhan after her Geema. We held each other when little Euzhan died, too. I've watched the long hours she puts in on the Elder Council, sacrificing herself so that everyone would be better off. Do I get furious with her? Absolutely. Often. Do I understand how others might view her as cruel and harsh? *Hai*. And I know I'd also miss her terribly. I would miss *all*—''

But I had no chance to finish.

From down the hall, from the SaTu's room, there came a horrible, strangled scream.

CONTEXT:
Euzhan Allen-Shimmura
of the Rock

"GERALD'S GOING TO BE BADLY SCARRED FOR THE rest of his life," Cuauh had told her. *"He'll also have an audible speech impediment which may only get worse. The grumbler ripped loose or tore half the tendons on the left side of his face, and I'm not sure he's going to regain control of them entirely. I'd also expect arthritis to set in at the mandibular joint. I'm sorry, Geema. I wish I had better news for you, but I don't. Right now, with this kind of deep injury, I have to worry about infection—if we get that . . ."* Cuauh had shrugged. They both knew what that meant.

Euzhan shivered, remembering. She found herself gripping the smooth wooden knob of her ancient cane as she stood at the window of her study, as if the pressure of her grip could change what had happened. Outside, looking down the steep, rocky flank of the Rock, she could see people moving in and out of the main entrance; the checkerboard squares of the cultivated fields in the valley, and the shining ribbon of the Green River as it snaked toward its collision with the Loud River, kilometers away. The *Ibn Battuta II* was in, docked at Old Bridge, ready to leave in the morning for AnglSaiye. Beyond the river, on the far hillsides, the bubble-trees were beginning to turn, their fruit glistening as it ripened.

It all looked so normal. So pastoral. So eternal. Yet she could overlay it with memories a century old. She alone of anyone here knew how much things had changed, could remember all the hard work and effort, the blood and pain that had gone into creating that scene before her.

Blood and pain. Shifting her focus, Euzhan saw her own reflection in the glass before her, the same young-looking face she'd seen gazing back at her for decade upon decade—unlike the land, always unchanging.

A sham, she thought, glaring at herself. *A false shell of youth, and inside I'm stiff and old and broken.* She turned, her body rigid as always, and walked carefully back to her desk, supporting herself on the cane. It took her several seconds to convince her joints to loosen enough to allow her to sit at the chair behind the desk, her knees cracking, her hips grinding in protest. When she was finally settled, she leaned the cane against the arm of her chair, took a small brass key from her jacket pocket, and unlocked a small drawer. She pulled out a folded sheet of paper.

She stared at the paper a long time, holding it in her fingertips, watching it tremble in her hand: an ancient piece of rag paper, the edges frayed and feathered, splotched with stains, the folds nearly worn through the paper after all the years. Carefully, she opened the stiff paper, smoothing it down on her desk, and looked again at the spidery handwriting there, the ink faded to sepia on the ivory background of the parchment.

My Dearest Euzhan:

    I hope this letter manages to get to you. Elio told me that he'd do his best to smuggle it past your Geeda Dominic, and I pray that he's successful. I'm writing to you because I want you to know that you are the one person I regret leaving behind. I don't know what Dominic will tell you about why I had to go (nothing good, I suspect—your Geeda tends to hold his grudges), but I still keep the hope that one

*day he'll relent and let you come to see me. I think
you would love the island, Euzhan. There is so much
here, and every day I discover some new surprise that
makes me appreciate the Miccail more . . .*

*Euzhan, I love you as much as if you were my own
daughter, and I miss you terribly. Every time I looked
at you, I saw your mam Ochiba—her face, her eyes,
her mouth. I miss Ochiba, too. She was the best friend
I had, and no matter what Dominic may tell you,
there was nothing wrong with the love I felt for her,
or she for me. As I write this, I can look up on the
wall and see the drawing of her that I did, many years
ago. Maybe one day you'll be able to come here and
see it yourself.*

*I wish that you'd been able to know your mam,
Euzhan, but I can tell you that even though Ochiba
died giving you life, that is a sacrifice she never, ever
regretted. For the few days she was able to be with
you, she held you and kissed you and loved you as
much as any mam could. Ochiba was a wonderful,
open, and giving person. Be like her, Euzhan. Listen
to her* kami *because I know she will always be with
you.*

I had to leave, mali cvijet. *I would never have gone
away from you otherwise. You'll come to understand
why when you're older, but even though your Geeda
and I can't agree on things, I do know that in his
own way, he also cares about you as much as I do.
You are a special child, and I'm certain there's a
great fate in store for you. I hope that you always
remember me well: how you used to sneak into the
clinic just to watch me work, how we used to play
hopbox down on the landing pad, how you once gave
me a flower to put in my hair at a Gather—because
it made my eyes look pretty, you told me. I still have
that flower, pressed in the pages of my journal.*

*Maybe one day I'll be able to show it to you.
Maybe one day, I'll be able to give you a Gather
blossom of your own. I hope so.*

Remember me, Euzhan. I will never forget you.
                        Much love to you, always,
                                        Anaïs.

Euzhan's finger traced the writing of the signature, feeling the slight ridges the ink had left on the paper, looking at the blurred edges of the letters: the spike of the "A," the way the final "s" was separated from the other letters. Carefully, she refolded the paper, placed it back in the drawer, and locked it again. She reached for the cane— Geeda Dominic's cane, and once patriarch Shigetomo Shimmura's cane. Two centuries of hands had used this, had rubbed the knob of Earth's oak smooth with their palms and polished the grain with the oil of their hands.

"Damn you, Geeda, for infecting me with your own poison," Euzhan whispered to the cane. "And damn you, Anaïs, for being what you were." Euzhan's fingers, youthful and long, curled around the knob of the cane. Lifting it, she pounded it twice hard against the floor, as if she could summon their *kami* with the noise.

Instead, a few minutes later, a muffled voice came from outside the door, with a tentative knock. "Geema?"

"I'm hungry," she answered with a sigh. "Bring me some soup and bread." As footsteps skittered down the stairs toward the kitchen, Euzhan lifted the cane again, resting the cool smoothness of the wood on her cheek.

To her touch, there was very little difference between the two.

VOICE:
RenSa

"WHAT *DID* YOU COME HERE FOR, IF NOT TO HELP me, FirstHand?" CosTa asked, with far more gentleness than I might have had for myself. She seemed genuinely puzzled, even if JairTe fumed out in the entrance to TeNon. Outside, through the open doors, I could still hear the chanting continuing, a sea roar in the burial chamber.

"I don't know," I answered honestly. "But I can feel how wrong this is. CosTa, the Black Lake is gone. It dried up *terduva* ago after KaiSa sacrificed kerself there to become the Sa Beneath The Water. Now ke rests in Angl-Saiye—VeiSaTi's promise was fulfilled, and the Black Lake is nothing sacred anymore."

"It was our land, and they took it."

"It was," I agreed, "and if you try to take it back now, then hundreds of CieTiLa will die in the effort. You know the technology they have, the weapons they can create from graystone. They will kill you with your *lansas* still in your hands, and for what? For land that means less than the land here at TeNon, which is at least blessed by the presence of your grandfather. Black Lake is *gone*. There is no need to spill blood over it."

"So what would you have me do, RenSa?" CosTa asked, waving her hands. "They have murdered our people, over and over again, and they have refused honorable *xeshai* to settle the matter. If I ignore them, do you think they'll leave us alone? Do you think that will satisfy the *kahina* of those who have died? Tell me how to ensure that we can live together with the *KoPavi*, and I will do it. Do you have that answer?" She lifted her head into my silence, the tips of her claws just emerging from her fingerpads. "I thought so," she said quietly.

"The humans were sent here to bring us back," I persisted, "as the Sa Beneath The Water promised. They have given us back our *KoPavi*."

"And that purpose isn't valid any longer. Now they're like spring floods that have lasted into summer—no longer useful, only destructive. The gods brought them down but didn't take them back to the cloud world; they've left that task to us."

"Now you know what the gods intend, CosTa?"

"No," CosTa answered sharply, then she repeated the

word again, softly. "No, RenSa, I don't." Coming over to me, she touched my face, the back of her hand stroking the side of my face. Her eyes, the blue of a high noon sky, stared at me sadly. "Tell me, RenSa. You know the humans best. Do they think of us as equals? Can they?"

"Do they? Most of them, no," I told her. I caught her hand and held it to my skin. "But can they? I don't know. Some at least, yes. But I know this also: If we could learn to speak with the same words, we have much to teach each other."

Her eyes searched my face. I held her gaze, not knowing what she saw there. At last she sighed and dropped her hand. I let it go, listening to the slap of flesh on the cloth of her *shangaa*. "I'm afraid that it's too late for that," she said.

JOURNAL ENTRY:
NefSa, FirstHand to Anaïs Koda-Levin, O'Sa

THIS IS AWKWARD, THIS HUMAN HABIT OF TRANS-forming events into words written on paper. Yet there is a power to it, as there is power in carving the runes into the stone of a *nasituda*. I write to an unknown future, so that they will understand, whether they be human or CieTiLa.

Later, I will erect a *nasituda* and write this there as well. *Nasituda* writing is so different—I will carve the symbol for Sa, and place over it the line of the clouds: the symbol for the O'Sa. I will also carve the crescent moon, and over it the cloud line: the symbol for the Cha'akMongTi. And I will carve the fire line, with the earth line under it, and above them the wavering lines of a *kahina*.

Here the O'Sa and the Cha'akMongTi died.

So spare, the words. So full.

How would O'Sa have written this? Differently. With more words and prettier images. I suspect ke would have danced around the events, would have tried to explain them. I won't, because I cannot. I do not know the human language well enough to dance with it, and I know my words will be plain. I will simply state what I know. Forgive me if my plainness offends.

We came to Hannibal early in the morning. A human runner brought the news that the humans and QualiKa had clashed again the night before, and that several on both sides were dead—the rumors were that the Cha'akMongTi was among those killed, though no human had seen his body. The humans were arrayed close to the CieTiLa encampment, with an open field between them. When we arrived, O'Sa went immediately to the scene of the battle. Several of the people with ker, myself included, told ker that we should meet first with one side or the other, but ke would not listen. Instead, ke began walking out into the field, with the rest of us following closely behind. We could see the humans to our left, the QualiKa to the right. "Here," O'Sa said. "This is where we will camp. NefSa, I want you—"

We heard the bark of a rifle shot from the human side of the field, then O'Sa grunted, doubling over. Ke collapsed to the ground, and when I ran to ker, rolling ker over, there was blood spilling over ker fingers.

So much blood.

"O'Sa!" I cried, and ke opened ker eyes and saw me.

"It hurts, NefSa," ke said, as if in wonder, and held up ker hand to her face, the fingers trembling under the thick red. "It hurts so much."

"We will get you away from here," I told ker, and waved my hand to the attendants standing around in shock.

"No!" O'Sa shouted to me. "I must stay here. Bring them to me, NefSa—QualiKa and human. Bring them to me here." She closed ker eyes then, ker body relaxing in my arms. "Let me rest until then," ke said, ker voice no more than a whisper. "Bring them here to me."

"I will try," I told ker. "I will try."

VOICE:
Ishiko Allen-Shimmura <u>of the Rock</u>

I RAN DOWN THE HALL BEHIND CAITLYN AS KE burst into the SaTu's room. "Gods!" I heard Caitlyn cry, and then ke was pulling the SaTu away from Linden, who clutched at ker throat and the thin cord wrapped around ker neck. Blood was streaming down the side of Linden's face. At ker feet, a stone axe lay on the floor, more blood staining the carpet underneath it.

I saw the sacrificial bowl, set in its stand, and a flagon of water alongside it. I could smell the *jitu.*

I went to Linden as Caitlyn wrestled the SaTu back to ker bed. Terri was screaming, scratching, and biting at ker, a mad thing. "Damn it, I must complete the sacrifice! VeiSaTi has told me to do it! Don't you understand? Can't you see? It's the only way, Caitlyn, the only way . . ."

I helped Linden drag the cord from around ker neck. The fingers of ker left hand were bleeding, caught under the cord as the SaTu had tried to tighten it around ker throat— that had saved ker. Linden choked and gasped, gulping in breaths of air. "Ke . . . was going . . ." ke started to say, and I held ker, watching Caitlyn struggling with the SaTu, who suddenly went limp and began weeping.

"We know," I whispered to Linden. "We know." I was staring at Caitlyn over Linden's shoulder, and ker eyes were on mine as ke held the SaTu, sobbing and bent over as ke sat on the bed.

I saw iron in Caitlyn's light eyes, a hard certainty. "I knew," Caitlyn said, looking at me. "I think I knew as soon as we saw Rashi's body, but couldn't say it . . . Couldn't really comprehend it . . ."

At the mention of Rashi's name, Terri looked up again, ker face bleak, ker long, gray hair stained with Linden's blood. "I told Rashi that the *KoPavi* told how we must sacrifice, that VeiSaTi had come to me. You have to understand. It's the times, Caitlyn. The times demanded it: the QualiKa returning, Euzhan's refusal to send Fianya—these were all signs. I sent Rashi to take Fianya, so ke could give ker to VeiSaTi . . ." Ke stopped. Ke glanced around at the three of us, all staring at ker. "I *had* to," ke said. "Don't you see? I *had* to."

Caitlyn glared at ker. "And afterward, you made sure that I was the one sent to investigate, because you were sure that I was the most likely to fail, that no one would ever find out the truth. Isn't that right, SaTu? You wanted me because you were certain that I would bungle things."

I heard the pain in Caitlyn's voice at that, and the way ker body sagged as the SaTu wordlessly nodded.

"I would have told them, but no one would have understood," Terri cried. "You have to see that, don't you? They wouldn't have understood the importance. They would have thought me mad. They can't understand. They won't understand."

Terri began sobbing again. Caitlyn let ker collapse onto the bed, staring down at ker as if ke wanted to strike the old Sa, ker fists balled at ker sides. With a visible effort, Caitlyn turned from ker and came over to help me get Linden to ker feet. I took a towel from the drawers alongside the bed and tried to staunch the blood from the wound on Linden's temple as Caitlyn supported ker.

"Ke attacked me when I turned around," Linden said. "When I came up with ker, ke kept talking about a sacrifice, and I thought ke was going to kill another guffin. Ke took *jitu*, and I didn't try to stop ker, thinking that afterward ke'd settle down. Ke took the axe out of the stand and . . ." Linden's eyes closed in pain; opened again. "Ke was going to kill me, was going to make me the sacrifice that Fianya was to have been. We have to take ker back to AnglSaiye, Caitlyn. We don't have a choice now."

"I knew," Caitlyn said again. "Inside, I knew." Caitlyn gave another angry glance back at the SaTu, still weeping helplessly on the bed and staring at something on the walls that only *jitu* could see, then ke nodded. "You're right, Linden," ke said, but ker gaze was now on me. "Right now I don't want to leave, but this is something we have to deal with. We'll leave on the *Battuta* in the morning."

Together, we helped Linden stagger from the room and took ker into the kitchen to clean ker up. As Caitlyn sprinkled powdered *kalava* on the jagged cut, and I cleaned the blood from Linden's face with a damp towel, Caitlyn looked at me. "Will you go with us?" ke asked. "With me?"

I smiled at ker. I touched ker sweet face with my left hand as I felt salt burn in my eyes.

"No," I told ker. "I can't. I'm sorry."

VOICE:

Caitlyn Koda-Schmidt <u>of the Sa</u>

ANGLSAIYE.

I should have felt relief as the *Ibn Battuta II* steamed out from the mouth of the Loud and into the bay, giving us our first glimpse of the familiar cliff-walled island. Home. Squnting into the sunlight, I could see the white dome of the Sa temple, at the top of the long stairs to the summit. Not many people climbed the five hundred stairs now, preferring the less-dizzying safety of the elevator compartments, winched slowly upward from the summit.

AnglSaiye: I took in deep breaths of the familiar salt air and let the wind off the ocean tousle my hair with its rough, cold fingers. Being here meant that I could give up the charge given to me almost two months ago now, could lay down the burden of the responsibilities I'd been given. I'd been told to find the person who'd been responsible for

Fianya's death; I'd done that, even though the trail had led back here. My task was done.

Once, I would have been ecstatic at the thought. Now, I wasn't sure that I wanted it to be over.

Four hours later, the *Ibn Battuta II* docked, and we disembarked. Within two hours, Linden and I had completed our purification rituals, the Sa Council had convened, and Linden and I were called to give our testimony. They listened to SaTu Terri as well. By late that night, Terri was no longer SaTu—ke was stripped of ker title and held under guard in ker room, to be given over to the Elder Council of the Rock on the *Ibn Battuta II's* return trip to be judged in the death of Fianya.

With Rashi also dead, Linden was now the oldest of the Sa. Considering ker part in the investigation and ker experience, Linden was named as the new SaTu for the Community. As for the Miccail portion of the Community, if RenSa was found alive and well, then ke might be elevated to FirstHand. In the interim, the current ThirdHand—JolSa—was raised to SecondHand and given control of the Miccail Sa.

Such bare words. So plain . . .

"What are you going to do now?" Linden asked me. We were sitting together in the SaTu's quarter's—Linden's quarters—at the table where Taira and Terri had always sat. Linden was wearing the white *shangaa* of the SaTu and looking a bit uncomfortable in it. A midnight meal had been set out for us: plain bread, some goathen cheese, and ale. Through the windows, I could see Quali just rising over the bay, the moon's light pearling the waters. "I need someone to take Terri back to the Rock when the *Battuta* leaves tomorrow."

"I don't know," I said. "SaTu . . ."

" 'Linden,' " ke corrected me. "I think you still have unfinished business there, Caitlyn, and I also believe that we need someone there to represent us until the current crisis with CosTa and the QualiKa is over. Right now, everything's in upheaval here because of what's happened, and I can't leave. We still don't know *where* RenSa is for certain. You've been involved since the beginning—taking Terri to the Rock for the Council's judgment will put closure to that part of things, at least. What you do after that . . .''

Linden shrugged. ''I trust you to know best, Caitlyn.''

VOICE:
RenSa

STANDING BEFORE THE ENTRANCE TO TeNon, I could see the entire valley in the dawn, looking as if the very stones had come alive. Everywhere there were CieTiLa, scurrying about, striking tents and gathering possessions, gathering together as the various Hands of the QualiKa took command of their groups, their marker flags fluttering from poles on the saddles of their *konja*.

A sight like this had not been seen since the time of DekTe and CaraTa, when they arose to conquer most of the TeTa and overthrow the rule of the Sa. The thought made me shudder—I hoped that the comparison was not an omen. DekTe and CaraTa's rule had been short, leading directly into the sacrifice of the Sa Beneath The Water and the long fall of the CieTiLa into *terduva* of oblivion, from which O'Sa Anaïs had finally delivered us.

The QualiKa prepared to march, and I shivered in the cold wind, wondering what I should do now. I felt helpless, small and insignificant against the power arrayed below me.

''RenSa!'' The call came from the foot of the steps. Lost in my own reverie, I hadn't heard the *konja*'s hooves approaching. CosTa was there, astride a huge, black-haired *konja*; behind her, JairTe sat on his own steed, facing away from us with an air of disapproval. CosTa clutched her *lansa*, set in its holder on the saddle, the blackstone tip glistening in the morning sun. "We are about to leave. Will you ride with me?"

It was the question that I'd been hoping she would not ask. I would have been content to have been left behind, to watch from TeNon as the QualiKa masses moved through the jaws of the valley pass, then find my way back to AnglSaiye. I'd taken *jitu* the night before, and sacrificed a guffin, hoping that VeiSaTi would give me guidance, but the images had been as confused and scattered as my own thoughts. "This is not something I believe in, CosTa," I told her. "In the heart of my *kahina*, I feel this is a mistake."

CosTa grinned at me. "Then let it be a glorious mistake." She waved his hand toward the QualiKa below. "Look! A thousand or more of us, all going out to take the Black Lake."

"There is no Black Lake," I told her as I'd told her before. "There is a pond, and marsh. The Black Lake has gone and changed, as we must, too."

CosTa shook her head into my arguments. "Then come with me because I ask. Because you know that, whether you agree with me or not, you want to be there to see. Because, perhaps, you care what happens to me."

I lifted my head, feeling the sun graze my *brais*. JairTe was still staring stiffly away, though I know he heard. CosTa's hand was out to me, the long fingers curled in invitation.

I hesitated, looking down again at the valley and the army.

Then I went down the steps and took her hand.

CONTEXT:
Komoko Allen-Shimmura
of the Rock

THE KNOCK ON THE DOOR STARTLED HER. "JUST A moment," she said, wiping at her eyes with a sleeve as she went to the door. Ishiko stood there in the hallway.

"Can I come in, *mi* Komo?"

Ishiko had been crying as well. Komoko could see it in the redness of her eyes, the puffiness under them. She stood aside from the door. "Come inside," she said. "Please."

Komoko's room was dim, with a window that opened out into the large Common Room, but no exterior windows. She had candles lit, and a peat fire crackled in the hearth, giving the room a wavering, warm illumination. Ishiko's glance went to the bed, and the framed drawing that was still lying there: Fianya's face, crudely dawn—Komoko had done it herself, and she had little talent for likenesses. Still, it reminded her of what Fianya had looked like. When she saw the drawing, she saw her child's face rather than the spare ink lines.

"I'm so sorry, *mi*," Ishiko said. "None of this should ever have happened to ker."

"It did," Komoko said, trying to say the words without the bitterness that she wanted to add to them, the extra accusations, and not succeeding. She looked at Ishiko, her eyes gone dry. "Are you going to tell me that I'll get over it one day, that the pain will go away? I won't ever forget, and I won't ever stop feeling the hurt."

"I know," Ishiko said. "I still feel the loss of my own."

269

Komoko nodded. She sat down on the bed, cradling the picture on her lap and staring at the flames lapping at the sides of the peat bricks. Ishiko sat alongside her. Komoko could hear Ishiko start to say something, then stop. Finally, Ishiko's right hand touched Komoko's, laced around Fianya's picture. "I never gave you the support I should have, when you were pregnant with Fianya and after, when Geema was doing all the yelling and screaming."

"You never said anything bad to me, Ish."

Komoko heard Ishiko sigh. "I never really said anything to *anyone*, to you or Geema," Ishiko continued. "And that's the problem. I should have. I should have told Geema that she was being cruel. I should have said that you did what any of us might have done." A pause. "What I *did*," she finished.

Komoko turned to Ishiko, setting Fianya's picture aside. "Ishiko—"

"Did you love ker, *mi*? I mean, did you want to be with ker more than the one night? Was ke something special?"

"No, not really," Komoko answered. "I . . . I thought ke was pretty, and I wanted another child so much, and I thought that Geema would never find out." Komoko stroked Ishiko's hair. "It's different for you, isn't it, with this one."

Ishiko nodded. A faint, inward smile flickered along her lips. "I don't deserve to ask this of you, *mi*. But I would like your support, because you understand. Because you've been where I am now."

Komoko sighed. Opening her arms, she pulled Ishiko in to her, head to shoulder. She kissed the top of her head gently. "I'll help you," she said. "It's time that our Family began to change. I'll help you."

VOICE:
Caitlyn Koda-Schmidt <u>of the Sa</u>

I WAS PREPARING TO LEAVE THE TEMPLE AND GO down to the *Ibn Battuta II* when Banu Koda-Schmidt, at four years old the youngest Sa, came running in. "Caitlyn," ke said breathlessly, "the SaTu wants you to come to ker office right now. Hurry!"

I dropped the *shangaa* I was folding and ran past Banu.

I could hear Linden's voice and another, unfamiliar one from the office. The door was already slightly ajar; I pushed it open and entered.

". . . don't have a good choice here, Linden. That's what you must understand." Ghost glanced up at me. He was an elderly Caucasian man with white hair and glasses, a sharp nose set between eyes that looked large behind the thick lenses, dressed in a dark suit and tie that looked to be from the mid–twentieth century. His voice was high and raspy, almost contentious, with a faint nasal twang. "You won't talk me out of it either, Caitlyn."

"Talk you out of what, Ghost?" I asked.

"CosTa's on the move, with her QualiKa," Linden answered from behind ker desk. "Ghost is insisting on dropping himself on them."

"Not all of me," Ghost said. "Just a part. Enough to end this." His voice was eerily calm. He might have been talking about stepping on a spindle-leg.

"You can't do that," I said automatically, looking from Ghost to Linden. "Ghost, I know you talked about this before, but you can't."

Ghost took a cloth handkerchief from his pants pocket, took off his glasses, blew on them gently, and polished

271

them. Settling them back on his nose, he cleared his throat. "Do you know who I am?" he asked.

I looked at him again, at that ancient gray suit that looked like it belonged in an ancient black-and-white movie. "No," I said.

That garnered me a faint smile. "You are really such a poor student of history, Caitlyn," Ghost said.

"*I* know," Linden said. "And whether that person made the right choice has been argued ever since. Ask the children of Hiroshima, Harry."

Ghost took in a long breath, his thin face pained. "I know," he said. "I understand. But because this is also a hard choice doesn't mean it's a bad one. I'm talking now with the Rock as well, and most of the Elder Council there agrees with me. CosTa is heading for *them*, after all. She's two days away at most. If she gets to the Rock, we're going to lose people. I can stop her now, before that happens."

"By killing all of them," I said.

Ghost looked at me calmly. "Caitlyn, my interest is in human survival on this world. That's all."

"Look ahead, then. If you destroy CosTa and the Quali-Ka, you make them martyrs. A year from now, five years, ten—the Miccail will remember, and someone will take up the mantle of the Cha'akMongTi again, and it will be this act that will be their rallying cry."

"Or this may give the message to the Miccail that this *can't* ever happen again. I don't know, Caitlyn. I can't predict the future. All I can do is what I can do *now*. After all, I don't have a future beyond the now. Whatever happens, I will be gone."

"Then fire a warning shot," Linden suggested. "Drop something right in front of them, create a big enough explosion that they realize that to go forward is suicide."

Ghost's old man shoulders lifted and he sighed. "I can't. I have only one shot at this, I'm afraid. CosTa is already closer to the Rock than I would like, and the *Ibn Battuta* herself is too big to bring down with the kind of precision we need here. I've run the scenarios a thousand times, trying to decide what would be best. The *Battuta*'s made of too many components, and I couldn't control the breakup in the atmosphere. I'd do damage over most of the area and probably end up killing as many of you as I did QualiKa. The *Ibn Battuta* has to come down over the ocean, where the impact will do the least environmental damage. What I *can* control well enough is the main fuel tank. CosTa's been moving at a steady rate and direction since dawn, following the valley out of TeNon, so I know where she's going to be. The explosive bolts holding the tank to the *Battuta* still respond to the system, and I can program the network to vent the last of the fuel, timing the descent to have the tank strike where the main portion of the army will be. It's going to be a spectacular and very deadly impact. But in doing that, I also seal my own fate: The loss of the tank leaves me with no way to control the rest of the ship at all, in an orbit that will rapidly decay." Ghost blinked behind the glasses. A ripple of static went through the figure, and I knew he was drifting out of range. "So you see: one shot. I need to make it count. I can't take any chances."

"Ghost, we need more time to think about this," I said, trying to talk quickly. "This kind of decision needs more thought."

"There isn't time. My calculations are already made, and the window's very short." Ghost glanced at an old stem-wound watch on his wrist. "In fact, the time . . ." He looked up. ". . . is now."

In the holographic field, his figure shivered once, and we heard a distant *k-chunk* and a sinister hissing that slowly faded. "It's done, and it can't be undone," Ghost said. His figure morphed, became that of Gabriela Rusack, who had programmed the computer over two centuries before. "I'm sorry," she said. "I'm so very sorry." The figure shivered and dissolved into static, then returned.

"Wait!" I said, reaching for her even though I knew the gesture was meaningless. "How long until it happens, Ghost?"

"Three orbits. Eight hours." She shrugged. "That's all the time CosTa . . ." Her voice faded, the figure went transparent, then disappeared entirely. I stared at Linden.

"This is insanity," ke said. Ker face was ashen. "We

can't even warn them, not in time. Even sending a runner . . ."

I went to the window, looking out over the plateau of
AnglSaiye at the sloping hillside, where the mingled dwellings of human and Miccail sat alongside each other, and
thinking that it was all going to end soon. I remembered
my years here, remembered the last time I'd sat in this room
talking with Ghost, with SaTu Taira. . . .

I slapped the windowsill.

"Linden," I said. "There may still be a way."

JOURNAL ENTRY:
NefSa, FirstHand to Anaïs Koda-Levin, O'Sa

WE LAID O'SA ANAÏS DOWN ON A BED UNDER THE
gauze tenting. I had done what I could to stop
the bleeding, but I knew the damage inside was too great,
and I also knew that O'Sa Anaïs could see ker death in my
eyes. But ke said nothing, did not complain but only asked
for a little water to ease ker throat.

Ke looked like a *kahina* already, ker skin pale and ker
gray hair spread out on the pillow.

We sent for the leaders of both human and QualiKa.
NagTe did not come. We did not know then that he was
already dead, struck down during the last battle and his
body carried away. It was LarXa, NagTe's SecondHand,
who came instead, and when she told O'Sa Anaïs that
NagTe had been killed, ke wept with her. "Tell your
daughter that I will miss Nag, and that I will look for his
kahina in the ShadowWorld," ke told LarXa, for ke knew
that NagTe had fathered a child on Lar.

Elder Micah Allen-Shimmura entered the tent then, along
with a representative of each of the other Families. Though

Micah had been appointed spokesperson for the human delegation, he would not look at O'Sa Anaïs, as if the sight of ker wounded on the bed pained him. Afterward, it would be whispered that Micah had fired the shot that felled O'Sa Anaïs. Perhaps that was true, for O'Sa Anaïs gestured to him. "Sit here," ke said, and Micah knelt down beside ker bed. O'Sa Anaïs touched his shoulder and he finally lifted his eyes to ker.

I wish I could remember exactly what O'Sa Anaïs said then, so I could set them down here as they were spoken. I cannot, though, and my approximation will have to suffice. I tried to remember all ker words, but ke spoke softly in ker pain, and there was the noise of all the others in the tent, and afterward I could only recall some of the words. "We must live with all that has happened," ke told Micah. "The past can't be changed, not by me, nor by you. All you can do is change what happens from this point. It was blind hatred that brought us here to this point. I tell you now to open your eyes. Open your eyes." O'Sa Anaïs looked at Micah, at the other humans, and at LarXa. "We must all do that now, or we won't be able to find a path that allows us to leave here in peace."

"O'Sa—" someone began to protest, and O'Sa Anaïs lifted kerself up from the bed with an effort.

"No!" ke cried. "We stay here, all of us, until we agree on a way to end this stupidity. Anyone who walks from this tent now says that they are a true coward, and you condemn yourself and your children and their children to more pain and more death. We stay, and we negotiate a truce." Ke fell back then with a groan, closing ker eyes. When I started to go to ker, fearing the worst, ke rallied again and waved me back.

"We start now to change the future," ke said. "Agreed?"

What could they say? How could they refuse ker, dying as ke was? They stayed, all that day and into the next. And finally, when they left, LarXa went to the QualiKa, and they struck their tents to vanish into the misty hills to the north, where NagTe's body had been taken, and the Families of the Rock left Hannibal to the control of AnglSaiye and the Sa, revoking their claim on the land.

O'Sa Anaïs lingered for another day. Sometime during that next night, when I went in to look at ker, I found ker body still and cold. As I gazed sadly at ker empty body, I thought I felt the rushing of air as ker *kahina* slipped past me to wander the world.

Don't worry, I thought it said to me as it passed. *I am still here. I will always be here.*

VOICE:
Caitlyn Koda-Schmidt of the Sa

I SCREAMED.

The yelp of fright and terror came involuntarily as I felt myself going over the edge of the AnglSaiye cliff. Then the wings of Ely's plane caught the air, the engine coughed and roared like a mythical dragon. The wind shrieked in my ears, through the guy wires and over the canvas panels, giving voice to its own fright at seeing this machine invading its domain.

The goggles over my eyes fit poorly, and the cold, rushing air made me squint tearily at the dizzying sight. We were a hundred feet over the waves, with nothing between the bay and us but empty air, with the clouds rushing by just above so close I almost felt I could reach out and touch them.

It was terrifying. It was glorious.

It was noisy as hell.

"Bet you thought you were about to meet VeiSaTi there for a second," Ely hollered, turning his head from the pilot's seat in front of me. His hair whipped around the edges of his leather helmet.

"I still do," I yelled back. The smell of exhaust made

me lose my breath for a moment. "But I'm enjoying this while it lasts."

Ely gave a laugh that the wind tore away. "Don't worry. I told Linden—this flying beauty's fixed this time. Got some fine steel from up north last shipment. Had the engine going for hours last week. Made a successful run around the island, too." A gust of wind caught us—the plane rose ten meters in an instant, then fell again. I nearly threw up, gulping with the motion, and Ely laughed again.

Ely turned the rudder, flaps creaked and moved, and we began a long, slow bank to the right. The steep hills ringing the bay swung by in front of us at an angle. The engine's pitch rose a half-tone and we began to rise, higher and higher, until AnglSaiye's summit lay far below and behind us. Underneath me, the headlands rolled and the winding, green ribbon of the Loud passed away into haze.

I relaxed the death grip I had on the edges of my padded wooden seat and actually relaxed slightly. We were still flying, Ely seemed confident even if I wasn't, and we were moving faster than anything I'd ever seen before.

I actually began to have some hope.

Half an hour or so later, we passed the confluence of the Loud and Green Rivers. Not long after, in the distance, I saw the shape of the Rock. The engine continued to roar, defiant. Ely was humming some tune, obviously enjoying himself. We banked and turned toward the rising green hills to the left, where TeNon lay just south of North Lake.

The winding river that flowed through the valley had carved terraced hillsides on its own way to the Loud. The old Miccail highroad moved through the valley as well, with seven arcing bridges that crossed the river's curving path.

And we saw them. Like a dark mass of insects, they swarmed in the middle of the valley leading from TeNon, following the highroad that arrowed toward the Rock: the QualiKa. They had seen us as well—as Ely descended and swung into a gentle turn to take us over them, I saw the glinting of *lansa* and upturned faces. I looked for RenSa among them but didn't see ker, though I could make out, on a *konja* to the front of the army, the banner of the crescent moon, and I knew that must be CosTa. "Set us down over there!" I called out to Ely, tapping him on the shoulder and pointing toward an open field near them.

"I see it!" Ely called back, and we began to descend. As we came down, the land began to rush by us, a streak of green and sepia on either side, then the wheels touched with a lurch and a bounce that slammed me back into my seat. The engine roared even louder, and the plane wheeled around hard before Ely cut the engine.

The sudden silence and stillness was disconcerting. I sat there for a moment, stunned, as Ely let out a whoop that echoed from the hills. "That was *fantastic!*" he said. "Caitlyn, I never thought . . ."

He stopped. The *konja* with the crescent moon of Quali had pounded up to within a spear's throw of us, clods of dirt flying from its hooves, and others were following. A familiar form was clinging to waist of the rider.

I pulled myself from the cockpit and jumped down to the ground. My ears were still ringing with the engine's roar. "CosTa!" I called to the rider of the *konja*. "I've come from the SaTu of AnglSaiye, and I must speak with you." And then I spared a moment to smile at the person behind her. "RenSa," I said. "It's good to see you again. I'm going to need your help . . ."

VOICE:
RenSa

I COULD HEAR THE RAW DISBELIEF IN COSTA'S voice.

"You say that a *kahina* in the sky will throw a huge stone at us and crush us, *all* of us." CosTa spread her arms to encompass the valley, thousands of strides from east to west, in which the QualiKa masses stood—more CieTiLa gathered than I had ever seen before, but still tiny against the immensity of the land. Then she laughed at CaitlynSa. "Your *kahina* is more powerful than GhazTi Himself, then."

"No," Caitlyn said, "but what I'm saying is the truth. This has nothing to do with your gods, but with *technology*." Caitlyn used the human word as ke gestured to Ely's flying machine behind ker. Ely stood beside the stinking thing of wood and cloth and graystone, ringed by QualiKa *lansas* and looking terrified. CoSTa blinked at the sound of the human speech, harsh after the soft CieTiLa syllables. "This 'stone' is from a . . . a made thing," Caitlyn continued. "A machine like this one, only far larger." Ker gaze caught mine, pleading. "RenSa, please. I don't speak your language well enough. You've seen Ghost. You know our history. Tell CoSTa that this is real."

But I found it difficult to comprehend myself—a piece of Ghost's ship, so huge and moving so fast that it would destroy everything in this valley when it struck, that the very ground would tremble for a day's walk around . . . I looked at the green walls of the hills, blued with haze and distance, and at the swelling ranks of the QualiKa. All of this gone in an instant? How could that be? It seemed impossible.

"I've talked with this *kahina*, yes," I told CoSTa. "The human history says that before they came down here they dwelled in the clouds in a machine so large that it took a day to walk from end to end, all of it made of graystone. They say that the star we sometimes see moving at night across the sky is that crippled machine, so far away that it appears only as a speck of light. You know the history our sages tell as well as I do, CoSTa: how the humans first came down in graystone fireships, how we watched them carve the rock by the Black Lake with lances of burning light." I touched my bandaged shoulder. "Even if the humans can no longer do that, we still know how well their rifles can kill from a distance, and we've seen and felt the awful explosions when they mine the rocks from which they make graystone.'' I shivered. "I know that CaitlynSa is telling you what ke believes to be the truth, CosTa,'' I said finally. "Ke would not lie to you.''

"The stone will crush all of you the way your foot smashes a scuttler into the ground,'' Caitlyn said. "CosTa, you must believe me.''

"*I* don't believe ker,'' JairTe spoke disdainfully from alongside CosTa. "Even if it were possible, GhazTi would not allow it. The flatfaces are frightened of us, that's all. They would do anything to keep us away. This is another lie, another trick.''

CosTa listened to the Te gravely, then inclined her head to Caitlyn. "Why would you come here to tell me this?'' she asked. "JairTe is right: This could be a deception, so that I don't take my people to the Black Lake.''

"If it's a deception, then all you lose is a day,'' Caitlyn answered. "You should be safe once you're over the ridge, but there's not much time. You must move your people quickly out of the valley. If I'm wrong, then tomorrow you can march toward Black Lake again.''

"And if there is no lie, then why even tell me? Why not let it happen?'' CosTa moved closer to Caitlyn, staring at ker with that compelling gaze that I'd felt myself many times in the last several days, that dominant presence.

"Because that would not be the *KoPavi*,'' Caitlyn answered. "Because one violence only leads to another. Because my SaTu and I believe that what's been done in the past is wrong. Destroying the QualiKa and the Cha'akMongTi will not solve anything; it will only give your people a hatred for us that would last centuries. Because . . .'' Caitlyn paused. Ker teeth, so white and strange in ker flat, ugly human face, caught at ker lower lip. A breath lifted ker shoulders. "Because if it *does* happen, and I have saved your life and those of the QualiKa, I would ask you to return to TeNon. We've given you this warning because it's right to do so; we can't force you to do anything. But we ask you as one gift in return: Go back to *TeNon*. I will bring the Family leaders there. Let the Sa—human and CieTiLa—talk with both you and the Families.

Terrible mistakes have been made, by all of us. Give us the time we need to find a path.''

"There it is," JairTe grunted in mocking laughter. "The Sa lies. They are afraid of us, as I said. A rock from the sky . . . *phaah.* My *brais* feels nothing moving there.''

My *brais* felt nothing either—even while understanding Caitlyn's warning and knowing that we would see nothing until the instant before impact, biology and instinct told me not to worry: *Your Sun's Eye is quiet; there is nothing dangerous above you.* I could sense CosTa's own indecision, and then she moved.

Her hand flicked out, a quick blur, and she lifted Cailtyn by the throat so that the human's booted feet barely touched the ground. Caitlyn's skin puckered around CosTa's opened clawtips; ker eyes were wide, ker mouth open gasping for air, and four rivulets of blood drooled down Caitlyn's neck onto the collar of ker *shangaa*. CosTa's footclaws rose, as if she were about to kick out and disembowel Caitlyn.

Calmly, CosTa looked again at the valley, at the QualiKa Hands waiting patiently for her orders, at the thickets of *lansa* dark in the sun, at the QualiKa ready to kill Ely should the Cha'akMongTi gesture to them. CosTa glanced up, squinting into the light with her seeing eyes as if she could witness something hurtling toward her, but there was nothing. Nothing but a still, deep blue brushed with white.

CosTa looked down. Looked at me. "Tell me, RenSa," she said, still holding Caitlyn in her deadly embrace, the muscles in her arm quivering from the effort. Caitlyn's face had gone red as ke struggled to breathe, and ker hands pulled at CosTa's arm desperately. "Is *this* why you were sent to me? So you would be here now?"

As she said the words, I felt their truth. "It may be," I told her. "Only VeiSaTi knows for certain. Maybe I was sent to remind you that the Sa are willing to die for their beliefs and the *KoPavi* when it's necessary, as did the Sa Beneath The Water.''

CosTa's brow furrowed, and I could not tell if it was anger. "RenSa, when I kill this human Sa, what will you do then?"

I tried to look at CosTa, not Caitlyn. I didn't move, didn't try to interfere—what could I have done? "I will mourn ker death," I said, "because ke will have died honorably. Then as the *KoPavi* says, I will build a pyre for ker and set it alight. I will make a sacrifice for Caitlyn's *kahina* and pray to VeiSaTi that you are right and my SaTu and Caitlyn wrong, and then I will follow you to Black Lake. And when the stone comes from the sky to kill you—and it will come, CosTa; it will come—I will die with you."

CosTa gave a wild cry. I saw muscles bunch in her calf, and she lifted her foot from the ground, kicking suddenly toward Caitlyn's body. I waited for the blood and the entrails.

But CosTa's footclaw stopped, trembling, just touching Caitlyn's *shangaa* at ker abdomen. For a moment, the tableau held. Then CosTa lowered her foot to the ground and relaxed her claws. Caitlyn fell to the ground, gasping for breath, while the paleness slowly returned to ker face.

"We will leave the valley," CosTa said, raising her voice so that the Hands heard her command. JairTe's protest died with CosTa's warning gaze as she pointed to nearest hills. "We will go there. We lose nothing by waiting . . . and we will see if the Sa's stone comes from the sky."

VOICE:
Ishiko Allen-Shimmura of the Rock

WHEN I WALKED INTO HER OFFICE UNAN-nounced, Geema was reading what looked to be a letter, which she refolded hastily and stuffed into her desk drawer. She looked up at me with an annoyed grimace as I shut the door behind me.

"You've forgotten how to knock?" There was a flush in her too-perfect cheeks. She brushed back short hair with her fingers, as if ridding them of the feel of the paper, and arranged herself stiffly on her chair. Her frown sent all the carefully prepared words tumbling into oblivion.

"I'm pregnant," I told her without preamble, my hands folded in front of me as if I were already cradling the swelling mound of my stomach. "I . . . I wanted you to know that before I told the rest of the Family."

"Through the Sa," Geema said, the last word nearly spat out. Of course she knew that my pregnancy was because I'd been with Caitlyn—Geema always knew whenever someone stayed overnight with one of the Family or when one of us wasn't home all night. She knew I hadn't been with anyone else.

I nodded. "*Hai*," I told her. "Through Caitlyn." Her mouth tightened, and I rushed to finish before she spoke, the rest tumbling out of me like water released from a dam. "I don't need your approval, Geema. That's not why I'm here. I'm happy to have another chance to have a child, and I'm happy that it was through Caitlyn, through someone that I care about. All I need to know, Geema, is whether you're going to treat me the way you treated Komoko, because I won't stay here to take the abuse. Komo didn't deserve the grief you gave her, and I don't either. Being part of a new life is a wonderful thing, Geema, and it's time we realized as a Family that we need to accept the way things are on Mictlan and work with them, not defy them. I don't know what happened between you and O'Sa Anaïs so long ago. I don't know who or what poisoned you against the Sa or how you came to be so sour about everything, and I don't care. Look around you—the world has changed, and you can't keep it the way it once was. The Sa aren't going to go away, and quite frankly, we need them." I raised my left hand, displaying the unbending, fused ridges that were my fingers. "The other Families may not say anything to you, Geema. You're the Eldest, and they're used to staying silent when you talk. But I hear them. I hear the jokes they make about our Family and the little 'deformities' most of us have. I notice that at the Gathers, we're often the last ones chosen. I notice that we're the smallest of the Families now, when once that wasn't true. Do you really want us to die out like the Koda-Levins? A hundred years from now, do you want there to be only four Families? Maybe it will just be you left, Geema, still looking the same and all alone.''

The words and my vehemence ran dry. The silence was loud, and Geema's sharp, unblinking gaze would not let me look away. "Are you finished now?" she asked. "That was a pretty speech, and I'm sure you worked very hard at putting it together." She clapped her hands together in mock applause as I felt heat rising from my neck to my ears. Not trusting myself to say more, I turned and started to walk away from her. I was ready to leave Geema, to leave the compound and my Family and go to AnglSaiye. But Geema's voice brought me to a stop, my right hand on the knob of her door.

"I'm sorry, Ishiko," she said.

"Geema?" I didn't move. I could feel the cold glass of the knob in my palm.

"I'm not apologizing for feeling the way I feel. I'm saying I'm sorry that you think I'd hurt you. That's not what I want, ever."

Now I turned, though I kept my hand on the knob. "It's not just me you're hurting, Geema. It's the whole Family."

"I don't believe that. All I've ever done is for the sake of the Family."

"Then, for the sake of the Family, admit that the time's come to change—not just with us and the Sa, but with the Miccail, too."

She didn't answer. I opened the door and started out.

"Ishiko," she said behind me, "congratulations on your pregnancy. It's been too long since I last held a child of yours, and I'm looking forward to doing it again."

I looked at her. An uncertain smile gave her doll's face an animation it usually lacked. I tried to smile back at her, and nodded.

I shut the door.

VOICE:
RenSa

"I HAVE TO GO TO THE ROCK NOW," CAITLYN SAID. "They have to know what we've done, and I have to convince them to come to TeNon with me"

"They're not going to like it," I told ker. "Euzhan will have apoplexy."

"Maybe not," ke insisted. "Maybe this time she'll realize that it's past time to make peace. She needs to know that CosTa has made a concession, and that she needs to make one as well. Tell CosTa that I must go, that I will return with a delegation from the Families . . ."

I stood on the crest of the eastern hillside of the valley with CosTa and JairTe. On the steep slope below us, the rest of the QualiKa were struggling upward. Down along the river field, Ely's machine was moving, a faint whining roar coming to my ears as the plane accelerated impossibly, a thin trail of black smoke following. It lifted into the air, the wings dipping right, then left, and then it rose, moving higher and higher until it was above our heads, moving downriver toward the Loud and the Black Lake. Sitting behind CosTa on her *konja*, we watched for several breaths, then CosTa clucked her tongues at the *konja* and turned the mount, starting to head down the far side of the hill.

Behind us, I heard a percussive cough, and then silence.

I twisted around in the saddle. It was easy to find Cailtyn and Ely: The smoke trail of their flying machine had become thick and dark. The machine was falling, wings spinning in the air, and there was no noise, no noise at all. "Caitlyn!" I screamed to the sky: uselessly, helplessly. Just before the machine struck the ground, it straightened and leveled out, and the engine coughed once.

Then it disappeared behind trees and low hillocks near the river. A faint sound like splintering wood came to us, and a column of smoke rose.

It all seemed so small and distant, so sudden and quiet, yet in my heart I felt a sudden dread.

"CosTa!" She had stopped, watching the accident herself. Now she looked at me. "I have to go to ker. They may be hurt."

She looked at me with her calm, wise eyes. "The human Sa's stone is coming, RenSa. They are alive and can leave the valley themselves, or they can't and are dead. One or the other. If what the human said is true, there's no time for you to go after them—the sun has already fallen halfway down the sky, and they said the stone would strike before it touched the western hills." She cocked her head slightly. "Or are you saying now that you think the human lied?"

"No." I glanced again at the plume of the smoke. JairTe watched us from his *konja*, not a stride away, restless. "I didn't lie. I'm certain the stone will come, but there still may be time, if I take your *konja*."

"And then the Sa rides away to AnglSaiye, leaving us," JairTe spoke, leather creaking under him. "Maybe that's the trick, CosTa. Maybe the flatfaces *want* us over the ridge, because that's where this stone of theirs is really going to land. Maybe RenSa is only looking for ker own escape, and this was the plan they devised to accomplish it."

"CosTa," I said, not even looking at the Te. "The *KoPavi* gives the Sa the responsibility to sacrifice. We're taught that sometimes we must even give ourselves, as did the Sa Beneath The Water—because that is what is demanded of us. I'm not afraid to die with you. I promise you that if I can, I will come back to you." I reached out, showing her my hand with the claws hidden, then touched her face, staring into her eyes. "I would come back to you because that is I what I would most want to do, CosTa. But

CaitlynSa is out there, and ke needs me, also. *We* need ker."

"Ke's a flatface," JairTe scoffed.

"And ke is a Sa and thus part of me," I answered, still looking only at CosTa. "As will be the child I have given you, CosTa." I saw myself reflected in her eyes. "Let me go, CosTa. Let me try."

CosTa clasped my hand in her own. Abruptly, she swung down from her *konja*. Standing alongside the mount, she handed the stiff leather reins to me.

"Go," she said.

CONTEXT:
Caitlyn Koda-Schmidt of the Sa

"CAITLYN?"

The voice was faint and came from some great distance. It was very dark. The sunlight had vanished.

"Caitlyn?"

Caitlyn felt something brush against ker face. Ke tried to slap at it, but ker hand didn't seem to work. Ke tried to open ker eyes, but the eyelids were glued shut with a sticky substance that only yielded slowly. The light, when it finally came, was nearly unbearable. Ker head pounded with its impact.

"Caitlyn?"

"What, damn it?" ke said, and ker voice was harsh and cracked, and ke tasted blood in ker mouth. Ke tried opening ker eyes again.

Ke was looking up at the sky. Someone's face was framed against the light, and one of the wings of Ely's plane ran a black diagonal against the thin clouds. Ke could smell something burning nearby. "Ely?" ke said.

"*Hai*," Ely said. His silhouette moved closed to Caitlyn,

and ke saw Ely's face in reflected light. Ke didn't like the frightened concern ke saw in the man's eyes. "How are you?"

Caitlyn took inventory, and had to bite ker lip to stop from screaming when ke tried to move ker legs. Something grated harshly in ker hip socket, and ke couldn't seem to feel ker left leg at all. When ke brought ker right hand up, ke saw white bone protruding from the skin halfway down ker forearm. Ke nearly fainted again, then, and had to take several deep calming breaths before ke could answer Ely. "I'm hurt," ke said simply. "You?"

"I was thrown clear when we first hit. I'm scraped and bruised, but I'm mobile. Let me get you out of there." Ely reached down and tried to pull Caitlyn out of the plane, and this time ke did scream from the pain, and the blackness swirled at the edges of ker vision. "No!" ke shouted. "Ely, stop! Stop!"

Ely eased Caitlyn back down, and the world slowly came back to ker. Ke licked dry, split lips. "You have to get out of here, Ely," ke told the man. "Run as fast and as hard as you can for the valley wall."

"Caitlyn—"

Caitlyn shook ker head into the protest. "I can't walk, and we won't make it if you try to carry me. You only have an hour or two, and we're sitting in the middle of Ghost's target. Someone has to get word back to AnglSaiye and the Rock about what we did here. Go on." Ke could see Ely hesitating, caught between wanting desperately to get the hell out of there and feeling guilty at leaving Caitlyn, and ke waved ker left hand at Ely. "Go!" ke said again, and finally Ely started moving away.

"Ely!" ke called after him, and heard ker stop. "When you get to the Rock, I want you to find Ishiko Allen-Shimmura. Tell her . . ." Ke stopped. There were no words to contain everything Caitlyn wanted to say. Ke closed ker eyes against the sun and tried to remember her face, her touch, her voice. Ke wondered if she would hate ker for what the Sa had done. Ke wondered . . . and ke realized that time was passing and Ely was still waiting. "Tell her that thinking of her made this easier. Tell her that. Now get out of here."

Ely tapped the side of the plane, and ke heard his footsteps moving away.

And then, for long while, ke went away.

"Caitlyn?"

A face drifted above ker, indistinct and shadowed. Whatever had been burning had gone out. The sun had moved, nearly ready to touch the edge of the western hills. "Ely, you idiot—I told you to *move!* Didn't you understand?" Ke wanted to cry, to weep from pain and frustration and anger. "Didn't you understand?"

"Caitlyn, it's RenSa."

Ke squinted upward through the blood haze, the pounding in ker head, and the fog of pain. *Hai*, there was a snout and the ridged face of a Miccail. "RenSa? You're supposed to be on the other side of the valley."

"I saw Ely's machine fall. I came to help." Ker shadow grew larger and Caitlyn felt the plane's fuselage move under RenSa's weight, jostling ker body. Ke cried out, and RenSa stopped moving.

"Damn it, RenSa. Don't you realize it's too late now? *Khudda!* You've just killed yourself."

RenSa glanced upward over ker shoulder at the sky. "I see nothing, Caitlyn. Maybe the stone will come late. Maybe it won't come at all."

"It's coming, RenSa. I know it is." Ke laughed. "So maybe SaTu Terri wasn't wrong about what was being asked of the Sa, after all."

"Let me get you out of there," RenSa answered. "I have a *konja*, and we can still."

"It's too late for that, RenSa. Can't you feel it? I can— like a spear aimed for my heart. We're already dead, RenSa."

Caitlyn felt RenSa's hands again, stroking ker hair, smoothing it away from ker face. "Then our *kahinas* will stay here to watch over this place," ke said to Caitlyn, whispering the words, ker shadow shielding ker from the aching sunlight. "We will stay here, together."

Caitlyn saw RenSa lift ker head, ker nasal vents widening as if ke were sniffing at the air. "It comes," ke said.

CONTEXT:
CosTa

CosTa FELT IT FIRST. HER BREATH WENT HEAVY in her lungs, and icy fingers stuttered down her spine, raising the hair of her spinal mane. "No, please . . ." she whispered, suddenly afraid as she never had been during all the fighting, and she craned her neck to look backward to the crest of the hills behind them, hoping to see RenSa come riding hard over the lip of the valley. She reached for JairTe at the same time, wanting the comfort of another person, but her hand never reached him.

It happened.

There was the briefest moment, the barest glimpse of fire plummeting like a god-thrown spear from the sky. In that instant, she heard the startled cries of the gathered QualiKa—"Cha'akMong-"—then the sound came.

CosTa had never heard a roar like this: the tormented screaming wail of the world itself, howling in outraged agony. The bass thundering slammed into her like a physical thing, the sound battering her again and again and again, seeming to last forever, punctuated with the sharp crack of trees splintering and rocks breaking. Over the crest of the hill and rising from the valley they'd just left, a column of darkness boiled upward, gray and sullen and turning ever darker as it blotted out the last failing light of the day.

Night came in an impossible moment, enfolded in thunder and cloud.

The ground lurched under CosTa's feet, sending her falling heavily to the ground and throwing JairTe the other way. CosTa twisted on the shaking, frantic ground, trying to see.

At the summit of the hill, the trees were flattened, crushed by an invisible hand. A thick cloud was spinning and foaming downhill toward them, like a storm-tossed wave crashing over a breakwater. As the roar subsided and the ground settled, CosTa tried to get to her feet. "Jair!" she cried.

"I'm here, my Ta," he said from somewhere, gasping, and she heard the disbelief and terror that riddled his voice. He was alongside her, unexpectedly, and then as quickly dragged her to the ground again, covering her with his own body as rocks and clods of dirt rained down from the fuming sky while the cloud of dust and dirt enveloped them. CosTa could hardly breath in the thick air, and she heard a *konja* screaming in pain from close by. A rock struck her exposed leg, and JairTe grunted as he was pelted by stones. CosTa coughed, choking and spitting out gritty dust. Her *brais* was blind and sore. The deluge of rocks subsided, and she felt JairTe's body lift from hers. Still coughing, she rose to her feet, blinking away the worst of the dirt.

Everywhere, the QualiKa were getting up in the cloying twilight. Above them, the cloud was still rising, the top now torn and smeared by the upper winds. A silence had settled on them, broken only by moans, coughing, and curses. Dust lay thick everywhere, and it was a rare person she saw who was without a cut or injury of some sort.

But they were alive.

"I have to see," CosTa said. "I have to look at this."

JairTe frowned. "Cha'akMongTi, I don't think—" he began, but she was already wading through the debris littering the slope. JairTe sighed and went after her, waving to the Hands that started to follow him. "Stay here," he said. "Make an encampment, tend to the wounded, and wait for us."

It was nearly full dark before they reached the crest of the hill, climbing over tangles of fallen trees and piles of huge stones. The land was covered by a fingertip-deep coating of fine dirt, and the air was still thick and irritating with it, bands of it falling from the sky. JairTe worried about how they were going to get down in the dark, but CosTa simply continued to climb. When she reached the top, her shoulders sagged under her torn and filthy *shangaa*. "By GhazTi . . ." she whispered, her voice husky and awed. A few seconds later, JairTe was standing alongside her.

Through the blurred filters of haze, distance, and deepening twilight, they could see the valley spread out before them, but it was no longer the valley they'd left a few hours before. A god's hand had reached down and smashed every tree, flattening them harshly to the earth, the trunks all pointing back to the center of destruction. Where the river flowed, where the highroad they'd been following crossed the flowing water with the fifth and highest bridge, the god had plunged Her hand into the soft belly of the earth, gouging out a great pit that looked to be almost a half day's walk across. The river foamed as it plunged over the steep ramparts of earth into the great hole, a mist rising from the heart of the new waterfall.

Nothing lived there. Nothing moved in all that desolation.

"By the gods . . . RenSa . . ." CosTa said, touching her stomach as she said the name.

"Ke's dead," JairTe answered. "You told ker not to leave. Ke should have listened to you."

CosTa sank to her knees in the dust, and JairTe hurried over to her. "Cos—"

CosTa shook her head, shrugging him away. "RenSa is dead, CailtynSa is dead—they're out there, in that awful hole. There's nothing we can do here." She looked up at him. "Tell the Hands that we must prepare to leave."

JairTe could barely hide the smile that came with the words. "To the Black Lake," he said, nodding. "I will go down and tell them . . ." he started to say, but her gaze had gone cold and harsh, and she stood again.

"We go to TeNon," she said to him. "As we promised

Caitlyn and RenSa. We return and wait for them to come to us.''

JairTe shivered in disbelief. "To TeNon? Cha'akMong-Ti, the flatfaces will expect us to be dead or fleeing. If we hurry to Black Lake now, we will catch them even more unprepared than we'd hoped. We can't waste this opportunity.''

CosTa stared at him. "So we should break our promise to the flatface Sa who told us of the sky stone?''

"Yes," JairTe answered heatedly. "I have been your SecondHand since you became Ta of the QualiKa, and I have never failed to do what you asked. But this time I ask you to listen to me—because I am your SecondHand, and because you have called me Te. Because we have made our hearts one. This is our moment now, Cha'akMongTi, the moment for all CieTiLa. We must take it. We must.''

CosTa backhanded JairTe across the face. The blow turned JairTe's head and sent him staggering a step backward in surprise. As he put his hand to the burning mark on his cheek in bewilderment, CosTa turned her back on him, staring again at the crater in the valley, now almost invisible in darkness.

"This is what I think," she said into the night. "If RenSa would give ker life for CaitlynSa, then there is something within the humans worth saving. Because of ker, I will keep my word. It is my gift to her *kahina*.''

CosTa turned back to JairTe. She held up the hand with which she'd struck him, palm up. "Someone has to make the first gesture, or it never stops, JairTe. Not until every last one of the humans is dead. I don't think either of us could carry the burden of all that death. Do you?''

Without waiting for an answer, she started back down the hillside to the waiting Hands. After a moment, his face still burning as if branded, JairTe followed.

BEGINNINGS

My dearest Mary,

Before this note reaches you I shall have fallen as a soldier in the cause of Irish freedom. I write to bid you a last farewell in this world.

If you really love me teach the children in your class the history of their own land, and teach them that the cause of *Caitlin Ni Uallachain* never dies. Ireland shall be free from the centre to the sea as soon as the people of Ireland believe in the necessity for Ireland's freedom and are prepared to make the necessary sacrifices to obtain it.

> —SEAN HEUSTON,
> Unit Commander of the Irish Volunteers,
> letter to his sister before his
> execution, May 1916

VOICE:
Ishiko Allen-Shimmura of the Rock

I DON'T KNOW WHAT I EXPECTED IT TO LOOK LIKE, though of course I'd had it described to me several times, starting with Ely's breathless tale on his arrival at the Rock. The picture painted for me by all the words had been different somehow. Certainly nothing had prepared me for the tremendous *scale* of it all.

Ghost's Lake was two kilometers across, and nearly circular. The *Ibn Battuta*'s tank had come down directly on the wide river winding through the valley leading to TeNon, gouging out an impossible divot in the veils of greenery, shattering an ancient highroad bridge, and laying waste to the trees for another few kilometers around the jagged circumference of the impact crater—deadwood littered the landscape, scattered like tinder. The crater had quickly been filled in by water rushing down from North Lake, creating a new body of water.

A black lake, silty and nearly opaque with the dirt and debris.

Somewhere under the still waters, under the waves ruffled by the wind's hands, were Caitlyn and RenSa.

The two Sa Beneath The Water . . .

I'd heard that some of the Miccail have already come here, visiting this valley as they once had the Black Lake near the Rock, venerating it as a sacred place. I suspect that some of us humans may do the same.

I know I will.

In the twilight, I saw a Miccail emerge from the ruffle of quick-growing reeds near the river's entrance, stepping out onto the stair-stepped, muddy flats around the lake. A

297

nasituda stood close the shore where she walked, carved with Miccail symbols that I could not read. I waved to her; after a moment, she gave a wave in return. I wondered whether she might be QualiKa, and I felt an urge to go and talk with her, to have her tell me what the speaking stone said. The child jumped inside me, and I cradled my swelling belly, watching the last sunlight turn red and orange on the tips of the wavelets—since the devastation here a few months ago, our sunsets have been particularly gorgeous. Strange to see such beauty deriving from such destruction. I started to call to the Miccail, but when I looked again, she had gone back into the reeds.

Perhaps that was just as well. There will be time for words later. There's still much healing to be done between our two species, and there are those (like Gerald and probably Geema) who will never come to forgive or forget, even if they eventually submit to change. In the fading light, I went back to the tents where Linden and the others were camped, by the foot of the hills. As I approached, I saw two people waiting for me near the SaTu's tent, one of them illuminated by some unnatural light. "Ishiko," Linden called. "Ghost's here."

Ghost wore the appearance of O'Sa Anaïs. Ke was wrapped in an orange *shangaa*, white hair wisping over the shoulders from a wrinkled, timeworn face that spoke of an open heart. "Ishiko," ke said. "You're looking well—and bigger. I wish I were going to be around to see your child."

"I wish you were too, Ghost. I still get startled every time I see my profile in a mirror, but I'll get a lot bigger yet." I rubbed the mound beneath my coat. "I was out looking at your lake," I told ker.

Ghost glanced toward the dim shores of the lake, where a flock of migrating sand skippers rested near the reeds. Life was resilient, if nothing else—in another year, this place would be fully alive again, green and noisy. "I'm sorry," Ghost said, giving me a soft, sympathetic smile. "I wish this could have ended differently. I really do."

"Caitlyn wouldn't say that. Ke'd say that things have come out better than ke had hoped. Our first meetings with

CosTa went well enough, and most of the Rock Elders understand that we need to keep the dialogue going. I think Linden and our delegation will make even more progress.''

"I'm sure you will," Ghost said. We didn't say anything for a time, listening to the quiet sounds of the river and the lake, the soft muttering of the sand skimmers as they settled for the night, the nickering of the *konja* by the wagons and the muted conversations of the other people with us. "Well, I guess it's time," Ghost said finally. "I'm glad I could say good-bye to the two of you. I hope you understand— I did what I believed I had to do. That's all."

"We understand," Linden and I said together, nearly in unison, and we smiled at each other with the serendipity. Ghost's body shimmered, and ke morphed again, this time changing to the image of Gabriela Rusack, wearing the *Ibn Battuta* dress uniform. She seemed to take a deep breath, lifting the wide shoulders of the dark blouse. Static was starting to flicker through her body and we could hear a hissing rush like a great wind in the audio. The snout of the holographic projector, set on the ground near the tent, pulsed erratically with shifting colors that played over her body. "We'll miss you, Ghost," I said to her.

I don't know if she heard me or not. "Watch," she said in her static-garbled voice. "Over there." She pointed to the sky above the eastern hills. We both looked up. In the purple twilight, a shooting star burned, arcing across the sky toward the west. In a moment, the fireball sputtered, then shattered into three separate pieces, each streaking silently westward, their passage burning in our eyes. Only a few seconds, and they had moved overhead and vanished again, beyond the valley walls toward their eventual destination well out in the vast ocean.

"Ghost—" I started to say, turning to her, but the projector had gone dead, just a hunk of metal and plastic and circuitry that would never work again, our last link with old Earth. We were truly aliens now, our fate tied to Mictlan. I patted the cold metal. "Rest well, Ghost," I whispered. Linden was still staring at the sky, where the myriad stars were appearing one by one as the sky darkened. The moon Faraway—Quali—was rising, full and bright. I touched Linden's shoulder, and ke patted my hand. As I moved away from the firelight, ke called out to me.

"Where are you going, Ish?"

"Back to the lake," I told ker. "I think . . . I just want to sit there for a while."

"Ke loved you, you know."

I smiled at ker. "I know," I said.

I left Linden and went to the shore again. In the moonlight, I sat on the rough bark of a fallen amberdrop and listened to the sound of the waves lapping at the shore, and I tried to hear in their rhythmic serenity ker voice.

APPENDIX

A BRIEF COLONY HISTORY

NOTE—Years are given in Mictlanian years, which are 1.365 Solar years. Dating is from Year 0, the year in which the colonists found themselves orbiting the planet which would become known as Mictlan.

Year 0:

The *Ibn Battuta* (the culmination of a multinational scientific effort, and crewed by approximately a thousand men and women, most of them in LongSleep compartments) arrives in the Tau Ceti system and parks in orbit above the fourth planet. The planet is largely water, with two large landmasses, one mostly in the northern hemisphere, the other nearly opposite and mostly in the southern hemisphere. Once it is determined that the planet is within acceptable Earth standards, the artificial intelligence that runs the ship—named "Ghost" by the crew members—awakens those in LongSleep. The first survey shuttle sent down returns with the surprising news: Another intelligent race evolved here. The first ruins of the Miccail's civilization are found in the southwest corner of the continent in the northern hemisphere (though not in the southern hemisphere's continent), but there seem to be no surviving members of that race. Dating of the ruins shows that none are more recent than 1,000–1,500 local years.

Following established procedure, the crew of the *Ibn Battuta* sends a message back to Earth via tachyon packet impulse, letting them know where they are and what they have found.

There was no answer. For whatever reason, there would never *be* an answer.

Year 1:

Two bases are established on the planet's surface and are rapidly growing, supplied from the *Ibn Battuta* stores via shuttlecraft. One of the two shuttles is beginning docking manuevers with the *Ibn Battuta* when a fuel relay bursts. The resulting wild acceleration slams the shuttle into the *Ibn Battuta*'s drive units. The shuttle and drive units both explode, sending shrapnel flying, which holes the living quarters of *Ibn Battuta* in several places. Nearly everyone there dies in the next few seconds. The drive units are crippled, the *Ibn Battuta* is sent reeling from its geosynchronous orbit into an elliptical, tilted one. The other shuttle, which was already docked on the *Ibn Battuta* for repairs, is destroyed. On the ship, the remaining crew members work to save the ship's computer and its links to the small colony below—they manage to maintain power to the computer and some of the ship systems, though the ship remains airless and unrepairable. The crew members aboard *Ibn Battuta* do not live long, though Ghost continues to operate the crippled computer network.

On Mictlan, there remain some twenty-four people on the two bases. The majority—six women and nine men— are located at the base in the southern hemisphere.

Year 2:

The southern base stays in contact with their northern brethren and Ghost only for another ten months. A huge storm system slams into the southern continent during that winter; when it passes, all contact with the southern base is lost. It is never again regained.

At the northern base there are only nine people: four men, five women. Akiko Koda and Shigetomo Shimmura had already formed a relationship; Rebecca Allen and Guy Levin quickly became a couple as well, as do Maria Martinez and Antonio Santos. Gabriela Rusack, while a friend to some of them, never formed another sexual relationship—she had been involved with a woman who died on the ship, and remains celibate and deliberately childless (despite considerable and growing pressure from the others) for the rest of her life. Jean Delacroix and Robert Schmidt are temporarily left outside of any relationships.

The first children of the colony are born late this year, Kaitlen Allen-Levin and Shigetomo Koda-Shimmura.

Years 4–10

Monogamy never particularly worked on Earth, where adultery is common—it doesn't work here, either, and it's much harder to hide ... Rebecca Allen and Shigetomo Shimmura become lovers, and the pressure splits apart the Allen-Levin and Koda-Shimmura relationships. It's also obvious to the colonists that from a strictly biological point of view, monogamy dangerously limits their genetic diversity. A few point out that the storm of four years past may have destroyed only the southern colony's computer and radio links to the *Ibn Battuta*, and that the people there could well be still alive: They argue that there is no need to do anything drastic. But as the months continue to go by without contact, their protests are increasingly weak. Gabriela steadfastly refuses to reproduce, but Robert and Jean are (unprotestingly, it should be noted) drawn into the task of survival.

Rebecca and Shigetomo have a child in Year 6. So do Akiko and Robert. The breeding program is put into the virtual hands of Ghost, whose holographic image can be transmitted down to the colony from *Ibn Battuta* whenever the ship's new orbit takes it overhead. This is not an easy decision, and there are many emotional, angry confrontations in succeeding years as the program solidifies. Still, they all realize that the next generation will find whatever arrangements they make "normal." Chemical birth control is impossible—the technology doesn't exist. The only effective birth control measures are barrier methods, and the production facilities for these are limited. It hardly matters—to allow humankind to survive, reproduction is paramount. With the continuing silence from Earth, for all the colonists know they may be the only remnants of their kind left anywhere.

Despite this, the four women of the first generation will produce only fifteen progeny.

Year 11:

Gabriela becomes the first person to be shunned, ostensibly in punishment for her refusal to participate in the breeding program. This first shunning was for six months; afterward, she still refused—angrily—to participate.

Year 16:

The first of the third generation is born to Adari Koda-Shimmura: Tozo. Given the breeding program, it's obvious that the old method of naming children with the paired names of their mother and "father" is ludicrous, given the fact that—without blood typing or DNA tests—the identity of the father is questionable in many cases. The birth of the Families is in the decision to give only the maternal name to the offspring of any union: children "belong to" the mother alone, and to her extended family.

Year 21:

Gabriela is declared shunned once more, this time for establishing a relationship with a younger woman in the colony, Adari Koda-Shimmura. Gabriela is banished from the colony altogether, living apart from the rest on the Rock and having little to no contact with them. The rift between Gabriela and the others (with few exceptions) would never be closed.

Year 23:

A furious storm much like the one that struck the southern base rakes the settlement and six of the original nine colonists (Akiko, Maria, Jean, Robert, and Shigetomo) are killed, along with three of the second generation. The sudden population decrease is frightening. Any last remnants of the old social structure are swept away with the furious winds. The first of the Family compounds arises: The Koda clan builds what will eventually become the Koda-Schmidt compound. Long ago, the shuttles' lasers had carved out a series of interconnected caverns with several entrances in a large hill alongside the river—the hill was actually one large rock, much like Uluru in Australia. The Koda clan partioned out one cavern as their own; the other new Families quickly followed suit. Over the next several years, a complex series of buildings were erected: mostly underground, some above, but all connected to each other in a warren of passages.

Years 39–41:

A disease, evidently mutated from some Mictlanian virus, runs through the group, killing mostly those eight or younger: the Bloody Cough. The illness devastates the new fourth generation in particular, and leads to another drastic reduction in population. In the next few years, nearly everyone who shows the symptoms which gave the disease its name dies. However, the virulence of the plague eventually lessens. Some who catch the Bloody Cough survive. Still, through succeeding generations, almost two of every five children born will succumb to this plague.

Year 50:

Kumar Allen-Levin and Kemeul Koda-Levin embark on an ocean voyage to reach the southern continent and find any survivors of the lost colony there. They are never heard from again.

Year 66:

The skeletonized body of the last of the original colonists, Gabriela Rusack, is found in her cabin several kilometers from the Rock.

Year 96:

The last of the second generation, Robert Allen-Delacroix, dies.

Year 101:

The well-preserved body of a Miccail Sa, or midmale, is found in the bog near the Rock. It is given to Anaïs Koda-Levin, one of the two doctors in the colony, to examine and dissect. Anaïs will soon discover that ke, too, is a Sa.

Year 102:

A Miccail Sa is born on the island of AnglSaiye. The discovery is made that the "grumblers" are actually the much-changed remnants of the supposedly extinct Miccail, and that certain tribes of the grumblers have retained a veneer of their culture.

A human colony is founded on AnglSaiye by Anaïs Koda-Levin, Elio Allen-Shimmura, and Máire Koda-Schmidt after Anaïs is shunned by the Families on the Rock for her relationship with Máire. Others of various Families join them over the next few years.

Year 103:

A child is born to Máire Koda-Schmidt. Gabriela, as she is named, is the first human child conceived via a human Sa.

Year 120:

With other human and Miccail midmales being born, Anaïs Koda-Levin forms the Community of Sa, both human and Miccail, roughly based on the tenets of the ancient Miccail Sa community on AnglSaiye. Anaïs will become known as O'Sa (Great Sa) and be revered as the Second Founder.

Year 125:

A cooperative venture of Miccail and humans (mostly from AnglySaiye) begins the long undertaking to repair the old Miccail system of highroads and wayhouses.

Year 140:

Despite the increased interaction between Miccail and human, there are still occasional violent clashes between the two species, usually involving land and resources, to which both groups feel they have claim. In 140, the QualiKa ("Souls of the Small Moon") sect is formed by the charismatic NagTe, who claims divine inspiration from GhazTi, one of the darker gods in the Miccail pantheon. The symbol of the sect is a crescent moon tattooed on the chest. The QualiKa preach separatism, and violent confrontation if necessary. In the years following, there will be skirmishes between the human colonies and the QualiKa. especially in the mountainous region around the lakes named Castor and Pollux, where iron ore and copper deposits have been discovered.

Year 149:

Despite protests from the Miccail, a steel-smelting operation is set up at Lake Pollux. This will eventually become known as Irontown, under control of the Elders of the Rock.

Year 164:

Anaïs Koda-Levin dies while ending the Hannibal Massacre. In addition to Anaïs, five other humans die there, along with a dozen or more Miccail, including NagTe, the leader of the QualiKa. Afterward, each group would point to the other when asked who started the hostilities. All that can be certain is that the precipitating event was when Mahesh Allen-Shimmura killed a member of the QualiKa sect (though Mahesh claimed he acted in self-defense.) The situation escalates when NagTe and the QualiKa demand Mahesh's life in payment, and the Elders of the Rock adamantly refuse. The Elders of the Rock instead send an armed delegation toward the Miccail encampment; Anaïs, hearing of the original incident, hurries from AnglSaiye to defuse the escalating situation. By the time she arrives, the fighting is already under way. Anaïs, despite her advanced age, insists on walking openly down the highroad between the encampments in company with a mixed delegation of human and Miccall; she is struck, undeniably, by rifle fire from one of the humans, though no one will admit to having fired the shot. The striking down of the O'Sa horrifies both sides. Refusing to be moved from where she had fallen until she meets with the leaders of both sides, the mortally wounded Anaïs negotiates a peace.

Anaïs dies two days later in Hannibal. Over the next several years, perhaps as a result of the loss of NagTe, the QualiKa movement loses momentum, with only occasional eruptions of trouble since.

Year 166:

Two sisters, Lev and Henriette Koda-Schmidt, and two brothers, Agadir and Algernon Martinez-Santos, set out for the southern continent in an oceangoing sailing craft, leaving from the island of AnglSaiye. As with the expedition a century earlier, none of them are ever heard from again.

Year 168:

Euzhan becomes the Eldest of the Allen-Shimmura family after the death of Andrea Allen-Shimmura.

Year 185:

The granddaughter of NagTe, Cos, is born. She will, in the first years of the third century, revive the QualiKa, and will be called CosTa.

Year 200:

Fianya—a Sa—is born into the Allen-Shimmura family, even though the Allen-Shimmura expressly forbid their Family members to have sexual relations with the Sa. Fianya will die two years later, after Euzhan refuses to give her to the Sa Community on AnglSaiye as custom demands.

APPENDIX

ORIGINS OF THE QUALIKA

The QualiKa ("Souls of the Small Moon") sect was formed by the Miccail NagTe in Year 140 of the human colonization. NagTe, depending on who is telling the story, was either a charismatic leader led by the visions of the Miccail deity GhazTi, or a murderous fanatic bent on destroying the human element on Mictlan. The reality, as is often the case, probably lies somewhere between the two.

His birth is announced on a stele located slightly east of the Rock. The dating of the stele entry is Fourth Quali, Six Finger Winter, which translates to the early spring of Year 119. NagTe was eldest child of the TeTa who ruled there, FasTa and SefiTe, who were also known to the humans as Dottó and Whitetuft, both of whom had once saved O'Sa Anaïs's life when ke was shunned by the colony of the Rock. NagTe no doubt led a relatively privileged early life, and as eldest stood to possibly inherit the title of Te upon his father's death.

NagTe claimed that he had visions from the Shadow-World from earliest childhood, with many of the prophetic dreams involving the major deity GhazTi. However, he experienced a true spiritual epiphany in Year 138, when his father, SefiTe, was killed by the human Srivaya Martinez-Santos, who was a member of a mapping and exploratory team from the Rock searching for copper and iron deposits. Details again vary depending on who tells the story . . .

THE HUMAN VERSION:

The tale brought back to the Rock was that VarTe and a large contingent of his XeXa—including NagTe—came

to the human encampment late in the day, when only Srivaya and Kuro Allen-Shiummura, another team member,
were present. The Miccail chieftain threatened the two humans and was obviously distressed with the invasion of his
territory. Hopelessly outnumbered, Srivaya and Kuro were
in fear of their lives, and when SefiTe showed his claws
and advanced on Srivaya, she fired on the Miccail Te, killing him instantly.

One of the XeXa immediately slew Srivaya with a foot
strike—this was NagTe, according to Kuro's retellings of
the story in later life, when NagTe became infamous among
the humans. Kuro also fired, wounding or killing another
of the XeXa, and fled with the Miccail in hot pursuit.

Kuro managed to elude the Miccail in the forest, find his
other companions, and warn them. Fighting off occasional
ambushes from SefiTe's people, they fought their way from
SefiTe's territory and returned to the Rock.

QUALIKA VERSION:

According to QualiKa folklore, SefiTe, accompanied
only by his eldest child NagXe, learned that several humans
had invaded their territory without coming to the TeTa as
they should. Worse, they were violating the land, digging
into the earth without the proper rituals and thus risking
the spiritual well-being of all the CieTiLa by disturbing the
earth *kahina*. SefiTe had come to offer his people's help in
assisting them with the rituals, to show them how to appease the *kahina* so that there would be no earthquakes or
other repercussions, and to forgive them for their impolite-
ness in not coming before the TeTa.

When they arrived at the encampment, SefiTe and
NagXe initially believed the area to be deserted, until they
heard noise from inside one of the tents. Entering, they
found the two humans engaged in sexual intercourse. The
humans, lost in their passion, did not notice the CieTiLa
until SefiTe spoke in the CieTiLa tongue, telling them (as
any CieTiLa would who had interrupted friends in the middle of things) to finish and that he and his eldest would

speak with them afterward. And, with the casual attitude CieTiLa had toward sex, they started to crouch down there to wait.

But the humans had already broken apart, shrieking like crazy animals and confusing SefiTe and NagXe. The woman reached for her weapon. Before SefiTe or NagXe could react, she had pointed it at them and fired. NagXe saw the side of his father's head explode, and he was spattered by brains and blood. Instinctively, NagXe lashed out at the naked human female, his footclaw eviscerating the woman in one strike as the human male fled the tent shrieking.

NagXe would have pursued, but he could not. At the moment he'd slain the female, the strongest vision he'd ever experienced clutched him, holding him tightly, and GhazTi came to him . . .

Where is the truth in all this? (For there are other alternate versions of the event as well, though none by eyewitnesses.) The truth can never be known with any certainty, since both surviving participants in the event, NagTe and Kuro Allen-Shimmura, are long dead. In all likelihood, both designed their versions of the tale to fit their own agendas.

True or not, the vision that NagTe claims came to him then was the genesis of the QualiKa society he would form just a few years later. In that vision, GhazTi appeared in His Spirit Warrior aspect holding the *LansaTi*, the God-Spear. The horn of crescent Quali was set in his forehead as his *brais*; a gigantic, perfectly rounded wingclaw feather was carefully braided into His spinal mane.

Reaching down to where SefiTe's body lay huddled on the ground, GhazTi dipped a finger in SefiTe's pooling lifeblood and with it traced the image of a crescent Quali on NagTe's chest. Then GhazTi bent over the dead human and lapped at her lifeblood with his tongues. Finally, GhazTi embraced NagTe, kissing him fiercely, and NagTe could taste the metallic sourness of the human blood. The blood burned in him, rushing through his body; when it reached his chest, where GhazTi had sketched the sign of Quali in his father's blood, his skin was seared from the inside, burning the sign of Quali forever into NagTe's flesh.

"The CieTiLa have abandoned the ways the gods have taught them," GhazTi said, His voice as harsh as rocks, as stern as a thundercloud. "Too few perform the old rites, too few observe *KoPavi*, the path of the Open Door, and that has weakened all CieTiLa. You must bring the CieTiLa back to *KoPavi*, or the CieTiLa will fall into human ways and be lost. You have felt how CieTiLa blood and human blood cannot mix together. They will try to change the *KoPavi*, they will claim our land as their own, and they will use their tricks to change the CieTiLa into something else. I will send you signs and omens to keep you to the *KoPavi*, but you must be alert and have the courage to stand with the *KoPavi* against even the resistance of other CieTiLa.

"I tell you this: The earth will drink blood. The *kahina*, the spirits of earth and fire and air, will all rise up with you. You are Cha'akMongTi, the GodMouth, and your words will be my words. You are CheVeyo, the Warrior Spirit. You are also LansaTi, the GodSpear, and you will prepare the *KoPavi* with blood if you must.

"If you fail, it will tell you that the CieTiLa are still too weak, still lost from your long sleep, and I will take you with me into the ShadowWorld. But I will eventually come to another of your line, Te or Ta, and I will make that one the new Cha'akMongTi."

So saying, GhazTi picked up the body of SefiTe in one hand and devoured it in a single gulp, swallowing it whole. Thunderclouds formed in the sky above Him, the earth shivered underfoot, and a thousand *kahina* in the shape of lightnings wrapped themselves around Him and bore GhazTi back to the ShadowWorld. NagTe was knocked unconscious as the electrical bolts snapped around him, and did not recover for a full hand of days.

That was the vision of NagTe, the beginning of the QualiKa, who were named for the moon symbol burned into NagTe's chest.

We know the historical facts of the next few decades all

too well. In the wake of SefiTe's death, FasTa declined to claim another of the Xe as her mate, and so as eldest child of the Ta, NagXe became NagTe to rule with her. But the vision still troubled him, and by Year 140, NagTe had left his home with a small group of followers, the seed of the community that would become the QualiKa, and wandered the land for some time.

NagTe sought out the Miccail of the territories through which they traveled, talking with them of the *KoPavi*, relaying his vision, performing the rites and making the required sacrifices. Each time he stopped, NagTe gained more followers. Eventually, he came to AnglSaiye, and for a few years dwelt there with his followers. As once had his parents, he became a friend of Anaïs, the human O'Sa, and he helped ker to reestablish many of the old customs of the Sa, so that they had their own *KoPavi*. However, he could see that O'Sa Anaïs had a personality as charismatic and dominant as his own, and NagTe realized that the Community of Sa, both human and Miccail, would never completely align itself with his vision of the *KoPavi*. In the last few months of his time at AnglSaiye, in Year 151, there were clashes between the QualiKa and the human settlers of AnglSaiye, and with much sadness, O'Sa Anaïs eventually ruled that NagTe and his followers were to be shunned, banishing NagTe and the QualiKa from the island. NagTe refused to leave, however, and the QualiKa were forcibly removed in a violent incident that left two humans, the FirstHand of the Miccail Sa, and three of the QualiKa dead. NagTe and O'Sa Anaïs exchanged bitter, harsh words before the QualiKa were taken away from the island.

For the next several years, there were regular bloody encounters between the QualiKa and the humans. The symbol of the crescent small moon became feared by the humans, and many of the Families began to regard all Miccail with suspicion. Like similar human apocalyptic sects, the QualiKa were roused by the fundamentalist passion and fervor of their beliefs in the *KoPavi*, and this passion often manifested in fury: both toward the human society, as well as toward those Miccail who refused to follow the *KoPavi* as preached by NagTe. The violence escalated, reaching a zenith in Xear 164 with what would later be called the Hannibal Massacre.

When work crews from the Rock arrived at the point where the Green River met the old Miccail highroad and began to build a small settlement as a shipping point for ore from the Twin Lakes region to the north, the outcry from NagTe was immediate and loud. The humans had asked not asked permission of the TeTa of that territory, had not performed any of the rites needed to appease the *kahina* of the earth or the river, and the location of Hannibal might disturb the traditional migratory route of the nik-nik, whom the Miccail hunted in the fall. The *KoPavi* was being ignored, NagTe ranted; the humans ignored NagTe and continued building.

Frustrated, NagTe led a group of over a hundred of his followers to Hannibal. Afterward, each group would point to the other when asked who started the hostilities.

The precipitating event leading to the final confrontation was the killing of a QualiKa by Mahesh Allen-Shimmura. Mahesh claimed that the act was pure self-defense, that the QualiKa attacked him as he walked down the highroad toward Hannibal. This is possibly true, but Mahesh was one of the more militant in attitude toward the QualiKa of the already unsympathetic Allen-Shimmura Family. The QualiKa, for their part, claimed that the murder was entirely unprovoked, and that is also entirely possible.

The Families in Hannibal told NagTe that he must leave; NagTe, in defiance, settled the QualiKa in tents across the highroad, refusing to depart. The situation deteriorated further when NagTe demanded that Mahesh be turned over to the QualiKa to be executed accordlng to Miccail law. NagTe insisted that the *KoPavi* was entirely clear on this, Mahesh's death being the only way reparation could be made to the offended *kahina* of the area. The Elders of the Rock, not surprisingly, given the Allen-Shimmura influence, adamantly refused when this demand was brought to them. The Elders instead dispatched an armed delegation to relieve their Family members at Hannibal. At the same

time, O'Sa Anaïs, learning of the original incident through
Ghost, departed from AnglSaiye to attempt to defuse the
worsening situation. Ke would be too late.

Mahesh was killed by one of the QualiKa while walking
sentry duty, though whether the murderer was NagTe himself remains a question. Open fighting had already begun
by the time Anaïs arrived, the QualiKa armed only with
spear, bow, and claw since the *KoPavi* did not permit them
to use captured human weapons. When Anaïs stepped
ashore at Hannibal, five more humans were already dead,
as were a dozen or more QualiKa, including NagTe, who
was seen to fall after being shot leading the charge of the
QualiKa across the highroad to where the human troops had
gathered. NagTe's lifeless body was carried from the battle
by his followers only hours before Anaïs's arrival, and
would never be seen by human eyes again.

Anaïs, despite ker advanced age, insisted on walking
openly down the highroad between the warring factions,
accompanied by a mixed delegation of human and Miccail
from AnglySaiye. For a moment, the fighting stopped as ke
approached, the gunfire and shouts fading. There would be
one last shot fired, however: the bullet struck Anaïs, who
crumpled to the stones of the highroad, clutching ker side.

The wounding of the O'Sa horrified both sides, for even
though the last meeting between NagTe and Anaïs had been
marred by anger, a deeper respect for the O'Sa remained
in NagTe's heart. He had often declared that the human Sa
were protected by the *KoPavi*, and had honored the Miccail
Sa who came to the QualiKa in their ritual wanderings, all
his own offspring being conceived through the Sa. For ker
own part, O'Sa Anaïs had always defended NagTe to ker
own people as a true visionary, insisting that the *KoPavi*
held the best path for both human and Miccail while la-
menting the violence of the QualiKa.

Anaïs refused to be moved from where ke had fallen
until the leaders of both sides were brought to ker. Ke was
visibly distraught on learning that NagTe was already dead.
However, with the force of ker personality, the mortally
wounded Anaïs negotiated a truce.

O'Sa Anaïs died two days later in Hannibal. Though the identity of ker murderer would never be known, suspicion is often placed on Micah Allen-Shimmura, then one of the Elders of the Family. Over the next few years, almost certainly as a result of NagTe's death, the QualiKa movement lost momentum and dissolved. For the next several decades, the QualiKa, if they existed at all, remained hidden.

It would remain to CosTa, NagTe's granddaughter, to revive the QualiKa.

APPENDIX

COMPARISON OF THE MICCAIL AND HUMAN SA

Despite the obvious similarity of possessing both male and female genitalia, the human and Miccail midmales are more different than alike. Some of this is grounded in the fact that both are species alien to each other, each with its own sexuality and with no possibility of cross-fertilization. Evolution is a creative artist, and the canvas of the Miccail is utterly distinct from that of the human race. Even though at first glance, both human and Miccail Sa might appear to fulfill the same function and perform in the same manner, they do not.

Even the appearance of the two types of Sa are very diverse. The Miccail Sa has a vagina well above the anus and just below the end of the spinal column, with a normal Miccail penile structure in the front. This facilitates the usual mode of the Sa-involved sexual act for the Miccail: The Miccail Sa is penetrated by the penis of the male via ker rear vaginal opening; the midmale in turn penetrates the female in much the usual manner. This double copulation is performed by all parties at the same time, rather than separately. The semen of the male passes rapidly through the vaginal sheath into a seminal canal that passes along the pelvic floor of the Sa. The canal quickly transports the semen via orgasmic muscular contractions to the Sa "prostate," where it is combined with more ejaculate from the Sa kerself and released through the midmale's penis into the female. All of this happens within seconds, the male orgasm invariably triggering the Sa's extended release a few moments later.

The human Sa, in contrast, is more traditionally her-maphoditic, with an erectile penile shaft—both shorter and thinner than that of the human male—sprouting from where the clitorial hood would normally be in a human female, the vaginal opening just below. This makes double copu-lation awkward if not impossible, and human Sa generally engage in single acts of intercourse with a male alone or a female alone. The human Sa "stores" the seminal fluid of the male within ker altered "uterus" (which also connects to the penis), where the semen is revitalized and kept active. Viable sperm can be released into the female up to three or four days later.

The ejaculate of the two species is also very different, though in both species, the midmale serves as an evolu-tionary "stabilizer." The vaginal secretions of both human and Miccail midmales act as a biological "filter" for the male semen, culling sperm carrying mutated DNA while adding prostatic acid phosphatase and fructose (an addi-tional energy source) to the remaining seminal fluid. This altered, energized semen can then be ejaculated from the midmale into the female. However, research has shown that the Miccail Sa also contribute genetic material of their own to the mix. The human Sa has no testes or prostate; the Miccail does possess a gland much like a prostate, and that gland also dispenses genetic material. Lacking the technol-ogy to study the actual genes and DNA structure involved, anything further is speculation, but we know that this ma-terial attaches itself to the head of the Miccail male's sperm, and is thus injected into the egg along with the male's ge-netic information when the egg is fertilized.

The human Sa contributes no genetic material to the mix at all. They serve only to pass to the human female a re-energized and stable version of the male's semen.

Along with the above-mentioned genetic stability, as wanderers the midmales—both Miccail and human—also serve as dispersers of new genes, the human Sa by carrying (knowingly or unknowingly) the DNA of Families from one to another and the Miccail Sa by adding their own genes to the mix. Both human and Miccail can (obviously) reproduce without the Sa, but the midmales increase the genetic diversity of their respective population, significantly decrease the occurence of mutations, and increase the viabilty of offspring, thus fulfilling their role within the reproductive process.

APPENDIX

A BRIEF COMPENDIUM OF SELECTED FLORA AND FAUNA

Amberdrop
Amberdrops are deciduous trees with purplish, thick leaves. They have multiple trunks, and a grove of them is more a single organism than a collection of individual trees. Amberdrops prefer moist soil along streams or swamps. There are several subspecies, only two of which become good-sized trees. The leaves vary from species to species, but all are characterized by the ability to seep a thick, yellowish substance. Insects are attracted to the sweet-smelling substance, and become trapped and quickly covered, so that they do not decay. By late summer, a single amberdrop tree may have "collected" several thousand insects and the occasional small bird or lizard. In fall, the leaves shrivel—forming upright cups—but do not drop from the tree, and the sap become thin and runny. The entombed insects fall into the funnel formed by the coiled leaves and are there absorbed by the tree.

Bell Root
A medicinal plant with analgesic properties. Bell root is found in dry, rocky soil, and is characterized by spiked, hard leaves and a shallow root system with knobby protrusions.

Bluefern
A common lowland plant fond of swampy or moist soil. The bluefern has thin, feathered leaves with a distinct azure cast.

Bumblewort
A furry, placental mammal about the size of a terrier. Slow, thick-bodied, the bumblewort looks clumsy as it waddles through the brush searching for the succulent roots which are its primary food source. The bumblewort has sharp claws and teeth, used for digging and tearing, and can defend itself quite well against its enemies, despite its timid appearance. Bumbleworts are generally brown with black stripes, though one sub-species is tiger-striped.

Coney
A small, agile mammal inhabiting brushy fields and forests. Coneys have the third sightless eye, and are quick to startle with changes in lighting, making swift, bounding leaps away to cover. The coney's muscular back legs are nearly twice the length of their front paws, and they are generally bipedal, reverting to four legged locomotion only in flight. Unlike their Earth namesake, the coney is not particularly rabbitlike except for the hopping flight mechanism. They have no outer ears at all, only earholes, and more resemble a meerkat than a rabbit.

Curltongue
A small, beakless bird, several species of which are brightly colored. Curltongues feed on flowering plants and amberdrop sap, sipping the nectar with their namesake long and agile tongues.

Ebonyew
A dense, dark wood with pure white grain lines. Ebonyew trees flourish well to the

south of AnglSaiye and the Rock, reaching well over a hundred feet in height, with trunks sometimes three or four meters in diameter, and a thick canopy of leaves that grows at the very summit of the tree. The wood is highly prized as durable, insect-resistant lumber, and is also sometimes used for sculpture because of its beautiful grain.

Faux-wheat · A wheatlike grain, which when milled produces a slightly sweet, coarse flour suitable for bread-making. Faux-wheat has a reddish cast, and bread made from the flour is dark.

Globe-Tree · Not a true tree at all, but more a giant fern, sometimes reaching heights of twenty-five meters. The leaves are variegated, profuse, and large, growing from ground to peak. The name comes the spiky extensions that sprout from the middle of the ferns, at the end of which grows a round fruit the size of a basketball. The inedible seedball ripens through spring and summer, until in fall it cracks explosively, the sound audible from some distance, scattering seeds up to a quarter-kilometer away. There have been reported injuries from people being hit by a globe-tree seed, though no deaths.

Goathen · A large, flightless birdlike mammal with downy feathers. Goathens can grow to the size of the Earth ostrich. The head is cluttered with several knobby extrusions, and the goathen's demeanor can be decidedly belligerent at times, especially in the wild. The goathen has been domesticated in the last several decades, and is kept both for its meat and for the thin milk it provides.

Groundslug

A large, unshelled land mollusk, dark brown with bright green irregular spots. The groundslug can range up to a meter long. The slimy covering of the groundslug is caustic, and can cause chemical burns to unprotected skin, and evidently acts as a deterrent to animals that would prey on the slow, otherwise defenseless creature.

Honeydipper

Flying insects about seven to eight centimeters in length, with thick, brightly colored bodies. Honeydippers are not hive insects, but solitary. They feed on the nectar of flowering plants, but do not process it as food. Rather, they take the nectar and deposit it around their burrow, using it as bait to lure unwary insects into range, which are then killed by specialized forearm pincers which both hold the victim and at the same time inject a fast-acting neurotoxin. Honeydipper poison is toxic to humans, though rarely life-threatening.

Ice-Borer

The bane of wintering animals. Ice-borers inhabit lakes and pools in rivers and streams. Hibernating in the muddy lake bottoms in the warmer months, they awake in late fall when ice begins to form. Ice-borers are able to detect infrared radiation via a specialized organ in the middle of their heads. When they detect heat on the ice above (usually a jaunecerf or some other animal looking for water, though careless humans are not immune), the ice-borers, usually working as a quartet consisting of two mated pairs, will rapidly use the hard, ridged spines that line their spines to open the ice around the prey animals—the spines are substantially warmer than the rest of the ice-borer, and that heat aids the ice-borer in opening the hole. Once the prey animal falls into the icy water, the ice-borers attack, gripping the animal in their strong jaws and dragging them underneath the ice to drown and be eaten. During its mating season in early winter, the ice-borers call to their potential mates in long, melancholy grunts.

Jaunecerf
A deerlike animal hunted for food by the human colonists of Mictlan. The jaunecerf has a yellowish coat in the summer, which darkens to nearly orange in winter. Like many Mictlanian animals, it has a third, sightless eye high on the forehead that registers changes in illumination, and a doubled tongue.

Land Barnacle
A shelled creature infesting trees and rocks in moist environments. The shell is much the same shape and size of the Earth sea barnacle, though the shell is smooth and brightly colored, different species sporting different colors and patterns. The land barnacle, however, is not a mollusk, but a shelled reptilian creature, feeding on fungi growing on the surface it inhabits.

Nik-Nik
The nik-nik is a fleet four-legged mammal with a light, woolly coat, large ears, and heavy, cloven hoofs. Nearly blind, the nik-nik relies on echo-locating clicking calls to navigate through the forests it inhabits—hence its name. The adult nik-nik has a series of horny spikes along the spine and down the legs which the nik-nik can raise in danger.

Pear-nut   A small, bushy fruit tree with tiny, spiky
                  leaves. The pear-nut fruit is about the size
                  of an orange, bright green when ripe, and
                  hard-shelled with a granular interior that
                  when scraped yields a whitish paste. The
                  taste, according to the original colonists,
                  is somewhat similar to the Earth pear,
                  though pear-nut paste is generally balled
                  and left to harden and served in that fash-
                  ion, sometimes garnished with spices

Proto-wolf   A carnivorous pack animal, though not
                  overly wolflike despite its name, looking
                  more like the front of a jackal grafted
                  onto the rear of small horse. The proto-
                  wolf has spiky gray-to-brown fur, a thick,
                  smashed-snouted nose, lean body, and
                  short clawed paws. The back legs are
                  longer and more muscular than the front,
                  lending the animal a sloped, crouched ap-
                  pearance even at rest. The packs com-
                  municate with high-pitched squeals which
                  are audible over long distances at night.
                  Packs out hunting are afraid of nothing,
                  and will attack animals far larger than
                  themselves. Circling the chosen prey, the
                  proto-wolves dart in whenever an oppor-
                  tunity presents itself to nip at legs or
                  flanks, slowly wearing down the opponent
                  until it falls exhausted, at which point it
                  is doomed. The pack attacks in concert,
                  ripping and tearing at the prey.

Puffwort   A small relative of the globe-tree, the
                  puffwort is a prolific bush with greenish
                  to purplish fan-shaped leaves. Like the
                  globe-tree, the puffwort grows a central
                  spike from which dangles a seedball that
                  ripens in the fall. Unlike the globe-tree,
                  the ripe seedball remains intact until con-

tact by some animal, bird, or large insect causes it to rip open, usually enveloping the poor victim in a cloud of whitish, sticky spores, which adhere for a time to the hapless victim before dropping off, thus spreading the seeds over a large area.

Redwing

A large flying insect, with bright red, translucent wings over a handspan wide, now rather rare. The founders of the human colony on Mictlan told of huge swarms of redwings filling the sky, so many that the sun was dimmed and bloody through their wings. Not much is known of the redwing owing to their current scarcity.

River Grouper

A large fish inhabiting the rivers around the colony. The adult river grouper is one to two meters long, thick-bodied, and slow. The river grouper's usual feeding tactic is to sit on the muddy bottom of the river with its mouth open and its long tongue extended—the end of the river grouper's tongue has a knobbed shape that resembles a small fish. By wriggling this "lure" the river grouper attracts schools of small, minnowlike fish. The river grouper will then rush from its resting place and feed. River groupers can be easily snared with seines, though they are muscular and can put up a tremendous fight before being subdued. The meat of the river grouper is white and succulent.

Sawtooth

A large carnivorous seabird with a gray breast and white wings with pale orange stripes. The head is large, sitting atop a long neck, and it has exceedingly keen sight. Adults can reach the size of a condor and can present a threat even to humans. The sawtooth is not actually toothed, but the large beak is lined with toothlike, razor-sharp ridges, hence the name. The sawtooth rarely ventures more than a few kilometers inland, and prefer offshore islands where the winds are reliable. An adult sawtooth is too heavy to fly on windless days, and is itself vulnerable in that state.

Skimmer
Skimmers are brightly colored birds who prefer swampy or boggy land. They scoop up insects, water plants, and fish with their wide beaks as they fly over shallow pools, their white-plumed breasts seeming almost to touch the water. Skimmers leave distinctive cloverleaf tracks in the mud.

Spindle-leg
A colony insect, with eight long legs and a thick carapace. The spindle-leg is a burrowing insect, creating colonies that may range over several meters with several entrances and exits. Usually found in dry soil, though the red-backed species prefers the muddy ground near the river. Spindle-legs will bite when threatened, though they are nonpoisonous.

Starnose
A burrowing mammal, with clawed front feet, dark fur, and a distinctive, fleshy nose. The starnose is blind and deaf, having no organs of sight or hearing at all. It does possess a keen sense of smell, and can evidently feel vibrations through its body. It feeds on worms and grubs, as well as the roots of succulent plants. In the faux-wheat fields, it is a destructive pest.

Stink-flower
Aptly named, the stink-flower is a smallish tree, no more than six meters high,

with a thick, ridged trunk and large flowers that bloom year-round. The stink-flower produces a strong odor that attracts insects and small birds from long distances, but in the interior of the cup-shaped flower is a pool of tarry material that traps the victim. Oddly, unlike its cousin the amberdrop, the stink-flower does not consume the insects or birds that it traps. The stink-flower lives in a symbiotic relationship with crustaceanlike creatures that lurk in the long splits in the trunk. The crustaceans exude a chemical that allows them to walk in the tarry vessels of the flowers without becoming stuck. They eat the prey caught there, then return to their homes in the trunk. The stink-flower gets sustenance from the droppings (quite malodorous themselves) of the crustaceans, which fall into the earth around the trunk of the tree. While the stink-flower is not a pleasant neighbor, the tar (odorless itself) has uses for creating watertight and flexible seals.

Sweetmelon   A sprawling ground vine with large, thick-veined leaves. The sweetmelon produces brilliant white blossoms in the early summer, and large varicolored melons in the fall, the meat of which is sweet and juicy. Sweetmelons must be picked before they become too ripe, however, for the juice ferments inside the melon quickly. Wildlife eating too-ripe or rotting sweetmelons have been found intoxicated and sick.

Tartberry   A prickly vine with bright yellow leaves and a red fruit. Growing on sandy hillsides, the tartberry forms thick, nearly impenetrable brambles. The fruit is marginally edible, though extremely sour even when fully ripe.

Thorn-vine
A vine whose main trunks, when injured, drip a thin, viscous oily sap that dries quickly to seal the cut. The thorn is nearly leafless, the entire surface chlorophyll-filled. The thorn-vine produces long, daggerlike namesake thorns, which make a formidable hedge. The sap has found several uses, including medical ones.

Toothworms
More accurately, "toothed worms." These are earth-boring carnivorous worms about twenty-five to fifty centimeters in length, whose mouths are ridged with tiny, spiny teeth. Blind, a toothworm turned up in a shovelful of dirt will bite at anything radiating heat. The bite is painful, as the toothworm injects a small amount of poison into its victim. The bite could be potentially fatal to infants, though not to adults.

Tree-leaper
Lemurlike, tree-dwelling marsupials inhabiting the western portions of the northern continent of Mictlan. Tree-leapers live in communal groups, are extremely territorial, and will defend their nesting trees against much larger intruders, such as humans. A lone tree-leaper is no match for a human, but the swarming attack of a tribe of them can be dangerous.

Verrechat
A small, catlike marsupial with transparent or lightly tinted skin and muscles. Sometimes domesticated.

White-bean
A semidomesticated bush which yields pale-colored beans in bunches of six to ten. The bean is sweet, with meaty kernels.

330 APPENDIX

Whitewood

A tall tree with heart-shaped leaves with three to five lobes, light purple above and hairy underneath. The outer layer of cream-colored bark peels away to reveal wood that is nearly white. The hard, coarse-grained wood is used for furniture, boxes, and woodenware. The fruits of the whitewood are a string of three or four "buttonballs."

Wizard

Literally, "winged lizard." Tree-dwelling lizards with scaly feathers and a large flap of loose skin running the length of their bodies. A large, mutated forefinger nearly half the body length of the wizard is attached to this flap—when extended, this wing allows the wizard to fly short distances. This is true flight, not merely gliding. There are several species of wizard, each with characteristic patterns, with the adults varying in size from ten centimeters to over a meter. The Blue Wizards are particularly gregarious and form large colonies, which may number up to several hundred members.